PRAISE FOR *RIDDLE OF S...*

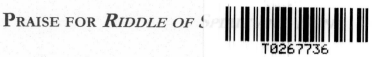

"In nineteenth-century America, orphan... ... ... the world to make their way—but this Jane Austen-like story is entwined with an archeological mystery when human bones are unearthed in contemporary Buffalo. Like roots wrapping a skeleton, the story of the cousins is itself enfolded in spiritualism, women's rights, and a landscape being changed by new methods of transportation. Each time period is distinctly and beautifully drawn, the descriptions as sharp as though limned in pen and ink by a master artist. Carolyn Korsmeyer has delivered a dual page-turner in *Riddle of Spirit and Bone*!"

—Valerie Nieman, author of *In the Lonely Backwater*

"The past meets the present when the skeletal remains of a young woman are discovered by a utility worker in Buffalo, New York. Long-buried secrets are exposed in this gripping dual timeline tale of innocence lost, deception, and the ultimate betrayal."

—Gail Olmsted, author of *Landscape of a Marriage*

"Spiritualism lures three impoverished women down a devastating path in a brooding gothic mystery. I savored the spooky theme and dual timelines, anticipating the reveal with sad anticipation along with the modern-day characters."

—Sandra L. Young, author of *The Divine Vintage* series

"Carolyn Korsmeyer's atmospheric mystery *Riddle of Spirit and Bone* is a dual-timeline treat. Moving effortlessly between 1851, when three newly bereft women become caught up in the murky new world of spiritualism and seances, and 2015, when an excavation for replacement of gas mains in a Buffalo neighborhood reveals the skeleton of a young woman entangled in tree roots and launches local archaeologists in a search for her story, this subtly told tale ruminates on knowledge and deception, representation and vision."

—Karla Huebner, author of *In Search of the Magic Theater*

RIDDLE OF SPIRIT AND BONE

Carolyn Korsmeyer

Regal House Publishing

Published by
Regal House Publishing, LLC
Raleigh, NC 27605
All rights reserved

ISBN -13 (paperback): 9781646035403
ISBN -13 (epub): 9781646035496
Library of Congress Control Number: 2024935074

Cover images and design by © C. B. Royal

Regal House Publishing, LLC
https://regalhousepublishing.com

Printed in the United States of America

For David

1

Bone

It was a bone.

There was no mistaking it. A bone. It fell at his feet, brown and sere except where a chip from the edge shone white against the packed earth lining the trench. For a moment Dan stared in disbelief, his eyes striving to see a stick, a twig, a length of rusted pipe, or anything more likely than a bone. He bent and gingerly picked it up, sensing its lightness, its age, oddly regretting the injury his pick had dealt.

The man digging next to him turned, dropped his shovel, and exclaimed at the find. "Boss! Hey, Carl, come here! Better take a look!"

A large man approached. "What's going on?"

Dan handed the bone up to the foreman, who held it distastefully between two fingers, first curious, then dismayed, then furious that it should be here. Last week it had been an arrowhead, which he had quickly hidden beneath his steel-toed boot and no one had been any the wiser. And then there were those pieces of blue and white tile unearthed with a giant bite from the backhoe. He had been confident they were nothing more than discards from an old bathroom floor, hardly worth notice and certainly not enough to stop digging the trench. Those he had flung into the dump truck without hesitation, not even bothering to hide them.

But a bone. Not a dog bone, not a piece of rawhide withered and twisted with age. Not a soup bone or the remains of someone's chicken dinner. Nor probably an animal bone like one from the sheep that—he was told—used to graze long ago in the park to the north, though it did look pretty old. But sheep had thick, short bones, at least if you could judge from a leg of lamb. This bone was long and slender. It looked suspiciously—ominously—like it once had supported the body of a person.

And this time he could not follow his impulse and bury it hastily in the dump truck, for he had not been the one to find it. It had fallen free from the side of a newly dug trench just when they had reached the depth where the new main pipe would be laid. To make matters worse, the digger named Dan, not even a regular who could be trusted to keep his mouth shut but an extra hired on as a favor to the contractor, had handed it up with a reverent expression, like he had just unearthed buried treasure. And the other man in the trench looked almost as fascinated at the find. Their eyes followed the bone, their tools set aside, their hands idle.

"Goddammit to hell," muttered the foreman, but only under his breath. The guy who manipulated the backhoe with indispensable skill was a newly converted born-again who had already admonished him twice for taking the Lord's name in vain. But a compound curse was called for when you find a human bone in the middle of a trench when you're trying to replace the gas mains for a whole city neighborhood. Residents were getting peevish.

"There's more, boss," said Dan. "Look at this."

Awed, fascinated, and slightly queasy, Dan stood shoulder-deep in the trench and pointed to the excavated area just above his knees. The ground in this section was less rocky than the rest of the channel had been. They had counted themselves lucky to have finally reached a small part of the neighborhood that didn't rest on bedrock. The work had gone quickly today, slicing through what was basically packed earth. But their luck was short-lived, for here, poking out from a dense network of dead tree roots, were two delicate curves that just had to be ribs.

The contractor would not be pleased. The city would not be pleased. The neighbors would not be pleased. They were already complaining that the work was taking too long. But there was no help for it. The foreman whistled loudly and caught the eye of an inspector down the street, extracting him from an examination of a lateral pipe connecting to the new main. An aggravated homeowner watched, arms akimbo, as the inspector followed the summons and crossed the street toward the park. "Got a problem here," said Carl, trying for a casual tone. "Site maybe needs to be checked. Should we call in the boneheads, do you think?"

The inspector ran his finger down the length of the bone that had fallen loose and balanced it in his hands. It had a slight, graceful curve that was almost pretty in a grisly sort of way.

"Jesus Christ. It looks human. At least, I think it does. What about the police?"

The two paused, pondering the same question. Who would take less time, archaeologists or police? Which brand of interference was the bigger pain in the ass, historical or forensic?

Word was spreading, and other workmen were drifting toward the trench with curiosity. The inspector had found artifacts before on various jobs, but this was his first skeleton. Unlike Carl, his first response had been a moment of awe, though awe was quickly replaced by their shared aggravation at the thought that the work would be interrupted.

Well, there was no help for it. Bones trump gas lines.

"Better call 'em all," the inspector declared.

Sighing, Carl dialed the contractor. Then the police. Then, giving in to the inevitable, he dialed the number he'd been given in the unlikely event (*unlikely!*) that they discovered artifacts of historical interest. He gestured down the trench and the backhoe went idle, then silent.

If only there had been more rock here instead of a patch of earth deep enough to cover what looked to be a grave—makeshift, perhaps, but sufficient to hide a body. After a month of delays during which two hand shovels and a pick had broken against the resisting ground, he never thought he would want to hit more rock. But that just goes to show that you never know what truly counts as luck.

Uneasily, he thought again about that arrowhead, so easily snatched from under the noses of the diggers. Where exactly had he been when that little item had tumbled out of the mouth of the backhoe? Had they been close enough to this site that the arrowhead might be connected to this goddamn bone? He thought they had been far down the street or even on another block, but he had secreted it under his boot and then slid it into his pocket so swiftly that he wasn't paying much attention to exactly what part of the construction zone they were on. What a catastrophe it would be if they had stumbled on an old Indian graveyard. The project would never be finished then. He had given the arrowhead to his nephew but thought now that it might be prudent to retrieve it.

His phone rang. The contractor, issuing the instructions that he expected: Stop all work for the day. Worse yet, remove the equipment. They were sending a flatbed to take the backhoe and the small cat tractor to another job. That spelled a long delay, and now Carl was going to have to inform the neighbors. Including the man down the street, who was still standing in his driveway with his hands on his hips, no doubt wondering why the inspector hadn't finished approving his new hookup.

The diggers began to disperse, but the workman named Daniel still stood in the now-silent trench. It was just wide enough for him to crouch down until he was eye level with the bones. From the little that was visible, the skeleton appeared to be caught in a twisting embrace, torqued gradually by the clasp of roots that had grown over and through the bones until they had formed a network that was both supporting and invasive. The ground was full of thick, reddish clay in this patch, though there were zones of darker earth that made him think that maybe this land had once been a farm. Or maybe not a farm, for you wouldn't expect to find human bones in a pasture. He now began to wonder if they had dug their way into an old cemetery.

He set aside his shovel and picked up a small, sharp rock and delicately used the point to scrape around the bones. He loosened the edge of a knot of clay that fell away in a chunk, revealing another bone, then another, all in a curving line. Now it was unmistakable. He knelt before a pale cage that could only be a set of ribs. And all at once he could imagine an entire body lying in front of him behind all the dirt. Being so close, he felt a weird companionship forming.

He vaguely recollected that long ago a battle had been fought nearby, 1812 or maybe 1813. Could this be a fallen soldier, his body overlooked for burial? The ribs looked small, but they might have shriveled over the years. Was it a woman? A child? It seemed somehow wrong just to walk away, even though whoever it was could hardly care at this point. Tentatively, he stroked the bones with one finger. The contact felt intimate, forbidden. He wondered if they would be able to remove the rest of the skeleton intact from its dense net of tree roots, and if there were others in the vicinity. If they had dug their way into a graveyard, the replacement of the gas mains would require diversion. Or perhaps the graves would need to be removed to another cemetery. Either way, the work would halt for a while in this area. With that thought he realized that, oddly, he didn't want to leave. He was caught by a strange feeling of attachment to whoever lay here.

A voice overhead disturbed his reverie. "Dan! Get out of there. Have you fallen asleep? We have to cover the trench with a tarp and wait for the boneheads to come."

Reluctantly, Dan climbed back into the sunlight.

2

DEATH MASK

TROY, NEW YORK. APRIL 28, 1851

"You'd better put more salts in your pocket," said Lydia. "Auntie is likely to have another swoon on the way to the cemetery."

"Do you think she'll try to throw herself into the grave like Mrs. Fielding did last month?" asked Jane.

"Probably not. It's too muddy."

The cousins smiled at each other, their gazes crossing in the long mirror above the mantlepiece. The glass reflected the pale waves of one, the straight brown hair of the other.

"A heartless remark, Liddy," said Jane. "Auntie is certainly dramatic, but she is sorely affected by Uncle George's death. The loss of a husband is a grievous matter."

"Of course, you're right," said Lydia with a shrug. "I don't mean to be unkind. I know she was fond of him. She certainly has accumulated enough pictures of him. It's as though she's afraid she'll forget his features."

"Oh my, yes. And now they are all she has left. Dear mementoes of the dearly departed. And displayed at present for all of us to remember." Jane's tone was both sad and slightly sardonic. "My own efforts at limning were hardly good enough for her. She has kept our local artists in business with the silhouettes, the profiles, their double portrait, two miniatures, and that awful death mask. Uncle George wasn't a handsome man in life, but to keep his image in death, well—"

"Hush! Don't say it." Lydia giggled nervously, glancing around as if their late uncle might be in a position to overhear. If that were the case, he certainly had plenty of places to hide. The large house was designed with numerous alcoves and bays, all now festooned with black mourning draperies. She finished adjusting her veil over her hair, its yellow glinting through the netting.

"You look lovely, Liddy," said Jane, "even in these drab mourning clothes."

Lydia smiled. "We had better hurry. The carriage is waiting." She quickly replaced the black bunting hung over the mirror and hurried out. Jane followed more slowly, wondering what it would be like to live here now that their wealthy uncle was gone. One more death to add to the others, first Lydia's mother and then her own. Life seemed very tenuous and unpredictable these days.

The cortege that made its way slowly through the streets was a long one. It was led by a hearse drawn by four horses decked with black plumes, a closed carriage carrying the closest female members of the family—in this case, just Aunt Madeleine and her two nieces—and a trail of mourners on foot. A bevy of citizens stood on their stoops and watched its progress. A few murmured at the impropriety of ladies accompanying the hearse to the cemetery, but times were changing, and the younger members of the crowd were less disapproving. Respect was in the air, the men hatless, the women sober, acknowledging the passing of this worthy collar maker. More than one was heard to wonder if the sons would handle the manufacture as well as their father had. After years away, it might be difficult for them to step into the shoes he had so recently vacated.

The wind was high on the cemetery hill, and Aunt Madeleine's long veil whipped around the heads of her nieces, whose own headgear was tangled in an excess of black tulle. She teetered at the edge of the open grave, and when collapse threatened, she was grasped from behind and held firmly upright by her husband's brother. As the coffin was slowly lowered to its final resting place, he kept her steady, providing a murmur of comfort and also dreading the moment when the last will and testament of his brother would be read. It was not yet generally known that George Talmadge had failed—by neglect or design was unclear—to alter the list of those to whom he bequeathed his property, which had dwindled in the last few years but was still enviably substantial. The second Mrs. Talmadge, wife for only three years and now a widow, was in for a nasty surprise.

That revelation, however, was delayed by the throng of mourners who crowded into the house afterward. Attendees from both the windy burial and the funeral service held previously in the church gathered in such numbers that several swags of mourning cloth were dislodged from their perches. The tributes, civic and personal, were many. Conversation ebbed as accolades to the deceased commenced and then flowed again as the speaker finished his homage. There were nods and appreciative murmurs and the occasional tear, discreetly blotted away in flutters of white linen. Sometimes the flutter disguised an eye that was regrettably dry, but no one doubted the weight of the occasion, for the deceased had been an important man.

The many portraits of George Talmadge that his wife had commissioned were propped on a long table laden with pies and cakes, cold meats, biscuits, and a large bowl of punch. It was rather as if the man himself were hosting a meal. Profiles of Talmadge flanked a tray of sliced ham and two miniatures were interspersed among cheeses. Looking out from both sides of the table were water colors of Talmadge and his second wife Madeleine, gazing across from each other and stiffly sitting in straight-backed chairs. Someone had considerately removed the death mask to the pantry.

Conversation subsided as the mayor stood and, after a noisy throat-clearing, launched his own encomium to the upright citizen, now lost to his community. This speech was bound to be longer. Those positioned near the laden table shifted from foot to foot and tried not to chew too loudly, though at the edges of the room a few people bent heads and murmured quietly.

Jane whispered to Lydia, "Who is that tall gentleman so solicitously attending to Auntie? I believe I saw him on the edge of the gathering at the cemetery, but I don't recall meeting him before."

Her query was noted by a group of sharp-eared women standing nearby. "His name is Mr. Lewis," one helpfully hissed. "Alexander Dodge Lewis. He is visiting from Poughkeepsie, where he is quite the personage among some circles. And we understand that he is on his way to Little Falls, but we have wondered ourselves just why he is here."

"Well, we do have our suspicions. I have heard that he is often to be glimpsed after a funeral," said another. "He is rather handsome, isn't he?"

Lydia murmured agreement. The elegant figure of Mr. Lewis was bent over Aunt Madeleine, apparently whispering comforting words. He was a man of commanding appearance. Dark hair sprang away from his brow, his high collar was impeccable, his suit sharply tailored. The hands that clasped hers were long-fingered and meticulously manicured. The widow smiled tremulously and nodded, lifting her veil and dabbing her eyes with a lacy handkerchief. He pressed something into her hand, raised it to his lips in a courteous, formal gesture, bowed vaguely to those looking curiously in his direction, and made his way quietly into the hallway and out of the house.

"How kind of him to offer consolation to Auntie," said Lydia, "even though he must be a recent acquaintance. I wonder if we shall see him again."

"If, indeed, it is consolation he was offering," said Jane, who hadn't been able to see him very well from her position behind a broad-backed man. She was thinking of Uncle George's reputed fortune and the newly minted wealthy widow, who, although past her first youth, was still pretty enough to turn heads. Behind her there was a faint snort that might have been meant for a comment, but when she turned to inquire further, the informative women had dispersed to other conversations.

Jane did not like crowds, especially swarms of people in a room that was growing dim with the waning afternoon and an atmosphere of pipe smoke. Her head was aching and her eyes were beginning to water in the close air of the room. But it was too early to retire to her own chamber, so she stood patiently through the mayor's speech, feeling comfortably insignificant and hoping that no one would engage her in conversation. Lydia's social ease and facility with small talk was a source of occasional envy, but much of the time Jane was content to remain on the sidelines, a curious spectator but unnoticed herself.

So she was somewhat surprised when a woman drifted into focus in front of her and introduced herself as Mrs. Talmadge. And then, noting that Jane's eyes sought her aunt with blinking puzzlement, she clarified: Mrs. Herman Talmadge, wife of the deceased's elder son. She gestured to a woman at her shoulder, her sister-in-law, Mrs. Rupert Talmadge, who joined them.

"How do you do," said Jane, mustering a smile. "My name is Jane. Not Talmadge but Woodfield." She laughed slightly, for of course these women would already know that she was no Talmadge. "You probably recall that my cousin, Lydia, and I have resided with our aunt Madeleine for just over a year. She has yet another name: Lydia Strong. We are the daughters of Auntie's late sisters." Jane glanced toward Lydia, who had made her way to the table and was cutting a slice of cake and chatting with a neighbor. The mayor had finished his speech and was spearing ham.

The two younger Mrs. Talmadges nodded and smiled, each trying to recall the tangle of surnames that had ended up residing in the home of their distinguished father-in-law after his second marriage. They had met his wife briefly at their wedding but had seldom visited since that time. Both were now feeling rather as if their side of the family had faltered in the duties they ought to have performed. (How often does a death bring such thoughts to the fore.) They hoped to make up for the lapse quickly, if only for the sake of appearance. "We haven't been present, perhaps, as much as we should have," one murmured.

When Aunt Madeleine joined their circle there were exchanges of sighs and condolences. Mrs. Herman and Mrs. Rupert Talmadge squeezed her hands and murmured consolations. In sympathy, they lowered their veils to match hers. Perhaps they were not in full agreement with her declaration that the loss of a husband was not to be compared to their own bereavements. But they kindly forgave her the thought, because the sentiment was not unreasonable, and the occasion was understandably fraught.

It was evening of the next day before the family could assemble in private and listen to the reading of the will. This time, Aunt Madeleine really did swoon.

3

Eviction

"To be turned out of my own house! It is too unjust, too cruel!" Madeleine wailed. She dropped a sheaf of letters onto the floor and sank into a chair, head in hands. "And so soon after losing my beloved husband. It is not to be borne!"

Jane patted her shoulder and murmured soothing words, which, although sincere, were becoming stale, for she had been uttering the same phrases for days. Lydia waded through the upturned contents of a wastebasket and sorted once more through a box full of discarded pen nibs and bottles of dried-up ink.

The room looked ransacked. Every drawer and cubby hole of George Talmadge's capacious desk had been emptied, every paper scrutinized. The cushions of the chairs had been turned over, the edges of the rugs lifted. Lydia had even lain on her back beneath the desk and tapped the bottoms of the drawers, hunting for hidden compartments that might conceal a codicil to the will that so dismayingly omitted mention of his second wife. Jane had examined the backs of all the pictures on the walls to see if there was anything taped behind. Neither she nor Lydia thought it likely that a paper of such importance would have been concealed at all, for there was no reason to keep secret a bequest to a legal wife. Still, it was puzzling that Madeleine had not been included among the legatees. Her distress was understandable, so they humored their aunt and joined her in the fruitless hunt.

"I know, Auntie, but there appears to be no help for it," said Jane. "The will was quite clear, and Mr. Bailey has confirmed that Uncle George did not consult him about amendments, nor anyone else at the law firm. It is a pity, but they are bound by the terms of the registered testament."

After more than a week of the same litany, there was little more to

say. Aunt Madeleine swung from weeping to fury, from nervous collapse to manic activity, all the while berating her late husband's family
for not acknowledging that there must, there simply *must*, be another
will. Jane sympathized but at the same time had to admit that her aunt's
complaints, however justifiable, were also getting tiresome, becoming
more rant than lament.

"I am certain that Uncle intended to make a new will," said Lydia,
repeating the calming statements that she had been uttering for days.
"Obviously, the press of business delayed his actions, and he had no
reason to expect that a will would be—er—required so soon, being
a person of ordinarily robust health. He most certainly expected to
recover from his last illness and to rise from his bed before any legal
adjustments were needed. But since he did not, and since the sons are
moving to Troy to take over the business as soon as possible, it is natural that they would want to occupy his father's house as well."

She did not mention the whispers overheard among the servants
that Mr. Talmadge might have considered the considerable largesse he
had already displayed to be sufficient for a second wife. Nor that a
similar sentiment might have been expressed to his lawyers. No reason
to repeat a hurtful rumor.

Tears spouting, Aunt Madeleine pounded one small fist against the
other and responded with the energy of indignation. "It may be natural
that they should assume the business," she said. "But it is not natural
that they should fail to respect their father's wishes. And those wishes simply must have included the well-being of his wife. That should
be clear to anyone. Absolutely anyone acquainted with George would
know beyond doubt that he would have provided for me. I was his legal
wife and hence deserving to inherit! That there should be any doubt
whatsoever is most dismaying."

Her voice became stronger and louder as she repeated these sentiments, and she leapt up and began to pace about the room, crumpled
papers scattering at her approach.

"Unfortunately, it is the will that specifies the wishes in their official
form—"

But Jane's tired remark was overridden immediately.

"There is more than one way to indicate wishes," said Madeleine
with a resolve suddenly quite at odds with her previous surrender to
distress. After another circuit of the room, she plopped down into her

husband's desk chair. Her febrile gaze was fixed, though now it seemed not to be directed at anything in particular but at some thought that had just arisen. After a silence that neither Lydia nor Jane were quite sure how to assess, she rose to her feet. The tears had dried and her voice was firm, the tremor of upset replaced by determination. Her nieces regarded the abrupt change of demeanor curiously.

"You will both please continue the search of the house, but I intend to investigate other grounds to challenge the will. We may not be able to locate George's explicit instructions, but I shall not give in so easily to this miscarriage of justice. I am going this minute to see Mr. Bailey again. Perhaps if I confront him at his office in the presence of his colleagues, one of them will help persuade him of the justice of my cause. I shall be strong this time, no more weeping widow to soothe without satisfying. I gave up too easily the last time." Madeleine Talmadge strode from the room, then turned and said, "And if that isn't successful, there may be still other means to pursue. I am not done with this. Not at all."

Her nieces paused, surprised at the decisive declaration from their normally irresolute aunt. Then they surveyed the disorder left behind.

"Well, I, for one, consider the search of this room complete," said Jane. "We have been at it all day, and looking at the same papers over and over will not change one word of what they say."

"Or more exactly, what they don't say," agreed Lydia. "Poor Auntie. It really was a terrible oversight of Uncle George not to have changed his will when he married again. One would not have thought it of a man of business. But I agree. Any more attempts to discover a lost document here would be a waste of time."

The mess of the study was turned over to a tight-lipped maid, and the cousins retreated upstairs. They watched from a second-floor window as their aunt bustled down the street, her brisk speed at odds with her mourning attire. Her bright curls, almost a match with Lydia's, bounced with energy, and in the breeze her veil blew back from her head like the tail of a small black comet.

"The younger Mrs. Talmadges would disapprove of her going out like this," said Jane. "I suspect they consider her to have been an unworthy second wife to their father-in-law, despite their three happy years of marriage. Recall that Auntie told us they considered her background to be less than respectable, which was most unjust. But her behavior now

would confirm that view. I'm sure they believe that she ought to observe deep mourning, keeping to her bed, refusing food, seeing visitors
only one at a time. Or at least keeping to the house with the windows
darkened. Certainly not striding down the street in broad daylight on
her way to the law offices."

"Well, I admire her for it," said Lydia. "Even if Aunt Madeleine did
not meet entirely with the family's approval, it was really too bad of
Uncle George to neglect his affairs as he did. For surely, she is right that
he would not have wanted to see his wife turned out of their home,
even by his own sons."

"She is not being turned out precisely, though, is she? They have
made it quite clear that she could stay if she chose."

"I don't blame her for refusing," said Lydia. "I would do the same.
They may have asserted that she could remain here, but their invitation
was offered reluctantly, and they are surely pleased that she has declined
to stay. Furthermore, in my opinion, three Mrs. Talmadges in one house
is two too many."

"In any event, it makes little difference to us," added Jane. "There
would be no room for us even if Auntie did stay."

"No, you're right. We two are turned out in any case." The cousins
regarded each other with smiles both sad and wry.

"At least we shall share the same fate, whatever it is," said Jane. "And
Uncle George's family surely will not leave us without any resources at
all. Still, if we must leave, we might as well begin to decide what to pack
and take with us."

Neither Jane nor Lydia had taken much from their old homes when
they moved in with their aunt and her prosperous spouse the previous
year. A pottery cup or two, embroideries stitched by their mothers, a
few trinkets that served as mementoes of happy childhoods before
grievous losses had interrupted their lives. Each had also kept the few
books that comprised their fathers' libraries, dull tomes treasured for
the memory of those who had read them. Each still wore the necklace she had received on her sixteenth birthday. Lydia had declared she
would never take hers off, and although it sometimes tickled her neck,
Jane usually followed suit.

In truth, this departure from the Talmadge home, upsetting as it was,
was easier than the one that had come a year before when their own
mothers—already widowed young—had died, both victims of sudden

morbid fevers that had taken them within weeks of each other. Of lon-ger-term misfortune were the arrears that lingered from their fathers' joint and ill-advised business ventures. The plans and expectations of two congenial households disintegrated into a set of debts that had no hope of being discharged, and the two daughters were left nearly penniless and quite on their own.

United in shared catastrophe, the cousins had gone to live with the one relative who wanted them: sweet, light-hearted, pretty Aunt Mad-eleine, who had welcomed them like the daughters she never had. The man they soon came to call Uncle George had surely not contracted a second marriage with any anticipation that there would be two ex-tra young women residing in his house, but nevertheless he had been generously accommodating. But now Lydia wondered aloud if perhaps failure to include his second wife, not to mention her two nieces, from his will might indicate that his real feelings about his unexpectedly expanded household had been rather different from his hospitable out-ward expressions.

"I wonder if our presence influenced his failure to include Auntie in his legacy," she said sadly. "He never hinted anything like that, but now the possibility occurs to me. I hope that Auntie doesn't harbor the same doubts."

"She doesn't seem to. I think she always assumed that Uncle George was as fond of us as she is. Maybe she misjudged him. But in any event, she is quite determined to claim her just share of his legacy," said Jane.

Lydia sighed. "I'm beginning to feel rather nomadic." Her eyes filled with tears, quickly brushed away. As the older cousin, she felt obliged to be strong in the face of adversity. Jane, with her head in a closet, had not seen the tears, but she detected the tremor of voice at the end of that dejected sentence.

"Don't despair, Liddy. Our period of prosperity has been brief, but it need not be final. Aunt Madeleine might be losing the house, but the Talmadge sons surely will grant her a generous sum to tide us over until our luck turns. They would incur disapproval if they did not, and their wives strike me as women who are sensitive to social sanctions. At any rate, we should be in decent shape for the time being."

The words were uplifting, the mood behind them not quite so op-timistic. Jane considered herself the more realistic of the cousins and as such also felt obliged to be strong in the face of adversity. It would be a contest, she thought, to see which of them would first give in to melancholy. She noticed that her cousin was fingering the locket at her throat and guessed that she was thinking of her mother, whose portrait on a shaving of ivory lay inside.

"What appears substantial now may not seem so in a few months," said Lydia, uttering a sentiment more practical than sentimental. "It is not easy for a woman without funds to retain her social position, especially with no home of her own. And we are by no means sure if this cousin in Rochester will welcome two unknown nieces, are we?"

"I hope just long enough for you to find your own rich husband, Lydia, dear. How lucky we all are that you have such a pretty face." Jane's tone was teasing, but at the back of her mind was real concern about the sudden removal of their temporary prosperity. Lydia laughed ruefully.

"What an old-fashioned sentiment," she said. "A woman should not need the wealth of a husband to make her way in the world."

"Easy to say if you have an income already," said Jane. "You do realize that the other Mrs. Talmadges probably consider Aunt Madeleine to have landed a husband for just that reason. And I suspect that the absence of provision for her in Uncle's will would confirm their suspicions."

"They might, but it would be unfair. Auntie was a devoted wife. Uncle George was not the husband I would choose for myself, but they suited each other quite well, I believe."

They both thought of the multiple images of George Talmadge, now removed from display and carefully stacked in packing cases. The death mask had been wrapped in linen—like a small shroud, Jane had observed—and placed in its own box.

Lydia straightened and spoke with sudden vigor. "Of course, we must go with Auntie and help her settle into her new life. But we should also bear in mind that her circumstances might not be satisfactory for us in the long run. The time has come for us to make our own ways. One cannot both face adversity and remain passive."

Jane regarded her cousin with admiration. "How I envy you your courage, Liddy! I should not be nearly so brave in the face of our immediate prospects if it were not for you."

Lydia smiled. "If we stick together, we shall be fine, I'm sure. We managed before, and we will again." She pulled out a dusty traveling bag from under a bed. "Do you think that the luggage we have at our disposal will be adequate for this move?"

"Oh my! I must not forget to pack my paints." Jane removed a small artist's kit from a shelf along with several sheets of charcoal-smudged paper. "I was trying my hand at portraiture when those traveling limners came through last fall. They displaced me when Auntie hired them to render pictures of herself and uncle."

She surveyed the unfinished portraits critically. Those she had sketched in profile weren't bad, but she had tried a full face view of a person now quite unidentifiable. Lydia came up beside her. "In my view, your efforts aren't so inferior to the ones downstairs. You really are talented, you know; much better than the other girls at Miss Willard's. Perhaps you could set yourself up as a painter. That would supply some extra income while I track down that rich husband you have in mind."

Lydia was joking, but she planted a seed. Indeed, perhaps I can, thought Jane. There are sure to be places along our way where a traveling artist might pick up a fee for a portrait or two. She wrapped her pencils and brushes in a loose cloth and tucked them into the corner of her bag.

A noise outside brought her to the window. "Is that Auntie already on her way home from the lawyers' offices? Come look, Liddy, I can't make out whom she is talking with."

Lydia joined her and peered through the patchwork of leaves on the tall oak at the side of the house. "That must be her, and she is speaking with two women. I can't see their faces very well. Oh yes, I know who they are. It's the Spencer sisters. They were at the house after the funeral and we both spoke to them. Remember the women who recognized the man who spoke with Auntie? A Mr. Lewis, I believe his name was. I can't recall why they were able to identify him, but that is two of them for sure."

The conversation outside was being carried on in voices too low-pitched to overhear. Through the leaves they could see that the three women had bent their heads together in the pose of those guarding a secret. A paper was being passed among hands, read with apparent interest, prompting gasps and more intense whispering.

When Aunt Madeleine entered the house she had no good news from the lawyer to report. Without clear evidence of intent to change the disposition of George's property, Mr. Bailey had insisted, there were simply no grounds to challenge the will. But her nieces were puzzled at the tone with which their aunt delivered this discouraging news. She was not weepy, she did not rant against fate, she did not swoon. She seemed pensive. They were reluctant to pry about the conversation outside that they had witnessed, for it had carried an air of privacy. And she did not volunteer its substance. She was unusually thoughtful as she commenced packing her own things for the road, but it was not for some days that they discovered why.

4

THE DIG

"You shouldn't wear sneakers when you use a pick ax."

Jacob was startled by the voice above him. The point of the pick missed its target, swung by his tattered sneakers, and buried itself in the earth. He shook it loose in irritation, scattering clumps of dirt across his feet. The stranger standing above him was silhouetted by the slanting afternoon sun. Jacob squinted to bring the face of the man into focus. From his position in the trench, he was eye-level with a pair of knees.

"What? Who are you?"

"The gas work has been halted here," asserted Jasmine in her head-of-the-dig voice. "No one is supposed to be in this area until the archaeological analysis is complete." She was so short that her head barely cleared the edge of the trench, but she spoke authoritatively.

"That's right," said Karen, the third person in the trench. "I'm afraid you'll have to leave." She placed the shovel she had been wielding in front of her feet, shielding the fact that she was wearing sandals. The ax had come alarmingly close. Of course, she knew perfectly well that she should have worn closed shoes for heavy work, but no one had told her that brushes would not be used today. The earth rimming the trench was thick with clay and compacted tree roots.

They had already shooed away four other gawkers, but this intruder was wearing the reflective yellow vest of the gas works, and a circular indentation around his hair indicated a recently removed hard hat. He might be more difficult to get rid of. He also might know what he was talking about.

"I see you removed more turf," he observed. "Neat job. Why don't you try to get at the bones from the top?"

Jasmine paused. Senior to the others, she was temporarily in charge, though the small crew that had been quickly assembled to examine the trench and its unexpected inhabitant was presently made up of only three graduate students. The police, observing with relief that the clutch of old roots indicated that the skeleton had lain in place for too many years to fall under their remit, had ceded the job of recovery to the archaeologists on call. But the faculty advisor, who handled consultation for the city when backhoes plunged into the earth, had not expected anything at all to be discovered from the work on the gas mains. After all, the area had been excavated twice in the last century, a fact repeated defensively over emails and a staticky telephone call. He was hastily preparing to return to supervise this wholly unexpected find. But for the moment it fell to Jasmine to make decisions.

What they were doing wasn't secret, so she figured she might as well answer the question. "The skeleton is trapped in all these old tree roots," she replied. "We're trying to loosen the ground beneath first to see what else might be buried. Don't want to damage anything."

The man nodded. "But they're roots from a dead tree," he said. Dutch elm disease and city development had destroyed the large trees that used to grow in the vicinity, though the replacement lindens were already tall. In this particular patch, however, there were few remaining trees at all, and in the absence of shade the sun was punishing.

"True, but we need to see how much of it grew into the skeleton. It will help to date the bones. Besides, thanks to the trench that's already dug, it's easier to get at them from below." Jasmine wondered why she had to explain anything to this person, but somehow it seemed right.

"Makes sense," the man said. "Want some help?"

"You really shouldn't be here," Jacob repeated.

"Maybe not," said the intruder, "but I wouldn't mind helping."

The others hesitated. They were hot, they were filthy, they were tired, and the narrow scope of the trench made it awkward to use the heavy tools that the unforgiving ground demanded. Besides, they observed the stranger's steel-tipped shoes and their feet suddenly felt very vulnerable.

"I'm not sure that we should," said Jasmine. "What's your interest in this, anyhow?"

A brief silence. The man looked around, studied the sky, looked down at them again. He appeared oddly embarrassed.

"I found her."

"You're the one! Awesome!" said Karen. "That must have been amazing."

Amazing. Exciting, strange, nauseating, weird, mysterious. Awesome. Dan was a little discomfited at his own sentiments. He had been captured by these fragments of a former person, her pathetic, unnamed remains. His work on the mains at another part of town had finished early today, but rather than going home he had found himself returning here, a vaguely proprietary feeling drawing him back to the bones.

Though there was no reason to grant him any official standing with their project, the other three had to admit that finding a skeleton would prompt special interest. They regarded him with greater respect. He in return studied them: one tall, thin young man with lank hair, two women, one dark with curly black hair pinned up on top of her head, the other fair and rather freckled from the sun, all three dirty and tired-looking.

"Why do you say 'her'?" asked Jacob. "We haven't identified the skeleton yet. Could be male or female."

"It's a guess, of course. But judging from the small rib cage, at least the bits that can be seen, I would say a woman, wouldn't you?" Dan figured there was a fifty-fifty chance he was right anyhow.

"Oh, all right, go ahead." Jasmine hoisted herself out of the trench and shook the dirt out of her gloves. "But be careful. We're trying to carve out the space below and around the bones to see how far to mark off the excavation site. At the moment, those roots might be all that is keeping the skeleton intact, and the position of the body needs to be maintained. Also, keep an eye out for other artifacts that might be around. So far we've found some scraps of cloth, and everything—absolutely everything—needs to be preserved. Don't just hack away. Every time the earth is loosened it will need to be checked."

"Of course," said Dan, tamping down his delight. "Better get out of the way, though. It takes room to swing a pick efficiently."

The others followed Jasmine out of the trench and watched as Dan took their place. With surprisingly graceful strength, he swung the pick back along the lateral space of the trench and brought it into the earth in an upwards arc. His muscular arms were tan from shoulder to wrist; paler skin showed at the edges of his shirt as he swung the ax. A large clump of clay webbed with roots broke free. He handed it up, and the archaeologists carefully broke apart the earth in search of bone fragments or small articles that might have dispersed into the earth as the tree's roots spread.

"Nothing," said Jasmine.

Dan continued his work, gradually hewing away at the ground below the bones and sending up clumps of earth for inspection. After a while he set aside the pick ax and took up one of their sharp pointed trowels. Jasmine hopped into the trench and joined him, followed by the others. The quarters were cramped but excitement was brewing. The four of them now worked side by side with small tools, crouched uncomfortably and nearly eye-level with the emerging bones. The smells of earth and clay and sweat surrounded them in an oddly sociable miasma.

"Careful!" said Jacob. "Look. That could be part of an arm beginning to show."

The outline of a foot demanded a stiff brush, plied by Karen until Jasmine sent her—somewhat belatedly—for the camera to document the stages of discovery. Long bones began to appear, and a bulge that might be an ankle. The delicate segments of the hands seemed to be folded against the body. The skull was the prize, the seat of the person, now just a small globe hidden in the earth.

It was Jacob who first detected the circular outline emerging. As he scraped around the edges they could tell that her head—they had adopted Dan's pronoun—was barely attached to the spine. Several inches askew, it was canted back and sideways. Painstaking and slow as the work was, they could not take their eyes off the emergence of the skull.

"Cool!" said a voice above. They all started and looked up. A gaggle of children wearing soccer uniforms were crowding around the trench. Their small spiked shoes stood amid the clumps of sieved earth, some of it now tumbling back into the trench.

"I'm afraid you have to stand back!" Jasmine clambered up and herded the gawkers away, noting with concern that there were several others drifting in their direction and that the loosely draped caution tape was now trampled on the ground. She could hear car doors slamming and the raised voices of parents calling their charges to pick up the balls and get on their way. Clearly, they needed a better way to shield the site from onlookers.

As they all climbed to the surface, they realized that more time had passed than any of them had realized. Exciting as the discoveries were, fatigue was setting in and no one fancied working into the evening. The contractors had left large sheets of plywood to cover the trenching for the mains, and the archaeological team had brought along their own heavy plastic sheeting. Jasmine realigned the posts around the dig and added another emphatic loop of caution tape. Dan went to his truck and supplied two traffic cones and a set of flashers. He wasn't sure if he was supposed to lend out such equipment, but after all, the dig was in the vicinity of the mains. And besides, his uncle was part-owner of the sub-contracting company. And what the hell, this was just a summer job.

Before securing the cover, the four tired diggers surveyed the results of their work. A shallow ledge of thick, clayish dirt now protruded into the widened trench, the length of the skeleton just barely visible in its sarcophagus of earth.

"We got a lot done," said Jacob.

"Yes, we did. All of us." Jasmine turned to Dan. "Thank you for your help. Without you we wouldn't be nearly as far along. If you want to come back, please do. But I'm afraid there is no money to pay you. You'd just be a volunteer."

"Okay," said Dan. Thinking: nothing could keep me away.

"I hope it's not going to rain," said Karen. "Look at the sky."

"Oh my God," said Jasmine. "If water gets into the trench, the bones might fall. We need to build a support, and fast."

The region desperately needed rain. Leaves were curling on the bushes, grass was parched, and sprinklers were running overtime. The air had been thick with dust from the gas line excavation for weeks. But what a terrible time for those heavy clouds to advance from the west. A wicked little breeze suddenly puffed around them, promising a deluge and plastering yet more dust on their sweaty faces. Dan returned to his truck and came back with another sheet of plywood, this one narrower, as well as a set of sawhorses. Together they reentered the trench and erected a makeshift platform beneath the skeleton to secure it against falling. The sawhorses were too large for the space, but one placed on its side effectively held the strip of plywood steady beneath the bones. Over it all they spread the plastic sheets. It took all four of them to hold them steady in the suddenly rising wind, and they scurried to the piles of excavated earth for rocks to weigh down the edges.

"Thank you," Jasmine said again after the site was battened down securely. I hope I didn't offend him with that comment about payment, she thought. Dan's expression was hard to read.

He's kind of cute, thought Karen, looking covertly at those strong arms. I hope he comes back. "I hope you come back," she said. Dan glanced at her with a faint smile.

"Before I forget," he said, "I actually came by to give you something."

Another trip to the truck and he handed Jasmine a plastic bag.

"This is her bone. The first one we found. It dropped into the trench when I was digging." Carl had given the bone to Dan. He had wanted nothing more to do with the damn skeleton.

"It should have remained in situ," said Jasmine, thinking as the words left her mouth that she might sound academic and snobby. "I mean, in place. You shouldn't have taken it away."

"It was already removed," said Dan, who had understood the first locution perfectly well. It was annoying but typical that a hard hat makes some people think you can't read. "The foreman showed it to the inspector and then the police before your team was called in. But now you can have it back."

"What should we do with it now?" Jacob asked. "Doesn't make much sense to put it back in the trench, does it?"

"No. I guess I'll take it home for tonight," said Jasmine. And where would it go at home, where her dog roamed freely and indulged in investigative chewing? Potential disaster. Maybe in the desk drawer of her bedroom, if her boyfriend wouldn't be too weirded out by sleeping near a skeleton.

"I think it needs to be in the lab," ventured Karen. "Dr. Killian can decide where to put it when he finally gets back here."

"And one more thing," said Dan, oblivious to their uncertainty. He handed over another plastic bag. "The foreman thought you should have this too. Though frankly, I'm not sure where it came from. He didn't find it in this trench for sure, so it's probably irrelevant. But just in case."

Despite the wails of his nephew and the recriminations of his sister, the foreman had retrieved the purloined arrowhead and added it to the booty to be handed over to the boneheads. Jasmine looked at it with consternation. Then she thought of a job for Dan, who was turning back toward his truck.

"Please try to find out where this came from, would you? It would complicate our job here a lot if we thought it was nearby. But you guys are working all over the city. Do you think you can ask him where he picked it up?"

"Sure, I can ask," said Dan, slightly mollified. He was pretty sure that Carl hadn't intended to report the arrowhead at all, but sharing the fiction of his upright honesty would serve everyone better than accusations. Dan was pleased at Jasmine's request, for now he had yet another reason to return to the bones.

5

AN INKLING OF THINGS TO COME

TROY, NEW YORK. MAY 26, 1851

Neither Jane nor Lydia could sleep. They knew they should be well-rested for the journey commencing in the morning, but nerves and worries about leaving had keyed them to such a pitch that both were too jittery to relax.

The previous days had been filled with the details of leaving: bidding goodbyes to friends, obtaining items needed for the long trip across the state, and laundering and tidying all the clothes that would soon be stained and worn from the rigors of travel. The packing itself was complicated, as many things had to be boxed for shipment down the canal to their ultimate destination. Or what they anticipated would be their ultimate destination. Aunt Madeleine had been kindly if rather vaguely offered room at the home of an obliging relative in Rochester, but so far the inclusion of her two nieces in that invitation was more hopeful than certain. The relative had agreed to collect and store their trunks and boxes when the shipment arrived, even if their owners were delayed, and Madeleine had interpreted the tone of that agreement to mean that they all would be welcomed. "A large house, there will be lots of room to accommodate us," their aunt had said, brushing aside Jane's doubtful queries.

But Jane had glimpsed that welcoming letter before it went into Aunt Madeleine's pocket, and she thought she might also have seen the lines *...at least until the girls find other lodgings.* Perhaps I misread, she told herself.

Sufficient clothing and other goods needed to be carried in hand luggage for the long journey, for their route would be peculiarly indirect. Their aunt insisted on making several stops along the way for reasons that were not entirely clear, though she indicated a desire to visit various kin and friends. And besides, she said, my Rochester relatives are about to move to their summer cottage and won't be ready to receive us for a little while, so we can take our time. Jane's naïve suggestion that they go west by the Erie Canal was met with summary rejection and a reminder of the dirt and rough life of the canal, as well as the unsavory crowds of immigrants pouring in from Ireland and heading for laboring jobs at the Buffalo terminus. With a wave of the hand, she also dismissed Lydia's tentative rejoinder that some canal travel was perfectly respectable, and a direct journey by rail was rejected for unspecified reasons. A series of shorter trips by coach had been arranged, some purchased, some merely planned. It seemed that Aunt Madeleine was in no hurry to establish a new home.

And yet—she was eager to leave this one.

Their plans for travel had been determined with unexpected speed, for the younger Talmadges were not scheduled to move into the Troy house for another two months, and Mr. Bailey had made it clear that there was no reason for Aunt Madeleine to depart any sooner than was convenient. But the second Mrs. George Talmadge was adamant. Lingering any longer than necessary was both undignified and fruitless, she declared. No longer would she tarry in hopes of convincing someone of her rightful ownership of the home she had shared with her late husband. With that possibility scotched and her protestations about her husband's last will and testament falling on deaf ears, she would go as soon as transportation was ready.

Suspicious at her sudden haste, Mr. Bailey had sent an emissary to the house, ostensibly to attend to the widow and to offer assistance and reassurance. His additional charge was to determine if this precipitous departure was a means to abscond with household items that ought to remain in place. But while Madeleine's trunks were large and packed to the brim, there was no indication that she was taking anything that was not arguably hers, and she had brought no real property into the union that ought to remain in her husband's estate. One might cavil at the set of silver flatware or the imported china dishes, but the claim that they had been wedding gifts was not worth disputing. Nor was there any question about the sparkling ruby necklace, the two diamond rings, the emerald earrings and the pearls, for a local jeweler attested to the fact that they had all been purchased by her husband as wedding gifts. The embroidered cushions, draperies, and petit-point chair covers were the products of her own busy needle. And certainly she was entitled to take the many painted, sketched, and silhouetted portraits of her late husband. And, of course, the death mask. In short, the lawyer had no reason to believe that any covert purloining was afoot.

Strange as it seemed to members of the legal firm who had been the object of her many fruitless, angry petitions, it appeared that Madeleine Talmadge simply wanted to leave without delay.

It seemed strange to Lydia and Jane as well. After days of weeping and storming around the house at the injustice of having to abandon her home, after multiple appeals to Mr. Bailey to dispute the will, after two passionate letters to her dastardly stepsons that failed to elicit a satisfactory response, and finally after a long, tear-stained missive pleading with her brother-in-law who, to no one's surprise, sided with the sons—after all of that, she had suddenly calmed and started to pack.

That calm had descended after another colloquy with the mysterious group of ladies glimpsed on the sidewalk, the import of which, so far, she had failed to disclose. And now enough time had passed to make it awkward for her curious nieces to inquire.

"Liddy, are you awake?" whispered Jane.

"Yes. Are you?"

"Obviously. I'm getting up and going downstairs. I'm hungry."

"Dinner was awful. I doubt you'll find anything worth eating."

But they were too restless to stay in bed. Both got up and put on their wrappers and tiptoed past their aunt's bedroom. Gentle snores issued from the half-closed door. Madeleine was having no trouble sleeping after her habitual dose of sleeping powder. They crept down the stairs, light-footedly careful to avoid the squeaky parts.

In the dark of the hallway landing, Jane walked into a pile of trunks and cases and suppressed a gasp of pain. Several small bags balanced on top tumbled to the floor, and her left slipper stuck under a piece of luggage. She limped to the kitchen with a bare foot and a bruised toe, cursing herself for not remembering that the hall was full of things to be shipped and carried away.

"Do be quiet, that was quite a thud," said Lydia unsympathetically. "Shall I light the stove? We could have some tea."

"The stove and also a candle, if you please. This tile floor is cold underfoot. I want to go back and retrieve my slipper. And please try to find something left over from supper. If tomorrow begins in the manner of today, Auntie will be in too much of a hurry to depart to give us time for a substantial breakfast."

"She is still of the view that young ladies ought to eat sparingly," said Lydia, who did not share that opinion. She rummaged quietly and discovered a hoard of dried apples and half a sponge cake to go with their tea. The cake didn't look familiar, confirming Madeleine's suspicion that sometimes the cook prepared dishes too delicious to make it to the dining room. But their kind and somewhat feckless aunt had never indulged in petty worries about household economy. On the other hand, here was a nice cake ready for the taking, and the cook could hardly object if they partook of a dessert that had been baked on the sly. There were also biscuits and a tin of jam on hand, and Lydia made note of a few other items of food that might be packed to eat later during their trip.

Jane's slipper must have landed in a place that was hard to locate in the dark hall, for their midnight feast was laid on the table and ready to eat by the time that she reentered the kitchen. Not only was the slipper back on her foot, she also carried a clutch of papers in her hands.

"Liddy, look at this! I found something strange in Auntie's bag. I wonder if it might account for her change of mind and our hasty departure."

"What? You went looking through her bags? What can you be thinking? Auntie will be most displeased. She does not like people poking through her things, nor would you. Just remember what she said after that nosy lawyer came to scrutinize her packing. His pretense of assistance was a poor excuse for inquisition as to her intents. She was quite resentful, and rightly so."

"I know, of course you're right. But these were in a bag at the top of the pile, and it fell to the floor when I bumped into the heap of luggage. The compartment wasn't secured shut and the contents spilled out. Of course, I had to check around with the candlelight to be sure that nothing got lost. I intended only to take a quick look to be sure that nothing had landed on the floor, but then my eye was caught by this. And I couldn't help but read it."

Jane held out a thin newspaper, small enough to be considered a pamphlet, but with a banner headline that proclaimed: *The Dead Speak!* The words aroused a shiver, and both girls glanced into the dark corners of the kitchen.

"It isn't ours. We shouldn't read it," said Lydia, but now without conviction. "Besides, I'm not sure I want to hear from the dead at this moment."

"I believe we should. It might affect us too if it explains why we are leaving just now," said Jane. "Especially if it accounts for our making these strange stops along the way that Auntie has planned. We have a right to know why, do we not?"

This was more than temptation; it was a positive invitation to read further. The girls put their candles close together to shed a shared pool of light on the paper and pored over the printed text.

> Little Falls, New York. 3 May.
> If there still be doubters after last evening's dramatic events, they would be wise to reconsider their skepticism before it is too late. Attendees at the Temple of Eternal Communion were witness to phenomena we have long proclaimed possible, for spirits of recently departed loved ones appeared to those assembled. In voices faint but clear, they testified to the fact that the death of the body need not entail the disappearance of the spirit it used to house.

"What do you think it means, 'before it is too late'?" wondered Jane. "It almost sounds like a threat, don't you think?"

"Surely that isn't the point," said Lydia. "The more important thing is that these people saw the spirits of those they mourned. And even spoke to them!"

Jane uttered a skeptical snort. Then she glanced around the dark kitchen just to be sure that they were still alone.

> Under the guidance of our distinguished visitor, Mr. A. D. Lewis, two faint emanations appeared at the edges of the room, and soon they were identified as a grandparent and a cousin of Mrs. Lucy Wright, a longstanding member of the Temple and a well-regarded citizen of this town. Four other members sat around the table and can confirm her report. The hovering spirits drifted toward the ceiling, at first uttering humming noises as though not yet able to form words. But after a few minutes, voices could be distinctly heard, one female, one male.

Both Lydia and Jane shivered. The shadows of the kitchen seemed to press closer, and they bent near the warmth of the candle. The scent of singeing hair prompted them to draw back, but they continued to read intently.

> Their messages were soothing. The grandmother uttered, "All is love. All is love." The cousin's message was less clear, but it is

thought he said, "Peace, peace"—a hissing sound that some present found mesmerizing. After some minutes of their awe-inspiring presence, the candles flickered and went out, although no window was open. And when they were relit, the spirits had gone.

"Oh my, can it be possible?" said Lydia. "I have heard others speak of raising the spirits of the dead, but our minister has scoffed at the idea. In fact, just last Sunday he declared the very possibility not only preposterous but against the teachings of the Bible. But perhaps he was wrong, for here is testimony!"

"Here is a story at any rate," said Jane. "And it certainly is an interesting account. Do you think, Liddy, that this is the paper we saw being passed to Auntie the other day by the Spencer sisters?"

"You know, I think that's very likely. I could not see what they were discussing from the vantage of our window, but what else could it have been?"

"What is this publication? I never heard of it before."

One of the candles had burned out. They squinted in the flickers of dwindling light. The top of the thin newspaper read *The Sign*, and in smaller type below: *A monthly publication of the Temple of Eternal Communion. A group dedicated to the truths of Spiritualism which invites all those of open mind and heart into its midst.*

"But what could Auntie's interest be in this? Do you think she believes in ghosts? Surely not. But oh—could it be possible… No, it isn't likely that—oh my…" Lydia did not complete the thought.

The two cousins stared at each other and pondered the possibilities just opened. A strange idea, thrilling and terrible, occurred to them both. They thought of their aunt, newly widowed and in mourning, harboring a grievance about the last will and testament of her late husband, and seeking in vain for evidence that the document did not represent his actual final wishes. With no physical evidence to the contrary, and with Uncle George unavailable to comment on the decision of his lawyers, could she possibly be in search of his lingering spirit in hopes that he might be persuaded to issue a rebuttal?

Oh yes, they agreed. She could.

6

THE JOURNEY BEGINS

LITTLE FALLS, NEW YORK. MAY 28, 1851

"It's such a pity that you arrived just after Mr. Lewis left to continue his trip across the state," said the woman called Miss Essie Everett. "He is ever so much more attuned to the souls who have passed to the Other Side than are those of us who will be here tonight, although we shall certainly do our best to summon the spirits of those you seek. Especially as you so urgently desire a message from beyond."

"Yes, indeed, it is too bad," said Aunt Madeleine, sounding somewhat peevish in her disappointment. "I did write him in care of *The Sign*. I had every expectation that he would receive my note in time for our arrival. He was so kind at the funeral of my late husband, informing me of his availability, should I desire further conversation. I had hoped he might be of assistance. After all, he gave me his card." She held it out: *Alexander Dodge Lewis*.

"Assuredly he could," said Miss Evangeline Everett, "but perhaps we shall be able to take his place. And if not, I am certain you will be able to catch up with him by the time he reaches Utica, which was his next destination. The chapter there is large, and he is likely to stay for some time as his sister lives there. We are but a small group here, although our numbers are growing as the word spreads of the success of our endeavors."

Jane looked around her a little anxiously. The sun had set and the room was already becoming dim. The house they had entered had once been home to a large family, and now the many rooms were full of things accumulated over two generations. The area was cluttered with ottomans and small tables laden with fragile-looking bric-a-brac. She became clumsy when nervous, and there were abundant opportunities for collision. Lydia had no such qualms. She was already inspecting the perimeter, weaving around chairs and occasional tables, reading posted testimonials pinned to mounted boards and peering at several dour portraits on the walls. I'll sit next to Lydia, thought Jane; we'll be all right together.

Their departure from Troy had been delayed by the tardy collection of the trunks to be shipped by canal boat, which required a postponement to a later coach, which was then troubled by the amount of hand luggage to be loaded for Mrs. Talmadge and her nieces. Fortunately, there was only one other traveler with them, a tolerant man who graciously took a seat next to the driver rather than occupy a space squashed with bags, hatboxes, and a lopsided case that threatened to fall off the rack overhead. It was obvious to Jane that her aunt was more upset about leaving her home than she would admit, and that a certain amount of dallying was the result of her reluctance to depart. Aunt Madeleine had descended the steps of the house but then whirled around to ascend and make one final check of her bedroom, left again but returned to speak once more to the housekeeper, left and returned twice more, until at last, blinking back tears, she and all her gear were loaded into the coach. Her two nieces with their lighter loads jammed themselves in beside her.

And now they were at Little Falls, the first of the stops she had arranged, the purpose of which confirmed her nieces' midnight speculation. The prospect was bizarre, but Aunt Madeleine, it seemed, had given up on lawyers and was pursuing the possibility of directly confronting her late husband to discover just why he had mishandled her legacy. And, presumably, what he might do about it now. She had not mentioned this transcendent purpose in so many words, but now that they were about to gather for a session to call forth his spirit, it was obvious that she had elected to try out an alternative route to her single-minded goal.

Three more women entered the room, followed by two men who carried more chairs and set them in a circle around a square tea table covered with a tasseled cloth. The space seemed to shrink with the increase of population. Madeleine, Lydia, and Jane stood as they were formally presented to the monthly meeting of the Temple of Eternal Communion. There were welcoming nods and sympathetic murmurs on learning that Aunt Madeleine had come on a quest that could not be satisfied by earthly means. Jane exchanged a glance with her cousin, who looked expectant and eager. She felt her pulse increase.

After all were seated, there was a spontaneous folding of hands and bowing of heads.

"We always start with a brief prayer," said Miss Evangeline Everett, the elder of the two sisters and apparently the leader of the group. "We find that it settles the mind and makes it more receptive. I should caution our newcomers that spirits do not like to enter a place where there is agitation of any sort. Anger, resentment, fear—all negative feelings need to be left behind. You must clear your minds and calm your hearts."

Heads dutifully bent as Miss Evangeline murmured a request to heaven for serenity so that souls of the departed might cross over the Great Divide between Eternity and the Present and speak to those assembled. Jane clutched Lydia's hand, which trembled slightly. Both were more than a little nervous at the thought that ghosts might appear, although Miss Essie had stressed that "ghost" was not a respectful term for the lingering spirits of the recently deceased. "They have not returned to haunt," she insisted, "merely to communicate."

"They are truly desirous of assuring us that death should hold no fear," another attendee confirmed. She had introduced herself as Mrs. Lucy Wright, widow of Little Falls, she to whom the spirits had spoken in the account from *The Sign*. Now that she had been the object of a spiritual visitation, she counted herself an expert. And after all, they were meeting at her house.

"I am not feeling very calm," Jane whispered to Lydia. "I feel quite jumpy and rather queasy. I think this unease probably counts as a negative feeling. I hope it doesn't prevent Uncle George from communicating."

Someone made a gentle shushing noise and she fell silent. Jane lowered her lids in the hopes that if anyone looked, her eyes would appear dutifully shut. She peeked around and saw that Aunt Madeleine was already glancing expectantly about the room, even though they had been instructed to keep their eyes closed until bidden to open them.

They sat in silence as the sky outside the curtained window grew ever darker. There was murmured debate about how many candles should be lit or whether the room should remain dark. Three candles of different lengths were chosen. One of them started to gutter and caused some excited gasps before someone thought to trim the wick. They sat longer. And still longer. Miss Essie murmured an indistinct incantation and hummed a little. A general humming spread around the room, and it did sound soothing and serene. Then a man at the table cleared his throat loudly and was hushed. Perhaps his rough noise deterred the entry of spirits readying to attend. The group continued to sit with the patience of those who trust that something is worth waiting for. Jane began to wish she had visited the privy before the Temple convened its meeting.

One of the candles suddenly went out. All eyes fixed on the coil of smoke ascending from the wick.

"There was no wind," whispered Mrs. Lucy Wright. "No wind. A spirit approaches." A dribble of wax bubbled from the drowned wick and pooled around the base of the candlestick.

"Do you feel it?" said Miss Essie in the quietest of whispers. "The cold. The air has turned cold."

And, yes, they all felt it. A chill passed through the room. There were shivers and gasps of anticipation. Jane gripped Lydia's hand harder. It was definitely colder than before, and there seemed to be a thin fog rising around the table. Her heart pounded so loudly she worried it would drown out the voices of the arriving dead.

All at once, Miss Essie inhaled with a sharp hiss. Her head fell back as though her neck had snapped, and her eyes flew open and stared upwards. Jane chanced a glance toward the ceiling but saw nothing out of the ordinary.

"Sister, what do you hear?" whispered Miss Evangeline. "Is there a presence?"

"Yes," sighed Essie after a pause. "I can feel a presence."

"So can I," said Lucy Wright, she whose dead grandmother had appeared to her in this very room. Similar testimonies spread through the group in a series of breathy exhalations as those assembled began to sense the arrival of spirits of the dead.

"Most definitely."

"More than one, I do believe."

"The air is full of power."

The cloudy atmosphere in the room grew denser, rather like a concentrated evening damp.

"I think I feel it too," whispered Lydia. "Like a tremor going through me. Auntie, do you feel anything? Is it Uncle George?"

But before Madeleine could reply, a hoarse, masculine growl filled the room. The sound issued from Essie but sounded not a bit like her.

And while it was hard to discern words, the indistinct rumble was unmistakably an attempt at forming speech. Some gasped, some cowered; Lydia winced as Jane's grip on her hand tightened.

"Can this really be Uncle George?" Jane said. It didn't sound much like him.

Miss Evangeline seemed to recognize the presence. "Eustace, is that you?"

The growl uttered a noise that was taken to be assent. Several around the table nodded and relaxed. Eustace had visited before.

Lydia pried Jane's fingers loose and patted her hand. "It's all right, Janie. This spirit is known here. I sense we are not in danger." Lydia seemed intense but not fearful. Her pupils were dark; she exuded a kind of avidity that her cousin found both perplexing and enviable.

"I wonder if Eustace has met Uncle George," Jane whispered back.

Miss Evangeline expressed the same thought. "Eustace, we beg your assistance, please. There is one among us who desires to hear the voice of her late husband. Might you be a conduit for a message from…from whom, dear? Remind me of the name."

Aunt Madeleine required a nudge from her niece. "My husband, George," she said faintly. "Mr. George Talmadge." She sat rigid, her eyes darting around the room in search of the spirit behind the voice.

From across the table Mrs. Lucy Wright was gazing at the opposite wall, giving the impression that she could see Mr. Talmadge standing behind his wife. Both Jane and Lydia chanced a glance, but Uncle George did not reveal himself.

Essie uttered another groaning sound and the fog in the room thickened.

"George? Is that you? George?" Auntie's voice was high and plaintive.

And then all the candles went out. Jane could not suppress a small shriek.

"Do stay calm," commanded Miss Evangeline. "There is no need to fear. Please sit still." This proved impossible for Jane, who felt the chair beneath her jostled by another presence. She thought she might faint from the nearness of the spirit.

But it was neither Uncle George nor Eustace who was the cause of the upset but a small newcomer who had opened the door abruptly enough to knock Jane's chair askew and to set up a breeze that extinguished the candles.

A short, pudgy boy stood in the doorway, his silhouette faintly visible against the somewhat lighter hallway.

"John Edward! You know you are not to come in here when we are in session," exclaimed Lucy Wright.

"But I'm hungry," said John Edward.

Mrs. Wright was full of embarrassed apologies as she ushered her son out of the room to satisfy his shamefully prosaic needs. Exasperated and ruffled, she expressed the hope that Eustace would not have been unduly disturbed and the session could continue.

"Unlikely," said Miss Evangeline with a hint of reproach. "Once interrupted, spirits are reluctant to return of an evening."

She stood and relit the candles, and there was a scraping of chairs as the assembly began to break up. Shared glances of disapproval darted around the table at the inability of their dedicated member to control her child, but it is hard to criticize a mother in her own house. Still, despite the lamentably brief moment of spectral communion, the arrival of Eustace had been sustaining.

The Everett sisters turned to Aunt Madeleine. "I'm very sorry, Mrs. Talmadge. We have disappointed you," said Miss Essie. "But I hope that what you have seen here has allowed you to believe that a summons to the afterlife is far from impossible. As you continue on your way, I predict that Mr. Lewis will be able to afford the satisfaction you seek. No, please do not weep; there is no call to be discouraged. It sometimes takes a while before a recently departed spirit is able to appear amongst the living. Give him time. Your husband will come to you, I am sure. This evening has not been in vain."

7

Afterthoughts

The presence—and the absence—of spirits visiting from beyond left a disturbing residue in their minds. Excitement, fear, hope, apprehension, confusion, all combined to produce disquieting dreams and frequent wakefulness, eyes peeled against the dark to detect faint apparitions, ears attuned to footfalls where no foot trod, skin atingle with the sense of presences nearby. The discomfort of their accommodations did not help. When Madeleine fell into a doze, she snored, disturbing her nieces. When Jane slept, she dreamed and moaned, and when she turned and tossed in her narrow bed every fiber in the mattress set up a rubbing squeal. Lydia spent the night in a state somewhere between wake and sleep, seeing or dreaming or imagining spirits hovering in the corners of the room.

None of them was well rested, but in the morning, Aunt Madeleine was suffused with febrile energy. Unlike her usual habit, she awoke early and returned to the home of the Miss Everetts to seek further information about the whereabouts of Alexander Dodge Lewis. She was gone for some hours and on return reported that she had agreed to another attempt with them that evening, but if George failed to appear, she was determined to seek out someone whose voice might have greater summoning power. She tossed her bonnet on a chair, sat down hard, and sought a handkerchief to stem the sudden tears pent up from the morning's efforts.

"Dear Aunt Madeleine, calm yourself," pleaded Lydia. "Your distress is understandable, but take heart from what Miss Everett said last night. It will take time for Uncle George to appear to you. As she said, the spirits are rarely summoned so readily. With patience, I am sure he will be among those who come."

Jane stared at her cousin. The reassurance was kind, but could Lydia possibly believe that the solution to their problems lay beyond the grave? She herself had spent a terrible night fleeing horrid dreams and had awakened with the vivid memory of her own dead mother, those dull, sunken eyes and the slack jaw exposing her leaking, foul gums before it was bound shut. And worst of all, the lingering smell of the disease that had left her body an alien thing. Commanded to kiss her mother farewell, Jane had closed her eyes and only approached the dead flesh with her lips, permitting her hair to fall forward to hide the fact that she avoided that final touch.

Were her mother to appear among the spirits, would it be that horrid corpse that she had been at the end? Or the loving, lively woman that Jane preferred to remember? What form do dead souls retain after their bodies lie corrupt? She didn't want to find out. Commanding their return seemed a ghastly and hazardous business.

Those questions stuck in her throat, for Lydia's sympathetic gaze at their aunt also looked a good deal like eager anticipation. The atmosphere of the room the night before had repelled Jane, but Lydia's reaction had been different, almost excited. They had both confessed to being afraid, but fear takes many forms. The fast-beating heart, the shallow breathing, the sense of threat. Jane had felt dread approaching. Clutching her cousin's hand, she looked at Lydia and saw the pulse throbbing visibly in her slender neck. Her posture erect, her lips parted. At once fearful and electrified. How I envy her bravery, thought Jane.

Exhausted from a night ill-slept, Madeleine fell into a doze in her chair.

"Liddy," whispered Jane, "do you think it wise to encourage Auntie's hopes like this?"

"Why not? What has she to lose with this hope? And, indeed, it is not only I who offer encouragement!" Lydia's reply was quick and emphatic. "It is the very possibility of communication with the dead. You were there yourself. Did you not sense that spirits might be nearby? Did you not feel the change in the air?"

"I did sense a chill," Jane admitted. "But it might have been simple fear. I often shiver when I am afraid."

"Miss Everett did not think so prosaic an explanation appropriate, nor did Mrs. Wright. And that voice! We all heard that voice. And for a certainty, it did not belong to anyone present in the room. No one living, that is."

Recalling the dreadful rumble of Eustace made Jane shiver again. But now it occurred to her to wonder how that odd growl issuing from the throat of a small woman had come to have a name. The situation was both horrifying and absurd. Thinking of the comic aspects of a grumbling ghost helped to calm her agitation. As did the thought that if spirits could be deterred by the simple entrance of a hungry child, they might not be so fearsome after all.

"Perhaps you are right," she conceded. "I confess that I don't relish the thought of the dead returning to us, at least around a table in a stranger's house. What is more, I think it very likely that they do not return at all, despite the strangeness in the air last night. Nevertheless, Auntie will be sorely disappointed if Uncle George fails to appear. But even if he does, I don't see how a ghost will be able to convince a lawyer to overturn a will."

"It is truly all very new," admitted Lydia. "Though I am not ready to dismiss the possibility that we are on the brink of new discoveries with regard to the afterlife. You should keep an open mind, Janie. However, you are right that lawyers are apt to be skeptics about such things. Perhaps what transpires this evening will be more assuring. And even if it is not, Aunt Madeleine will not be satisfied until she meets this Mr. Lewis again. He may be able to succeed where others have failed."

"Perhaps he might. He certainly captured Auntie's attention. And I believe we can well guess why he turned up after Uncle George's funeral, for he was probably suggesting to Auntie the possibility of calling forth the dearly departed. I hope he is not one of those comely men who prey upon widows."

"There is no need to be suspicious." Lydia's tone was confident and reassuring. "The Miss Everetts know him well and testify to his good character. And at any rate, it isn't as though Auntie has all that much to be preyed upon, does she? Not with the will leaving her out. She carries her worldly goods with her, and they don't amount to much more than some jewelry and the banknotes that were given her by the lawyers to cover the journey west."

"Yes, that's true, although the jewelry is very fine. Still, if Mr. Lewis consents to help her under these circumstances, it would be difficult to discern an ulterior motive."

On the other hand, thought Jane, if a spectral message were somehow to loosen the ample purse Uncle George had left to his sons, the person who brought that message to his grateful widow might have something to gain. She quashed the idea as an unworthy suspicion.

8

KAREN'S QUEST

BUFFALO, NEW YORK. JUNE 30, 2015

"Here you are. You're a hard man to find."

Dan turned and squinted up at the voice to discover Karen at the edge of his trench. She was wearing a short skirt and high-wedged sandals, quite a contrast to the clothes she had worn while digging around the skeleton. Attractive, but not very appropriate for visiting a gas line excavation. Her bare toes were edged with dust.

"Dan!" yelled Carl from six houses away. "Bring another coupling down this way."

"Hang on a minute." Dan vaulted out of the trench, sprinkling more dirt over Karen's shoes. She stepped back and stumbled over a pile of rocks, barely missing a fall. She watched as Dan selected something from a pile of other somethings, told Karen to watch her step, and delivered the something to a spot half way down the block. It wasn't quite the welcome she had hoped for.

She moved back farther into a driveway, noting with curiosity that the trench was open where sidewalks had been laid but had somehow been drilled beneath the concrete of driveways. She scanned the long hole, thinking how marvelous it would be to find more artifacts, but here the narrow opening was lined with nothing more than dense tree roots and rock. Lots of rock.

"Lots of rock," she remarked as Dan returned.

"You have no idea," he said. "Those bones are in an unusually non-rocky part. Most of this part of the city is bedrock."

"Yes. Even though it isn't a real grave," said Karen. "Not in a cemetery anyhow. There are none of the typical signs of formal burial. And of course, she was the only one there." Her words were more academic than the casual, friendly banter she had planned. But now that she had found him—having borrowed Jacob's car and visited all the gas work sites on the west side—she was unexpectedly nervous. "But who knows, it was a long time ago."

"How long ago do you figure?" Dan was sorting through his tools and showing signs of wanting to return to the trench, so Karen sped up her chat.

"At least a hundred and fifty and maybe two hundred years. Long ago for this part of the world."

"Unless she's Indian."

"Right. The arrowhead. But the bones aren't nearly old enough to be associated with arrowheads, which would be the products of a more ancient culture." (Of course, he knows that, she thought. Stop sounding so stuffy.) "Did you find out where it came from?"

"Not precisely. Frankly, the guy who picked it up probably doesn't remember exactly where it was. But it wasn't near your dig, as I already told you. Look, I can't talk now. Gotta work."

"Okay, but wait." Karen followed him back to the edge of the trench. "Aren't you going to come and dig with us some more? After all, you found her. Aren't you curious to find out more?"

Dan paused. "I drove by the other day and no one was there," he said. "I figured you'd stopped excavating."

"We stopped work briefly to wait for Craig. That is, for the faculty advisor who supervises local things when something old turns up unexpectedly. But he had an accident and was delayed. But then he called again and said to carry on, and now we're back at work digging around for surrounding artifacts." Karen saw his curiosity pique and thought sadly, He is interested in the dig, not in me. Then she was annoyed with herself for feeling that way, maybe even for coming here at all. She continued. "And we've found some that look pretty interesting. Some kind of chain, maybe a necklace. Wouldn't you like—"

"Dan!" A command from down the trench. Dan turned to go. Karen felt her opportunity slipping away.

"Wait, I also came to ask you about something else." It was worth one more try. "Would you like, do you maybe want to go to a concert tomorrow night?" Dan turned back questioningly. "The team is all going." His face was unreadable, and she began to feel even more awkward. I shouldn't have come, she thought. I should have stuck by my resolve to give up men for a while. She could tell the blood was rising to her cheeks and hoped the day was warm enough that Dan would assume she was merely hot. "Think about it. It'll be down at the marina. And there will be fireworks. You should come too." And as his expression remained tentative, "You're part of the team as well. Please come."

"Dan! Yo, Dan! Earth to Dan!"

The commanding admonition was coming from Carl, who was really just trying to make Dan uncomfortable by calling attention to his pretty diversion. At that moment the gas inspector was walking by, making notes about the new hookups. Dan snagged the pen from the inspector's clipboard and grabbed Karen's hand.

"Here's my number. Call me tonight with the details. I have to get back to work." He wrote seven digits on her forearm and returned the pen to its amused owner. Then with a slight smile at Karen, he vaulted back into the trench.

She read the numerals inked on her skin between the large fingerprints left by his work gloves. "Okay," she said to the air before leaving the work zone and the beam of inquiring eyes she sensed following her down the street. The meeting hadn't gone exactly as she had hoped; he hadn't seemed all that delighted to see her. But at the end there had been that little smile. The roughness of his gloves and his firm grip stayed on her skin. She thought about not ever washing her arm again, reminding her of fifth grade when Paul Ruff had given her wrist a flirtatious pinch. She hadn't thought about that crush for years. Funny how a sensation can awaken a memory.

Carl lumbered into the trench beside Dan. His bulk made it hard to work in the narrow space. "The Black chick is hotter," he said, raring for a tease and hoping to rile the younger man.

Dan didn't take the bait. His retort was stalled by competing emotions: offended on Jasmine's behalf for the label, and also defensive with regard to the less-hot Karen. She is perfectly attractive when she's not covered with dirt, he thought. Or actually, even with the dirt. He thought of her flushing face and wondered how rude he had appeared. No one else from the archaeological group had made any attempt to find him, even though he had twice driven by the dig, still covered with a tarp but with no signs of continued activity. He had assumed that they had shut up shop and forgotten him and his connection with the skeleton. Disappointed, he had even felt mildly aggrieved. Now with an explanation, he was somewhat mollified.

And he had to admit that the prospect of digging to discover what else had lain for years beside those bones—rather than to lay a pipeline—was inviting.

9

LUCILLE

The windy gusts had been a tease. For two days huge clouds dark with rain gathered overhead only to be blown east, adding a stir of humid dust to the excavated neighborhoods. Thirsty gardens wilted, home-owners who had scurried outside to mow the grass before the deluge arrived watched with frustration as their balding lawns further shriveled. Taunting sheets of gray rain could be seen drenching a distant horizon.

For the young archaeologists it was a blessing, despite their clogged sinuses and irritated throats. They—including Dan, who now tried to exit his job at the earliest possible moment each day—worked to widen their trench in search of artifacts accompanying the skeleton, but the need to be careful slowed their progress. Patches of rock and obdu-rate roots hindered their efforts, and the clay clung to everything so that they had to take apart sticky clumps with their fingers to be sure no clothing shreds or other objects were stuck within. Although their roped-off zone had been extended, so far only a little more had turned up. Some scraps of fabric, a broken necklace, a twisted object that had once been a shoe. Whoever lay there seemed to have died alone and empty-handed.

At some point they had named her Lucille, though whether after the Leakeys's famous Lucy—mother of us all—or after B.B. King's guitar was in dispute.

She sings to me, said Jacob, to whom the name had first occurred. There was no particular reason it should have; he was just in a fine and energetic mood that day. Karen didn't bother to say that she had never heard of B.B. King.

Jasmine crabbed that the skeleton shouldn't have a name at all, not at this point. One needs to remain disinterested, and a name makes one feel too emotionally connected. She was nervous that they might have made some procedural mistakes that would be pointed out when their faculty advisor finally returned, and she might be held responsible. The whimsical name might make them seem even more unprofessional. Her scruples were overridden.

Jacob insisted that Lucille was a nice name, but he conceded that there was no good masculine equivalent should the skeleton turn out to be male after all.

To which both Dan and Karen had chimed, "Lucifer!" in unison. Dan grinned and punched her lightly on the shoulder and Karen felt warm. Warmer. The nasty breakup with last year's boyfriend was beginning to recede. I hope this isn't just a rebound, she thought.

"But surely she's female," said Jasmine. "That necklace wouldn't have belonged to a man."

"Unless he stole it," said Jacob. Such speculative banter kept them going during some of the stickiest weather of the summer.

Their faces were streaked with runnels of sweat beneath sticky, scalp-plastered hair. Karen had worn mascara only one day before deciding it was better to look a little sparse around the eyelids than to have commas of black next to her nose. She envied Jasmine the luxurious lashes bequeathed from her West Indian father.

Dr. Killian finally joined the team, jet-lagged and yawning after having endured a long, bumpy jeep ride and two badly delayed flights to come back from his Utah dig to superintend the site. Streaks of dark bruises decorated his shins, and he carried a set of crutches but set them aside to look into the trench. He pronounced himself reasonably content with the work done thus far and approved of the decision to leave the skeleton in its grip of roots until the entire packet of earth and bones could be removed. Jasmine breathed a sigh of relief. Dan was quietly pleased that the explanation for his presence was accepted. At first, Killian had looked at him blankly, as if worried he might have misplaced the face of a student. Noting his expression, Karen had quickly reported how much help Dan had been. And besides, he is the one who originally found her, added Jacob. Extra muscles had come in handy as they labored with the packed and stony earth.

"Ah, our Howard Carter," said Killian with a smile, shaking Dan's hand.

Jasmine refrained from identifying Howard Carter for Dan, who was fairly certain that Killian was really comparing him to an anonymous native digger in the desert rather than a real archaeologist. One of those dark-skinned background characters in the movies who never appear in the credits.

Actually, he soon decided that Killian wasn't such a bad guy. He was younger than he imagined a senior professor would be, maybe only in his forties. And he didn't mind getting dirty either. Of course, if you didn't like dirt, you would need a different line of work, for the past is buried in dirt. Killian had arrived at the site in worn cut-offs with a ludicrous number of fraying pockets that indicated he was wearing the tattered remains of cargo pants. He was casual about the line of bruises and recent scabs that his attire failed to conceal. "Slipped off a ladder last week," he said. "Nothing serious." His bandages needed changing before long, but he ignored how quickly they became soiled. He had a pair of protective gloves, but they stayed in his back pocket because he preferred to work with his hands. "Skin has feeling," he said. "Gloves don't." His nails were cracked and filthy, but he stroked the emerging bones with the sensitive pads of his fingers like a musician testing an old violin. "Glad you guys didn't try to pry the bones loose yet," he said approvingly. "You were right to document them right here on the scene."

Finally the clouds made good on their promise and the rains did come. Now the site was topped with a waterproof tent to protect their work, so they had to shout to each other above the drum of raindrops and the occasional rumble of thunder. Dan was privately delighted at the bad weather, since his job on the mains was suspended for the duration. The tent kept their heads dry, but the rain still found them, snaking in around their feet with such sly warmth that they were ankle deep before they knew they were wet. This was the disadvantage of setting up a dig along a utility site, for the trench that had been opened for the new lines stretched for three long blocks and could be neither completely covered nor drained. After half a day of downpour they were soaked in water so filled with silt and clay that a dropped tool took minutes of fumbling on hands and knees before it could be retrieved.

The earth finally relinquished Lucille. The task of extracting her from the cage of roots was saved for the lab, for their tight embrace had protected her from complete disarticulation. Except for the detached femur that had first signaled her presence, her bones appeared to be more or less connected, although it was the network of roots that had kept her skeleton whole, gradually warping its original shape with the slow growth of the now long dead tree.

A probe around the skull indicated that her lower jaw might still be missing. "Not uncommon," said Killian. "The hinge of the lower mandible is often the first to come apart. No doubt we'll find it eventually, though it's kind of odd that it didn't remain in place, given the disposition of the other bones."

"I hope it wasn't carted off with the backhoe," worried Jasmine.

"I don't think it could have been," said Dan. "The skull is lodged in those roots, and the hoe didn't go into them. You see how narrow and neat the digging has been." Straddling both excavations, he felt he needed to defend the gas line work.

Craig nodded in agreement. "It'll turn up," he said optimistically.

Lucille was lifted from the trench on the piece of supporting plywood that had been her bier all week. The few artifacts found with her, a frail segment of chain with a dented locket and some clothing fragments, were piled at her feet. She was laid on a section of muddy grass half protected by the makeshift tent while Karen shot more photos. Dan felt the urge to say a prayer, which surprised him since he hadn't been to church in three years and probably hadn't prayed then either. Jacob would realize later that he was chanting the Sh'ma under his breath.

"Are we right, Craig?" asked Jasmine. "Is it female?"

It seemed that graduate students were on a first-name basis with their professors, so Dan had decided he was too.

"Hard to say for sure at this point," said Dr. Killian. Craig. "From what I can see of the shoulder width, I would say probably female, or perhaps a young boy. The pelvic bones need closer examination when we get her—or him—into the lab and cleaned up."

"How long do you think she's been in the ground?" It was hard to give up the feminine pronoun.

"Not sure yet. Many years, though. The bones have absorbed a lot of the pigment from the clay around them. This is not a recent burial. But I've been wondering why we've just found her now so many years later. Why wasn't she discovered earlier when the gas mains were first laid?"

Dan could answer that. "These trenches are in a new location," he said. "The old mains run down the center of the street. These new ones are under the walks on either side. But I've been wondering something else. Isn't it kind of strange that there are only bones here? I mean, there are some remnants of clothing, but not much. Wouldn't you think that there would be something left other than her skeleton?"

"That's a good question," said Killian. "Of course, if she was there long enough, organic fibers would have decayed. Bugs and worms and mold—nature consumes everything eventually. The speed and thoroughness of the decomposition depends upon the composition of the soil."

"But doesn't it seem like a hasty burial? And suspicious?"

"Good question," Craig said again. Perhaps that was his habit with students. "In my view, it is. But there may be other things nearby that were displaced over time and by the growth of what used to be a tree here. It's likely that we just haven't found them yet. We'll keep sifting through the earth removed from the area. There is likely to be more evidence of clothing too, just so coated with clay that it isn't clearly fabric. The site will have to be kept cordoned off for a while before we determine that we've gotten all there is to find."

Dan was glad to hear that prediction. He didn't expect to be invited to follow them into the lab, but he could return to the site, since he seemed to be included in that *we*. Still, he doubted that the site could remain roped off as long as Craig hoped. His suspicion was immediately confirmed.

"Unfortunately, the city is eager to get this street work completed," added Killian. "We're under some time pressure, because the residents around here are protesting and want their sidewalks back. So we'll have to work as quickly as we can. And although the lack of a coffin indicates that this was a single, quick burial—which as Dan says, is kind of suspicious—and also the absence of tombstones suggests the same, we still have to be sure that there was never a graveyard here. Even a small churchyard or a family plot."

"There wasn't," said Dan. "I already checked."

Everyone stared. Dan shifted his feet uncomfortably. He had meant to introduce that fact more smoothly.

"How do you know that?" asked Killian.

(Thank God you knew that, thought Jasmine, who was thinking that she should have checked herself.)

Well, it was bound to come out sometime. Dan drew a long breath before saying, "For one thing, the gas works have maps of the underground infrastructure in the area. Water mains and so forth. Cables. Their positions have to be checked before any deep digging takes place. Plus…" He sighed. "Plus, I kind of know some people who work with the local preservationists. They were hanging around that little museum down the street last weekend when I was helping out there with the removal of old wallpaper. I asked about this site. Everyone is interested that there would be a skeleton here. And of course, it's been in the newspaper. Anyhow, they assured me that no graveyard is on record for this area."

"Preservationists!" exclaimed Killian. "Of course! Our natural allies. They are always on the side of halting change and digging up the past."

"Well, they also will want the new gas lines to function," cautioned Dan. "But they'll probably help buy you some time."

"Excellent suggestion!" said Killian. "I should have thought of that right away. And I should have remembered the museum nearby. An old historic house, isn't it? Been closed for a while, I think, but planning to open again soon. Renovating, are they?" He took out his cell phone and scrolled through his address book with fingers so muddy the screen was smudged. "And now that you mention it, I know just who to call. I think I still have the number, maybe. Ah yes."

Dan couldn't see the number he dialed, but he was pretty sure he knew who would answer.

10

LYDIA'S PORTRAIT

UTICA, NEW YORK. JUNE 3, 1851

The warm air carried the scent of peonies and clover. Jane sat in the dappled shade of high trees, feeling calm and optimistic. The apprehension lingering from the disturbing evenings in Little Falls had finally dissipated, and she no longer felt the need to look behind her to check for strange shadows. Doubtless there would be more murky evenings in store for them all, but at the moment she simply luxuriated in the sunshine.

Uncle George had again failed to appear, but following the suggestions of the Miss Everetts, Aunt Madeleine had finally tracked down the whereabouts of Mr. Alexander Dodge Lewis. Now they were slated to stay for a while in Utica while she persuaded the acclaimed spiritualist to call forth her late husband. Her intentions were explicit now. She was bent on finding Uncle George. His spirit, that is.

"But, Auntie," Jane had ventured, "surely the lawyers won't be convinced—"

"All I want is a proper farewell," Aunt Madeleine had tartly interrupted. Not, perhaps, unreasonable under the circumstances. So they were on a search for whatever phantom wisps might linger from the corporeal George Talmadge.

Jane put that shivery thought out of her mind for the time being and reveled in the fact that they were no longer in transit. Time to do a bit of washing, time to explore a new town, time to unpack the bags.

From the latter Jane had unearthed her paints and brushes, her charcoal and crayons and her scanty supply of uncreased paper. Now all of this was arrayed before her on a makeshift easel, little more than a slanted board, but enough to establish a plausible image as an artist. A limner. A portraitist. A small stack of completed drawings lay by her side, suggesting that her brush was swift and skilled and that her creations might be worth paying for. In fact, they were earlier products of her brush that she had brought from Troy, but no matter; they were hers. She had placed the best ones on top.

Her model was being less than cooperative. "Please do stop peering around so much," said Jane. Lydia sighed and straightened her posture.

"Apologies, but you have set me looking in the most boring direction you could. All the people in the park are walking behind me, and I can't see what is going on. There is simply this dull pond to gaze at. The ducks are of limited interest, you have to admit. Three of them have gone to sleep, and there is nothing more tedious than watching a sleeping duck. They are just feathered lumps. And this stool is far from comfortable. How long will you take to finish?"

"The point is not finishing, as you well know." Jane was familiar with her cousin's habit of animated conversation when in the grip of tedium. It was best ignored. "The point is to be observed to be in the process of rendering your portrait so that others will want theirs done too. In fact, I am working as slowly as I can, so be patient."

"Well, I wish you had set me facing in the other direction."

The portrait was going rather well, Jane thought. It was composed in the popular style of a seated figure in profile, but she had turned the shoulders so that more could be seen of Lydia's neck and arms, rather as if she were glancing over her shoulder. Faces were difficult. It was much easier to sketch clothing and jewelry and hair, and Lydia's attire was emerging in precise detail. As soon as the form of her sitter was sketched in, Jane planned to add a sheltering tree and a wavering horizon of water to indicate a lake. It would make for a more pleasing composition than that afforded by the small duck pond—hardly more than a puddle—where they now sat. There were a few marks of erasure around the nose, but once the profile had been drawn to her satisfaction, it had been fairly easy to place eyes, mouth, and even ears on the rest of the head. Well, the ears had been a little troublesome at first, but those improvised coils of hair covered them nicely. The image was coming to life on her paper.

It was the kind of day that Jane loved most. The sun thoughtfully kept its rays from sending piercing reflections from the small pond, and the high shade cast through the windless trees permitted full light without the flickers of blowing leaves. A day perfect for looking, for studying the shapes and colors and shadows of everything around, for testing her observations. When she had first begun to paint, she had assumed it would be easy, for isn't drawing just putting on paper what is displayed to the eye? But the slippage between eye and hand was profound. When she managed to render a shape, a shade, a color, or most of all a person accurately, it was as if a whole world opened in miniature. But it took time and patience, as well as tolerance for failure and repeated trying. Lydia might desire to move, but Jane was comfortable and content to sit still and study her form. The water view was pretty, she thought, describable as picturesque, and if Lydia would curb her energy for the time being, even she might enjoy the tranquility.

A young couple strolled past and paused to see what Jane was doing. She shot them a smile but concentrated on the folds of Lydia's dress. The presence of onlookers at her shoulder was sufficiently unnerving that the girl in the drawing soon appeared to have three knees. The couple moved on and Jane set about with her gum eraser.

"Auntie says she has plenty of money for our trip," said Lydia after the couple was out of earshot. "I don't see why you think you need to commence being an artist already."

"Well, we might not be with her forever. She has yet to receive assurance of our welcome from her Rochester cousin. It won't hurt to earn a few more pennies here and there. Besides, I'm enjoying myself."

"Also, it might violate her sense of propriety, your being out here in a public place for all to see." This sentiment was uttered with little conviction, for Lydia was a young woman of advanced views and usually had scant regard for propriety. It was just more idle chat to occupy her lively mind.

"It is perfectly proper for a young lady to draw and to paint," Jane retorted. "Indeed, it is part of our standard education, as you well know. You chose clanking a keyboard over learning to draw. Mine at least is a quieter pursuit, even if it sometimes falls short of rendering a pleasing scene. Although I grant you that selling the products of pencil and brush is not the chief purpose of the art of a proper young woman of the highest caliber. Perhaps someone in my impoverished position simply isn't of that station, and if someone wants to buy my paintings, I'll be grateful."

"I consider ladylike daubing a waste of the female brain," Lydia persisted. "And there is no keyboard for me to clank, as you so flatteringly put it, now that we have left Troy." Jane didn't reply. She recognized boredom seeking diversion by trying to raise an argument.

Two children appeared at her elbow. "What are you doing?" said one. "Dancing a jig," said Jane.

Being literal minded, the children stared in perplexity. But they stayed, and soon their mother appeared.

"Oh, what a lovely picture. How talented you are!" she exclaimed. And thereby became Jane's first commission.

It wasn't easy to draw squirming little boys, but once she managed the matching pug-nosed profiles, it was a matter of minutes to supply their little blue suits and squared-toed shoes. She had set them on the ground facing each other, the one holding a ball, the other reaching for it. There had been a squabble over who would hold the toy, but it was quickly settled by four hands touching it together. Jane painted it as she imagined, consulting the models only occasionally. The boys scampered off to throw pebbles at the ducks long before she was finished.

The mother was pleased with the result.

"And what may I pay you for your labors?" she asked in a light tone that hinted the question was merely for the sake of politeness and the hope that this young woman was sketching portraits as an idle pastime.

"Thirty cents, please," said Jane, and fortunately the woman was carrying her purse.

The news of her earnings prompted mildly insulting surprise.

"Really? Someone paid you to draw? How very gratifying." Aunt Madeleine was only briefly impressed. She had put on one of her nicest dresses and was fussing with her hair before the mirror. Ruby earrings sparkled against her carefully arranged curls.

"You look quite dazzling, Auntie," said Jane.

"Thank you, dear. Now, please, do change for the evening as soon as you can. Mr. Lewis will be meeting us just at nightfall. He is a busy man and we'd best not keep him waiting."

Apart from the brief glimpse at their uncle's funeral, neither Lydia nor Jane had seen Mr. Lewis, though judging from their aunt's description it was clear that she had found the right man. The gentleman had greeted her pleasantly, she reported, and had remembered the details of her husband's funeral and the occasion when they had met.

Bright-eyed and febrile, Aunt Madeleine had learned the streets of Utica quickly. Her step quickened as she approached a tall man, well-dressed and broad of shoulder. Jane and Lydia held back and noted approvingly how he bent to greet the much shorter Mrs. Talmadge with winsome thoughtfulness.

He was just as handsome as they remembered. His waving dark hair curved over his skull and nestled at the nape of his neck. His brown eyes were both warm and probing, as though he sought to understand perfectly not only what was said but the mind behind the words. His own fluent speech was uttered after the faintest of pauses, for he weighed his words carefully in order to address both the speech and the sentiments of others. He greeted Madeleine by recalling again the details of meeting her just after her grievous loss and expressing the hope that she was well in mind and spirit. After assuring himself of this, he turned to the younger women and bowed with courtesy and a dash of courtliness.

Lydia was immediately captivated. Jane smiled at the sight of her pretty cousin flushing with delight as Mr. Lewis bent over her hand, almost bestowing an old-fashioned kiss. Perhaps this will be the rich husband who will set our course aright, she thought. How nice it would be no longer to occupy the role of penniless and orphaned cousins. She let her imagination roam into the future. Though he was considerably older, Lydia and this man would make a handsome pair.

She assumed that Mr. Lewis was a man of wealth, judging from his fine clothes. The cuffs of his shirt were pristine and sharply pressed, and brass buttons with a raised design of oak leaves marched down his sharply tailored waistcoat. He presented the confident picture of a man of means, and his manners were amiable. Jane felt herself succumbing to his charm as well, her own cheeks warming at the touch of his hand, smiling in response to his greeting.

This evening, as was only appropriate, his attention was chiefly directed to Aunt Madeleine, who took his offered arm as they walked. Lydia positioned herself at his other side, and Jane trailed slightly behind. The bricks of the street were uneven, and she had to watch her step in the growing dusk. It would be embarrassing to stumble. She paid little attention to their murmured conversation and concentrated on keeping up with their pace.

Mr. Lewis escorted them to a large house at the end of a street lined with stately chestnut trees.

"My abode when I am in Utica," he said. "It belongs to my widowed sister, Mrs. Grace Sibley, to whom I shall introduce you. It is one of several places I stay during my frequent travels. Humble but adequate for our purposes, I hope." The door was opened by a housekeeper, and they passed through connected hallways from which two elegant parlors branched. To Jane's eyes the house hardly qualified as humble. Eventually they reached a small room set off from the dining area.

"Here we shall not be disturbed," Mr. Lewis assured them. "My sister is a member, indeed a founder, of the local spiritualist community, which is correspondent with the Temple you visited recently at Little Falls. It is crucial that those of us who are the pioneers of this new science coordinate our endeavors and prove the soundness of our beliefs against their many decriers. I consider her a kindred spirit and a woman of great discernment. She is well apprised of the quiet and privacy required for the task before us. But first, may I offer you some refreshment?"

Aunt Madeleine was inclined to refuse in her eagerness to begin, but Mr. Lewis soothed her impatience and ushered her to one of the upholstered chairs.

"I urge you to have just one or two sips of this calming tea, madam. It is a mixture of my own, and I have found that it relaxes the mind in a way that is most conducive for spirits to visit. They, being unencumbered by the gross physical attachments that ground those of us who still inhabit the living world, are highly attuned to our mental states. A tranquil and open mind is needed for them to appear."

He poured a fragrant liquid into teacups edged with gilt. It was still hot, clearly prepared just recently. Jane wondered if his sister had boiled the kettle, having intuited their immanent arrival, but was too daunted by their host to inquire. The tea was a striking crimson in color, pleasantly sweet offset with a tang of sharpness.

"Rose hip?" she ventured, and was rewarded with a smile from Mr. Lewis.

"A discriminating taste, Miss Woodfield," he said, and she was pleased at his approval—and also by the fact that he had registered her name. With her cousin and aunt bearing different surnames, so many acquaintances just referred to them all as Talmadge.

"Rose hip indeed," he continued. "From the garden just behind this house. Enhanced by honey from local bee hives. Nettles, roses, bee balm, borage. A bit of valerian and just a hint of lavender, which is so strong a flavor that it readily overtakes the others. Most healthy and sustaining."

"It's lovely, thank you," said Lydia.

All agreed that the tea was tasty and revitalizing after a long day. The ladies drank their cups to the full while night gently fell outside and the windows darkened.

Then Mr. Lewis placed three tall candles at the center of a table, and they settled down to wait.

11

A NATURAL MEDIUM

UTICA, NEW YORK. JUNE 3, EVENING INTO NIGHT

The candles emitted a scent that was both sweet and dark. The light they cast seemed to shrink the space of the room to a globe of faint gold. The walls around receded into shadow.

"It will take some time to prepare your minds and bodies to be receptive to visits from those who inhabit the afterlife," said Alexander Dodge Lewis. "And, therefore, I judge it best to begin our task with just the three of you. Later others may join us, but for now, please relax and wait."

"I thank you for this thoughtfulness, Mr. Lewis," said Aunt Madeleine. "The group at Little Falls was larger, although everyone was welcoming and most kind. But perhaps the spirits sensed that the three of us were not yet attuned to them, and we disturbed the atmosphere of the group."

When did she come to that conclusion? Jane wondered. Both her aunt and cousin were nodding and looking hopeful. Jane sought to imitate their demeanor.

Mr. Lewis bent his head in acknowledgement and continued his explanation. "Indeed, a peaceful atmosphere is most important. One must be receptive. Sometimes it is I who speak at gatherings such as this, but you must not assume that spirits will only communicate through me. Any of us may become conduits for their messages."

Jane felt her heart quicken at that thought. It was both exciting and dreadful to imagine that a spirit might single her out for its message. But Mr. Lewis did not indicate that there was anything to fear. He believes that spirits are benign, she thought. But how can he be sure?

"You must be tranquil, feel peace," he said as if reading her unsettled mind. "A spirit may come at any time, whether day or night, though I myself find a darkened room to be propitious. The candles that I have just lit will act as an aid to prepare your minds and hearts, for they are imbued with a substance of harmonious purity that, if you take into your selves until it permeates your spirit, will come to match the essence of the ethereal presences we invite into our company."

Harmonious purity, thought Jane. She looked at Lydia for some guidance about this mysterious directive, but her cousin's attention was intensely, avidly, fastened on Mr. Lewis. Taking her lead, Jane turned and studied him as well. Her nervousness gradually abated as she saw that he sat in a tranquil attitude, neither insistent nor hesitant, merely offering an invitation to join him on a foray into the spirit world. With the warmth of the tea spreading through her limbs, she too sat back and relaxed.

"The sense of smell represents an intermediary between the physical and the spiritual domains," he intoned. "Unlike other human senses, it partakes of both worlds. Think of how differently the senses engage us. Vision and hearing are vast in expanse, producing no bodily sensation. One sees, one hears, almost as if disembodied. In contrast, taste and touch remind us of our physical being, gross, heavy, material. But smell—ah, our sense of smell provides a pathway between them both—the spiritual and unearthly and the physical lives we lead day to day."

I have never thought about these things before, thought Jane. How wise he is. It is all becoming clearer to me now.

"But this pathway only opens for those who attend receptively to its powers. Odor emanates from physical things, for all creation has its own scent. When we smell, fragrance enters our body but produces no sensation. Rather, it lifts us upward beyond the physical. Can you not feel yourself rising even now?"

Yes, Jane thought. I am lighter. The burning candles permeated her senses until she felt filled with their scented flame.

"I advise you to inhale deeply, ladies, but slowly. Do not seek to hasten the process. Focus on the atmosphere created from the fire of the candles. Small fires, but how they burn—burn away the preoccupations of the everyday, leaving us open to the eternal. Feel their warmth, absorb their quality, lose yourself in the surrounding air as if you were but a petal fastened to earth by the frailest stem."

They inhaled in unison, following the voice, itself becoming as disembodied as the scent surrounding them. Jane imagined what it would be like to float, her tether barely fastened to the ground. Perhaps it was like being immersed in water, drifting with a gentle current. Her head began to whirl slightly. It was both pleasant and unsettling.

"Relinquish your worries, your fears, your doubts. Let care fade away and prepare your mind for a visit from those for whom all cares have ceased. It will take time. With patience, you will feel the moment that a presence arrives."

The candles burned steadily, their flames gradually lengthening as they reached into the air.

"Breathe, feel," said Mr. Lewis, his voice soft and captivating. "Let yourself go. Be without effort or tension. And wait, wait with patience. And as from a wave, like the sea that at a distance appears dark but when close becomes transparent, there will appear visions that confound all we previously thought we knew." He repeated his words more and more softly until his voice seemed a mere hum.

One of the candles flickered slightly, as if a moth had fluttered by. Lydia sighed. Another flicker; the moth passed through the flame but was not burnt.

Were those wings? thought Jane. Part of her wondered how much time had passed, but another part didn't care if she stayed forever.

Lydia sighed again. "A presence," she breathed, "a presence." Her words were but an exhalation. It was as though she was venturing into a foreign language, tasting the syllables, waiting for the meaning to become apparent.

Lewis paused, anticipating more. Jane and Madeleine looked at her, but while Lydia's own eyes fluttered open, she gazed without focus at the ceiling and said no more. Her lids drifted shut again as she emitted another long sigh.

"Shut your eyes against the distractions that surround you in the physical world. Listen only for voices," Lewis continued. "Not my voice, I am here only as a welcomer. Listen for those softer, subtler voices from beyond. Close your senses against the material world that weighs down our surroundings, lift your souls and let the spirits enter."

Jane's lids were heavy, her eyes bathed in darkness. She was dimly aware that Lydia next to her was beginning to sway, her head canted back, her lips slightly parted. The arriving presence held her in a dance. It could be felt drawing near. Jane felt a coolness by her shoulder, and now she had to look, quelling the needle of fear that had made its way through the tranquility of the candle flames.

"Liddy," she whispered, "do you hear something?"

Lydia tipped her head as if listening, but she only uttered a slight breathy sound, and Jane didn't know if it was assent or denial. Gently, Lydia swayed from side to side. Then suddenly she sat up straight and stared ahead. Involuntarily, the other three followed her gaze, even Lewis, but they saw nothing.

"Lydia, what is it?" asked Jane.

"George?" Aunt Madeleine's voice was tremulous. Her eyes searched the room, her head moving from side to side to see into the shadows.

"It is too early to call forth a spirit by name," said Mr. Lewis softly but repressively. "Be patient. Wait quietly. It is the quiet that will permit him to join us."

Lydia gradually relaxed her posture and leaned back in her chair. Slowly, her head tilted back like Miss Essie Everett's had been. Her lips parted and her eyes drifted upwards until it seemed she could see into her very skull, then they closed. Jane watched her cousin's unexpected behavior with interest and curiosity but no alarm. The needle had gone and she, too, was relaxed and utterly trusting.

"Is it Eustace?" she whispered. "Has he followed us from Little Falls?" Aunt Madeleine uttered a little squeak, quickly suppressed.

From Lydia there came a long, drawn-out breath, so long that it seemed at first there could be no air left in her lungs. Then her chest rose and her body seemed to lift from the chair.

"Ah," she whispered softly. "Oh, *oh*."

Now all their eyes were on her. Mr. Lewis leaned forward and gently extended his hand. Though he did not touch her, Lydia's fingers fluttered toward him as though attracted to the warmth of his skin.

"Lydia," he said softly. "Who is there?"

"George?" said Aunt Madeleine hopefully. "Is it you? Have you come?"

Lydia moaned. Abruptly, she went rigid again, staring sightlessly ahead. And then just as suddenly she slumped and began to slide from her chair. Lewis was at her side in a flash. He caught her and held her upright until her eyes opened and she looked around in bewilderment.

They were all standing now, their chairs shoved back or toppled with the energy of whatever had propelled them to their feet.

"My dear Miss Strong," said Lewis, his voice harboring a wondrous tremor, "you fell into a trance. Can you recall what you saw, what you heard?"

Lydia blinked and looked around her. "I did? What happened? I can't remember."

Aunt Madeleine sighed in disappointment. "Nothing, my dear? Nothing at all?"

"No matter," said Lewis. "We are at the very beginning of the journey. And how rare that a path forward should be disclosed so soon." His smile was exultant. "Lydia, my dear, you are a natural medium."

12

MRS. SIBLEY

Rain hammered against the tall windows, smearing the view outside into wavering greens and browns. The mottled light it cast across dusty shelves and faded chairs made the library look more inviting than did the new draperies, tightly upholstered settees, and polished finish of the front rooms downstairs.

Jane chose a chair by a table where the most light fell, and watery shadows dappled her drawings. She selected the recent one of Lydia in the park. Her graceful form sat gazing at a sun-spangled lake. Her hands rested in her lap, her feet were planted before her, her expression calm. The wiggly impatience that had beset the sitter was not apparent in the serene scene. Jane began to apply light cross-hatching around the figure, enhancing the folds of her dress and the shadows beneath her chair. She filled in the neckline with its small locket, using her own matching necklace to check the details. She added deeper color to the background and darkened the shadow cast by the tall tree behind. Under her fingers, the seated figure moved forward against the scene behind.

The picture was developing nicely. It was easier to finish it here in the library, her hand steadier now that she was seated at a table rather than sketching in the open air, although alone in this room there would be no potential clients passing by to notice her work. The storm was keeping all but the busiest citizens of Utica indoors, and there would be no strolling and admiring of her pictures today. She was eager to resume her outdoor drawing; it was pleasant to sit outside. What is more, she had earned several dollars already and appreciated the financial confirmation of her art. Many young ladies plied pencil and brush, though only a few made it pay. If the need for reward suggested that she no longer occupied a secure social position, so be it. Jane was enjoying herself, and absorption in the effort of rendering sight into image eased the anxiety of being in transit to an uncertain future.

That uncertainty magnified the longer they were delayed in their westward journey. The spiritualist interruption engineered by Aunt Madeleine had begun to slice though the shared goal of finding a new home. At the invitation of Mr. Lewis and his sister, they had moved from their hotel and were now occupying rooms in Mrs. Sibley's house. Aunt Madeleine and Lydia were pleased, but while their abode was now certainly more comfortable, Jane felt awkward about being here. Neither her aunt nor her cousin shared that scruple. Worse, Jane felt at risk of falling behind on the thrilling path that was now opening before her cousin, for Lydia appeared to be transported by her unexpected communion with the world of dead souls. The thought that their lives might take separate directions was unbearable, and from time to time, a tingle of dread skittered across her mind.

Drawing calmed her and focused her mind as she attended carefully to details of everything before her in an attempt to capture it all in a picture. Jane valued the clarity of vision that drawing fostered. At least I can see what is before me, she thought, if not another world. Not the world where spirits abide and where, if Mr. Lewis is correct, scent might lead us. Not a world of apparitions speaking from the Other Side. During the day, Jane could scoff at the very possibility that spirits might visit, but she could not quell a stab of envy for her cousin, for whom a new world had opened.

The portrait of Lydia was nearly complete. Jane set it aside and withdrew from an envelope a set of theorems. It had been an indulgence to purchase them with her first earnings, and had she been in her own home she would have attempted to make the stencils herself. But here as a guest in someone else's house—really a hanger-on admitted in the wake of others—she did not feel free to rummage around for the needed materials, even though most households contained things like heavy paper, varnish, and sharp, pointed knives. In any event, the cost of her purchase might be justified if she could manage to sell any products from her hand. Theorem paintings were popular, and those who didn't desire to have their likenesses taken might be moved to buy a decorative stenciled still life.

She had bought a set of five theorems, a series of fruit and flower outlines that could be overlaid and arranged in different patterns. The fruits looked like they would be easier to render than the flowers, whose multiple petals would require deft design and the mixing of subtle hues to capture their gradations of color and the shadows they cast.

A simple design of a melon in a shallow bowl flanked by two peaches and a cluster of grapes was a good place to start. She began with the melon, sketching lightly its curving outline, placing the smaller peaches in front, then surrounding them with the outline of a bowl with grapes dangling off one side. Her paper was full of erasures to correct haphazard overlaps before she figured out a composition that didn't look like a random set of circles. Decision made, she began again with the melon stencil and filled in shapes with the first layer of color. She would have liked to use her paints, but in someone else's library the possibility of drips and spills seemed unwise, so she contented herself with freshly sharpened pastels. They tended to smear, but at least they wouldn't run off the table onto the carpet.

It was an everlasting source of marvel that from pictures of humble items a whole world could emerge. Under the hand of a skilled painter, the curve of a peach or a vase cast shadows that hinted at things hidden, carrying portent and meaning just beyond grasp. This particular small fruit bowl would be little more than pretty, but as she worked, Jane imagined more complex arrangements, darker backgrounds, combinations of shapes and sizes, flowers both in full bloom and in bud, petals strewn on tables. Glasses half full of gleaming wine, figs split in their ripeness, knives crossing plates set aside by a person who has just left the room or perhaps still stands beyond the frame.

She had seen copies of such paintings in books and wondered if her simple schoolgirl theorems could ever approximate their complexity. The stencils were convenient, the outcomes pretty, the formulas limited. She set aside the melon and placed the peach outline on the paper, working intently and carefully. Then she shifted the stencil to one side, positioning it to add another peach, its outline lighter than its companion. She shaded one side of the overlap, and as a shadow came into being, one peach slid behind the other. The drawing seemed to grow in volume beneath her fingers. The grapes were harder to render, each oval plump on its stem, the cluster dense. She blended layers of rose and violet over them, adding just a touch of pale yellow where sunlight might gleam. A bunch just ripe for tasting began to bloom on the paper.

"My, how talented you are."

Jane's hand jerked and a streak of red slashed across the design. She leapt up and nearly collided with the woman standing at her shoulder. She found herself face to face with Mrs. Sibley, Mr. Lewis's sister and the owner of the house, and not a person to whom one could safely vent one's aggravation.

"I do beg your pardon," said Mrs. Sibley mildly. "I had no intention of startling you, and now you have spoilt your pretty picture. Please forgive my interruption and permit me to supply you with more paper."

Jane found no words; her heart was hammering and her breath short. She watched in vexed silence as Mrs. Sibley examined the damaged theorem picture, then turned over each of her drawings and scrutinized them one by one, making approving noises from time to time and greeting other images with opaque silence. The woman was annoyingly proprietary, but after all, it was her house. Jane was little more than an interloper, and an expression of resentment seemed out of order.

"Have you had training?" asked Mrs. Sibley.

"Only a little." Jane was pleased that her voice was almost steady, far steadier than her pulse. "Just the usual drawing instruction that one is apt to have growing up." Where did those casual sentiments come from?

Mrs. Sibley nodded, studying the faces of two portraits, the landscape behind two others.

"Obviously, you have a gift," she pronounced.

"Thank you." Somewhat belated, not entirely sincere, perplexed at the compliment. The woman was looking far more keenly at her pictures than they merited. A silence descended, and Jane suddenly felt bound by manners to speak.

"Forgive me, but I haven't yet had the opportunity to thank you for your hospitality," she ventured. "We are all three so grateful that you have opened your house to us."

"Oh, but it is my pleasure," said Mrs. Sibley, setting down the drawings and turning to look intently into Jane's eyes. "My home is always open to friends of my brother's, and most especially when he brings those spiritually attuned."

"That is kind of you," said Jane, taking a step back. Mrs. Sibley was one of those persons whose conversation prompts them to stand just a little too near. She was tall and stately, like her brother, and wore an assertive lavender scent. Jane had to tilt her head upward to look her in the eyes. She continued her disclaimer. "But I'm not at all sure that I am so attuned. It is an unfortunate shortcoming, I'm sure, and I wish it were otherwise. But it is my cousin Lydia who has the gift. Apparently. That is, it appears that she might. We are both quite new to this."

Mrs. Sibley took Jane by the shoulders and turned her toward the window. In the flat light from the rainy sky, she peered deeply into her eyes. "Blue," she said dreamily, "but not quite blue. Flecks of gold and green, and a ring of darkness around the iris. The color of one slightly different from the other. You have seer's eyes."

"What?"

"There are depths in you, my dear Miss Talmadge, that have yet to be plumbed. Do not presume that only your cousin has the gift of insight. Of receptivity. None of us should close our minds to possibility."

Jane stood still, wishing the hands would relinquish her shoulders but feeling constrained by manners to remain in place. Finally, Mrs. Sibley let go and smiled.

"But time will tell," she said in a lighter tone. "Nothing to worry about, naturally. Either your vision will come or it will not." She looked again at Jane's drawings, the portraits, the unfinished theorem, the stencils now smudged with color. "It is possible that your vision will appear under your fingers, you know. In your art."

"Really?" Jane was thinking of the dimness that Mr. Lewis preferred for spiritualist gatherings. Without light, there was no image to render.

"Perhaps you have not yet heard of spirit writing. Or in this case, drawing," said Mrs. Sibley. "To those inclined to communicate by means of pictures, spirits sometimes use the hands as a conduit for communication. Under your fingers, under your touch, pictures will appear, and they will tell their own stories. If, of course, your path to sensitivity opens in that direction. Just wait, Miss Talmadge. Perhaps you ought to carry your paper and pencil with you at all times. You never know when a visiting presence may move you to draw."

"Actually," said Jane, hoping to bring the conversation nearer to earth, "I am not Miss Talmadge. That is my aunt's married name. I am the daughter of one of her sisters. My name is Jane Woodfield. I'm sorry if you were under a misapprehension."

And then, having opened the subject, Jane fell again under Mrs. Sibley's inquisitive gaze and felt obliged to tell her the whole story of the different names of the three women whom she had so graciously welcomed into her house. The orphaned girls, the generous aunt, the move to a new city. And then the tragic loss of an uncle after only a short time living under his roof. And why were they not to stay under that roof? Reluctantly, the troubling story of the will and the grown sons who were even now moving into the house. Before she knew it,

Jane had more or less emptied her history onto Mrs. Sibley, who listened with such intensity that it was hard to stop talking. Jane could not recall if anyone had ever treated her with such attention before. It was both flattering and unsettling. And yet, those inviting, sympathetic eyes kept the words spilling out, and it would seem churlish not to speak. At last, Jane managed to stop, and there was a long pause before the other woman spoke.

"I beg your pardon for the error of your name," said Mrs. Sibley. "Of course, you and your cousin were introduced to me properly. My apologies for the lapse of memory."

She smiled with great friendliness, although, on reflection, Jane could not help thinking that the error might not have been an accident.

But Mrs. Sibley was as good as her word. She whisked out of the library and soon returned with several sheets of good paper as well as a length of pale velvet stained along one edge.

"After you have perfected your skills with those designs, my dear, perhaps you would make me one of those clever paintings. I have seen pictures such as those you are practicing produced on soft cloth such as this. They are quite lovely, and I would treasure one from your hand. As you can see, this fabric has been soiled and is no good for the jacket I had in mind, but there is plenty left to serve as a canvas for your art."

This statement was too fulsome for the scanty evidence of success now scattered across the desk, but Jane agreed readily, thinking that a gift of one of her theorem paintings, assuming it came out decently, might count as a kind of payment for the room she presently occupied. She thanked her hostess sincerely and promised to do her best.

More relaxed now and eager to return to her drawing, Jane agreed to bring her pencils and paper to the next gathering. She shivered in anticipation. The prospect was a bit alarming, but how wonderful it would be to discover that she shared her cousin's gift. If a spirit could seize Lydia by the throat and speak with her voice, perhaps another would take Jane by the hand, and she might draw a picture that revealed a message from the world beyond. She examined her hands, extending them in the pallid sunshine now leaking through the streaked window panes. The scoffing attitude receded, and her fingers trembled with excitement at the possibility.

13

BUTTON

Her phone was ringing. On and on. Because it usually took a long time to locate, Karen had set the voicemail to kick in after twelve rings, by which time most callers had given up. Eleven blasts of Morning Trumpet ringtone had already pealed before she found the phone next to the front door under the T-shirt she had worn the night before. Her greeting was so groggy that she had to clear her throat twice before her voice actually formed hello.

"You forgot, didn't you?" said Jasmine. "Hurry on over to the dig. It's going to rain again later and we're doing one more sift before letting the gas works resume. Craig is already there and has invited someone else to come and take a look. He thinks he's found something important, and we should be there too." Then, "Do you have Dan's number? I ought to call him too."

Since Dan was at that very moment still asleep in her bed, Karen hedged. "Not ready to hand, but somewhere. I'll call him myself. We'll be there right away."

"Okay," said Jasmine, without comment on the plural pronoun. Karen put down the phone. Conflicting thoughts skipped through her head: How unlike me to fall into bed with someone I've known such a short time. So much for my vow to give up men until I finish my degree. And so much for avoiding a rebound relationship after last year's disaster. What must he think of me now? But what a nice time we had last night at the fireworks. At least I did. And finally: how handy that he is already here.

Karen searched her memory for recent instruction to report for work on a Sunday morning, but her brain was still foggy from too many beers. She was naked and starting to shiver and figured another couple of minutes warming up under the covers wouldn't hurt. There were still a few sticky patches on the sheet, though most had dried by now. She could hear the shower running and thought about joining Dan to get warm that way instead, but when the water shut off she decided that a quick brush of her hair was the better choice.

"I've just put on some coffee," she said as Dan emerged, damp and rosy. "We've got to hurry. They're at the dig already for a final sift of the soil. They might have found something. Plus Craig has called in some expert, or maybe just a friend, who is heading over now."

"Why so early? Does it matter if we're late?"

Dan caught her around the waist and kissed the back of her neck, but Karen, remembering her unbrushed teeth, pirouetted away with a smile and headed for the bathroom, where with luck there might be a couple of gallons of hot water left in the tank.

Clean but hungry, they drove to the site in silence. Dan behind the wheel with an unreadable expression on his face, Karen wondering if he was regretting their impulsive night together. Plus worrying slightly if the attraction she felt for him was greater than his desire for her. He was oddly reluctant to go with her back to the dig this morning, even though they all had worked side by side for long enough that he should feel part of the team.

They arrived at the site of Lucille's final resting place just as another car was pulling up behind them. Jacob emerged looking sleepy and less than eager. Dan hung back for a short time before joining the others, who were peering avidly at something Jasmine was holding. Cradled in her palms was a brown, uneven lump of root and clay with a shallow depression in the center and tiny scratch gleaming out from the earth.

"I don't know how we missed it," Jasmine was saying, a little defensively. "We went through everything around her so carefully."

"Where was it?" asked Karen.

"At the bottom of the trench way down there at the edge of the region we cordoned off." She pointed to a spot below them and said again, "Craig and I got here early and found it, but I simply don't understand how we missed it earlier."

Dan glanced into the widened trench. "If I remember correctly, that's near where her bone fell when the backhoe made the first cut after the walk was removed. It had rolled to the side and wasn't directly underneath the rest of her. This probably landed with other pieces of rock and clay that flew to the side. At that point no one was expecting to find anything but tree roots."

Actually, the cuts for the gas line were neat and produced relatively little scattering, given the size of the job. The backhoe operator was highly skilled and manipulated the huge jaws of the machine with deft precision. But Dan felt sorry for Jasmine, who seemed to carry her responsibility as head graduate student for the project with exaggerated anxiety. Craig didn't look nearly as disturbed as she did.

"I'm afraid that if there was other stuff surrounding the bones, it might have been carted away with the other fill," she said mournfully.

"There can't have been much," said Dan. "The line replacement stopped immediately."

"But what is it? A coin?" asked Karen.

"Maybe," said Craig. "It's metal obviously. Could be a button."

"From Lucille's clothing?"

"I doubt it," said Craig. "It looks too heavy for a button on a dress. I've started to wonder if we might have dug up a young soldier. Maybe a boy, given the slight stature. This could be a button from a uniform. And if we've got relics from a battle, we might have a reason to request a delay for resumption of the utility works for a little longer. We'll know soon."

"What's the rush on a Sunday morning?" asked Jacob, somewhat crabby after a late night and an interrupted lie-in. "After all, she's been in the ground a long time. Would another day have made a difference?"

"Well, it's pretty important to the people who live around here to finish our work and get the sidewalk restored. I called one of those preservationists that Dan mentioned the other day. She agreed on the importance of this site and had been reading about the skeleton. She was interested in what we were turning up, so I felt it only courteous to invite her to see this latest."

Yup, thought Dan, here it starts.

"Besides," Killian continued, "it may save us some time, because she knows about the history of this region and the artifacts that sometimes turn up around here. An interesting person. Met her at a lecture a couple of years ago. She's head of that museum down the street. Ah—I knew she'd be swift to arrive. Can't pass up an opportunity like this one. Here she is."

A car door slammed and an elegantly dressed woman emerged. She looked to be in her mid-fifties and at first seemed a little lame, as her stiletto heels were sinking into the ground and impeding her progress.

"I drove the wrong car," she said as she neared. "I've been out and didn't want to bother to go home and change after I got your call, Craig. I usually have a pair of boots available in the trunk, but not today."

Craig smiled broadly as the two shook hands. His was slightly muddy, but she didn't seem to mind. "Team, meet Priscilla Cavendish, director of the museum at Bigwell House, just down the street a block or so from here, as well as a local historian and an expert on the War of 1812."

Ms. Cavendish nodded a greeting. "Good morning, all! So this is the dig I've been hearing so much about. I've been meaning to come by and see what you're up to. Identified your bones yet? Sure about that date? Of course, too early to be certain. Well, let's take a look. Oh, hello, dear." She stepped forward and gave Dan a glancing kiss on the cheek. "I hoped you might be here."

The others froze, Jasmine with her hands full of earth, the others staring, Karen stepping back a bit and looking startled.

Dan smiled sheepishly. "This is my mother."

There was a perplexed pause while curious eyes shifted between him and the woman who had dispensed this unexpected greeting. Dan surveyed the group, reckoning that more than one of them was taken aback by the combination of gas line digger and elegantly dressed woman.

"I told you I had a connection with local preservation efforts," he said, thinking, *Well, this is awkward.*

"So you did," remarked Craig. Passing over the surprising moment, he took the clot of earth containing the glinting object from Jasmine and held it out for viewing.

"Haven't cleaned it off yet, Pris. Didn't want to remove the clay either. There is a dense network of fine roots that have grown around everything here, and we want to proceed with caution in case there is more buried within. There might be something else attached to this thing, which we are provisionally identifying as a button. Given the history of this area, I thought it might be from a uniform of some sort. Thought you'd like to look at it in the raw, as it were. That's why I called you here so early. If you look down at the side of the trench, you'll see that we've put a marker where it was situated, although as Dan has said, it was probably displaced by the digging for the gas mains."

Priscilla Cavendish tilted as her left heel sank. She righted herself and focused her attention on the object in her hand. She fished in a pocket and brought out a pair of glasses. Mud filled her vermillion nails as she carefully scraped away some of the clinging earth from the rounded top of the object, muttering, "How remarkable. It does look like a button. Perhaps off a soldier's uniform, not sure yet. Seems to be lodged against something. Could there possibly be a thread still here? Surely not."

It wasn't conversation. The woman thought out loud.

Jasmine was admiring the casualness with which a manicure was sacrificed to investigation. Karen was wondering if Mrs. Cavendish would be bothered if she knew that Dan had spent last night with her. She didn't seem like the kind of mother who would mind. And after all, they were both adults. But now she was also wondering just how much more about Dan she didn't know. Dan himself was studying the trees overhead.

"Well, it is indeed a button," said Priscilla. First names were the norm here in the mud. "But I doubt that it's from a soldier's uniform. And besides, this particular area was not part of a battlefield, as far as I know. Those were further downtown or else upriver. Of course, we can't rule out that some soldier just came here on his own. On the other hand, wouldn't 1813 be too early to match your skeleton? Dan said you thought it was only about a hundred and fifty years old."

"That's a very approximate estimate," said Craig. "Just a guess at this point. If that's really a button off a uniform, it would suggest an earlier date. I thought you could give us a reason to direct our research one way or the other."

Patricia held out the partly cleaned object for all to see. An edge of brass lightly scored on one side poked from the lump of roots and clay. A design could be discerned beneath the veneer of mud.

"This design doesn't match any of the uniform buttons I've ever seen," she said.

"It looks twisted," said Jacob.

"Yes, it does. Quite bent. But it's been in the ground a long time, and who knows what forces might have damaged it before the gas line excavation turned it up. And I think there is more stuck to the back side." She continued to poke with a fingernail. "Craig, if you don't mind, I'd like to free this from its surroundings right away. You've piqued my curiosity."

Craig made an invitational gesture, and Priscilla fished in her jacket pocket with her muddy fingers and came up with a sharp object that looked suspiciously like silver. Dan recognized it as a pickle fork from his grandmother's dinner service, commandeered long ago for more interesting uses than spearing gherkins, but he said nothing.

Priscilla began to probe daintily around the button, oblivious to the dirt that became lodged under her nails. Pick, probe, pick, probe in tiny increments, then occasionally blowing away crumbs of clay, once spitting on the brass to dissolve a patch of mud. Gradually, the thready roots began to unravel.

God, I hope she doesn't lick it, thought Jacob.

It was an expert and slightly alarming display of confidence.

"The shank seems to be trapped in something, perhaps a stone," she reported. "See how it is bent and doesn't want to come loose? I don't want to damage it further by forcing it away." She was oblivious to the crumbs of earth that scattered from her hands and landed on her dress.

More probing, tapping, one more spit. Jasmine shot a glance at Craig to see how he was receiving this method of inquiry. He had a small, intent smile on his face.

The delicate probing was having its effect. Under the prods, the button gradually emerged from its tomb of clay and its binding of fine roots. A clump of clay fell away. And now they could see that its shank was solidly stuck in…stuck in…

In between two teeth.

That discovery stopped even Priscilla. "Oh my," she said.

Gasps as the others recollected the skeleton's missing lower jaw, wrenched from its splintered socket.

"Oh my God, poor Lucille!" exclaimed Karen.

"I think we need to turn our attention now to the cause of death," said Craig after a stunned pause.

Before them all there arose the image of a girl whose final action on earth was to bite so hard that her teeth ripped a button away from a garment worn by the last person to see her alive.

14

FAILURE

UTICA, NEW YORK. JUNE 15, 1851

The rain persisted. Heavy clouds covered the sky and mist hung so low that steeples disappeared into murk. Once more, Jane stood by the library window, her mood as dark as the weather. The table was stacked with pictures again, but the paper on top was blank.

As blank as her mind the night before when the spirits appeared to everyone but her.

Although they had started the session early, the lowering weather had further dimmed the light from the curtained windows until the room was utterly dark. Thunder rumbled outside, rain swept against the glass in rattling swathes. The air was damp and unpleasant, and although it was almost summer, Jane had shivered beneath her shawl, barely warmed after two cups of the rosy tea.

Spirits, however, care little for weather, and when Mr. Lewis intoned his soft invitation, the candles soon began to gutter. Before very long, Lydia's head dropped back as though her neck had become boneless. She gasped with another series of soft *Ohs*, her eyes rolling up so far that their whites were crescents quivering by her lower lids. Her transport occurred so soon that Jane was still glancing surreptitiously around to examine the somewhat larger group that had gathered to commune with those recently departed. In addition to Mrs. Sibley, there were two men who had arrived late and not been introduced to her. News had spread of a new medium, a new conduit to the world beyond, a new adept who could communicate with the dead.

At the center of this interest, Lydia fervently embraced her role, eager to explore its possibilities. For several days she had marveled at her newfound talent and had come away from conversations with Mr. Lewis pale and excited, trying unsuccessfully to describe to her cousin what it was like to be so taken over by a spirit that it might speak through her.

She imperfectly explained the science that Lewis had recounted which made the phenomenon possible: The incorruptibility of the spirit, the endurance of self after death, the limbo of ether that sustains what remains after animating forces leave the body. The continuity of material particles from the familiar, solid objects of everyday to the ethereal world that lies beyond mortality. A comparison with the phenomenon of electricity—the sudden illumination emitted from what appears to be nothing.

Jane tried to understand, smiled and nodded, and wished fervently that she could be similarly swept away by what was happening. Her cousin seemed transported, in awe at her own capabilities. Lydia was by nature bold, even impulsive, and prone to fervent enthusiasms that were sometimes later regretted. By nature both more timid and more cautious, Jane envied the braver temperament of the other. At the same time, she was concerned.

Lydia had lost weight, and her skin was paler than it usually was at the beginning of summer, in spite of the walks they had taken and the hours of sitting in the park having her portrait sketched. Twice Jane had woken in the night to find Lydia's bed empty. Perhaps failing sleep, she had sought fresh air or new surroundings. But thinking of the spirit world while roaming a large house alone in the dark was not healthy. Jane was sure of this, even as she wished she could share in the pursuit.

And now last evening, yet another arriving spirit had wrestled to take her over. Jane regarded Lydia with alarm, worrying that her trembling body and breathy gasps indicated distress as much as transport.

"Liddy? Are you all right?" she whispered. It looked so uncomfortable to have one's head canted back like that. Hard to breathe even. Perhaps Lydia was suffering in her link with the world beyond. Perhaps it was too difficult for a human body to withstand the tension between corporality and the strains of disembodiment. She put her hand on her cousin's arm and felt the muscles tense and tight as strings drawn over the narrow bones.

"Liddy?"

How could someone she knew so well be so suddenly removed from her understanding?

"A presence," Lydia breathed. "A presence descends. Can you not see? He is here."

What could she possibly see with those unfocused eyes? Jane looked around the room and found that she was the only one who seemed baffled about what was happening. Most had their attention avidly fixed on Lydia, some looked upward as if they could see through the ceiling to the heavens beyond.

Aunt Madeleine suddenly sat upright, uttering a small gasp. With her own eyes cast heavenward, she whispered, "Oh yes. Yes. I see the faintest of pale streaks in the air above. Is that what you see? Is it my husband? Is it George? Oh, don't fade, don't fade. Stay." She searched the air above her head, raising a hand as if in greeting.

Jane looked too but saw nothing.

"Do I see beyond?" Aunt Madeleine quavered. "When will I know when my husband appears?"

"Be patient, my dear Madeleine," said Mrs. Sibley softly. She sat between Jane and her aunt, and with the chairs crowded around the small table her shoulders occasionally touched theirs. "There are many spirits who visit us from time to time. If we are calm and receptive, they may bring with them those whom we seek. It does little good to call. One must wait."

"Lydia?" whispered Aunt Madeleine. "Who is it?" Her eyes filled with tears.

Mrs. Sibley patted her hand firmly and repeated: "Wait."

Following Mrs. Sibley's suggestion, Jane had brought pencil and paper to the gathering. She scanned the room, wondering how one would draw a spirit. Would her pencil render a streak of white? But why should spirits be white? Why should they be any color at all? But if they are only darkness, what could be drawn? What was Lydia seeing that she could not? She searched the dark for a sign. She closed her eyes and willed her mind to see; some trailing efflorescence, some wispy specter. No matter how fearsome, she wanted at this moment, above all, to *see*. But there was nothing at all. Not for her; nothing. Almost angrily, she opened her eyes again and searched the room for the presence that visited others.

She felt something touch her hand and she jumped before realizing that it was just Mrs. Sibley, her fingers too warm for a ghost. "Keep your eyes closed, my dear Jane," she murmured. "Don't seek, don't strain, just wait. Wait for a touch. Your hand will be guided. Do not hasten the influence of the visitors. Let them speak in their own time, let them take our earthly powers into themselves and convey to us the knowledge that freedom from their material bodies affords."

Words meant for comfort, bringing little. The room was crowded but Jane had rarely felt so alone. The warmth of Mrs. Sibley's shoulder next to her felt reassuring, solid, human. And alive. Obediently, she closed her eyes and waited for her pencil to move.

But nothing had happened. Lydia had continued to utter her *Ohs* until finally they subsided and she opened her eyes in bewilderment.

"What did I say? Did anyone speak?" she asked.

The others shook their heads but appeared sufficiently satisfied that spirits were nigh, for most had also felt their presence. At the end of the evening, Jane was cold, discouraged, and felt utterly as if she did not belong.

If only her hand had moved. If only her pencil had sketched something. Just a line would have sufficed. But the page had remained blank.

And now in the light of day, albeit a day dimmed with rain, that page lay on the library table. Oddly, Jane did not feel it right to use for an ordinary drawing the same sheet of paper that had awaited a spirit message. The paper from the séance should not be used to render a theorem, a profile, a landscape. Despite her failure, the presence of this very paper at the session had made it the agent for a spectral drawing, and it had to wait for its moment. Don't be superstitious, Jane told herself, but still she set aside the page and took another paper from her dwindling supply.

She was working on a sketch for Mrs. Sibley's promised theorem painting and was not yet confident that she could apply the colors to velvet. The hues absorbed differently on cloth than on paper, and handling the nap was especially taxing. More practice was required to achieve the subtle coloring that she desired. It would not do to make a present to this woman that was not up to the best standard.

Mrs. Sibley was a woman who elicited the best from others. At least, that was Jane's thought as she experimented with arranging the theorems in the most attractive design. How else to account for the unsettling combination of feelings she aroused? The intensity of her gaze was both disconcerting and flattering; she seemed both critical and deferential at the same time. Above all, she inspired a desire to please. Jane was drawn to her, was not sure she trusted her, and held her in a bit of awe.

As if thoughts could summon their objects, the woman herself walked into the library. She appeared not to notice Jane at first but went straight to the shelves by the door and ran her fingers over a row of books. One she took down and bent over the pages, fluttering them back to front impatiently. Then a second book, then another, tossing them into a pile until she flattened one open with a gesture of satisfaction.

"Here it is!" She looked up straight at Jane. "Good morning, my dear. You are at your task early today."

"So are you," said Jane, surprised to have been noticed, then biting her tongue at the audacity of such a reply. But Mrs. Sibley did not find her retort disrespectful.

"Indeed, I am," she replied. "Both of us early birds, seeking our worms. Or in my case, our books." She approached Jane's table and held out one of the books. "And here is something that you might read yourself. I hope you find this of interest."

"*Insights from Swedenborg,*" Jane read. She stumbled over the name.

"A simplified rendering of his thoughts, of course," said Mrs. Sibley. "He wrote much longer tomes. But this summary is sound enough, I believe. It may help you to understand the communication we seek between the physical and the spiritual realms. It may, indeed, aid in resolving whatever skepticism may be impeding your own communion."

It was as though the woman had read her mind. Jane kept her eyes downcast, wondering if the spirits had seen into her heart and refused revelation to someone who harbored doubts. She felt a twinge of guilt, but she also resented the possibility that her sentiments had been detected. A mind should be a private thing.

"God has given us reason. Are we not meant to use it and to question that which we do not understand?" she asked.

But Mrs. Sibley had already swept out of the room.

15

DAN'S STORY

"So?" The diner was now nearly empty of other breakfast customers. The air conditioning wasn't functioning properly, and the room was becoming warm. Karen watched Dan make designs with a pile of spilled salt next to his coffee cup. "So?" she repeated.

"So what?" he said, glancing up.

"So, are you going to tell me more about your mother?"

"What's to tell? You just met her."

"You never mentioned her."

"Why should I have? Why would anyone mention their mothers? You haven't told me anything about yours either. Ah, thanks."

A plate of eggs and bacon and a biscuit oozing butter was set before him. Karen looked with regret at her virtuous fruit plate garnished with a dollop of yoghurt. The cantaloupe was unappetizingly pale. "My mother isn't the one who appeared at an archaeological site where no one expected her to be," she said. "Of course, I'm curious."

"Want a piece of bacon?" offered Dan.

"Nor does my mother turn out to be head of a museum just down the street from that site. Nor an expert in local history who was called to consult about the bones you found. Bones that, in fact, you had told her about." Karen took the bacon. "Not to mention arriving in the early morning dressed as though she was just leaving a fancy party. More glamorous than most mothers on a Sunday morning, for sure."

"So you're surprised to find that someone like Priscilla Cavendish is the mother of a manual laborer?" said Dan, rather aggressively. "A ditch digger?"

"That's not what I meant at all," said Karen, rather hurt. "Don't be oversensitive. No one thinks of you as a ditch digger, least of all me."

"Not slumming then? Are you sure?"

"Stop it!" Karen was growing angry. "Of course meeting her there was unexpected. And you're right, I wouldn't have tagged her for your mother. Or any of ours, for that matter. But she had no trouble acknowledging you. You're the one who hid your connection. How come?"

"More coffee?" Without waiting for a reply, the waitress poured a steaming brew into cups that were still half full.

"Notice how you get coffee refilled whether or not you want it?" Dan said. "Water too."

"Why are you avoiding this question?"

Dan sighed and pushed his plate aside. "Look. I didn't mean to hide anything. I joined your project kind of sideways, as you'll remember. It was a total accident that the skeleton turned up in my part of the trench. I had no idea that anything my mother is involved in would turn out to be connected to Lucille."

Karen took another piece of bacon. "She seems like an interesting person."

"You could put it like that. She has her fingers in many pies; I try to keep them out of mine."

"Mothers can be that way, I guess." Another piece of bacon disappeared. "How come? Does she interfere?"

"Not exactly, but she has ideas that I'm tired of hearing. She has too many interests, too much energy, too many opinions, and certainly too many about me and what I should be doing. I have a complicated family."

"Families are usually complicated."

"You have no idea. Plus, as you might have noticed, she has an absolutely incredible ability to get her own way. Such as getting an invitation to inspect a site that has been cordoned off from the public for weeks. Actually, I'm surprised she didn't intrude earlier. Are you going to eat all my bacon?"

"Sorry." Karen returned to her own plate and speared a piece of pineapple. "So, you have different last names, right? Are your folks divorced? Mine are. For eight years now."

Dan considered. It was clear that Karen wasn't going to let the subject go. By not telling her everything, he would seem to be concealing something far graver than in fact was the case. The more he failed to answer her questions, the more it would appear there was something to hide. He retrieved his plate with its cooling eggs and one remaining strip of bacon. "Okay, I'll give you the short version, but part of it I would prefer you keep to yourself. Agreed?"

"Yes. Of course."

"To your last question: My parents are not together any more, but they are not precisely divorced either because they were never formally married. That may be hard to believe given the way she now looks, so classy and proper, but that appearance represents a return to her kind of upper-class roots. Insofar as there are any around here, that is. She herself refers to her family as a remnant of the threadbare local aristocracy. Anyhow, she went through a rebellious, sort of anti-bourgeois phase when she was younger, so when she became pregnant with me, she refused to get married to my father. Maybe to spite her family."

Dan took a large bite of biscuit and chewed slowly. Karen refrained from observing that he was stuffing his mouth to delay the story. After coffee and a long swallow, he continued.

"Whatever the reason, my parents stayed together for some years. Until my mother met Ben Cavendish. Suddenly, marriage seemed to be what she wanted after all, but not to my father by that time. After she married Ben—and although Cavendish is a decent guy, I'll admit that I haven't completely forgiven her for that—I lived for a while with my dad. But he moved south when I went to college."

Dan paused again for a forkful of eggs, wishing the waitress would come by with more coffee. His cup was now too cool and the coffee tasted bitter and greasy. He gestured across the room for another cup while sorting through the information he was dispensing.

"Long story short," he resumed, breathing in freshly brewed steam, "when I finished university a year ago, I had run up a lot of debt. A lot. I'd had a stop-and-start career as a student, took two years off, went to live down south with my dad for a while, kept changing my major, that sort of thing. Anyhow, it took me a while to finish, and the debt mounted way beyond what I'd anticipated. I've been working since then, and this summer I took the most lucrative job I could find in hopes of paying more of it off. It's not a very uplifting story, and not one that I share with many people."

"But everyone has student loans these days," said Karen. "I have a lot myself, and when I finish my graduate degree there will be even more. Possibly more than you. Why make a big deal about something so ordinary?"

Dan gave her a long look. And then decided to trust her.

"Okay, I said I would tell you, so here is the part I would prefer you keep to yourself. It's not just student debt. I did something incredibly stupid and went with some friends to Turning Stone my senior year. The weekend got out of hand, and—long story short again, and I won't even try to give you the long version of this because, frankly, I don't remember it very clearly—I came away with a big gambling debt."

"Gambling? You're a gambler?" Karen tried to keep the shock out of her voice.

"Not anymore. Believe me, no. Once was enough. I never intend to set foot again in a casino. But I hung out with a bunch of guys for a while who had far more money than I did, and I simply—drunkenly if you must know—followed in their path. The casino doesn't serve alcohol, but we went with plenty stashed in the car, and with frequent trips to the parking lot, we all got sufficiently loaded to lose track of our bets. It's my own fault, but I fell into a difficult situation and needed money fast. So I tapped my uncle, that is, my father's brother, for a loan. He was alarmed and pretty angry about it all. But he's a generous guy, and he helped me out. Luckily, he's a subcontractor for part of the gas line replacement, and he arranged for me to work digging trenches this summer, which pays well. But he made it clear when he loaned me money that it was for the short term only, and I'm pretty much working for free until the debt is paid. I'm even living in his basement to save on rent."

"And your mother doesn't know about this?"

"Nope. Well, she knows I'm living there, and of course, she knows about the student loans, at least some of the amount. But not about the debt to my uncle. He and she are civil to each other, but there's no love lost between them. He holds a bit of a grudge about the way she left my father. And I really do not want her to know about the money I owe him. That's one reason you have to keep this between us. She absolutely must not find out."

This might need more explanation, but Dan was having trouble finding the right words to express his reluctance. "It's not that she wouldn't want to help me out, not at all. In fact, I expect she'd offer to pay the debt herself. I don't mean to say that she doesn't care, because I know she loves me—and I her too, in spite of what it might sound like. But it's the kind of relationship that works best at a distance. Judging from past experience, she'll have too many ideas about what I ought to do and who I ought to depend on. And if she did pay the debt, the situation would be even worse because I'd be, what's that old word? I'd be beholden. And stuck."

Karen paused, unsure about her response. Dan continued. It seems as if once uncorked, his story just poured out.

"In fact—" He laughed a little ruefully. "In fact, during my off and on university career, she admonished me about buckling down to work unless I wanted to end up a ditch-digger. So that's what I am, ironically enough, at least for the time being. And you can play psychologist and make of that what you want." His tone was challenging.

Karen finished her breakfast in silence. Dan put his coffee cup down with a sharp clank and looked at her. "Well?" Perhaps he had said too much.

"You can be sure that I won't pass along any of this, Dan. Not if you don't want me to. And I appreciate that you've told me. I really do. But honestly, it doesn't seem to me like all that terrible a story. One bad weekend. We've all had them, haven't we? Certainly, I'd like to turn back the clock and erase some of the stupid things I've done. Just how much did you lose at the casino anyhow?"

Dan laughed ruefully. "You don't want to know. In fact, it's still hard for me to imagine how I could have lost that much in one night. Even now, the numbers stick in my throat."

This was an unexpected side of Dan. He seemed vulnerable in a way that she had not seen before. Karen liked him all the more for it. She was also rather enjoying this exchange, feeling she had an unusual upper hand in what had seemed to be an imbalanced relationship—her wanting him more than vice versa.

"Okay, then," she teased. "So you can't say the number. Just write it down. Then we can burn the paper. It will be a kind of exorcism. I did that once with a terrible boyfriend, wrote his name down and burned it. With a photograph. And believe it or not, it helped." She smiled and squeezed his hands across the table, noting how cold they were in spite of the warmth of the room. "Don't be superstitious. It's just a number, saying it won't change it anyhow." She rummaged in her purse and took out a pen. "Come on, I dare you. How much did you lose?"

Perhaps it was the dare, perhaps Dan suddenly decided he was really quite fond of Karen and didn't mind trusting her. He pulled a paper napkin from the dispenser, took her pen and scribbled a figure. He turned the napkin around so that she could read it, and then he tore it in half and soaked the inked pieces in the remains of his coffee.

"Oh," said Karen, hoping her shock didn't show. "Well, maybe I'd better get the check."

16

UNCONGENIAL THOUGHTS

UTICA, NEW YORK. JUNE 20, 1851

Finally, the sun shone again and the world returned to what it should be on the cusp of summer. Jane and Lydia welcomed the clear skies, admiring the opening petals of flowers and the greening high boughs where leaves unfurled pale and fresh. They strode with unladylike vigor toward the park, lifting their skirts over lingering puddles and inhaling the warm, fragrant wind. As they entered the parkland, the blue overhead was background to a high tapestry of green and sunlit leaves. Arm in arm, they headed for the spot where Jane liked to paint.

"I know you are tired of sitting for me," said Jane, "but your presence makes displaying my skills so much easier. I hope to sketch one or two more portraits before we leave. I have amassed a little portfolio from our brief stay here but need a few more drawings to tempt future customers."

"I am always glad to sit for you, my dearest Jane," said Lydia. "You know that. I should think my pleasure must be obvious." Her wry smile acknowledged the fib, for Lydia might be pleased to sit for Jane, but she was never pleased just to sit. Jane was glad to see Lydia her old self again, not today the captive conduit for voices unheard and spirits unseen. Today she was the same friend, the beloved cousin, the same lively young woman, the same model of what Jane wished she herself might become in a few years' time.

"It's good to see you looking well again, Liddy," she ventured. It was a gamble to hint at the subject that they had both been avoiding, but Lydia's response was not what she hoped.

"I have not been unwell, Janie. Not at all. Please don't confuse the effort of being a medium with illness. Being a receptacle for spirits is taxing, for sure. But it is not an affliction. It is a gift, as Mr. Lewis says. A gift. And one that I am coming to treasure."

"Of course, of course," Jane hastened to say. "I'm reassured to hear you say so."

"And besides," Lydia continued, "you are not the only one adding a few pennies to our treasury. Others who gather around the table contribute to the enterprise as well. I fancy that my talents have attracted a few of them."

"You mean they pay for these sessions?" How did I miss that? thought Jane.

"It is a mere pittance that Mr. Lewis collects," said Lydia. Her tone was slightly defensive. "And it is hardly required. All who seek are welcomed. If they choose to leave a token of appreciation, then it is for the good of us all."

An awkward silence descended, and Jane wished she had not brought up the subject. Their moment of shared exhilaration at the beauty of the day was slipping away. Why can't I leave well enough alone? she thought. Why can't I keep my mouth shut? Now I have ruined our time together this morning.

"I am pleased for you, Liddy," said Jane. "Truly, I am. I can't say that I understand what is going on. Not with you, nor for that matter with anyone else around our table. What you have discovered remains closed to me. I am not adept at this new undertaking that means so much to you and to Auntie. I wish I were. I know that it has great importance for you. Forgive me for not being able to share it."

Her statement ended tremulously, and immediately Lydia stopped and put her arms around her cousin, blocking other strolling passers-by who, also pleased with the sunshine, looked on kindly. Jane's small portable easel was trapped stiffly beneath her arm, and she could not return the embrace.

"Oh, dear Janie. There is nothing to forgive! I am sorry that you feel left behind, and surely it is difficult to explain to you what I experience. But nothing stands between us. Nothing. Not now, not ever."

Jane sniffed and smiled, her anxiety only slightly palliated. They hastened on their way, she aware of—and Lydia oblivious to—the curious glances of those who had witnessed their exchange. Once more she envied her cousin's self-confidence and her immunity from the opinions of others. It was one of the traits she sought to emulate.

The park was crowded with citizens enjoying the warmth and the relief from rain. Jane set up her easel under her familiar oak. Lydia leaned against the tree in a picturesque pose and prepared to model. Her light mood seemed to have returned, and now, laying out her artist's tools, Jane felt herself enter a zone of contentment. She wished then never to leave, to stay with her pencils and brushes beneath this sheltering tree, warmed by the sun and confident in the companionship of her cousin, and most of all, far from the night that brought spirits between them. But the subject was not finished.

"You should draw all you can today," said Lydia, "for I believe we shall be leaving Utica before long. Did you hear Mr. Lewis's conversation with Aunt Madeleine last night? She has been so disappointed at Uncle's failure to appear at our sessions, and she wonders if somehow she is unworthy of his presence. But Alexander believes that it is more likely that Uncle George will come to her in another place. His consultants suggest a place near a body of water, or perhaps some place where they once enjoyed themselves early in their marriage. And, as a matter of fact, that place is not so far away—just to the west of here, still south of the mountains."

"Alexander?" said Jane. "You call him by his Christian name?"

"It is his wish," replied Lydia. "I suppose it is more proper to refer to him as Mr. Lewis, since he is, after all, some years older. But he believes that morally we occupy the same plane. That is his term—the same plane. And as equals, we might call one another Lydia and Alexander."

This information was all reported with a suspiciously casual tone, as if Lydia wanted to blurt out the surprising shift in the relationship and get it over with. She left the tree and began to walk rapidly back and forth, admiring the pansies in their freshly soaked beds, the irises clumped fragrantly together, their curving leaves still shedding raindrops.

It took Jane a few moments to recover from the newly intimate form of address. But why should she be shocked at it, for after all, nothing in nature should prevent the equal standing of a man and a young woman. But the news of an imminent departure was unsettling.

"No, I was not aware that we were to leave so soon," she replied. Dismayed and rather hurt, Jane felt once more as if she were merely riding the wake of others' decisions. "No one has mentioned it to me. I spoke with Mrs. Sibley just this morning at breakfast, and she didn't indicate anything of the sort. Will she accompany us westward?" She tried to keep her tone light and as a result sounded rather stiff, but Lydia didn't seem to notice.

"I don't think so. She has obligations that keep her at her home. She is, after all, at the center of the spiritualist community here, and as such she owes many people her attention. And besides, Alexander— Mr. Lewis—often leaves from time to time to seek spiritual presences elsewhere. She often does not accompany him."

"I suppose Uncle must be accommodated," Jane said, hoping to strike a neutral tone. "If he is to appear, we must make preparations for his arrival."

However, propelled by resentment that her own desires should not also have been consulted, she felt obliged to say again what she really thought about the entire enterprise.

"But, Liddy, I do wish that Auntie would forget this fruitless quest. Even if Uncle does appear, what could he possibly say that would convince the lawyers that she ought to be his heir? She says that she only wishes to say a final farewell, but I'm sure she remains beset with frustration at being left out of his will. Really, Lydia, I am surprised that you do not protest. Our aunt is wasting both her time and her remaining money. She would be happier if she would just accept what has happened and be on her way."

Lydia regarded her with a look of tolerant condescension.

"Spoken like an unbeliever, of course, Janie. I could expect no less. But the mounting evidence for the persistence of souls after death has scientific grounding, you know. I believe Mrs. Sibley recommended you read the philosopher Swedenborg. With more and more people recognizing that the spirit endures beyond the death of the body, it is but one more step to introduce the wishes of the departed into legal consideration."

This sounded very like the words of Mr. Alexander Dodge Lewis himself, but Jane bit back that observation. After a silence, she shifted the subject.

"Please return to the tree, Liddy. This will make a nice sketch. More relaxed and natural than sitting in a chair in a park. But turn away a bit, I need your profile."

"One of these days you should work on the front of the face. Humans do have two eyes, you know, and two ears. And I would think it easier to draw a mouth from the front." Lydia returned to the sustaining trunk of the oak and posed prettily, smiling again. Both of them were straining to keep the conversation from fraught topics.

"Yes, that's just the right position," said Jane. "But please don't smile so broadly. Teeth are hard to draw, and even if one is adept, they make the finest portrait look like a jack-o-lantern."

This brought a laugh, but Lydia obediently closed her lips.

"But you're right," continued Jane. "I do need to expand my abilities so that I can draw whole heads. There are too many young ladies turning out profiles. I would have less competition if I had greater facility."

"I have read that one can practice faces by drawing on an egg," said Lydia.

"I read that too. I suppose it works quite well, but only if one's subject is notably round. Or at least ovoid."

"Like Uncle." And they laughed together, thinking of the death mask in Aunt Madeleine's drawer, a face as plump in death as it had been in life.

It was good to turn the conversation to shared amusement, but Jane had to tamp down another observation. She did not voice her concern about Aunt Madeleine's pearl earrings, a favorite piece of jewelry worn so frequently in the past and now not to be seen. They were, after all, hers to dispose of as she pleased. Still, she wondered: Had they been sold to finance this trip west? Could it be that the money provided by the Talmadge sons was already running short?

17

Theorem

Jane had to steady her trembling fingers as she put the finishing touches on the painting for Mrs. Sibley. After several drafts on paper, the stencils on velvet were positioned in just the design she both favored and could execute with fair competence. A peach, two plums, a melon, and a drooping bunch of grapes nestled in a glass bowl. She was pleased that she had rendered the bowl in a way that the fruits within its interior were fainter, as though seen through glass. It only remained to add some outline shading to make the picture come to life, but the watercolors threatened to blotch if she could not control the shaking.

She put down the brush and rubbed her hands, annoyed with herself for the inchoate upsets that disturbed her. The unexpected news that they were leaving soon had taken her aback. On the other hand, it was not as though she wanted to stay in Utica indefinitely. From the start she would have preferred to speed their journey across the state so that a new home could be established as soon as possible. Now, however, it was evident that Aunt Madeleine was delaying progress to Rochester, not in order to see friends and relatives along the way as she had intimated at first, but to pursue the possibility that Mr. Lewis might bring her husband's spirit near. Perhaps to explain the will, perhaps just to see him once more. Both possibilities were forlorn.

The discovery that their traveling plans were being formed without her knowledge and with no heed for her own desires continued to upset her. Jane was all too familiar with situations where she had little voice in important decisions. As the younger of the cousins, and certainly as an orphan with no resources of her own, she was used simply to following the directives of others. She had been lucky so far that those directives always seemed to have her own well-being in mind. But with Lydia's awkward revelation of their imminent departure, Jane suddenly felt she had become quite incidental to the trip. The journey seemed now to be propelled as much by Lydia's newfound abilities as by Aunt Madeleine's desire to right the wrong she believed she had been done, even by summoning testimony from beyond the grave.

Jane's feelings were thoroughly muddled. She was glad not to be the one steering their path. At the same time, she was resentful that she had no say in their movements. She was both impatient to be on her way and eager to stay in Mrs. Sibley's pleasant library where, for some reason, she had been given full freedom to read, draw, and paint at will. And it was both hurtful and baffling that relative strangers should suddenly have decisions about her immediate future in their hands.

She admired Mr. Lewis and appreciated his attentiveness, yet she suspected his motives. But on the other hand, what could they be? She had suspicion without any clear evidence to ground it.

She respected and liked Mrs. Sibley but was also puzzled by her demeanor and her air of judgment. But who or what was the object of her lofty air of assessment?

Most of all, Jane was in a state of marvelous bafflement at Lydia's unexpected affinity with the spirit world, felt herself becoming distant from the affections of her best friend, and worried that they were all in danger of falling victim to something she did not understand. And precisely because she failed to understand it, she doubted her own doubts. That was perhaps the worst of it, not trusting her own mind.

"That is coming along quite nicely," said a voice at her shoulder. "Is it complete yet?"

Mrs. Sibley had an uncanny ability to approach silently. Jane was glad that her paints were not positioned over the artwork at that moment, or there surely would have been an unsightly blotch to fix.

"I am nearly finished," she said after only a momentary pause to recover after her start. "There are just a few more touches to add. But beyond those, I will not be able to progress further. I have discovered that we will be leaving sooner than I expected, and unfortunately, there will be no time to have the picture framed."

"No matter, my dear. It is stretched quite nicely as it is, and I expect there is a frame somewhere in this house that will suit it perfectly."

Certainly, the large house seemed to be filled with so many objects that it would be no surprise to find an empty picture frame or two just ready to receive the new theorem painting.

"Perhaps, but it still seems a paltry gift to give you, unfinished like this," Jane said.

"Not at all, not at all. It is very pretty, and I shall look at it with pleasure every day." Mrs. Sibley lifted the painting and held it admiringly at arm's length. She walked around the library, testing it in different lights, and nodded with satisfaction when she positioned it by the door where the light from the window fell on it gently. She returned the picture to Jane's table.

"And as a matter of fact," she said, "I have something for you as well." Mrs. Sibley took a small packet from the pocket of her skirt and placed it on the table. "Perhaps you will find these useful as you develop your skills. They are quite simple, designed for school children really. They belonged to my daughter. But anyone might use them to good end, and I hope you will do so and think of me when you are drawing." And she left the room as quickly and silently as she had come.

A daughter? This was the first mention that Mrs. Sibley had children. But her hasty exit suggested that it was not a subject to be pursued.

Jane opened the packet and found within a set of drawing cards— images to practice sketching in order to learn simple perspective drawing: houses, trees, horizon lines, a walking figure, roads receding into the distance. They were not particularly advanced instruction tools, but she could readily see how her work could be improved by copying them. Freer in their form than theorems, they could, with practice, be adjusted for different scenes.

"Thank you, you are very kind. What a lovely gift," she said to the empty room, and set aside her drawing materials to find a bit of paper to write Mrs. Sibley a proper note, warmed by the unexpected gift.

Later that evening before an even larger group gathered for another summoning of spirits, she ventured a query to Mr. Lewis. He was silent for a moment before replying.

"Yes, her daughter. She was a lovely little girl, died when she was eleven, along with her father. A terrible fever afflicted the whole town that year, and they were among its first victims."

"I am so sorry to hear it," said Jane. The words were inadequate. "How very hard for your sister."

"It was indeed. We rarely speak of it." Lewis shifted his weight from foot to foot. Rarely had she seen him ill at ease, but before she could assess his apparent discomfort he stood straighter and resumed his usual demeanor. "But it provided her the opportunity for her first encounter with the spirit world. And how soothed she was to hear the little girl's message. That is one of the great boons of the spiritualist movement, you know, the ability to reunite people with their lost loved ones. I realize, dear Jane, that you have had some doubts, which I hope are soon assuaged. Such a blessing it was to Grace to hear the voice of her little girl once more. So calming to know that she resides now in a better place. Therefore, I like to think of her daughter as having left her mother, despite her deep sorrow, with a great gift."

At that moment the room began to fill with others. As they gathered to the table, Mr. Lewis went forward to greet them, and Jane was left astonished and sickened at the idea that, under any circumstances, a little girl's death could be considered a gift.

18

A New Way to Draw

They set out westward on a day blessed with just the kind of sun and light that Jane would have welcomed for painting outdoors. The roadway was already busy with carriages and riders. From the window of the coach they could see the rise of the foothills marching into the great mountains beyond.

"There is a small railway being laid into those yonder regions," Mr. Lewis said, gesturing from the windows of the coach. "It will serve especially those from New York City and other places of great population who wish to benefit from mountain air. Perhaps we might take a brief sojourn there after we test the waters at our destination. Although it could be a strenuous trip. The roads are narrow and rutted in many places."

"But you have been there?" asked Lydia.

Lewis nodded, giving a small self-deprecating shrug. "I was quite a walker in my youth, and there are peaks in the Adirondacks to challenge and thrill those with strong bodies and venturesome souls. Perhaps I'll show you them some day."

"Your youth is hardly far behind you," said Lydia, and Mr. Lewis smiled at the mountains. Lydia leaned forward to feel the passing breeze on her face, which fortunately was blowing the dust and splatter from their wheels away from her. She was exalted by the moving countryside. Jane might have been as well, but her view was blocked by the plumpness of Aunt Madeleine, who was queasy with the swaying coach and kept her nose buried in a cologne-scented handkerchief.

"Perhaps next time we might find a town on the rail line and board a car as we travel farther west," said Jane. "We could make faster progress, for sure."

But her suggestion, one of several she had ventured since they left

Troy, did not warrant comment. Aunt Madeleine was disinclined to any-thing but a coach, preferably a private conveyance, and Mr. Lewis, now apparently a member of the traveling party, seemed to agree. Besides, he pointed out, his sister had plans that might permit her to join them at some point along the way, so the shorter, more episodic journey was opportune.

It did not take long to reach the outskirts of Rome and to check into their lodgings, a hotel built so recently that the scent of freshly sawn wood had not yet dispersed. They booked just two rooms, as Mr. Lewis claimed acquaintances in town where he might stay, and where he anticipated that the forthcoming assembly of spiritualists would take place. But before making his way to his friends, he acceded to Aunt Madeleine's request that they hasten to the lakeshore where once she had happily strolled with her late husband, and where the watery sur-rounds seemed promising for a visitation.

The exact spot was hard to recollect, as the outdoor party they had attended had been large and the evening dark. And, Madeleine admit-ted, the normally temperate guests had indulged in more wine than was their custom. She walked along the grassy shore seeking a glimmer of recognition, wondering if remembered trees had been felled or more had grown, seeking a garden where the heavenly scent of lilies of the valley had risen. Beside her on either side walked Lydia and Mr. Lewis, the latter repeating assurances of the likelihood that the spirit of the departed would be attracted to the place where their romance had pros-pered. He reminded them that one must not rush the spirits.

Jane let them ramble ahead, thinking cynically that for a loving hus-band, Uncle George seemed awfully reluctant to make an appearance to his wife. She hoped that the dread that had grabbed her at the previous séance would dissipate in the bright light of day. With a shiver, she firmly told herself that what had happened last night could not really have been what it seemed. Under the high sun, the possibility of com-munication with the afterlife seemed considerably less likely than in the murky rooms at evening. Wondrous as a visit from the dead would be, Jane preferred that the spirits stay in their own world.

Today, she had declared her intention to paint while the others sought a propitious site for a séance, and no one objected. This both pleased her and left her with the renewed sense that she was irrelevant to their pursuits. Shaking off resentment, she looked for a place to set up her easel where strolling visitors might stop and watch her draw. A brisk wind off the lake was riffling her papers, and the pebbles she picked up to hold down the corners of her drawings were not heavy enough to withstand the breeze. To make matters worse, her skirt was similarly swirled and caught at her legs.

She cut an awkward figure with these windy struggles and was grateful that most of the strollers on the shore were at the moment clustered some distance away. At first she thought that a traveling entertainer, perhaps a magician, might have set up shop there, ready to discover coins hidden in children's ears or to conjure rabbits out of thin air. What else could explain a group of people gathered around what appeared to be a man under a black tent? Jane clumsily made her way in their direction, dragging her easel, its legs tangling in the tall grasses. In the lee of a small grove of young ash trees she paused to secure her bag of paints and brushes and the folder of pictures.

And there it was again. The picture from the night before. It lay on top of the other drawings, although she was almost certain she had hidden it at the back of the packet. She had even considered throwing it away, but something had held her back. And now here it was positioned on top of everything else, almost as though, all by itself, it had made its way forward to command her attention.

The previous evening, distressed and sad at the disclosure of Mrs. Sibley's lost daughter, unsettled about the impending departure, and above all tired, so very tired, she had sat with the assembled group awaiting the spirits. Which stubbornly refused to appear. Not the faintest wispy streak of white, not even an *Oh* from Lydia, and certainly no grumbling Eustace. After an hour, just as she was thinking that they might give up, she felt her hand move. By its own volition. Was there also the gauzy touch of a spectral hand guiding it? Alarmed, she opened her eyes, and the movement stopped, leaving behind a line, a line that traced a gentle curve into a spiral until it left the page.

She might have shown it around at that very moment: evidence of a spirit presence who, this time, had selected her for its message. Both exhilarated and more than a little frightened, she had started to nudge the paper to the center of the table. She imagined how Lydia would gasp with pleasure, how Mrs. Sibley would smile knowingly, how Mr. Lewis... What would be his reaction? Surprise? Disbelief?

But immediately Jane had also felt mistrust. Much as she wanted some unseen hand to grasp her pencil, a fearsome prospect that would grant her full admission into the spiritualist group, she was utterly disconcerted that this might have happened. And worse, she suspected that it had not. Surely, it was far more likely that she herself had been the mover of the hand, half-asleep, apprehensive, desiring to impress her cousin with a twin ability. The fact that she was unsure was unsettling in itself. Being taken by a spirit was scary, but it was even worse to think that her own mind might be divided between what it knew it was doing and what it did not.

Now she made herself look closely at that waving line. I must have been mistaken about where I put it, she thought. Papers do not move on their own; surely I mistook its placement. But the recollection of a pressure on her hand that guided the pencil across the paper was still sharp. She shivered, firmly creased the paper in half, and opened her folder of drawings to put it away, this time definitely at the back.

A mischievous breeze forayed between her fingers and sent the papers flying. Jane snatched at the air and ran, leaving her easel perched like an awkward heron in the weeds. But the wind was steady and strong, and by the time she had yet one more paper to catch she was almost upon the crowd around the man in the black tent.

In the instant before she skidded to a stop on the slippery shore grass, she realized that it wasn't a tent at all but a black cloth covering half a man and an apparatus on stilts, that the man himself was just emerging from underneath the hood, and that her last drawing—the very best one of Lydia—was about to land on the very spot where his right boot was stepping.

"Stop!" she cried, but it was too late.

Seven heads turned and stared at this wild-looking girl, hair blown apart, bonnet hanging from strings around her neck, cheeks flushed, arms clutching papers, and fists full of pencils.

Gasping and mortified, Jane merely looked down at the man's boots. His gaze followed hers, and he lifted his foot and picked up the smudged drawing.

"Oh dear," he said. "I'm very sorry."

There was a pause—variously puzzled, awkward, surprised, annoyed, amused—depending on the individuals in the assembled company.

"A portrait in the older fashion, I see," said a woman at his side. She might have meant it kindly, redirecting attention away from the distressed intruder. "Very nice. But please, sir, do let us see the fruits of your own labors and show us what emerges from your machine."

Jane tried to catch her breath as the man, who she now saw was scarcely older than herself, put her drawing aside and drew out a quarter folio from the apparatus before him.

"It still requires finishing," he said, "but as you can see, the proportions and the relationships among the objects are just as nature presents."

He held a picture in his hands, a full-length portrait of a man in front of two trees, a row of shrubs in the background, and a horizon receding into the distance. The audience applauded.

"So realistic!"

"And so quickly done!"

"Miraculous!"

"I shall bring it to you at the end of the day tomorrow," said the young man. "Permit me first to add the final touches, and I shall deliver it to your home."

He shook the hand of a portly gentleman who looked very pleased, and more to the point, who looked quite a lot like the figure just produced on the page. Round head, wavy hair somewhat receding from a high forehead, narrow shoulders, a widening middle discreetly slimmed by the artist. And best of all, he stood on a ground that quite clearly was solid earth, flat beneath his feet, in front of sprouting vegetation that receded into the distance.

There was a general shaking of hands and nodding of heads, some further admiring talk, and the crowd dispersed. Jane approached the young man, who again held her own drawing in his hands and was studying it.

"How do you manage the likeness?" she asked. "And not in profile but a three-quarters face. I lose resemblance instantly when I try to place a nose in the middle of a face."

He smiled. "That is, however, where it is usually to be found."

Jane took her own drawing back and smoothed it. There was a boot heel print on Lydia's lap and some of her nicely limned gown had torn away.

"I'm sorry I damaged your picture," he said. "It is really quite nice. Or was, anyway. Who is it?"

"My cousin. Her name is Lydia. It was one of my best, and I kept it among my current work so that it might attract more people wanting their likeness taken. But I guess I won't have much luck getting customers with you around."

Jane surprised herself. She was not usually so bold—or so rude—talking with strangers, especially with men to whom a proper introduction had not been tendered. But this young man didn't seem to take her comments amiss.

"Some people will still prefer your style, I am certain," he said. "To many, my device is considered an unartful tool, too tricky to count as art. And indeed, if used alone with no extra skill to correct and finish the image, it produces but crude likenesses. Nonetheless, I find it an aid to sight itself. And when one sees more, one can draw more."

And he folded back the black cloth and showed her what lay beneath.

19

CAMERA OBSCURA

The object thus revealed did not at first seem to merit the flourish of its disclosure. Mounted on a tripod was a wooden box with oddly placed apertures and a reflecting glass on top. Jane frowned in puzzlement.

"Look inside," said the young man. He pointed to an opening at the near end of the box, and Jane bent down.

At first she saw nothing. Or rather, nothing clearly. Merely slants of light filled with sparkling dust motes that sifted across the fine grain of the interior.

"Just wait a minute," said the voice behind her, and she was suddenly engulfed in heavy darkness.

The black cloth weighed more than one would expect. Startled, Jane was momentarily alarmed, felt trapped. The dense woolen covering was too close, even slightly choking in the warmth of the day. But the grass beneath her feet was still sunlit, and the scuffed shoes next to hers did not seem to be making any worrisome advances.

"Look again in just a moment," said the voice, apparently not having noticed her startled reaction. "I'm going to move in front. The image should still be in focus, but let me know if I look blurry and I'll adjust it."

Feeling like a parrot under its cage cover, Jane peered into the slit at the top end of the box, just visible in the darkness. The slants of light were no longer mere glares. They took form, and she now saw a faint miniature world on the floor of the box. A few tiny trees, sprinkles of weeds, sky. Then there was movement and more blurs, and then a grinning figure appeared with such clarity that she exclaimed in delight. The grin widened.

"What do you see? Can you see me standing here?"

"Yes!" Jane gasped. "Don't move, don't move. Stay where you are. I want to look more!"

Inside the box was an exact image of what lay before her. The perimeter of the image warped and faded slightly, but she could see the path that snaked across the grass, a line of trees, a shimmer of water just where the lake curved. And in the center, a young man with his hands on his hips and a look of shared delight.

"It does seem like magic, doesn't it?" he said. "At first. Pretty soon you'll notice its limitations. But I had the same reaction when I first looked into a box like this."

"Yes. Oh yes. Like magic certainly. But it isn't, right? Just a very clever viewing box. No, don't move yet. Please stay there just a little while longer."

It was not only the image that caught her interest. Nor was her only discovery the possibility that one might sketch a picture from the reflections cast inside. How very cunning, she thought. With this device one can study another person without his notice that you are staring. And stare she did at the young man in miniature, a lanky figure with brown hair curling over his collar, sleeves rolled up to the elbow revealing tanned, sinewy arms, a cloth cap below which smiled a generous, open face.

Before she was done studying him, the figure before her disappeared and Jane felt the heavy black cloth removed. Her hair, already tangled from running in the wind, was mussed further and pulled over her head by the hood. She stood and clawed it away from her face.

"What is it? Show me how it works. And how you can draw with it." And belatedly aware that she was standing too close to this stranger, who was looking at her oddly, Jane stepped back and steadied her breathing.

"I beg your pardon. I'm sure I am being rude. I don't intend to be forward. But you have caught my interest."

"No apologies necessary," he said. "It's nice to meet someone—a fellow artist no less—who shares my enthusiasm for the camera obscura. Which is what this is. A small version, to be sure, and a homely one at that. In fact, I built it myself. Still, it's a never-ending source of amusement to play with the arrangement of mirrors and lenses. Not only for drawing but sometimes just for looking."

He loosened two screws at the sides of the box and lifted the top section. Now Jane could see how two mirrors were mounted to catch the image that she had just seen and reflect it downward through a large, clear lens onto the floor of the box.

"You made this yourself?"

"I did, but don't be too impressed. I didn't invent it. Can't take credit for the idea at all. In fact, it's quite an old kind of device, first made in Europe, maybe Italy. I've seen pictures of bigger ones that are whole rooms. In fact, *camera obscura* just means *dark room*."

Other dark rooms skated briefly across Jane's mind.

"But my uncle thought it would be useful to construct smaller, homemade versions that could be carried around. I followed his design in making this one."

He continued with his explanation, demonstrating the positions of the mirrors, showing how the image blurred and sharpened with the height of the lens that he could adjust by turning a dial at the side. Jane was entranced.

"Show me how you draw with it. Why did you say that you still need to finish the drawing you just made? Why can't you finish it while it's still in the box? Who was that man in the picture? Have you done other portraits? Can you show me how?"

The man laughed, but it was enthusiasm not ridicule. He slid a blank paper inside the box, gave Jane a soft charcoal pencil, and bid her under the hood again. The magic returned.

Later she could not recall just how long she stayed there, the suffocating cloth ignored, her pencil tracing reflected images, her delight when she removed a picture to the light and recognized the subject, her frustration when the shadow of her hand blocked what she was trying to draw. Her companion understood.

"Yes, as I said, there are limitations. But when you have sketched the outlines to your satisfaction, they can be later corrected. And you can add color and detail away from your model."

"How poor my own attempts look in comparison," said Jane, gesturing to the folder of her drawings that now lay at their feet. "The methods I have used sometimes include stencils, but their subjects are limited. Mostly I pose people in positions that one sees in other pictures. It is easier to render them that way. But rarely do I manage to paint what I truly see."

"I'm not sure one can ever do that," said the stranger pensively. "I'm sure you know that there is another kind of camera that records an image on a sensitive plate just from the light that enters the aperture, but it is a mechanical process. I prefer this kind because I like to capture what I see, though, as you say, there is far more in the world than one can take in all at once. In fact, the camera obscura makes me realize what more there is to be seen, and also what escapes the reflection inside."

"What escapes reflection," mused Jane. For some reason, she thought of Mrs. Sibley. She looked quizzically at her companion and saw that he, too, was regarding her with curiosity. And also with something more. She stepped back again, but not as far this time.

"Jane?" said a voice behind her. "Jane, my dear, what on earth are you doing?"

Aunt Madeleine, Lydia, and Mr. Lewis stood in a row and stared. All at once, Jane could envision the scene as if she had shot up into the trees and could see them all arranged in two groups. What a picture they made: two properly attired ladies, one mature, one young, on the arms of a dapper gentleman; and the three of them looking dubiously at two vagabonds whose clothing and hair were stirred by the wind, their sleeves rolled up and their hands smudged with charcoal. She almost laughed.

"Oh, hello, Auntie. I hope you have had a productive walk."

"Very pleasant," she said, a little blankly.

"And who might this be?" said Mr. Lewis, directing a sharp glance at the young man by her side. He assumed a proprietary air, the role of protector. It might have been appropriate, given the unexpected appearance of a stranger next to a young woman, though Jane felt as little in need of protection as she ever had in her life.

"I beg your pardon, permit me to introduce..." She looked up.

"Jed Porter, sir, ladies," said the man with a small bow. "Miss Jane and I have discovered our shared interest in the art of limning. Of drawing and painting."

Quick and smart, thought Jane; he caught my name.

It was Lydia who smiled and stepped forward. "How very interesting," she said. "Down the shore as we strolled along, we heard talk of an artist nearby making pictures. They must have spoken of you. And now here you are."

"Yes," said Jed. "I suppose they spoke of me. I fear, however, that I have caused the destruction of your own portrait."

He picked up the spoiled drawing. Jane was pleased that the likeness was sufficient that he recognized her cousin, and also impressed at the change of tone he had adopted when meeting her family. His flexibility of address was unexpected. And he had effectively deflected the tone of Mr. Lewis.

The latter was regarding this newcomer appraisingly as Jed Porter gave a shorter demonstration of his device to Lydia and Madeleine.

"Very ingenious," Lewis interjected. "I have seen such machines before, I believe. Smoke and mirrors?"

Jed laughed. "Just mirrors. And, of course, a lens."

"Did I overhear you rightly when we approached?" continued Lewis. "I believe you were saying something about what escapes reflection?" His tone was probing.

Jed nodded. "I only cautioned Jane, that is, Miss…"

"Woodfield," whispered Lydia.

"Yes. I was telling Miss Woodfield that the device has limits. It is helpful for sketching the outlines of what one wishes to draw, especially if one has difficulty rendering perspective. But the reflected image is faint and somewhat flattened. There is much that it does not capture."

"Ah." Lewis nodded. Jane thought he might have been a little disappointed in the answer.

"It is getting late, Jane," said Aunt Madeleine. "We are returning to our hotel."

So it was time to leave. Lydia gracefully urged her aunt and Mr. Lewis ahead while Jane managed a reluctant goodbye to Jed Porter.

"I have so appreciated your time, your tutorial I suppose I should say," she said. "I'm sorry to have taken up so much of your afternoon."

"Not at all. I enjoyed our conversation," he said. And then with a hopeful tone, "Perhaps you will be in the vicinity for a little while longer? I'll be occupied with a mural project in town over the next several days, but after that, I intend to return to the lake and do a bit more sketching. If you might be around, maybe…" He trailed off and for the first time looked ill at ease.

"Surely, I will!" said Jane.

Perhaps a proper young woman would not have been so adamantly forward, she thought, but an artist needs nerve.

He smiled. "Good then, I'll see you again soon."

She scampered after the others, almost forgetting to collect her abandoned easel from the weeds. Her arms encumbered, she chanced a glance behind her and saw that Jed Porter raised his hand and waved before he, too, collected his gear and departed. She realized only later that he had kept the damaged drawing.

20

WHAT BONES CAN TELL

BUFFALO, NEW YORK. JULY 9, 2015

Once Lucille was untangled from her roots, she was gently brushed free of dirt and laid out on a laboratory table. Her disarticulated bones fell into an awkward splay. Craig arranged them more neatly, their outline describing the slight frame of the girl they had once borne. The lower mandible was partial and in pieces and had to be laid next to the skull, the button still jammed between two teeth. Dan thought she looked naked and vulnerable and wished there were a more modest way to display the skeleton, and then he wondered at the oddity of that thought. For the moment, she was both an object of analysis and a teaching tool for Dr. Killian.

"We don't have the capacity for a complete forensic analysis here," Craig said. "But before we send samples to the lab, let's see what we can determine from a visual analysis of the bones. Two of you have studied anatomy, right? So let's review for the others. First, how old is she? One easy place to look for signs of age is teeth, and even though we have only the complete upper mandible and a partial lower, we can examine them for wear. Jacob, any opinions?"

Jacob peered into what was left of the gaping mouth, trying to recall what his own teeth looked like in the bathroom mirror. "To me, the teeth look pretty healthy," he said, "given that they've been in the ground for a while. There aren't any missing, except for those in the lower jaw that became detached and fell away when the jaw splintered. And even they aren't too worn down."

"And that would indicate...?" Killian prompted.

"She's young, right?"

"I agree," said Killian. "And we have been right to call the skeleton 'she,' because the other thing a visual examination shows is sex. See the pelvis?"

Everyone peered, and again Dan had to set aside a sense of impropriety. Indecency. Where was this prudish sentiment coming from? He glanced at Karen to see if she displayed any discomfort, but she was utterly absorbed in the study.

"Here we see a wider subpubic angle than one finds in males, see? As well as a ventral arc. So we know our skeleton was female and young, not more than twenty years of age, I would say. And look at the bone ends here." Craig picked up a femur, the very one that had fallen at Dan's feet, and drew their attention to the ends. "Only recently fused, it looks like. Also an indication of relative youth. Not a child, of course, but a person at the advent of physical adulthood."

He replaced the bone and surveyed the skeleton. "We'll know more after the samples come back from the lab. Plus I'm calling a colleague for another opinion about the pelvis and what appear to be those bone chips fused to the back of it. There were more small particles embedded in the earth that sifted into that part of the skeleton that I'd like him to take a look at too. But I'm going to send off some samples immediately so that we can determine as much as possible about our Lucille as soon as we can."

"Any indication of cause of death?" asked Jasmine.

"I see no signs of lethal trauma to the skull. The hyoid bone is cracked, which ordinarily indicates strangulation. But the neck was twisted slowly from the action of the roots so its position was compromised. The evidence of the button lodged in the teeth certainly indicates a struggle of some sort right before she died. And before she was buried. I think we have to presume that disposal of her body was improvised, given the absence of a coffin or a marker. As well as the relative shallowness of her grave. We can't be entirely certain, but it is probable, in my opinion, that she was asphyxiated, maybe by strangulation."

They all had expected that judgment, but still, it was chilling to hear.

The analysis from the forensic lab came back sooner than expected. At Karen's phone call, Dan hurried to join them during his lunch break, his shoes still crusted with mud. He hastily changed into sneakers in the truck before winding through the maze of the large building and locating the anthropology lab. Increasingly, he felt that he was living in two worlds. In one, he still stood in a trench and wielded his tools against the hard-packed earth. But in the other, he felt he was diving through that trench into the past with a group of people who, he was surprised to find, almost accepted him as one of their own. Almost. He still wondered whether without Karen's attention, he might have been politely shouldered aside and excluded from further investigation. No one had explicitly suggested as much, but Karen was perhaps too insistent that he was a welcome addition to the team. He guessed that the entry of his mother onto the scene was another factor that kept him included, given her fields of experience and that surprising facility with the pickle fork and the button.

How quickly his own life had changed in the last several weeks. The heavy physical labor of the summer had been welcome, for the tiring work left little time to worry about either his debts or the lack of direction his life now displayed. Better to focus on the earth, the stubborn bedrock hindering the excavation of the trench for the new mains, the heavy clay smelling of moisture and age, the rot of old tree stumps, and the invading lattice of roots that bound it all together.

And then, from that thick matrix, a bone had fallen at his feet revealing the remains of a young woman, her delicate ribs inches away from his hands and his eyes. It was an unexpected and somewhat ghastly intimacy. Stunned and awed, he had been caught in wonder, unable to look away. The shock receded, the curiosity intensified. And as time went on, it was joined by pity and a peculiar sense of mission. He felt he owed it to Lucille to find out who she was, why she died, and where she had once belonged. Had he not been the one to open her tomb of earth, maybe he would not feel so bound. But he had and he did. It was like feeling obliged to help someone in distress whom you come upon by accident, just because you are there.

Entering the lab, he saw that Craig held several pages of results from the stable isotype analysis and radiocarbon dating, plus a bone mineral density study. He distributed them to the assembled company. Dan took note that the number of copies printed out included enough for him. There were sections of the reports that made no sense to him, but the conclusions were stated clearly. The bone mineral study confirmed their earlier conclusion that the skeleton was of a woman who had died relatively young. The isotype and radiocarbon analysis indicated that she was a white female of western European lineage, probably from New England or eastern New York, and that she died between 150 and 170 years ago.

"Now we know just about all we can derive from examination of the bones," said Craig.

"Except who she was," said Dan. It wasn't enough.

"Right. Her identity remains unknown. There's a limit to lab analysis."

"We could try to find out who she was, couldn't we?" asked Karen. "There must be records of deaths or of missing persons. Don't you think there might have been people looking for her? Maybe there's even still family around."

"Perhaps," said Craig. "In any event, it's time to issue another report for the public. She has aroused a lot of interest. And, in fact, if there are any descendants of her family still living here, they might have stories of a missing member who disappeared long ago. Not likely, of course, after all this time. But still an outside possibility."

A draft of the report was already prepared, a joint effort of Jasmine and Killian. It only awaited confirmation from the lab analyses. One of Karen's clearer photographs of the skeleton shed of her root shroud was printed in the newspaper with a brief story beneath confirming earlier reports.

> The skeleton found buried on the east side of Delaware Avenue during excavation to replace the gas mains has been identified as a female of approximately twenty years of age. She died in the mid-nineteenth century, possibly the victim of an attack or an accident. She was of slight build and stood approximately five feet five inches tall. There was evidence of a broken collar bone, healed in childhood. Otherwise, she appears to have been a healthy young woman...

And now, they also had something else to add to that basic information.

Upon closer examination of the pelvic area, it seemed that Lucille might have a few too many bones. Small fragments trapped in the earth as her flesh fell away had needed further analysis before their identity could be confirmed. At first Craig had thought they might be mineral deposits or chips from elsewhere in the skeleton, but now it was fairly clear that there were also a few extra, very small bones lying against the pelvis. The forensic pathologist confirmed the condition of the girl at her death:

> ...who was two and a half to three months pregnant.

Two lives cut short in an instant.

"What will happen to her now?" asked Dan.

Craig hesitated before observing that the anthropology lab had space to house more bones. A teaching tool is always welcome, he noted, and with no family to claim it, the skeleton might as well stay there.

"I think she should be buried," said Karen. "Properly this time."

"So do I," said Dan. "Not that I have any say in this. It may sound strange, but I feel like I've come to know her somehow." He paused. It was hard to articulate the next sentiment. "And that in a way, I owe her something." He still didn't quite comprehend why that feeling was so intense.

But it was shared. The others nodded in agreement. They stood side by side and broadcast insistence at Killian, who slowly smiled. Any doubts that Dan still harbored about his belonging there evaporated in the moment.

21

Unsettled Waters

Oneida Lake, July 10, 1851

Rain was slanting down but Jane paced the deck, heedless of the fact that her skirt was becoming heavy with damp. Although the water was getting rough, she was grateful that Aunt Madeleine had consented to cross Oneida Lake by boat. The last thing she wanted today was to be compressed shoulder to shoulder in a carriage jouncing over uneven roads and sprinkled with mud. She had begun to feel ill in the middle of the night, and the need for fresh air overrode the discomfort of the weather.

She also needed some solitude, and a slippery deck was the best available place, since the other passengers had taken refuge in the crowded lounge. There was much to think about, especially the jumbled memories of the last two nights.

Memories which, despite her efforts, remained full of blanks and blurs.

"No need to be concerned, my dear," Mr. Lewis had said. "Do calm yourself. Confusion is not uncommon in the aftermath of a visitation." He patted her shoulder and offered a mint tisane to sooth her heaving stomach. "The first encounter with spirits often overwhelms one. Soon you will become accustomed to the experience, and your memories will not vanish afterward." His pat turned into a reassuring squeeze, as he grasped her shoulders and bent to look into her eyes. "We are delighted to welcome you fully into our company."

Aunt Madeleine had clasped Jane's hands. She marveled at what had happened and then became overwhelmed and collapsed onto a couch. And Lydia was overjoyed that her cousin was now a full participant in the spiritualist quest. Jane herself had smiled and expressed agreement. She assured them that, despite her trembling hands, she was so very pleased to have been able to contribute something to the gathering.

It was not entirely false. She was indeed relieved and even a little bit grateful that, after all this time, she might become a true part of the community.

So why now on a windy deck with the grassy lake shores and their muddy paths passing steadily by, could she not shake this unease? After all, she admonished herself, weren't you wishing for just this sort of thing to happen?

There had been three nights at the table with a new group of spiritualists gathered from the vicinity. (Or was it four? Her sense of time was blurry.) At the first session, Jane had felt as marginal to the proceedings as ever, both depressed that whatever spirits were hanging about remained invisible to her, and skeptically impatient at Lydia's rapturous exhalations and Aunt Madeleine's pleas to the air. The claims of the others to sense a presence did not persuade her, and she had noticed with dismay the transfer of coins from the hand of a participant to Mr. Lewis's pocket. Not a fee, she told herself; as Lydia said, a donation, a gesture of appreciation.

Then on the second night, she had experienced again a strange pressure on her hand, the very feeling that had occurred once before in Utica as she sat next to Mrs. Sibley. A chilly atmosphere at her shoulder, a tremor of the fingers, a smudge of the pencil on her waiting paper, though no image had appeared. She concluded she had simply been on the brink of a doze and her hand had jerked. She erased the mark and said nothing of it.

But last night—last night what had happened? Her body inert, her mind a blur, a helpless feeling almost like sleep. Yet her pencil must have moved, for on the page under her hand there had appeared a face. A face full of scratches and hatch marks, curling lines and blurs, and amidst the jumble, discernible eyes peering through the marks like a watcher in the dark, a swipe of pencil defining a chin, a curl of a lip and—most ominously—a smudge above that lip that was an unmistakable likeness to Uncle George's moustache.

Aunt Madeleine had fainted.

Lydia had applauded and laughed with joy.

Mr. Lewis had leapt forward and grasped her shoulders and all but kissed her. Jane thought she might have been smiling herself, but her lips were numb and she couldn't be sure.

Expressions of admiration at her accomplishment issued from the assembled company, a set of Mr. Lewis's acquaintance who had gathered for the session, including two elderly women seeking to contact their sisters. All of them had declared themselves delighted to discover a new medium, an additional conduit to the world beyond added to their lists. Lydia's affinity with the afterlife was becoming widely known, and now a spirit had made its presence manifest through the movement of Jane's hand. Lydia had gasped her *Ohs* and stared through the ceiling to the sky beyond, but Jane, unaware, had been the one whom the spirits seized. She had produced a picture. An actual piece of physical evidence that the dead could not only speak but communicate in other ways. Everyone agreed that they had sensed a presence as well, and how marvelous it was that Uncle George had finally come, and that he had chosen to appear in an image. Jane's skill, both spiritual and artistic, was confirmed by this message from beyond.

The event should have been uplifting. What more had she wanted than to be among the favored circle of spiritualism? And above all, to be once more in tune with her beloved Lydia.

If only she could remember more clearly. If only she felt pleasure and gratification in the event, as well as relief in the knowledge that she truly belonged in this company. If only there were not also doubt. And dread.

Doubt that hers was really the hand that drew the picture, for with no memory of having done so, how could she take credit? Dread that the credit was not due to her at all but to some spectral entity that had seeped into her will and taken command of her fingers.

Doubt that such a thing is possible; dread that it might be. Doubt that she could do it again; dread that she might.

And anxious that there was no way to determine the truth of the matter.

Jane thought longingly of Jed Porter. She wished that there had been time to see him once more before they left Rome. Even though it would have been embarrassing, mortifying even, to confess to him her role in such a strange event, his even temper and clear head might have alleviated the worries that plagued her now.

She had seen him on a number of occasions after their first encounter, and each time she wished the clock would slow. They had spent delightful daylight hours absorbed in the techniques of rendering likenesses, not only of faces and bodies but also of landscapes, of the waves on the lake, of the light that the sun cast as it traveled across the heavens. Sometimes they drew freehand, using the backs and margins of old papers whose creases and erasures made them soft. Good paper was costly and not to be used for practice.

When they tired of the vistas provided by town and park, she rode with him to different places to draw, traveling in his sturdy wagon. It was well-designed to serve as part workshop and part sleeping space, and it was drawn by a large, patient horse named Horace. Horace was strong but slow, but what's the hurry? said Jed. Eventually he and I will make it across the state to the project I'm heading for, and along the way I can practice.

Jed was traveling with three sizes of the camera obscura, each made for pictures of different dimensions, from the small lens ideal for a miniature to a larger one that might be used to render a vista. When he demonstrated their use, her fingers itched to try them all. Sensing this, he had permitted her to ruin a number of sheets of fresh paper before she realized how much of his stock she had used up. She replenished it, but the quality available in Rome was inferior to what he had brought with him. He was not angry and seemed to relish her company as much as she did his. Never had she felt so at ease with a recent acquaintance. Jed had moved from stranger to friend in the span of a few days.

Sometimes they did not try to draw at all but just looked, their awareness of the sense of sight heightened by the knowledge of what mirrors could reflect, how shadows define a space, how lines give way to tones and abstract shapes became images. Vision itself became a focus for attention: what could be seen, what could be inferred, what was opaque, occluded, missing. Vivid, beautiful. The more she looked, the more beauty there was to be seen. Side by side they stood and let their eyes drink in the world around, shoulders sometimes touching, hands sharing pencils and brushes.

Lydia had teased her lightly about her new beau. Jane's first response was to object in resentful embarrassment and to insist that the friendship was merely that: friendship. Her retort was prompted more by the teasing tone than the idea that a young man might fancy her. It would be a new experience, if indeed her cousin's assessment was accurate. Lydia had already accumulated several admirers to her credit, though no particular attachment. Jane, shy by nature and less blessed with a comely appearance, had caught no one's eye yet. Therefore, she presumed that

Jed Porter was merely glad to have the company of a fellow limner, someone with whom a discussion of perspective lines and the depiction of volume would not be tedious. But maybe, just maybe, he also favored her. She warmed at the thought, but then also worried that his good opinion of her might change were he to discover the spiritualist purpose of her travels and the ways that her evenings were spent.

How would he have regarded that scratchy portrait of Uncle George—her hand guided awfully and artfully by a ghost? She imagined the conversation that might have transpired had he seen the picture.

Jed might have remarked first on all the smudges and extra lines, wondering why it took so long to outline the face. On learning that the drawing had been produced unconsciously, he would have laughed and made a joke about how eyes lose focus when falling asleep. Then realizing that she was serious, he would have looked at her soberly, perhaps with worry, and inquire how that could be the case. And she might have said, *I don't know either; a part of myself seems hidden, even from me.*

And then would she have told him everything about the westward journey that she was taking with her cousin and aunt, filling in the deliberate gaps she had left when accounting for her travels? Would she have explained the role that Mr. Lewis had taken in determining their progress? That would require mention of Lydia's remarkable facility to communicate with the dead.

Would Jed have smiled and shrugged, dismissing their quest? Would he have scorned her? Or would he have been eager to learn more, to examine the possibilities of communion between the living and the dead? Would he know Swedenborg, would he countenance the possibility that spirits are composed of tiny particles that retain commerce with the grosser, heavier physical world? Mr. Lewis considered this a new science, but that was open to debate. Jed often mentioned his scientist uncle, the one whose pictorial devices they were using. Uncle Rufus, he called him, *almost a father to me. A man of great inventiveness and a sound, critical mind.*

It was the admiring account of Uncle Rufus Porter that stayed Jane's tongue and prevented her from disclosing the spiritualist quest of her aunt. She once mentioned a séance in passing, noticed a raised eyebrow, and quickly diverted to another subject. Had she shown him the image that had grown beneath her hand, he surely would have frowned at the notion that an unseen force could guide a drawing, insisting instead that the science of optics governs both sight and art.

Poor Aunt Madeleine. Her pretty face was becoming drawn with worry, showing her age, and she had not worn her fine jewelry for weeks. It still seemed improbable that she was truly pursuing her doomed objective. In the light of day, Jane was convinced that no one could be as gullible as she seemed to be. Even if a spirit were to make an appearance, it would not solve the problem that her aunt was facing. Surely no one could convince a lawyer to countenance a message from the dead, especially a message so advantageous to the widow of the ghost who uttered it. It was obviously beyond the realm of possibility. At least, it seemed obvious.

Until last night, when Uncle George's face had appeared under her own hands, released from invisibility by the pencil she gripped. The expression on that scribbled visage—fierce, admonishing. And so terribly familiar.

Jane shivered at the recollection. Why were not the others more afraid of meddling with the spirit world? Why assume that the dead do not resent those still living and perhaps take pleasure in doing them harm?

Oh, stop it! Jane admonished herself. Even if spirits were present, in their immaterial state, they could not possibly hurt anyone. Other than scaring them half to death.

On the other hand, if they could take a piece of charcoal in their ghostly fingers, then what else might they cause to happen? Jane looked at her own hands, thinking of how smudged she and Jed had become from drawing with charcoal. Had her hands been blackened last night? Had her fingers borne the imprint of the pencil? She simply could not remember.

Although the lake was shallow, the blowing wind made the boat heave and judder. She swallowed repeatedly to keep her gorge down. Usually Aunt Madeleine was the queasy traveler, but today it was Jane who felt sick. The motion of the boat was stirring her insides, and she moved to the railing just in case her breakfast decided to return.

She was sad to think that she might never know what Jed Porter would have said to all of this, and if his sensible, solid self would have settled her mind and leant comfort to her distress. If only the drawing had appeared the night before, when there was still time to meet him and share the disturbing account. But on the day they departed—a day much sooner than she had anticipated and once more chosen without her consultation—he was again engaged on the mural he was finishing.

Jane had tried to locate him, but the time was short, and he was not to be found before the boat left. Nor was Horace and the wagon to be seen in the vicinity of the streets she passed. The best she could do was to leave him a letter at the hotel telling him of their destination. And hope fervently that he would think to look for her again.

22

ILLNESS

By the time they docked, Jane's sickness had worsened, and it was not relieved by the return to solid ground. They had to stop once to let her out of the carriage to vomit during the long ride that took them miles farther to their lodgings at the head of a small lake. The rain had cleared, the sky was endless, and the late sun sparked on the water and set every blade of grass to gleaming.

Or so Lydia declaimed, joyful at the lovely day, enthusiastic at what lay ahead on their journey west. Jane gulped huge breaths of the freshened air and gripped her cousin's arm to keep from falling, as those blades of grass and sparkling sunlit water were now part of a spinning world where nausea eclipsed any beauty that nature could offer.

She was to have shared a room with her cousin, but Lydia gave their room over to Jane and moved her things in with Aunt Madeleine for the evening. Both of them fussed attentively over her, offering salts, tea, a light supper—emphatically rejected—until nightfall. Mr. Lewis had discreetly vanished, leaving the women to deal with the mess of illness. At last, after much insistence, Jane was left alone with basin and chamber pot to cope with her malady until, finally, her sickness began to subside late in the night.

She lay in a limp, feverish state, too tired to move and afraid that if she did the horrid vertigo would return. Between receding waves of nausea, she dozed when she could. After an indeterminate time, she opened her eyes and found that the ceiling had settled to a steady rectangle above four stable walls with a window at her left. The hotel was quiet. Even Aunt Madeleine's usual droning snore could not be heard through the wall of the adjacent room.

Carefully, she sat up, rearranged pillows, straightened the covers. It was such a relief not to be dizzy and retching that she almost felt well, even though her joints ached and her body was trembly and weak. Glimmers of moonlight slanted between the curtains, and she gingerly got up and moved to the window. She opened the casement and felt a clean breeze enter the fetid room. Her knees were weak and the cool air made her shiver, but she wrapped a quilt around her shoulders and returned to bed, huddling upright against the cushions, enjoying the air, the stillness, and the blessed sense that recovery was at hand.

Nighttime was so peaceful and lovely. On the rare occasions when she was up late, Jane often lamented that the beauties of the dark usually went unnoticed by those who dutifully sleep it away. What a pity that the habits of health and society hid the moon and the distant stars from more frequent attention. She dozed on and off again, but lightly, still aware of the room and the night.

The foul taste in her mouth roused her after another hour. Jane got up to sip from a cool cup of tea that Lydia had left on the wash stand. She bathed her face and hands, found a comb and tried to put in order the hair that had twisted into knots around her head. Her aching body longed for sleep, but she would be so much more comfortable if she could tidy herself from the lingering traces of illness.

Out in the hall she heard a creaking floorboard and she paused, hoping that no one was coming to check on her. Without doubt she had truly needed Lydia's earlier assistance, for she had hardly been able to stand. And Aunt Madeleine's hovering presence had been a motherly comfort of sorts. But there are times when illness is better coped with alone. The various remedies on offer had merely increased the nausea, and Jane did not welcome an audience when crouched over a chamber pot.

What a spectacle she must have presented yesterday. And what on earth could have made her so sick? It obviously could not have been the rocking ship or she would have recovered on reaching dry land. Jane hoped that none of the other guests had witnessed her arrival. If any had, perhaps she had appeared to be suffering only from the vapors or some other ladylike ailment. She had a sense that Mr. Lewis had been sufficiently repelled that he had simply withdrawn for the time being. Jane moved to the window again to take another breath of night air.

Sometimes the thought conjures the man. A full moon lit the few drifting clouds so brightly that they gleamed like pearls. It cast shadows that were sharper and more precise than those of daytime, the absence of color intensifying light and dark. A row of poplars sent long cones of black across the lawn; the twisting branches of a tall oak were lace against the sky. All was as quiet and as still as a fine ink drawing.

Except for one shadow that was moving silently toward the hotel. A tall man was taking leisurely strides, perhaps admiring the lovely night, certainly not creeping along in the darkness of the building walls. The shadows cast by his long legs slanted sideways, scissoring as he walked, bending around bushes and riffling over manicured garden plots. He was hatless and easily recognized, and while it was unusual to be abroad in the middle of the night, there was nothing furtive about his demeanor.

Mr. Lewis paused and looked up almost directly at the very window where Jane stood, as if he sensed a watcher. She drew back, her heart pounding. She wondered if she could be seen at the open casement but wasn't sure why that thought should make her apprehensive. She was, after all, simply standing in her own hotel room, and the opportunity to glimpse this night walker was pure chance. Of course, just as she questioned what he was doing out there, so he might puzzle over a girl standing at the window when she ought to be asleep.

Perhaps he was just enjoying a breath of night air. Or maybe he was waiting for someone. He seemed relaxed, as a man would be who had decided to take a walk on a beautiful moonlit night. Jane wondered what time it was. There were no chiming clocks echoing through the building, and the dark sky gave no hint of the hour.

It was so quiet that the faintest movement registered as a mere breath of the building, hardly more evident than the flight of a moth glancing against a window. Jane sensed a gentle click of a door latch somewhere in the hotel, a creaking board, this time maybe on the stairs. A faint swish as if a skirt brushed the wall.

Perhaps the maids were awake and readying for the morning. Could it be time for them to rise already? Surely not. The day would break early at this time of year, and the sky outside gave no hint of sunrise. Maybe she heard nothing at all but her own breath, the beating of her own heart. The rising of her own fever.

Which couldn't possibly make a sound. The pounding in her ears was a product of illness, not the detection of movement in the building. I need to go back to sleep, she thought; I'm getting delirious. Her bed was just behind her in the small room. But she lingered by the window, so tired that the effort of moving even a short distance seemed too much to undertake.

Out on the grass, Mr. Lewis stood still and looked at the stars. And then he lowered his head as though something had caught his eye. Curiosity warred with her aching fatigue, and Jane was just about to collapse back into bed when another figure appeared.

It was a woman, her head and shoulders covered with a shawl, her skirt brushing the grass. She seemed to be wearing a loose dress, rather like a nightgown, as if she had just arisen from her bed. Her appearance galvanized Jane to peer more closely, caring little now that she might be seen, for the two shadows were intent only with each other. She opened the casement further and leaned on the sill.

Who—

No. Certainly not. It could not be.

The shawl had fallen back around the woman's shoulders. Could it possibly be Lydia out there? Jane resisted the idea, but the moon was full, and surely the slim shoulders and upright carriage illuminated in its light belonged to her cousin.

Were they heading alone to a late séance? Jane had an unhinged moment of resentment that they would go off without her. Wasn't her spirit drawing enough for them?

But even as ill as she felt, she realized that her fleeting indignation covered a more likely worry: could this possibly be an assignation?

A cloud moved over the moon, but just before the scene below dimmed into gray, Jane was almost certain that she saw Lydia pass something to Mr. Lewis, something she held in two hands. But that was less disturbing than his reciprocal gesture, for he put his arm around her shoulders and drew her toward the veranda that skirted the side of the hotel. Before they disappeared into the shadows, it seemed he bent his head to meet hers, and the moon just might have lit an embrace.

By now, Jane was shivering hard and the room was beginning to tilt again. I am seeing things, she thought. I am ill. The fever has risen. I must sleep.

She closed the casement and fell into bed, too tired to think further about what she had seen. In the morning it will all be clear, she thought, and I will know that I've been dreaming.

23

RECOVERY

There was a warm yellow color washing the room. Someone opened the window, and Jane could hear robins chatting in the bushes outside. Discreet clinks indicated that the rank slop pails were being removed and the wash basin refreshed. A cool hand rested on her forehead and a voice proclaimed that her fever had broken. And then all was quiet again.

When she awoke fully an indeterminate time later, Jane found a cooling pot under a flowered tea cozy and a plate of sliced bread on the table by the door. And a note from Lydia.

> Jane, dear. How worried we all were, but this morning your head is cool and I didn't want to wake you from a healing sleep. We have gone to see an acquaintance of Mr. Lewis who lives in the next village, but I shall see you on our return this afternoon. The proprietors of this establishment are most kind, and the maid will bring you anything you might like to eat.
>
> I do hope that you are better for this evening's gathering!

The tea was still warm, but just barely, leading Jane to think that the morning was well gone. She was starving but made herself chew and swallow the bread slowly, cautious lest too sudden eating might revive her sickness. Apparently no one else had become ill, and as far as she could remember, they had all shared more or less the same food for the last few days. She concluded that she had suffered one of those passing illnesses for which no particular reason can be found. Just bad luck. After all, few people are in good health every minute of their lives, and those who claim that they are probably have poor memories. Or don't want to admit to weakness. But illness visits us all. What relief that her distress had been short-lived.

Washed, dressed, and lightly fed, Jane felt renewed. A sunlit room banishes the worries that cluster in the night. She went to the window and tried to recall just what she thought she had seen. It was the same view of a wing of the building, the path running to the door, a line of trees, a well-tended garden with a man now there wielding a rake. Gone were the bleak tones of night, the stark moonlight, the slanting shadow of a man.

Perhaps I dreamed it all, she thought. Her recollection of the night was both vivid and tentative, like one of those times when upon waking, one is unable at first to separate memory from dream. Even after recollection is sorted out, the feeling persists that something only dreamt truly happened.

Jane went into the hall. She was fairly sure that Aunt Madeleine and Lydia had shared the room directly next to hers. She tapped on the door, though of course, no one would answer if they had left for the day. She turned the knob of the likely room and was glad to find it unlocked and empty. How awkward it would have been to enter a stranger's room. The bed was tidy, the luggage neatly placed by the wall. There was a bowl of grapes by the window that looked tempting now that her appetite was returning and a napkin wrapped around two biscuits.

There was no particular reason to assume that this bounty had been taken from the breakfast room for her, but nonetheless Jane sat on the edge of the bed and nibbled contentedly. Lydia would not resent the theft of a few grapes. Aunt Madeleine had also been fairly sympathetic, although the older woman was becoming more withdrawn than she used to be and scarcely talked to Jane at all these days. Widowhood must be weighing heavily on her, bereft and homeless as she was. She was wan and now seldom wore her lovely jewelry. Jane felt sorry for her, but her pity was increasingly tinged with exasperation that her aunt insisted on pursuing her foolish quest for a spectral legacy. If Lydia weren't so charmed by her mediumistic powers, she surely would agree that Auntie was wasting her time and merely prolonging her distress.

Jane sighed and felt sad again about the gap that had opened between her and her cousin in the weeks since they had left Troy. She harbored some hope that perhaps her newfound talent at spirit drawing—or skill, or gift, or even curse; it was hard to know what to call it—would repair the friendship and restore the close alliance they used to have. She longed to return to the time when they laughed at the same things, shared secrets and memories, and privately mourned their lost mothers together. Surely, none of that was truly gone. Life brings changes, but friendships remain steadfast.

However, there was a large stumbling block that stood in the way of repairing their closeness. Lydia had been utterly delighted at the spirit drawing that lay under Jane's hand. But Jane herself could not entirely believe that she really possessed that strange, new talent. She could not account for the appearance of the image of Uncle George, but that a ghost had been the artist was beyond credibility. Her subversive doubts remained. It was difficult to enthuse with Lydia about the discovery of a world that existed on a spiritual plane and to extoll the hopes that one could speak with the dead.

Jane would have liked to believe that it was her greater rationality and level head that accounted for their difference, but she worried that Lydia was simply the braver of the two. She was the one who always welcomed challenges and who showed greater courage in the face of adversity. Those traits, combined with her generous affection, had eased her younger cousin's adjustment to the changes that their shared losses had necessitated. It was, therefore, not very surprising that Lydia would peek into the world of the dead with curiosity and verve rather than dread. Indeed, she seemed to welcome these spirit presences—if that is what they were—even going so far as to invite them to invade her very body, lending them her voice to utter their words.

However, what seemed from one perspective to be Lydia's courage bespoke more than a tinge of foolhardiness, and as Jane reflected on the astonishingly rapid ascension of Lydia to the role of medium, her cousin's attitude seemed not so much brave as reckless. Lydia strode into the world of spiritualism with heedless fervor.

Jane could not bring herself to think of the spirits of those who had passed over—*over what?* her mind kept inserting—as obviously benign ensigns from heaven. If the spirit lives on, shouldn't it be content to reside in its new abode? Eternity provides sufficient time to wait for one's loved ones to join the company of the departed. Therefore, if the dead were not really entirely gone to their own heaven but insisted on making occasional forays back to earth, it was hard to believe that they weren't issuing grievances from the world beyond. Not just assurances but terrors; not communications from loved ones but complaints that they had not been loved enough.

In short, marvelous though it would be to share her pencil with a spirit and thereby sustain the closeness with her cousin, the prospect terrified her.

As Jane finished the grapes and got up to leave the room, she noticed that Lydia's nightdress, which had been draped over a chair, had slid to the floor. She picked it up and smoothed the wrinkles before folding it to place at the foot of the bed. And then she saw that the edge was stained with marks that looked like streaks of mud, greenish where newly cut grass might have left a stain. And that the hem was still damp, a dampness best explained by a late-night walk across a lawn already accumulating dew.

She had not been dreaming.

For a moment, Jane sat stunned with the nightgown on her lap, refusing to acknowledge the true significance of what she held in her hands. Her heart sank, and she tried to resist the knowledge of what was now an obvious truth. It had been no feverish illusion. Beyond a doubt it had been Lydia whom she had seen from the window, hurrying across the grass in the moonlight and still in her night clothes, passing an object to Mr. Lewis, and then sliding alongside him into the shadows.

What Jane could not divine was why. Why Lydia had left the hotel room so furtively and at such an hour; and what she had given him in that handover gesture. And—above all—what had happened in the shadows afterward.

Oh, Lydia. My dearest friend. What are you doing?

24

CUPOLA

"It's an ill wind that blows nobody good!" declared Priscilla Cavendish. She gazed out the window at the torrents of rain lashing against the house. Dan detected a note of satisfaction in her voice, perhaps because with its new roof and the repaired foundation of the wide front porch, the old structure of Bigwell House was proving strong enough to withstand this assault of bad weather. But also, he suspected, she was doubly gratified because the ill wind had blown in terrible storms that had freed her son to help with the repairs to the interior of the museum, much needed if their schedule for a gala reopening was to be met. Dan gave a wry smile and shook his head at his mother's uncanny ability to commandeer his help. Even nature conspired with her desires.

The weather had been so foul for a week that once again the work on the mains had been suspended, and the street outside ran with water opaque with clay. Fortunately for some residents, much of the gas work was now completed, the lines connected and the sidewalks replaced, although the city's sketchy attempt at reseeding lawns had never been promising, and now both grass seed and topsoil had drained into the storm sewers. Unfortunately for others, in the sections of the city where the work was still in progress, soaked plywood bowed beneath the storm's onslaught and the trenches were flooded. The discovery of Lucille had held up work long enough that streets around the Bigwell House Museum were the color of rust. Bedrock and clay do not permit good drainage, and thick water formed curbside rivers.

Dan bundled an armful of old wallpaper into a garbage bag. As it crumpled, it exuded powdery clouds of ancient glue and dust, filling his nose and making him cough. Two restorers, student interns from the conservation program at the nearby state college, were meticulously cleaning the decorated walls of their remaining paste, but it fell to Dan to clear away the layers of carefully steamed-off paper that had covered for years the extensive murals that embellished much of the house. The work in the dining room was nearly complete, but the highest room, a low-ceilinged cupola that sat atop the building, still needed to be stripped of its paper. Although traces of paintings were visible up there as well, a series of leaks over the years had belled out portions of plaster, and Priscilla believed those upstairs walls were probably too damaged to be of the same interest as those in the main rooms below.

Dan was not terribly impressed by the rather flat landscapes that were being revealed downstairs, but his mother was delighted.

"Just in his style!" she said. "And larger than many of the other extant works. So lucky that the colors have been preserved by all those layers of paper. And what a discovery to find Rufus Porter murals this far west!"

"How can you be sure these are his?" said Dan. He had heard the story before but with half an ear.

"So far the evidence is circumstantial, as I've said. Do pay attention, Daniel," said his mother with mild reproach. "But if we can find a signature, that would be absolute proof, although Porter rarely signed his murals. But, as I told you, we have Bigwell's draft letter commissioning the painting, and that will be proof enough for the time being. I intend to display the letter in a central exhibit case for the opening along with a few entries from his journals and business ledgers. It will put us on the map and ensure funding for years to come!"

Dan found that he was softening his attitude toward his mother and her proprietary ways. Her delight was seductively contagious, and he had to be pleased for her, even as he recognized that her gently manipulative ability was deftly at work commanding his labor and those of his friends. All four of them would have been impressed into service to renovate the interior of Bigwell House, except for the fact that Karen and Jasmine were taking turns at the Historical Society poring over microfilmed newspapers in search of a notice of a young woman who went missing some hundred and fifty to hundred and seventy years ago.

"Send Jacob upstairs when he gets here," he said. "I'm going up to the cupola again to see if I can do some more caulking if it's not too damp."

Rain hammered at the new roof over his head and streaked the cupola windows, replacements for the old, warped ones that could not be saved. The outer seal seemed to be holding, so Dan ran a thin bead of caulk on the inside and smoothed it with his finger. This room was relatively small, like a top hat perched on the rest of the substantial structure. It held little furniture other than a couple of straight-backed chairs and an enormous wooden chest flanked with two narrow bookshelves. There was no way to heat the room; it had obviously been built only for the expansive view afforded over adjacent rooftops. Bigwell had hailed from Massachusetts, and the cupola was possibly also a vague echo of the older widow's walks of the New England coast. It was barely taller than the two chimneys on either side, their fresh tuckpointing still bright against the old brick.

Dan leaned on the newly repaired sill and gazed out, admiring the view afforded by this high vantage. If the clouds weren't so thick, he thought he might be able to see all the way to the river. From this distance, the original plan of the city was visible, the streets running like spokes away from Niagara Square, long avenues sweeping north and east, a canopy of trees swaying over what remained of once wealthy households. Only a few of the old homes still stood in the neighborhood, and from on high it was clear how many of the lots had been razed to make way for commercial structures. On this block of the avenue, only Bigwell House remained to remind everyone of the brief, past glories of the city. Modern hotels and flat-roofed cubes housing businesses and fast-food restaurants were the immediate neighbors on either side. Here in the cupola, resting against the wall and waiting to be hung, were several large photographs from the turn of the last century picturing the lavish mansions that once had dominated the street. A few of those structures still stood, but now they were the headquarters of law firms and local businesses rather than the residences of the richest citizens.

He looked down at the sidewalks that once were edged with lines of stately trees that were planted to form curving branches to arch over the street. At one time there had been a double line of elms, but when the streets were widened, those nearest the street had fallen to the ax. The remaining trees and their steadily growing, powerful roots had buckled the sidewalks into cracked humps in areas where the new gas mains had not yet been laid, demonstrating the patient triumph of nature over human effort. But nature had yielded to time as well. A line of lindens had later been planted to replace the older elms that had succumbed to an epidemic of Dutch elm disease. Dan could see

a march of trunks black with wet and topped with thick leafy green
fluttering in the stormy wind, their procession occasionally interrupted
by a fire hydrant or a driveway.

The street that fronted Bigwell House approached the terminus
of another, and Dan suddenly realized that from the southern cupola
window he could see where he and his companions had labored. From
his elevated view it took only a moment to identify what was more
familiar from the vantage of a muddy trench. On the next block in one
of the treeless spaces was Lucille's grave. It was still cordoned off with
fluttering caution tape and planked over with warped plywood. Despite
the distance and the cloaking rain, Dan could see it quite clearly across
the satellite dishes and steaming vents of an adjacent building.

As he stared out the window, a pattern began to emerge before his
eyes—the trees, the avenue, the covered trench. He leaned so close to
the glass that his breath fogged the view.

"Mom!" he called down the stairs.

But it was Jacob who was coming up, his hands full of molding
strips.

"She's unpacking a crate of paintings downstairs," he said. "I doubt
she can hear you. The conservators have a radio on."

"I just thought of something. Look." Dan pointed out the window.
"See that row of trees? They were planted along the street when this
area was developed. It was a fancy part of town where wealthy people
lived, and trees were put in on both sides. Those aren't the same trees,
obviously, because the original ones died off a long time ago. But the
new ones were planted in the same spots. And now look farther. Can
you see where Lucille was buried?"

Jacob cleared the windowpane with his sleeve. "I guess so. Oh yeah,
now I see it. I had no idea we were digging so close to here. There's no
tree there now, though."

"No. For some reason, that one didn't get another replanted in its
place. But there must have been one there for a long time, because it's
in the exact space where the first one would have been. You can tell
from the spacing between the others farther along. Which means that
the roots that held Lucille were probably from that first planted tree."

"Yeah, I guess. So?"

"So it must have been planted around the time that she was killed,
or actually a little before. Otherwise, she would have been found when

the tree was put in. Maybe her killer took advantage of the recently loosened earth. If we can find out when the original trees were planted, we can narrow down the years when Lucille was buried."

"Not a bad idea. That would certainly help Jasmine and Karen searching the newspapers. They could narrow their research to a more limited set of dates. But would there be records of trees being planted?"

"I'm not sure, but my mother might know."

"Might know what?" Priscilla Cavendish appeared in the doorway. "Oh, I'm glad you brought up those moldings, Jacob. Won't this room look nice when they are up? What a pity the original paintings were damaged when the roof leaked."

Jacob looked politely at the faded patches of scenery still visible on the walls beneath scrapes and plaster repairs. "I'm sure they were very nice," he said. "Are these by Potter as well?"

"Porter. Rufus Porter. They remain to be authenticated, of course, but I'm optimistic."

"I'm afraid I never heard of him."

"Such an interesting man," Priscilla declared. "A real nineteenth-century polymath. He was a man of boundless enthusiasms and curiosity and a scientist as well as a painter. In fact, perhaps Dan has already told you—" Dan rolled his eyes; once his mother got started, her own enthusiasms were also boundless. "—that he founded the *Scientific American*. And he was also an artist. He developed a camera obscura that could be used by amateur artists and wrote a manual of instruction for how to paint wall murals. I'm going to ask Dan to construct a model of his camera obscura to display at our opening."

Dan looked up. "What?"

"Porter painted some striking interiors that are still extant, although they are all in New England. At least, the only ones that are authenticated are there. But we have located a letter that Samuel Bigwell wrote to Porter commissioning murals for this very house. That is what is being uncovered by the conservators downstairs, and they seem to be in a remarkably good state of preservation. Usually a cover of varnish damages a painting, but in this case it protected it from the wallpaper that was put up later. It will be the centerpiece of our opening." She paused, noting Jacob's rather frozen expression. He appeared either fascinated or dumbstruck. "Would you like a tour?"

"Not now, Mom," interjected Dan. "We need to get the moldings nailed up, and it will be easier with two of us working together. But first, look out this window. Do you know when trees were planted on the street? The old ones, I mean, the ones that used to line both sides. Do you know the date?"

Priscilla paused, her eyebrows raised as if ready to dismiss the question. Then she almost palpably shifted gears and peered out the window beside her son. "Ah, you're thinking of your skeleton in her roots, aren't you? Oh my, I see what you mean. What a view. I never realized how far down the street one could see from up here."

"Yes. All the way to the next block where Lucille was found. She must have been put into soft ground pretty quickly, maybe into earth that was already loosened for digging." Dan waxed enthusiastic. "And maybe next to a young tree that was planted about the same time and that grew into her bones over the years. Because she must have been put there after the tree was planted, right? She wasn't discovered until now, and if she were already buried beforehand, she might have been found when the tree was planted. But anyhow, I think it's a good bet that the tree and Lucille went into the ground about the same time. So—do you know when the trees were planted around here?"

Priscilla smiled at her son, pleased to see his face intent with excitement and interest. "As a matter of fact, I do. Bigwell was one of the last people to build a home in this area, and the trees were beginning to go in on this part of the street just as his house was completed. He refused to have a big tree in front of his own house. He didn't want it blocking the grand entrance, so there was a small disagreement with the city forester. But he won the argument, and they skipped the area just in front of the mansion. But, of course, you can see all the others if you look down out that window. The new ones, of course, not the original plantings. But the landscape design was preserved, including the tree around your skeleton, which for some reason was not replaced when it died."

"Yes, but when was it planted?"

"The year the house was finished."

Dan ground his teeth. "And that would be?"

Priscilla sighed and gave an exaggerated grimace at Jacob. "Do you know how many times I've told Dan about this house? I would have expected him to remember at least one or two details."

Amused and curious, Jacob intervened in the family drama. "What year was it, Mrs. Cavendish?"

Priscilla looked at Dan, who took a wild guess.

"1851?"

"Right you are, dear. I knew you'd remember."

25

DISAGREEMENT

JULY 17, 1851

In the end, it took another two weeks before they could hold the next séance. Mr. Lewis went here and there consulting his spiritualist colleagues, whose numbers seemed to increase as they traveled west along the northern tips of the long, narrow Finger Lakes, each one pointing them farther across the state. Queries were made about propitious times for a meeting between Mrs. Talmadge (alive and eager) and Mr. Talmadge (deceased and stubbornly reluctant to appear). When some upright spiritualists balked at the idea that they could predict when and where messages would be received, Lewis cast his inquiries further afield and sought the advice of a few carefully selected astrologers. The consensus determined that the atmosphere for spirit invitations would be at its height on the shores of Cayuga Lake at the dark of the moon. Jane's heart sank, as the full moon that had disclosed those fevered, upsetting sights was barely waning yet.

And so there was to be more waiting, then more packing and rearranging, more bumping across roads in crowded carriages, more delayed visits with Aunt Madeleine's vague bevy of cousins whom they were supposed to see before they finally reached their final destination—a destination that seemed doomed to perpetual postponement. From time to time Jane mentioned again the possibility of heading for a town along the route of the new railroad, where speed and belching steam was both alarming and intriguing. However, suggestions that a different means of transport might be more comfortable fell on deaf ears.

By now it was obvious that Auntie was persuaded to this slow meander so that she could test the spiritual climate for the appearance of her husband. Her conviction was abetted by Mr. Lewis, who observed that water seemed to possess a significance for the romantic history of Madeleine and George, so this lake-filled area might provide a likely place for their communion. He also took the opportunity to make a few profitable side trips with Lydia, whose reputation had spread, and her remarkable receptive power was an object of hope and curiosity.

To Jane's frustration, Lydia was entirely caught up in spiritualist activities and had little time to spend alone with her. And it was only alone that Jane could confront her cousin about her mysterious night-time secrecies. Since there was no reason that Lydia would suspect that anyone else knew of her meeting with Mr. Lewis, Jane did not believe that this insulation from her company was deliberate. Nonetheless, it was a little hurtful to find that her cousin did not miss their previous intimacy as much as she herself did—the nighttime conversations when everyone else was abed, their private jokes at the expense of those they considered especially puffed up, and in pensive moments, their dreams and expectations of life.

Lydia's own dreams and expectations had taken a sharp turn. Just the previous morning Mr. Lewis brought to their breakfast table a copy of *The Sign* with a page folded back. In bold print a headline declared: *Miss Lydia Strong: A New Medium among Us.* It was followed by a glowing account of the spirits that had visited the various gatherings during the past weeks, virtually clamoring to speak through her voice, fusing their spirit with hers, proving beyond doubt that there were paths to communication with the departed. Lydia had flushed, then paled, smiled and uttered something self-deprecating. But it was clear that she was thrilled to the core with the acknowledgement of her talents. She had found her calling.

As usual, Jane mistrusted her own responses. While Lydia was not by nature either skeptical or cautious, Jane believed herself to be too much of both. She wanted to warn her cousin, scold her gullibility, guard her against impulsive actions. But she was unsure of her motives, fearing that her objection stemmed not only from worry but also from envy. Or some other unworthy emotion. She could not decide what she felt the most: uncertainty, hurt, or worry.

To make matters worse, Jane had not seen Jed Porter since leaving Rome. Despite the message she had left, he had not sought to follow her, and now she had all but given up hope of ever crossing his path again. Their travels had deviated too far from the itinerary she had de-tailed for him, so even assuming that he had received her message, the likelihood that he would locate her was slim. She kept her regret private, for their acquaintance had been too short-lived to make much of it. Also, she didn't want to invite probing questions and the inference that she had invested unwarranted hopes on an itinerant painter. After all, Jed had promised her nothing more than what he had already given: a string of lovely days of his company and the use of his drawing implements. Probably he had forgotten about her altogether.

Now they were headed for yet another diversion from the route that was supposed to take them to their new home in Rochester, a city that seemed to recede farther in the distance with each passing day. Jane's meager earnings from her paintings were nearly exhausted, and she suspected that Aunt Madeleine's supply of funds for their travels was also running low. The crooked path they were taking might satisfy her aunt's desires and provide her cousin with a newfound talent to explore, but it was becoming only a burden to her.

She had to speak up.

"Really, Liddy," she said, trying to keep the resentment out of her tone as they readied their bags for the coach, "don't you think that Auntie is extending herself too far by putting so much trust in Mr. Lewis and his acquaintance? Her confidence in his guidance extends beyond reason. I ask you again, can she possibly believe that these spiritualist groups are going to secure her a claim on Uncle George's legacy?"

"Is that what you've been worried about?" replied Lydia. "I've been wondering if your bad temper was merely the aftermath of being sick."

"My bad temper?" Jane was taken aback.

"Oh, not temper, perhaps. But you have to admit that your mood has been low."

"Well, I have, after all, been ill."

"Of course, dear. But you appear to be brooding, which is not good for you. You'll feel better soon, I'm sure." The others were outside already waiting for their coach. Lydia turned to go, but Jane put a restraining hand on her arm.

"Now, Liddy, don't you divert our conversation like that. We are not discussing my mood. I am truly worried about Auntie. Surely you don't think that there is any merit in her hopes to hear from Uncle George at these gatherings. His legal will was quite clear that his sons were to inherit. It is lawyers and the courts of law that determine these things, not ghosts. I've said before and I continue to believe that she is only prolonging her distress."

Lydia turned and faced her. "I know that you retain some skepticism about the spirits, Janie, although I was beginning to hope that it was subsiding. Indeed, we all were." Her expression was unusually stern, and Jane drew back. "But don't you see how Auntie is comforted by our sessions? Whether or not anything we learn will affect her legacy, or its lack, she is soothed by the voices she hears. Most of all, she seeks assurance that her husband did love her, in spite of his woeful neglect for her eventual welfare. That can be only to the good. Surely you agree, don't you?"

"She hears voices?"

Lydia raised her eyebrows. "She does. You have heard them too. Everyone has. They are now quite clear."

"I hear you speaking, but I'm not always sure what you are saying." There are blanks in my memory of these evenings, Jane thought.

Lydia looked pained at this. She shook her head sadly. "Dear cousin, please open your mind. It is not I who speak, but the spirits who choose to speak through me." With that statement, Lydia smiled and cast her eyes heavenward in the way that she so often did now, arousing both awe and exasperation in her cousin.

Finally, Jane gathered her courage for the final question. "Lydia, there is something else I must ask you before we leave. It has been difficult to broach, given that we seem always to be in company these days, but before we join the others, I must ask you—" The words stuck in her throat.

"Ask me what?" Lydia looked puzzled.

"Forgive me, but I must ask you what you were doing the other night. Late, outside, the night I was so ill. I saw you from the window. I am sure it was you. You met Mr. Lewis outside the hotel and gave him something. You have said nothing of it, but I cannot be kept in ignorance of what is going on any longer. Please explain yourself."

Lydia did not look affronted, as Jane had feared, but she did draw herself up slightly and pause before replying.

"I do hope you have not been spying on me, my dear, suspicious cousin."

"No indeed! Not at all. It was pure chance that I happened to be by the window. I needed to breathe some clean air after being sick. But what I saw disturbed me greatly, and I must ask you again—what were you doing?"

After a pause, Lydia smiled. "I am sorry to hear that my little errand has caused you worry. Be assured that I was merely giving Mr. Lewis a parcel that Aunt Madeleine had made up for him. He sent word that he would be delayed on his return from the house of some acquaintance, and Auntie was exhausted from looking after you in your illness and fell asleep. Therefore, upon his arrival, I went out and delivered it."

"What was in it?"

"How should I know? It was securely tied, and I did not feel it my place to nose around."

The admonition was clear, though the voice that delivered it remained mild. Jane's annoyance and concern were beginning to recede, replaced now with chagrin.

"Don't be angry with me, Liddy. I have been concerned that you might be rushing ahead into a situation that you might not entirely understand. We have known Mr. Lewis only a short time, after all."

That was not the right thing to say. The beatific look returned, mixed now with a dose of condescension. Lydia was only slightly taller than Jane, but she managed to look down her nose as from a great height.

"Never fear, Janie. I am quite at ease with my new activities. And before you inquire further, let me assure you that Mr. Lewis is a complete gentleman. I have no complaint to make against him on that score whatsoever. He has not forced himself upon me in any way, if that is indeed what you have in mind."

Jane flushed. "I'm sorry, Liddy," she stammered. "I don't mean to offend. But you have changed, you know. You have changed so much and in such a short time."

Lydia smiled and gave her a hug. "Again, please don't worry, Janie. These times are new to us both. Let us both embrace them. Now, we should make haste; the others are waiting."

Something in Lydia's demeanor indicated that she had had more than one private encounter with the gentleman in question, but before Jane could pursue the point, their aunt called them to come and board the coach. Lydia hastened away, and although she had spoken with conviction, as she turned to leave, Jane detected disquiet in her expression.

As they exited the hotel, Mr. Lewis glanced at Jane with what looked very much like a frown of disapproval. Taken aback, she wondered what he might be thinking, or even if, somehow, he had overheard their conversation.

26

STORM

CAYUGA LAKE. JULY 27, 1851

The dark of the moon fell on a night that was made even blacker by a heavy covering of cloud. There was not the faintest glimmer from a star, not a glow from a nearby window, not a lantern moving rhythmically on a swinging arm. Lapping waves from the lake at their backs could be heard but not seen. Every now and then a passing breeze stirred a heavier splash against the rocky shore.

This time the gathering was taking place outdoors on a small, disused pavilion once convenient for those enjoying the shore but abandoned years ago in favor of a structure in a sunnier location. The roof was intact but the open sides were splintery and the board floor was warped and uneven. An adjacent grove of pine trees whined in the wind, and sometimes needles brushed the roof with a rough gesture as if something begged invitation.

"The sky is ominous. Should we not begin the session before the coming storm?" Aunt Madeleine asked nervously. The air was thick with moisture and heavy with impending thunder. It was almost as though they were waiting for the clouds to break open.

"We are quite protected here," assured Mr. Lewis. "Sometimes unsettled weather invites the spirits in ways that calmer venues do not. You have been frustrated that your husband has not fully appeared, have you not, Mrs. Talmadge? Wouldn't you value more than the few words that he has whispered?"

Madeleine nodded.

"Then set your fears aside. The place, the time, the phase of the moon, and the sky itself are most promising for a visitation this evening." He grasped her shoulders and looked deep into her eyes, and she smiled up at him tremulously, submissive in his grip. "Trust me, Madeleine," he commanded. She nodded.

Lydia was electrified by the wind. Ignoring the hazards of the dark, she paced by the shore until summoned into the pavilion. Her shoes were wet, her eyes shone, her smile was febrile, her breathing shallow. She did not sit next to Jane.

They had only snatched a few words in privacy since arrival, and the conversation had not been soothing. Seeking to repair their abrasive exchange before they boarded the coach, Lydia had taken her cousin aside. "Janie," she said, "I am sorry if I sounded harsh. But I pray you, do not abandon hope. You may not be so attuned to the spirits yet, but just think—" and Lydia's voice rose and her fingers gripped the locket around her neck. "Just think of the possibility that we might hear from our mothers and see them once more! That we could call them forth around these tables. Just imagine! Each time we meet, I await my mother's voice. Some time, I am sure, she will be the one who speaks."

Jane's heart dropped like a stone. "Oh, Lydia," she had whispered and could say no more.

Again, there arose in her mind the image of her own stricken mother, transformed in death into something alien. The notion that such a wrecked shell could release a spirit and return to her daughter was appalling. Jane had found comfort at her mother's grave, its rough stone and newly planted grass confirming the finality of her loss but also bringing a kind of peace. There she could imagine, almost hear, the familiar soft voice that had guided her childhood. But her farewells had been said with her prayers, and to supplicate heaven for some ethereal visitation seemed an abomination.

But Lydia had found no such solace. Jane's sympathy went out to her, but the usual admiration for her older, more confident cousin was transformed to sadness.

In later weeks, she would recognize that moment as the first true rupture, a split sundering her from her beloved cousin. Jane's skepticism returned in full strength. And with it, renewed suspicions about their imperious guide and his tactics—including the cups of calming tea administered before the spiritualist gatherings. It actually tasted quite pleasant, flowery and sweet, so Jane often gulped hers thirstily. Its soothing properties were only to be expected from the combination of borage and valerian that was commonly dosed out for relaxation. Nothing at first had indicated it was anything but an innocent beverage. But after her hand produced that mysterious picture, she had begun to wonder if the tea might—sometimes—also contain something else. Had she herself drawn that image of Uncle George, perhaps dazed by some drug? Or had the drawing been slipped beneath her unconscious hand? She no longer even tried to countenance the possibility that some spirit had taken hold of her pencil and sketched the face.

There was one advantage to this present uncomfortable outdoor setting with its gusting wind. It permitted Jane to dispose of most of the evening's tea. "Oh, I've spilt a bit," she said, miming a mishap and eagerly refilling her cup from the urn. She pretended to take a mouthful and then moved into the shadows and spat the contents into the grass beyond the pavilion, rather proud of her execution of this deception.

To her surprise, Mrs. Sibley had turned up for this event, having sped from Utica and arrived before them at Seneca Falls. That very morning before the weather had turned ominous, she had greeted Jane warmly, took her arm, and marched her around the town pointing out her favorite landmarks. It was so pleasant to have a walk with this charming woman, so reassuring to be in the company of a person who seemed genuinely fond of her, that Jane strode alongside with delight.

"Perhaps you recollect reports of that wonderful convention that was held here just three years ago," Mrs. Sibley said, gesturing to a nearby church. "I was lucky enough to be among the congregation when those marvelous sentiments were determined. The age of the woman is here, my dear Jane! It is time for us all to recognize the rights and freedoms that we have been denied heretofore. It was a defining moment for me, for it encouraged me to speak independently, both within our spiritualist community and elsewhere. I do believe it changed my life, and at a time when I was most in need of sustenance. You must think of your own wellbeing as you grow into the future, my dear. Do not be bound by the restrictions of the past."

Jane was not entirely sure what Mrs. Sibley referred to, but she listened avidly to her glowing account of the gathering of women who had formally demanded their rights, the description of their leaders, and the splendid encouragement from that stunning orator, Mr. Douglass. And among the group, it was disclosed, were several distinguished sympathizers with the spiritualist enterprise. Jane let the words wash over her, mostly appreciating the welcome from this woman and her warm greeting. Despite her apparent, if questionable, talent at sketching the spirits, Jane was feeling more and more of an outsider, the growing hostility of Mr. Lewis almost palpable. Her mood lightened with Mrs. Sibley's words, as well as with the thought that she herself might qualify as a woman of the future, vague as that idea might be at the moment.

But now the sunshine of the day had disappeared. The sky began to grumble, and Mr. Lewis summoned them all to their seats. They hurried to take their places at the table, a heavy carved piece of furniture that had been transported for the evening from some nearby dining room, its carved, lion-clawed feet gripping rough boards rather than a carpet. There were nine of them gathered around three tall candles positioned in glass hurricane lamps. Despite their shields, the flames flickered and snapped.

"Perhaps we would have been better indoors, Alex dear," murmured Mrs. Sibley. But she took his hand at her left and Jane's on her right, making a connection between the now rival minds. Lydia and Aunt Madeleine sat across from them. Jane couldn't name the other four participants, although they had been introduced; two women of middle age, two somewhat older men who might have been husbands. One of the latter had intruded himself between Mr. Lewis and Lydia. These four did not appear nervous. Perhaps outdoor séances were a norm on the shores of Cayuga Lake.

A paper was slid before Jane and a pencil placed near her hand. Two stones were added to keep the paper from flying windily away. She nodded dreamily and permitted her lids to drop, feigning the moment that the tea would have taken effect. Her memory of previous events was dim, but since she had been so relaxed, it stood to reason that her eyes would close, her head drop slightly to one side. Alert beneath the guise, she tensed and waited to see what happened next.

Mr. Lewis had timed this session well. The thunder approached along with rising gusts. The pines began to sing, and before long Lydia's head arched back, her signature *Ohs* taken by the wind. Aunt Madeleine looked around, her eyes wide in alarm, but the others sat with their eyes closed and faint smiles on their lips.

"They come," someone intoned.

"They are here," said another.

Jane gently reached for the pencil. It did not require dissimulation to fumble, for the dancing shadows made the implement indistinct. With slow strokes, she began to smudge the paper, drawing thick marks across the bottom, turning her head from side to side as if peering at something hidden in her own mind. Beneath slightly open lids she could see candlelight flickering across the table, illuminating a finger here, glinting off a ring there. Raising her gaze higher brought a dazzle of light and shadow. The candle flames emphasized the darkness of the dark, imposed their glare without illuminating. They seemed to grow taller and to twist beneath their curls of smoke.

A moan issued from Lydia's throat. Aunt Madeleine gave a start. "George?" she whispered. "George?"

Lydia's head rolled on her shoulders. In her pale dress she might herself have been a wraith. She exhaled loudly, slowly, until it seemed there would be no breath left in her lungs. Then a hissing inhale sharp enough to make a wailing shriek.

As if on cue, a jagged lightning bolt lit the sky and a crash of thunder made the lake shiver.

And all at once he was there.

Light and luminous, the bulbous face of George Talmadge hovered at the edge of the pavilion. The image was unmistakable. Receding hairline, thick jaw, protruding moustache, all floating above wavering strings of translucent white like the trailing sinews of a severed neck. The apparition wavered unsteadily in and out of the candlelight, seeming to seek someone.

"George!"

The specter did not turn toward his wife's cry. He might not have heard her, for the interfering wind had set up a howl.

Jane's heart was pounding so hard she found it hard to breathe. All her skepticism was put to the test with this terrifying thing moving overhead. She told herself it could not be. Impossible. But there it was. She fought the urge to quail beneath the table to escape the range of his gaze.

The wind blew harder and George Talmadge turned his hollowed eyes on her.

A bolt of lightning split the night and shook the ground beneath their feet. A deluge assaulted them, and a rasping voice rose amid the dark and pounding rain.

Madeleine—

Madeleine, my love. My wife.

Truly, I have not forgotten you.

In a crash of breaking glass the candles overturned and they were engulfed in blackness and wet.

27

EVIDENCE

CAYUGA LAKE. JULY 27, 1851

The final lightning strike had been terrifyingly close, delivering an electric tingle that prompted them all to sprint to the home of one of their number as fast as sodden clothing and shrieking hysteria permitted. They were drenched and shivering, but the evening's tumult drove sleep away. Before a large fire that smoked more than burned, for the woodpile was only carelessly protected from rain during the summer, they collapsed in heaps of dampness and mud and reviewed the astonishing events in gasping bursts of revelation.

"Such evidence before our very eyes!"

"Who could doubt any longer!"

"Marvelous! Wondrous!"

"Indisputable proof that the soul lives on! And can return to the living!"

Aunt Madeleine, having been hauled back in a state of near insensibility, revived long enough to deliver an impassioned plea to the assembled company to pursue discovery of her husband's final wishes, so frustratingly truncated by the lightning that had sliced through the séance. The others were more than reassuring. They promised, they soothed, they uplifted her spirits with their generous and enthusiastic support. She collapsed in a chair and alternately wept and smiled, murmuring appreciation and relief that what she sought so fervently was at last at hand.

Lydia had been transfixed by the apparition. Mr. Lewis had yanked her away from the pavilion just moments before her outstretched hands touched the pale face of her uncle twisting crazily in the light from the second strike. Then amid pounding thunder she virtually flew back to the house, her dress diaphanous and fluttering so that she resembled a spirit herself. Once inside, she paced and laughed and breathed so rapidly that she fell into a brief faint as well. But when aroused, she only wanted to go back to the shore and return to that fragile, receptive state that invited more spirit visitation.

"I believe you have been visited enough for one evening," was Jane's tart response. She handed Lydia a cloth to dry her dripping hair. "You had better get warm before you catch a cold. We've all had enough of ghosts for now."

She adopted the brusque tone deliberately, partly to buck up her own spirits, and partly—scarily—to test the atmosphere just in case some phantom had followed them inside and wanted to prove its presence. Mrs. Sibley looked distressed and Mr. Lewis directed a terrible glare her way.

"My dear, surely you cannot deny the evidence of your own eyes," said Mrs. Sibley. "We have all had a shock, but it should be regarded as a welcome surprise, especially for your aunt. Do not scoff at her joy at seeing her husband once again."

But what did we really see? thought Jane. The flash had illuminated a spinning head, suddenly less ghostly in the blinding light. Still, pity for Aunt Madeleine led Jane to hold her tongue further. She managed to mumble an apology. But then Mr. Lewis approached her and held out still another token of spiritual visitation.

"The evidence is not just for the eyes, Jane," he said. His tone was deliberate and deep. "As we have seen once before, Lydia is not the only medium among us. You are yourself in that company, although regrettably reluctant to admit your place. But now regard what your own hand has produced!"

The paper in his hand was damp and crumpled, but it appeared to be identical to the one that had lain beneath her fingers at the start of the proceedings. The group leaned forward and gasped. Discernible through the smudges and muddy splashes were two wavering, blurry lines of script:

not forfeit my fortune only
my dear wife

"Oh," said Jane. It was a moment fraught with risk. She could feel herself at the center of intense interest, almost as though the eyes of others had attached to her skin. She was carefully silent for a time, aware of curtains of rain surrounding the house, isolating it from the rest of the world. Then she said, "I wrote this? Are you sure?"

Mr. Lewis nodded.

She thought very fast before saying, "I see. Yes. This is indeed proof."

She managed to meet Mr. Lewis' eyes and was relieved when his challenging expression lifted and he gravely nodded. Aunt Madeleine grasped the paper, read the words aloud, and fussed at the incompleteness of the statement. Mrs. Sibley declared that more would come soon, and Lydia knelt at her aunt's side uttering reassurances. Several people patted Jane's back in congratulations, and she managed to keep her expression wide-eyed and blank, as if stunned by her own facility not only to draw a spirit but to write the very words he wished to convey. Almost completing the sentences he had uttered as the thunder split the skies.

Eventually, the exhausted crew dispersed to sleep, claiming beds or wide chairs or a set of cushions on the floor in lieu of returning to their own lodgings. Jane curled on a narrow window seat wrapped in a blanket and stared out through panes of glass striped with rain. Only when she was certain that no one else was awake did she feel for the true paper that had lain beneath her hand, the one that she had shoved into her pocket when the lightning struck.

The first light of day found Jane scrabbling along the storm-washed shoreline toward the pavilion and the wreckage of the abandoned séance. The sun was barely peeking over the hill and the air was damp and cool. Her footsteps squashed into the saturated earth, but since her shoes were probably ruined already from the dash to shelter in the lashing rain, it hardly mattered. She had not slept the entire night and could not rest before returning to examine the place where George Talmadge had made his ghastly appearance.

Jane stepped around the fallen candles and broken glass from the hurricane lamps. She righted one of the overturned chairs and seated herself. The dampness of the seat was matched by the state of her skirt, which she feared might be ruined beyond cleaning. But of uppermost importance was the paper—the one she had clutched at when the lightning bolt sizzled to earth, illuminating their gathering with shocking brilliance. Nine stunned faces, writhing trees, lashing rain. And a peculiar white thing less luminous in the light than it had been when only candles flickered.

She removed the paper from her pocket and smoothed it against her knee. There were the smudges at the bottom that she had begun to make as she feigned a moment of spirit writing. And there was the mark made when her hand jerked with the thunder. But no fragments of writing appeared at all.

As she said to Mr. Lewis, here was proof. But not proof of what he had in mind. She replaced the paper carefully in her pocket and stood to examine the side of the pavilion where Uncle George had made his entrance. There was a nail protruding from the side of the roof where something might have dangled, but the structure was so derelict that it was impossible to be sure that it hadn't been there for years. She scooted a chair to the edge of the deck and stood to examine the nail.

Yes. A remnant of white thread.

She left it in place. A thread by itself could have come from anywhere, but this small piece of additional evidence fed her conviction.

Tangled in the underbrush beneath the grove of pines she followed another set of threads trailing from a filthy piece of gauze. Jane picked it up and examined it. There was no way to determine if it had made part of the apparition, but another bit of possible evidence suggesting a less than ghostly appearance gave her confidence. Unfortunately, there was nothing else suspicious around, and by itself this remnant might just be the tattered remains of a scarf or a piece of underclothing torn from a washing line by the wind.

How Mr. Lewis had contrived to have that disembodied head float into the pavilion was yet to be determined, but Jane's imagination was beginning to put together a plausible picture. That face—so familiar with its plump jowls and domed forehead. And its stiff moustache protruding over the lip. A moustache that had caused consternation and a snort of suppressed hilarity overheard when Uncle George's death mask was being made, for it had gotten stuck in the warm substance coating his face and left a few stiff hairs in the mold that required removal with a tweezers before the mask itself was cast. The final product recorded not a sleek moustache decorating a dignified face but stubbles protruding like an ill-kempt broom. Aunt Madeleine had declared it lifelike.

But how likely was it that a ghost would sport the very same set of bristles as a death mask? A moustache twisted and protruding over a plaster lip?

Heartsick for Lydia, Jane felt suspicion turn to conviction. She was now fairly certain just what her cousin must have given to Mr. Lewis in the hotel garden that night.

28

EXPULSION

CAYUGA LAKE. JULY 28, 1851

What happened next seemed to Jane to occur in a series of stark, rapid-fire flashes, reminding her of the lightning strikes of the night before. In the space of mere hours, her life was overturned with such speed that she almost felt she had been hit by one of those crashing bolts.

It had been a mistake to confront Lydia immediately upon returning from the pavilion and before getting some sleep to permit her to order her thoughts. But back at their temporary refuge, she had met her cousin coming out the door, smiling at the sunshine and blithely keen to continue the quest to call up Uncle George.

"Janie! Up already, I see. Such a grand happening last night, was it not? A storm to welcome the spirits. Magnificent! Sublime! I do believe that now I understand the meaning of that word. But how beautiful the sun looks this morning. I can hardly wait for tonight when we resume our gathering. Aunt Madeleine is in high hopes and also—"

"No, Liddy! No, you mustn't!" Jane burst out. "Stop, pray stop! And think." Lydia halted, surprised at Jane's passionate interruption. "Think of how improbable these last events have been. We have blundered into something that we didn't understand. It has all been a deception, a fraud, and I have found proof that we are being misled. We must get Aunt Madeleine out of here and be on our way to Rochester immediately."

Lydia looked astonished, and Jane rushed headlong into her discoveries: the thread on the nail, the false writing, the piece of gauze, the death mask floating into their midst, not a spirit but a conjuring trick.

But what seemed to Jane as obvious evidence of Mr. Lewis's deception failed to convince Lydia. The longer Jane went on, the more stumbling her account became as her fatigue and distress got in the way of her speech. Lydia protested that Jane had misunderstood, that she must not have seen what others had discerned so clearly. Had she seen what others did, she would have no doubts. Surely, she was wrong in her conclusions. She was not open to the possibilities that spirits might descend, and was therefore blind to truths that others could see. Lydia looked at her cousin with such disappointment and affection that it brought tears to Jane's eyes.

After a pause while she collected herself, Jane tried again. "Oh, Liddy, I am so very sorry to insist. I know that it causes you distress, but I'm sure that I am right."

And that brought a set of rejections that alternated between the severe and the cajoling, the accusatory and the reassuring.

"Jane, dear, are you still wondering about what happened that night when you were ill? You accuse me falsely now. I certainly did not hand the death mask over to Alexander. You were feverish and did not know what you saw."

"Then what—?"

"I merely gave him some items that Auntie wanted sold to help with our expenses on this journey. As I told you, my dear, suspicious cousin, she was tired and had fallen asleep, and she desired that I wait up in order to give Mr. Lewis what she promised him. Why do you doubt me?"

"I wondered why Auntie was not wearing her ruby earrings as much as she used to," said Jane, thinking of the sparkling jewels that used to bedeck Madeleine Talmadge. "But, Lydia, don't you see how this makes matters even worse?"

Lydia could not be persuaded. "Janie, perhaps you are frightened to discover that you also have the powers bestowed on a medium. It was your own hand that wrote those lines last night. Uncle George chose you for his message! You simply do not remember. Or perhaps you refuse to remember and to acknowledge what they mean. You have a gift, and you fear it."

"But I didn't draw the picture! I don't have any such gift! That was not the same paper at all!"

Her cousin just shook her head, smiling sadly.

Most stunning of all was Lydia's calm and confident declaration, delivered with some sternness: "You are misremembering even what appeared to us all last night, although I hardly see how it is possible to mistake recollection of such a recent event. It was not a disembodied head that appeared to us, my dear cousin. What can you be thinking? Impossible, and besides, that death mask is made of plaster and is rather heavy. It certainly could not float in the air in the way you describe, so that fact ought to put your suspicions to rest. But in any case, it was not just a head that appeared. It was Uncle George standing there—all of him. Head to toe. Surely you saw him yourself."

Jane's head now spun even worse than Uncle George's had in the stormy wind. She sputtered out more of her protests, tried her best to insist that they were all engaged on a fool's chase led by a man whose aims were more monetary than spiritual.

Lydia took her hands and looked deep into her eyes with such love and concern that Jane's words stuck in her throat.

"Janie, please. Calm yourself and get some sleep. You will feel better soon, and you will know that over the last few weeks we have all seen things we never would have imagined possible. It takes time to reconcile oneself to discovering a world previously not known to exist. But you yourself have seen and felt things from that world. And they are visions that others would long to see and feel. You should count yourself among the fortunate. The spirits frighten you now, but soon they will be as familiar as friends."

Defeated, Jane stumbled into the house and collapsed onto the same window seat where she had spent the night. She was so weary and confused that she could hardly think. Her muscles would not relax, she was still damp and chilled, and she fought tears of exhaustion and frustration before finally her body took over her mind and she fell into a deep and uncomfortable sleep.

The next lightning strike came from her aunt. Madeleine Talmadge strode furiously to the window seat and shook her niece's shoulder hard. Jane jerked upright, disoriented and startled.

"You! You ungrateful girl! After all I have done for you and for Lydia, to forsake us in this way when we are on the very brink of success. I simply cannot believe it. Indeed, I hardly recognize you, Jane! I cannot tolerate this rebellion, this lack of feeling, this disloyalty! Lydia has just spoken of your suspicion about last night's extraordinary vision, and while she makes light of it, I cannot. What she calls reluctance to acknowledge what we now all know to be true—well, I call it simple disloyalty. And I can bear no more!"

The words went on and on, more pouring out than Jane had heard her aunt utter in many days. For the last several weeks she had seemed to become fainter and frailer, not at all like the cheerful aunt of Troy. But now she was reinvigorated with outrage. She was again the woman who had stamped around her husband's study looking for a new will and who had thought nothing of violating the delicate atmosphere of mourning to go argue with the lawyers.

Jane struggled to her feet, but her mind remained half dumb with sleep and her feet tingled in cramps.

"But, Auntie," she began, hoping that a complete sentence would ensue. Why would her head not clear?

"Don't you 'Auntie' me!" declared Madeleine. "You have no claims on me, not any more. If it were not for Lydia, our work with Mr. Lewis and his associates would be ruined! Indeed, he has been warning me for some time that your presence at the table might be discouraging visitations from the spirits. We had all hoped that when you discovered your drawing was a medium of communication, you would come over at last and be one with us. But apparently you remain unconvinced. The spirits deigned to visit you, despite your doubts, and you still will not believe!"

"But, Auntie, Aunt Madeleine, I have discovered—discovered—that is, just this morning I have found disturbing evidence, indications—" Jane quailed beneath her aunt's glare.

"You see? Even you cannot make a case for yourself. Really, Jane, this is the limit. You simply cannot be a part of this quest any longer."

Madeleine's stony face softened when she saw tears well in her niece's eyes and spill onto her cheeks, smudged and dirty from the morning exertions. Her voice was gentler when she said, "I am sorry, Jane, I hate to part in this way, I surely do. I have loved you, I hope you know that. But I loved my husband too, and I desire more than anything to speak with him again. Please try to understand. Misfortune has visited us all. I must do what is best, and we have decided that you must go your own way from now on."

"No, Auntie, please! I do have your interest at heart as well, truly I do. But I am worried about you and what you are getting into. And now that I learn that you have started to sell your jewelry—"

"What I do is my own business!" The softer tone was replaced again with ire. "I would hope that my own nieces would not engage in tit-tle-tattle about my private choices. No, don't interrupt. I have heard enough from you. In fact, if it were up to me, you would continue to

Rochester on your own. You could take one of those rail cars that you have mentioned so often. But be that as it may, arrangements are being made for you to stay here for the time being while Lydia and I continue with Mr. Lewis. We are going north to the mountains for a short time. Perhaps we shall collect you on our return; that remains to be seen. I am sorry, but we must part." And with that final judgment, Madeleine turned and left.

Sick at heart, Jane subsided back onto the window seat. She was deeply shaken, but she could not take that summary rejection to be final. Surely she would not be left behind. No matter how upset the others might be, Jane could not believe that she would actually be expelled from their company. Lydia would never go on without her. Never. Despite their anger, they would not leave her by herself. Too shocked and fatigued to move, Jane slumped back on the bench and hoped that when she woke again, the last scene would have been only a dream.

The next flash began with the sound of heavy footsteps slowly coming near. And then that smooth, deep voice, once inviting, enticing. And now dreadful. The words were sympathetic in tone but their message was a threat.

"Jane, we are all most disappointed in you." He had to say it twice. Jane sat up, tried and failed to stand. "I see you are weary," Mr. Lewis continued, "and it grieves me to deliver this news when you are feeling so weak. Perhaps this will revive you." He handed Jane a bun still warm from the oven and a cup of tea. The homely gesture disarmed her, and Jane realized she was starving. She ate ravenously, giving no heed to the worries she had formed about taking tea from the hand of this man. This cup did not hold the same brew; surely it was safe to drink.

When she set the cup aside, slightly refreshed and more awake, Mr. Lewis seated himself beside her on the window seat. There was hardly room for both of them, and he sat so close that she could feel the heat from his thigh pressing next to hers. Jane shivered. He moved closer and rested an arm around her shoulders, engulfing her in his warmth. A gesture both protective and restraining. She tried to scoot away, but she was already against the frame of the bay and could not move farther. He was so close that she could study the weave of his jacket, note that the hem had come loose at the cuff, and that one of the handsome brass buttons of his waistcoat was hanging by a thread.

"You need to get that sewn on securely," she said, hoping to divert the conversation to a quotidian problem. "It's about to drop off."

Mr. Lewis looked down, momentarily off stride. "Yes, I suppose I should."

"I have always admired the design of those buttons," she continued. "A trio of oak leaves, isn't it? Does your sister keep your clothes mended?"

But the change of subject was not sustained. "You know, my sister, who has better things to do than sew on buttons, has become very fond of you," he said, giving her shoulder a squeeze. His hand felt too large as it cupped her small bones. Her arm felt numb. "She had great hopes that you would become a member of our little community and would join us in our search for truths regarding what lies beyond the physical world. A world that we all inhabit for such a short time. You should bear in mind, Jane, that the time before our birth and after our death is far greater than that given us in life. How many people are full of fear at the very thought of all that time! All that time that we will never know. But we have proof that existence does not end with the death of the physical self, nor is communication with loved ones halted after they pass to the other side. Spiritualist insights are on hand to assuage such worries about mortality. There is much hope and comfort in our discoveries, do you not see that?" His words sounded rehearsed, part of a speech, perhaps something he had read. Or written.

A pause. The clock on the mantel began to tick very loudly. "Only if they are true," Jane finally said. "Otherwise it is false hope, false comfort."

"And you doubt."

"I do." Jane thought about adding: I'm sorry. But she was not. The apology would have come only from trepidation.

"I regret hearing you say this," said Mr. Lewis. "Of course, I have suspected it was the case for some time now, despite the evidence of your own drawing. I would have thought the result of your own hands would convince you. But to hear this confession from your own lips convinces me that Grace was right."

It took a moment for Jane to remember Mrs. Sibley's first name.

"Moreover, my sister has worried for a while now that your presence in our midst is disruptive. It is impeding our efforts. She has tried to befriend you and to help you come into your own, to give you a sense of your own worth. Perhaps in order to offset the obvious jealousy you hold with regard to your cousin. But apparently to no avail."

Jealousy! Jane was aghast. "Preposterous!" she gasped. "I am far from jealous! Not in the least! Rather, I am concerned, worried. Most of all for Lydia!"

"I fear the charge of jealousy is not preposterous at all. And Grace concurs. Moreover, it is becoming more and more evident that your reluctance to participate with your whole heart in our sessions is preventing some of the spirits we seek from visiting. This is most especially grievous for your aunt, whose wellbeing should be the first object of your concern. Your worry should be directed to the fact that her husband has been slow to appear."

"What about last night? Didn't you think that was him at the séance? Is that not success?"

"Yes, finally. Last night he did come to us. And for all to see. For you to see as well, Jane. The time, finally, to believe and to commit yourself to our cause. It was, permit me to say, your last chance. But now I discover that you still retain doubts."

"More than doubts." Jane struggled to her feet and turned to face Mr. Lewis. The edge of her skirt was trapped beneath his leg. She was momentarily tethered to him and still far too close for comfort. "More than doubts, Mr. Lewis. I have proof that the lines supposedly written by my uncle did not come from my hand. *This*—" she withdrew the paper from her pocket "—*this* is the paper that lay beneath my hand. Not the one you showed everyone. This one, which I put in my pocket before we all fled for shelter. And as you can see, no writing appears."

Mr. Lewis did not even look at the paper. Although he was still seated, they were almost eye to eye, and he stared into Jane's eyes like a mesmerist. "I have little doubt that you believe what you are saying, my dear Jane. But I testify to you that I removed the paper I displayed last night from under your fingers when the lightning struck us. Doubtless you were too surprised to notice."

"I would have noticed had you done that. I was watching carefully. You were not next to me, and you did no such thing. Therefore, I conclude, you must have written those lines yourself."

There, it was out.

"So you say," he replied. "I say different. And which of us shall be believed?"

He stood abruptly. Her skirt released so suddenly, Jane nearly toppled backward.

"And now we have had enough of this interference!" he said. His voice was quiet but steely. "You will leave this company today and make your own way onward."

"Mr. Lewis, you may be able to command the actions of others," said Jane, taking a shaky breath, "but I shall make my own decisions. As will my cousin, I am sure. She will not be pleased to hear that I've been expelled from your group. Where I go, so she will go. And then you will lose your medium."

But Mr. Lewis did not look perturbed. In fact, as she turned to leave, she saw that he was beginning to smile.

29

Rufus Porter Revived

Dan crouched over a table and flexed his fingers. His hands were callused and sore. The cuticles were cracked, and his nails seemed permanently inscribed with mud. A pain in his wrist suggested he had pulled a small muscle that didn't want to be called into service for a while. But at last, the gas mains were finished, his summer job was complete, and his debt to his uncle was paid in full. A good portion of the large student loan still loomed, but it could be addressed over time and didn't require the same delicate concealment.

All that remained now was to figure out what he would do next—tomorrow, next week, and the rest of his life. Helping his mother prepare for the opening of Bigwell House was as good as anything to occupy his time for now, but that time was already hanging heavy. The languid heat of late August hung in the air, the university term had already begun, and at the back of his mind was a worry that soon he would lack the purpose that digging had unexpectedly brought into his life. The search for Lucille's identity was still underway, but so far nothing definitive had turned up. Her skeleton remained at the university lab; additional samples were still out at the forensics facilities but so far had not yielded any more precise information. And the spot where he had discovered her was now cemented over with a new sidewalk. A dog had trotted over it before the freshly poured concrete was dry, leaving sprightly paw prints over the woeful site beneath.

Dan sighed and turned his attention to the project at hand, yet one more assignment from his mother. He couldn't resent her request under the circumstances, since there was nothing more urgent calling for his time. The instructions for building a camera obscura of the sort that Rufus Porter had considered suitable for household use sounded simple enough. Construct a box, cut some holes, insert a lens, mount two mirrors. But as always, the devil was in the details, and details were scant.

The outcome of his labors was slated for a place of honor at the opening exhibit, a plan of his mother's that, to his mind, indicated how little else of Porter's there was to display if the wall murals were to prove impossible to authenticate. The vitrines would hold some letters by the hand of Samuel Bigwell, ledgers from his company with invoices and columns of figures in faded ink, and a few pages from his personal journal. More decoratively, a few paintings by obscure nineteenth-century artists were soon to be hung, most borrowed from the storage rooms of compliant collections. The walls already displayed maps of the inner harbor and the terminus of the Erie Canal, as well as photographs of mansions and dignitaries from Buffalo in its glory days. The latter were all dead and few of the former remained standing. The stately hulk of Bigwell House loomed on the street by itself, its companion mansions long demolished.

Three long display cases had been positioned at the edges of what once had been a living room to permit circulation of the guests at the opening gala. His mother was already concocting elaborate plans for the event. Observing standard museum practice, red wine would not be served. Too hard to remove stains when splashed about; white only. Especially in the dining room, where the colorful murals—optimistically Porter's—had been uncovered and cleaned. The images on three of the walls and part of the ceiling were in good shape. Priscilla had made noises about touching up places overhead where the painted sky had fallen away, but the conservators had insisted that no one of sufficient expertise was available on short notice. Dan was glad to hear that, as he could just picture himself on a teetering ladder playing Michelangelo with his mother issuing instructions from below.

That indignant thought, he recognized, was unfair. Priscilla Cavendish was a stickler for proper treatment of objects under her care and would never enlist an amateur on a restoration project. The camera obscura was at least a doable design made from scratch, a replica, not a restoration.

He consulted Porter's book again:

A Select Collection of Valuable and Curious Arts, and Interesting Experiments, which are well explained, and warranted genuine, and may be performed easily, safely, and at little expense.

Porter was the quintessential Yankee: all do-it-yourself practicality.

He told you how to gild, how to make ink (including invisible ink), to restore old handwriting, to wash and polish metal surfaces, to make elastic varnish for umbrellas or hat cases, to render a likeness, to make gunpowder and skyrockets, to light a candle with ice, to make a galvanic pile or battery. And to do what Dan was presently endeavoring himself: to make a copying machine. The printed instructions promised TO PRO-DUCE THE EXACT LIKENESS OF ANY OBJECT, INSTANTLY ON PAPER.

> A very convenient camera obscura, for drawing landscapes, or even portraits may be constructed as follows: Make a box of boards, in the form of a regular cube, being one foot in length, breadth and height; bore a hole of one inch diameter, through the centre of the top; and on this, fix a double convex lens, the focus of which must reach the bottom of the box.

Constructing the box had looked easy, though in his first version, the lens had required a boost atop a roll of duct tape in order that its focus reach the bottom of the box, and he had taken a shortcut by using an orange crate for the basic structure. Once it was sanded and painted, he had figured it would look decent enough. However, his mother had observed that his project was intended for a museum exhibit, not a science class project. He had started over with better wood and a dial to adjust the height of the lens.

Her comment smarted, largely because it again reminded him that he had no particular work lined up for the months to come. Now that his job on the gas mains was finished, the next year loomed emptily ahead, and the return of his new friends to their studies presented an uncomfortable contrast. Karen had been absent for a time to visit her parents in Virginia, and he had only heard from her twice. In his gloomier moods, he wondered if she intended to shift her affections to someone with a more academic future.

"I need a break," she had said ambiguously upon leaving.

"From me?" Dan hoped his question had sounded light.

"Of course not, silly." A smile and a peck on the cheek before she entered the airport dragging a large suitcase behind her.

He concentrated on the work of the moment, hoping that somewhere in the recesses of his brain a plan for the future would hatch.

The stubborn difficulty of the project at hand was the positioning of the mirrors around the lens, as well as attaching a dial to raise and lower its position.

On the top of the box on the right and left sides of the lens, fix two pieces of boards, which may be about four inches high, eight inches long, and three inches distant from each other. Between these boards, fix a piece of looking glass, three inches square, and facing from you; the lower edge of the glass, being near the lens, on the side towards you; and the upper edge inclining towards you about thirty degrees from a perpendicular. Directly over and nearly four inches above the lens, place another mirror, the centre of which must face directly towards the lower edge of the first.

How blithe that simple word "fix." But fix how? Standard clamps were not designed either for the angles or the materials he was using. Mirrors were not easy to glue to wood, especially when they needed to retain an adjustable tilt. Predictably, he had dropped one and watched seven years bad luck emanate wickedly from the shattered shards.

After that breakage, he had purchased two make-up mirrors on small pivoting posts. Now he took pliers and carefully bent one of the posts and then attached it to an adjustment dial repurposed from a dimming switch. He coated the edges of the boards—carefully mitered this time—with another application of glue and willed himself patient while it set. He had to hold it in place for a tedious period and entertained himself by reading Porter's instructions for landscape painting on the walls of rooms.

Dissolve half a pound of glue in a gallon of water and with this sizing mix whatever colours may be required for the work. Strike a line round the room, nearly breast high; this is called the horizon line: paint the walls from the top to within six inches of the horizon line, with sky blue (composed of refined whiting and indigo, or slip blue,) and at the same time paint the space from the horizon line to the blue, with horizon red (whiting, coloured a little with orange lead and yellow ochre,) and while the two colours are wet, incorporate them partially, with a brush.

Such straightforward instructions. Draw a line, call it the horizon. Forget vanishing points, forget perspective, forget chiaroscuro. Just paint like a child with a coloring book.

Rising clouds may be represented by striking the horizon red color upon the blue, before it is dry, with a large brush. Change some sky blue about two shades with slip blue and paint your design for rivers, lakes, or the ocean.

Despite the simplicity of the instructions, there was a strict method that informed them. Porter specified in inches the height of land that would appear within the first mile of the pictured distance, and then in decreasing dimensions the heights of islands and hills that would march into the distance four, six, eight miles apart. Ten inches, six, one. How to hold the brush, how to muddle the paints together to make more colors.

> The colours also for distant objects, houses, ships, etc., must be varied, being mixed with more or less sky blue, according to the distance of the object. By these means the view will apparently recede from the eye, and will have a very striking effect.

You had to admire the inventions that Porter had adapted for the amateur artist, the itinerant painter, the housewife longing to decorate a room, the school child with a project.

At the same time, the usefulness of the instructions presented a large problem for Priscilla Cavendish and her ambitions for Bigwell House. Their very simplicity compromised the attribution of the murals here to Porter himself. As more than one member of her advisory board had pointed out, the fact that the manual had been published and widely distributed meant that just about anyone could have followed the directions to decorate these walls. Priscilla had gestured to the draft of Bigwell's letter requesting Porter's artistic services, but in the absence of a reply on record, no one could be sure that he himself had done the painting. At the moment, she had to be satisfied with a "perhaps by" or "in the style of" description. Ever hopeful, she was preparing alternate explanatory texts: By Porter, School of Porter, After Porter.

The outer door opened with a heavy click of the latch, and Dan heard footsteps and Karen's voice. So she was finally back. He wondered why she hadn't called right away on returning. Maybe she had; he'd left his phone at home. She entered the dining room and greeted his mother. The two of them tilted their heads and admired the ceiling. A faint tinkling noise indicated that the central chandelier was being hung. Priscilla had chosen a broad medallion to hide the fact that a good deal of the painting around the original fixture had fallen away.

Dan's fingers were stiff from holding the boards in place, and he realized that at least one of them was glued to the side of the device. Carefully he freed it, noticing with odd pleasure that a distinct fingerprint remained on the top. He could buff it away with fine grained sandpaper before painting it. Or he just might leave it there as a tease for future generations to wonder whose mark it was. A mystery for someone to solve long after he was gone, should anyone be curious enough. He found that he was pleased to have brought a whiff of Rufus Porter into the museum, even if the wall paintings weren't by the artist's own hand.

One more tilt of the mirror, an estimate at thirty degrees, and a final squirt of epoxy for extra security. The thing had to hang together long enough to permit interested guests to try it out. Hopefully, the light in the museum would be too poor to entice many would-be artists to attempt actually to draw. Porter declared that candlelight would be sufficient, but Dan had his doubts.

> The rays of light, passing from objects in front, will be reflected from the first mirror to the second, and from the second, through the lens to the paper, where you will have a perfect similitude of the objects in view, in full colours, and true perspective, and may trace them on the paper, with a pencil or pen.

He looked up and saw that Karen now sat on the other side of the room scrolling through her phone messages. His earlier worry returned. I wonder how long she'll want to see me after she's back in class, he thought; maybe I was just a summer diversion. She hadn't rushed to his side when she entered, had not even spoken; rather she had greeted his mother and toured the dining room, admiring the freshness of the newly revealed scenes.

"Karen, come here a minute."

Karen put away her phone and approached. She had been watching from across the room, trying to judge from the play of expressions across his face what he might be thinking. He had looked both occupied and rather sullen, almost broadcasting a Do Not Disturb thought-balloon over his head. I thought I'd surprise him, but I guess I should have called first, she thought. Absence is supposed to make the heart grow fonder, but there is also the problem of out of sight, out of mind. Maybe he won't be glad to see me. Maybe I stayed away too long.

"Finished?"

"Almost. Sit down there. No, a little to the left. I need the light from the window to fall on this mirror here."

She positioned a straight-backed chair in front of him. "How's this?"

"I'm not sure. You're not in focus yet. I need to adjust the dial, but it keeps falling off." Frowning, Dan fiddled with the height of the lens. It took a while.

"You've been very quiet this morning." Karen's voice was tentative.

"Busy," he said. Then after a pause. "So, how was your trip?"

"Fine. It was good to see my family. Especially my sister, who just had a baby."

"Very nice."

"Is anything wrong?" He glanced up and saw that she was looking at him doubtfully.

Dan smiled, a little perplexed. What might she think was wrong? She was the one who had taken off for three weeks. He was the one in a position to worry. "No, just lost in thought." And then when she seemed to expect more, he added, "Lucille has been on my mind. In fact, I can't get her out."

"I dreamed about her last night," said Karen. In fact, she had not, but she was beginning to worry that Dan might be losing interest in her. How weird that a dead woman is my strongest link with this man, she thought. She wondered if his attachment to her would loosen soon, and if their relationship was only based on the work they did together.

"I've been thinking that she might have come here on one of Mr. Bigwell's canal boats," she ventured. "Or maybe not his, but on some boat or other."

"Why would you think that?"

"Because Jasmine and I found no notice of her disappearance in any of the papers that we've read. And believe me, we've combed through everything published in and around 1851, the date that she must have been buried, given the evidence of the tree roots. If she lived in Buffalo, wouldn't you think that her family would have reported her missing? Or that some kind of notice would have been in the papers? But if she had just arrived, maybe no one knew she was here and so she wasn't missed."

Dan sat back. "You know, that would make sense, wouldn't it? A newcomer. Of course, she might have traveled here some other way, not necessarily a canal boat. And it wouldn't be very common for a young woman to travel by herself back then. At least, I don't think so. The docks were pretty rough places. But I wonder if there are any records of passengers for that year."

"Maybe your mother would know?" Karen made to get up.

"Maybe," said Dan, "but stay there for a minute. I want to see if this gadget works."

Dan peered through the aperture at the top edge of the camera obscura and worked at the dial that raised and lowered the lens. "Too much light is slanting through the lens," he muttered. "I guess I need that black hood thing after all." It was comically startling to see him fling a dark covering over his head. By the time he focused the lens, he saw a miniature Karen laughing at him from the floor of the box. Beneath the hood, he lingered over her smile.

"Perfect!" he said, somewhat muffled.

He had no drawing implements to attempt sketching the reflected image, but he had a feeling it was easier said than done. The camera was supposed to be an aid for amateurs, but how useful was it really? Maybe he would practice with a picture of Karen. But later. He backed out from under the heavy cloth, his hair tousled. He looks like he just got out of bed, thought Karen fondly. I wish he had. I wish we had.

"Have you ever taken a trip on the Erie Canal?"

"No, I haven't," said Karen. "I didn't know that the canal was still functioning."

"Some of it is," said Dan. "Up in Lockport there are the deep locks that raised and lowered canal boats the distance of the Niagara escarpment so that water flowing at the level of Lake Ontario could join Lake Erie, and vice versa. I think there are five of them. They are quite a feat of engineering. Maybe we could take one of their excursions before it gets cold. If you want to, that is. And if you're not too busy with classes and all."

"That would be fabulous!" I hope that didn't sound desperately enthusiastic, thought Karen.

"Good. Let's plan on it," said Dan. He kept his voice casual but felt his mood lift.

30

EXPELLED

It probably wasn't a Sunday, because the church was nearly deserted. Only a few people came and went, women with brooms and cloths, a man inspecting window frames and making notes. They glanced with mild curiosity at Jane but did not approach her. Perhaps it was not uncommon for strangers to sit alone in a pew quietly contemplating their problems, their futures, their pasts. Life.

Her two travel bags lay at her feet, and she hoped that her paints and brushes had been placed into one of them by whoever had packed them before she was ejected from their lodgings and set down in the middle of town. She figured that only a day and a night had passed since the thunderous séance on the shore, but so much had happened that it was hard to grasp how it had all occurred in such a short time. Her fatigue seemed to have extended forever.

The actual break had occurred undramatically. It was still hard to believe that it had happened at all.

She had awakened alone in one of the upper rooms of the house that had sheltered them all during the storm. She had no recollection of having climbed the stairs, but a memory of a floating sensation and low voices led her to think she may have been carried. Her luggage had been retrieved from the hotel and sat packed by the door.

"Mrs. Wentworth will meet you on Oak Street before evening and take you to her home for the night," said the woman in the kitchen who offered her bread and milk and a round yellow peach. Jane never did learn her name. She thought she might be the housekeeper, although her manner was hardly subservient. The peach was firm and sweet and seemed the most real thing in the world.

"Who is Mrs. Wentworth?"

This question brought a frown. "How could you not know? You spent last night seated across from her."

Jane recalled a tall, bony woman with a sharp nose and a chin that receded into the old-fashioned ruff around her neck. The idea of being sent to the home of this woman was not appealing.

"I'm sorry, I must not have caught her name when we were introduced. I'm having a bit of trouble remembering things." The woman was silent but offered her another slice of bread. "Where is Lydia? Where is my aunt?"

"They have already left, I'm afraid. You were sleeping too deeply to wake."

"Was I? Did anyone try to wake me?"

No answer to that. "I am so sorry that you are unable to join the group tonight." The woman sounded sincere but not terribly upset. "It is a pity, for your skills would have been a boon to us. Here now, finish your food. You must hurry. Matthew will take you into town, but he has an appointment to keep before we leave for this evening's session." The woman betrayed no awareness of the fact that Jane's absence from the next séance was involuntary. Jane did not know if this was ignorance, innocence, or guile.

"Where is Lydia?" she asked again. It was all that mattered now. After the third query, and just as Matthew was calling impatiently from the yard, a letter was pressed into her hand.

Now sitting in this sunny church, its wooden pew hard against her back and its open windows admitting a warm breeze, Jane opened it again and read.

Dearest Janie,

I am so excited at the prospect of our next meeting, which will be held at a place that, in a sense, backtracks from our travels westward. The place is beautiful, by all accounts, and many spirits have visited there. Aunt Madeleine is optimistic that finally her quest will be satisfied.

But what a pity that you are so tired and perhaps even a little ill and cannot come along. Even if you did not participate in the séance tonight, (for I hear you have been barred. Never fear! I shall do my utmost to reinstate your presence) you could have enjoyed the trip. I hate to leave you, but the opportunity tempts, and I am assured that Mrs. Sibley will take good care of you and find you comfortable lodgings until you are well again, and I look forward to returning and telling you all that has transpired.

Janie, dear, if only you had permitted the light of our discoveries to shine into your heart, you would be with us now.

But all is not lost, this is but a temporary parting, and when we meet again I hope to tell you of news that will, finally, chase away your doubts.

Until very soon, dear cousin,

Your loving,

Lydia

P.S. I am not supposed to breathe a word of this, but oh, Jane, I cannot wait to give you the news. I am transported! I am sure now that the rest of my life will be spent at the side of the man for whom I am destined. Be happy for me, Janie, for I fear that Auntie will disapprove. But no more for now. They are calling me to board the coach. Till later, dear cousin! Rise refreshed from your weary state so that we can rejoice together soon.

It was Lydia's distinctive handwriting, the Os round and slightly open at the top, the Ss skating under the previous letter. That familiar hand that her teachers had criticized for failing to match the copperplate exemplar.

And it was Lydia's voice: warm, enthusiastic, forward looking.

But Lydia would never just abandon her cousin to the offices of some woman hardly known to them. She would only have written this note if she believed that she would soon be back—sooner than the need for Jane be taken to this Mrs. Wentworth's distant home. The gaps of understanding in the letter suggested that she had been whisked away with the promise of a quick return.

What is more, Lydia seemed to believe that Mrs. Sibley would be there to care for Jane should she truly be ill and not just exhausted. But that enigmatic lady was nowhere to be found, and Jane was being sent into the hands of some woman she hardly knew. An unfriendly face from that tumultuous last gathering. The prospect scared her to the bone, but she could not figure out what else she could do. She was alone, in strange territory, and her funds were nearly spent. The lack of options was paralyzing, and she dreaded turning herself over to Mrs. Wentworth, whoever she was.

And then there was the postscript, perhaps most worrisome of all. To whom could Lydia be referring but the seductive and dangerous Mr. Lewis? *Alexander.* The expert liar, the humbug, possibly by now also the seducer. Jane bitterly recollected her humorous suggestion that Lydia might attract a rich husband to offset their financial worries. Attract she had done, but this devious man was hardly the answer to their prayers.

Jane wondered how long she had sat in this church. She looked around and recognized that this was the very church that Mrs. Sibley had pointed out on their brief walking tour of Seneca Falls. The place she had attended three years before on the momentous occasion when women had declared their place in the world. "You will be a woman of the future," she had said, squeezing Jane's hand. "Do not settle for anything less." Mrs. Sibley had even paused in their stroll and taken Jane by the shoulders, saying, "You are dear to me, Jane. You must be strong. You will be strong. Even if you feel alone in the world, remind yourself that a woman by herself is as strong as she desires to be."

At the time, this sober declaration had seemed so out of keeping with the sunny day and their otherwise light conversation, that Jane had merely nodded, somewhat taken aback. On reflection, alone and scared and awaiting a stranger who might wish her ill, the declaration seemed more like prescient instructions. So how strong do I need to be? thought Jane. It was easy to desire to be strong, harder to figure out how to translate desire into action.

And where was Mrs. Sibley now when she needed her guidance? Was she with her brother and with Lydia? Could she possibly be part of some plan to separate the cousins? Or was she also the victim of her brother's deception?

Woman of the future Jane might be, but the immediate prospects for that future were hardly promising. Here she was alone in a strange town with no friend in sight and the feeble promise that this Mrs. Wentworth would collect her this evening. The barely recalled beaky face was becoming truly alarming in her memory.

Jane's energy was returning, and with it a degree of focus. She berated herself for drinking yet another cup of tea from the hand of her enemy. No wonder she had not woken when the others had left. Lydia probably believed she was still weak from her illness and from lack of sleep and therefore required rest. But now her sodden mind, as well as that terrible sickness that had visited her before, began to seem ominously as though they might have been another result from the hand of Mr. Lewis.

She was in a church, and what does one do in such a place but relinquish one's will to God's. She bent her head and uttered an incoherent prayer to heaven to deliver her from this terrible aloneness. *Heavenly Father, rescue me from this wilderness. Restore me to Lydia. Do not leave me bereft and alone.* It seemed a bit flowery to call the orderly town of Seneca Falls a wilderness, but the word seemed apt for a prayer.

Forming her fear in words only made it worse, and from worried and anxious she could feel panic beginning to arise.

That would not do. Panic is a useless emotion.

Think, Jane! Think! Use your brain.

But it was her brain that had gotten her into this fix. If she had not been so skeptically minded, if she had not sought to prove that they were being finagled, then she might now be with her cousin and aunt, joined with them in happy obliviousness. (When ignorance is bliss, 'tis folly to be wise, she remembered. Although never before had she thought that homily might be actually true.) *Think!*

Churches, she had read, were places of sanctuary. Or at least they used to be, and in the pages of certain novels they still were. Perhaps she could simply stay here in this building and refuse to leave. Or could at least wait until some good stranger took pity on her and offered assistance. Maybe she could paint another portrait and earn enough money to rent a room someplace. The idea of returning to her paints was cheering. That was something under her control: the image on a paper, the line of a pencil, the stroke of color from her brush.

On legs that now shook only a little, Jane got up and walked to the aisle. Two women on stools polishing a window looked down.

"Are you all right, dear? You were sitting so still we did not want to disturb you."

"I'm not sure," said Jane. And now that she was on her feet an urgent need was apparent. "Is there perhaps a convenience in this building?"

"Not in this building itself, no, but just outside to the left there is a very nice little privy. You will find that it is well-tended, and it is also well-screened from the street."

And so it was. A visit to the privy, a turn around the churchyard in the warm sunlight, and that brief snippet of sane conversation with the cleaners began to restore a sense of normalcy. Jane told herself that she was letting her imagination run wild. Mrs. Wentworth was not a witch. She probably didn't want Jane to stay long and maybe could even become an ally to persuade her aunt and cousin to take her back into their fold.

"Don't forget your bags, dear," called a voice. "We are leaving now, and soon there will be people arriving for an evening prayer group. You should not leave your things behind."

With the departure of the friendly cleaners, Jane's anxiety came flooding back. She took the two bags from their hands with thanks and smiles, but then she could think of no place to go from there.

Well, it would do no good just to sit on the church steps. She might as well find the street where Mrs. Wentworth was to collect her. "In the evening" was not a specific time, and with the long summer days, it could be hours before she arrived. If she arrived. There were only a few coins left in Jane's purse, and she hoped there were enough for a room if need be.

Weighted by her bags, she began to make her way in the direction of Oak Street, where supposedly the rendezvous with Mrs. Wentworth was arranged. She figured it had to be across the street from the church and farther along, as behind her there was only a narrow canal that ran between two nearby lakes.

An unexpectedly short walk took her to Oak Street. And there Jane beheld a miracle. She was so stunned she dropped her bags and rubbed her eyes in disbelief. God, or luck, or fate had answered her prayer.

On the next corner, amid a small group of onlookers, she saw a man bent over an apparatus on stilts, his head and shoulders covered by a long black cloth.

31

SAVED

Jane walked very slowly toward the corner. The man's face was obscured, but surely it was Jed Porter. It must be he. There simply could not be another itinerant painter with a camera obscura mounted on a tripod traveling through the area. Those long legs and scuffed boots must be his. And the horse tethered nearby most certainly was Horace, his scruffy tail switching away the flies, his rhythmic jaw crunching a leisurely meal of oats in the feed bag. She felt such a wash of relief to find a friend in this strange town that her legs nearly collapsed.

While the onlookers waited for the picture to emerge from the dark, Jane hovered on their edges collecting her thoughts and trying to subdue the emotions that rushed into her with such strength she felt almost sick. She had not seen Jed for some time, although exactly how much time was foggy. It was entirely possible that he had almost forgotten her. It was surely too much to expect that he would be as delighted to see her as she was to see him. For certain, he would not share her desperate need of the solace and company of a trustworthy person.

With such thoughts she tried to prepare herself for the likelihood that he would not be enthusiastic to see her again. But she could not suppress the hope that this barely known young man might furnish a path away from the worrying confusion of the last few days, might even provide an escape from the band of spiritualists who had caught her cousin in thrall. Her heart began to pound so hard it caught at her breath.

At last the head emerged from beneath the cloth.

And it was Jed. His hair was longer and his skin had darkened from the summer sun. He held out a drawing to a man in the crowd, who smiled and shook his hand and showed it around to the assembled company. As Jane moved forward, she saw that it was not a portrait this time but a finely rendered scene of the shops along the road, the receding lines of the street foregrounding a milliner's window, apparently situating this man's place of business at the center of commerce. There was acclamation at the realistic rendering. "I would know that street anywhere," said one. "What a miracle," said another. "One can almost see what lies behind. And how vivid are the hills and the light that shines on the grass."

Money was pressed into his hand, the company gradually dispersed, and Jed began to fold up his equipment. His eyes fell upon Jane, and there was suddenly a suspension of time, a gap in experience, as happens sometimes when two people are simultaneously stunned by what they behold. The clock stops while they gather their wits and prepare to resume awareness of the rest of the world.

"Jane," said Jed. Then again, "Jane?" Another gap, for her voice stuck in her throat.

Jane moved toward him, unable to speak, but now because joy and relief came near to strangling her.

"Why are you crying?" Jed seemed to be holding back any pleasure at seeing her again.

"I'm not."

"But you are."

And she was, which was not only confusing but more than a little mortifying and not at all the way she would have liked to present herself. Jane dropped her bags at her feet and rubbed her face with her hands. Her cheeks were wet and her nose was running, and it needed no mirror to tell her how terrible she must appear.

"I'm sorry. I know I must seem a fright. But I never thought I would see you again."

"No wonder," said Jed, "since you left town without a word. What did you think would happen?" His voice was raw. "I looked for you for days, but you were gone. What was I to think?"

And then it all came out. Jane's astonishment that he should think she would leave with no word; his puzzlement and indignation that she had disappeared with no warning; the absence of any message to be found for him at their Rome lodgings. That set them both aback—Jed realizing that his hurt and anger at her disappearance was unwarranted, her wondering if the hostile manipulation of Mr. Lewis had begun earlier than she had thought. Amid their mutual exclamations, the thorough misunderstanding that her departure had caused became clear; and Jane became even more convinced that she had been on the edge of danger, and that Lydia was venturing even deeper into trouble. But attempting to explain that all at once was too much.

"I'm sorry, Jed," she said. Her breath still came in sobbing gasps. "I'm beginning to babble. It's so hard to make sense of everything that has happened to me."

Jed dredged up an almost-clean handkerchief from one of his pockets, and Jane blew her nose and mopped her face. She was beyond vanity and merely wanted to feel sane again. While she collected herself, Jed tactfully moved over to his horse and hitched the harness back to the wagon. Horace ambled up to Jane and snuffled a greeting, and she wrapped her arms around his neck. His smooth coat was warm from the sun and he tolerated a hug, possibly surprised at her enthusiasm but, being full of oats, quite content to be petted.

"You seem even more pleased to see Horace than me," said Jed, but his tone was amused. Jane laughed, inhaling a strand of mane that made her cough. And then, just as they both were smiling, the lengthening rays of afternoon cast a long shadow drawing near.

"Miss Woodfield. What, may I ask, are you doing?"

The voice came from behind her. Jane froze, and all the relief she had felt for the last quarter hour flooded away. She stepped back from the horse and straightened her spine, giving her nose one more swipe with the handkerchief before turning around.

"Hello, Mrs. Wentworth," she said. The black eyes in the beaked face flickered between her and Jed. How like a crow she looks, thought Jane, her fear rising.

"I ask again, what do you think you are doing? And who is this person?"

Jed stood silent behind her. Jane wished she could see his face to gauge her next words, but she did not turn around to look. This is my choice, she told herself. No matter what.

"I have met an old friend in Seneca Falls," she said, proud that her voice sounded calm. "Mrs. Wentworth, may I introduce Mr. Porter."

Then she did glance back and saw that Jed was making a slight, gentlemanly bow. His mobile face bore a look of curiosity, but he only said, "Very pleased to meet you, madame."

Mrs. Wentworth gave the briefest of nods in acknowledgement. Jed resumed his silence behind Jane, but she could feel that he took a step nearer to her. Horace twitched his tail and stepped forward too. They formed a close triangle, and Jane felt their warmth at her back. The three of them waited, two of them curious, one also anxious, and one ready for more oats and a nap.

"It is time we were off," Mrs. Wentworth finally said. "Are these your bags? Pick them up and come along now."

"No," said Jane.

A thud of amazement as the sharp face looked at her in disbelief. Mrs. Wentworth was not used to back talk.

"No, I think not," Jane repeated. "I thank you for your offer of hospitality, Mrs. Wentworth. It is kind of you. But I have decided to stay here."

"Impossible," said Mrs. Wentworth. "It is not up to you. I am to have you for this night and the next at least. Mr. Lewis was quite clear about this." She stepped forward as if ready to grasp Jane's arm and drag her away.

"Not at all impossible, I'm afraid," Jane said, registering that the time she was to be gone from her aunt and Lydia now extended beyond what she had earlier been told. She heard in these words the shadow of a plan for her that she did not like at all. It made it all the easier to insist: "I shall not go with you."

Jed finally broke his pose and stepped forward, his movement a mirror of Mrs. Wentworth's.

"Perhaps you already know of Miss Woodfield's skill as an artist," he said, little knowing what a reference to Jane's drawing talent would mean to this forbidding woman. "She and I have collaborated on projects before, and I am pleased to tell you that I am offering her an opportunity to assist me on a large mural that was commissioned for a newly built residence. It is for the house of one of the businessmen who operate at the terminus of the Erie Canal, a wealthy grain broker and a patron of the arts. So it is quite the mansion. It will demand much of our time and our energies to complete to his satisfaction."

Mrs. Wentworth was confounded. Jed might look like a ploughboy with his heavy boots and rolled-up sleeves, but he was well-spoken. Moreover, he addressed her in a respectful but subtly authoritative manner. She could not detect that he had invented his invitation on the spot. She looked suspiciously at Jane, who hastily schooled her expression to fit Jed's astonishing declaration.

"As you can see, therefore," Jane said, "I no longer have need of your kind offer of a bed for the night." Or however more had been intended by the scheming Mr. Lewis.

"Impossible," Mrs. Wentworth repeated. "Impossible and entirely improper."

"Far from it," Jane persisted. "Not impossible at all. Because women of the future need not be bound by the strictures of the past. My plans are quite in keeping with the ideas of Mrs. Sibley." Mention of that woman's name caused Mrs. Wentworth to pause, unsure now if her earlier instructions had been superseded.

Inspired, Jane continued. "In fact, Mrs. Wentworth, if you would be so kind, would you please deliver a note to Mrs. Sibley when next you see her, as well as another to my cousin Lydia."

Jed's actions swiftly coordinated with hers. He reached into his bag and handed her a sheet of drawing paper. She tore it neatly in half and with one of his fine pencils quickly scribbled two notes.

Dear Mrs. Sibley,
I thank you once more for your guidance and your wise words. They will sustain me in my own journey into the future, where the new woman I aim to be will hopefully flourish. From you I have learned that unless one dares to risk, one will never know what possibilities may lie ahead. I am very grateful.
Perhaps one day we shall meet again. I hope so.
Yours very sincerely,

Jane Woodfield

Then something occurred to her, and she hastily added a postscript:
P.S. *I have also written to Lydia, who will explain more.*
The second note was harder to write.

Dearest Lydia,
It breaks my heart to leave like this without speaking to you, but it is now clear that your path diverges from mine. I have met Jed Porter again in Seneca Falls and have joined him to assist in a project for a large mural. How I look forward to painting again!

We will continue westward. Please write to me care of Aunt Madeleine's cousin in Rochester, where eventually I shall stop, perhaps to stay, but at least to collect my trunk.

Until we see one another again, dear cousin, stay well and be happy, and tell Auntie that I love her.
With much affection always,

Jane

Jane folded the pages in half and addressed each just with a name. She made no attempt to seal them, being sure that Mrs. Wentworth would read them no matter what. She handed them to the befuddled woman, who had little choice but to promise their delivery. Jane reckoned that she might have discarded the note to Lydia, but Mrs. Sibley was another matter, and once she saw the postscript, there would be no point in not delivering the note to Lydia as well.

After a long moment of hesitation and a disapproving sniff, Mrs. Wentworth left. She cast one sharp glance backward before hurrying away. Jane and Jed stood shoulder to shoulder until she turned a corner, and then they looked at each other guardedly and contemplated what had just occurred. Horace moved to a grassy patch and began to nibble. As his traces tightened, the wagon shifted and uttered a tired rattle.

"Well," said Jane, "that was unexpected. You have gotten me out of a tight spot, and I hope you are serious about your offer to assist on your next project."

"Are you quite sure, Jane?" said Jed. "My mode of travel is not luxurious, as you can see. I have little money for lodgings and often sleep rough. Nor is it, to repeat that woman, at all proper for you to travel with me alone. You obviously don't like her, but she is not wrong."

"Not proper at all," replied Jane. "But I am sure. Very sure. That is, if you don't mind. I hope you don't mind." Doubt crept into her voice.

Jed gave a long smile and tugged Horace away from his munch. He slung Jane's two bags into the back of the wagon alongside his own equipment. Then with an exaggerated, gallant gesture, he handed Jane up into the seat before vaulting in beside her.

"Who is Mrs. Sibley?" he asked, taking the reins.

"That's a very long story, and it will take some time to make sense of it all," said Jane. She was much too tired to launch into the spiritualist saga at the moment. "I promise to tell you everything, but not right this minute." She leaned back and lifted her face to the sun. As Horace picked up his pace, a warm afternoon breeze lifted her hair. "But I thank you, Jed. I thank you from the bottom of my heart for rescuing me from that woman and from everything else that is part of the story I have to tell. But first, tell me, is there really a mural project you're to work on? And may I truly help you with it?"

"Yes, there is," said Jed, "and I would be very pleased to have your assistance. As well as your company. But you might not be pleased to learn that you will have to come with me all the way to Buffalo."

32

WESTWARD THE WAGON

It was not easy to recount to Jed all that she had encountered since embarking on the trip across the state. Still, she owed him an explanation for why she had left Rome as she did, as well as what had caused her fraught behavior upon meeting him again. Not to mention her impulsive decision to part company definitively with her previous companions and join his own journey. She set aside making a decision about what she would do after Rochester, where she might (or might not) be expected to have a new home with Lydia, and traveling farther to Buffalo with Jed. She would face that choice later, after the turmoil of her expulsion from her cousin's side had faded.

Now in a wagon slowly rolling out of town, pulled by the steady, compliant Horace, she took a deep breath and plunged in. But fatigue tangled her tongue, and in the midst of a stumbling attempt to relate her story, Jane realized that she was also hampered by a feeling of protectiveness toward Lydia and even toward her aunt. And that she was more than a little chagrined to recognize how much she herself had been enthralled by their spiritualist enterprise at first. So much so that she had refused to act on her suspicions until it was almost too late. Almost too late for her, maybe already too late for her cousin.

"Start at the beginning," said Jed after a confusing series of sentences that began, then halted, then were followed by even more partial thoughts. "No need to tell it all at once. We have a long ride ahead."

So she settled against her bags, which were comfortably stacked behind her like a cushion, and started over. It was hard to decide just when the story should begin. She tried first with a long description of Mr. Alexander Dodge Lewis, but this required a backtrack to her uncle's death and the first time she had seen that treacherous gentleman. Then there was Aunt Madeleine's pursuit of Mr. Lewis after her husband was buried, which set them on their path immediately upon leaving Troy, and this required revealing that her aunt had, most unaccountably, been omitted from Uncle George's will. Then Aunt Madeleine's desire—sounding even more foolish in the telling—to hear a word of solace from the departed in hopes that she not only would have a chance to see her beloved husband once more, but also might belatedly gain something of his estate, and the resulting dive into the spiritualist community.

Jed let the tale unfold without comment.

"I think it might have ended after a couple of sessions," mused Jane, "except for what happened at the second one."

It was painful to recount how Lydia had been so quickly caught up in the strange gatherings—especially the discovery that she was herself a medium who could connect the world of the living to the spiritual residence of the dead. Her ecstasy at the revelation of her gift, the avidity with which Mr. Lewis and the others extolled her calling and embraced her as one of their own. And then the crooked path they all began to take, holding séances along the way westward in hopes that Uncle George would make an appearance, but also summoning spirits for others who sought to hear from a beloved departed.

"It took me a while to realize that Mr. Lewis was taking money for his services, and for Lydia's as well. I don't know how much, probably not a lot, because none of those people looked very rich. And come to think of it, I don't know if he gave anything to Lydia. They all began to keep me in the dark. I was never regarded as central or even very reliable."

In relating the tale, she realized that Mrs. Sibley had been more insightful than was comfortable to acknowledge. Jane had indeed been resentful of her cousin's affinity with spirits. But it was not jealousy she felt—that she would not grant. Rather, it was deep hurt that the person she loved most in the world should have been diverted so easily from her side.

"Looking back," she said regretfully, "I can see that Liddy began to leave me some time ago."

Jed opened his mouth as if to ask more about her cousin, but he glanced at Jane's sad face and remained quiet, waiting for her to continue at her own pace.

She resumed with a more comfortable topic: how she began occasionally to supplement their income with her portraits and theorems.

But Jed already knew about that, and while the subject was safer territory, it was not what needed to be told. So she returned to the gatherings, introducing guardedly the information that sometimes her own hand had drawn a spirit presence. She could feel Jed stiffen at that admission.

"I know that must sound strange to you, Jed. It was strange to me as well. At the beginning, there were just lines and smudges on the paper. I thought at first that they appeared because I kept falling asleep, and you know how sometimes your hand jerks when you are just about to fall into a dream? In fact, I kind of hoped that was the explanation. I confess that I welcomed how the others responded to my scribbles, because I was beginning to feel so left out of everything. They imagined that I would become one of them, and that I might contribute in the same way that Lydia did. Does. And I warmed to the idea, despite my lack of conviction."

Jane felt easier once having made this confession. She continued to relate how her skepticism began to arise, then subside, then arise again in a confusing ebb and flow. She found herself emphasizing the growing suspicions, hoping to appear more rational than the rest of the story might make her seem.

"But then one night when I was feeling particularly dopey, I drew a face."

Jed looked at her with eyebrows raised.

"It happened the night before we left Rome. A very messy drawing appeared beneath my hands, and within the smudges and lines we all saw Uncle George. And his moustache. It was quite clear, especially the moustache, which used to stick out like a prickly bush." She began to giggle and had to take several deep breaths for the hysterical moment to pass. "I was quite disconcerted, and then we left so quickly. Not my choice, but the others were going and I had to accompany them. That's why I could only leave you a note, which you didn't receive anyway. And now I wonder why that was. I'm so very sorry that you believed I had just left without a word to you. I hope you believe that."

Jed nodded. "I do."

Jane felt a weight lift. Telling her story arranged what had seemed like haphazard events into a chain of occurrences that confirmed the wisdom of her sudden choice to go with him. What had looked like whim born of desperation and fatigue was really sound judgment. She hoped he would agree.

Jed had remained largely silent during her halting narration. After a long pause, Jane said, "As I tell you all of this, I realize that we must appear exceedingly foolish. It is hard for me to believe that I was not suspicious of Mr. Lewis earlier. And that I did not act on those suspicions."

Receiving no reply, she probed nervously, "Do you have any experience with persons such as Mr. Lewis? Have you ever attended a spiritualist session yourself?"

And with his continued silence, "Perhaps I should not have told you so much all at once."

Jed glanced at her with an enigmatic smile.

"What you must think of me!" Jane wished she could stop talking, but his silence was wearing on her nerves. "I hope that you will not be sorry to have my company now that you know what has been happening."

The wind was freshening. Her hair blew back in an unbound tangle. Jed shifted the reins to one hand and reached around her shoulders and pulled her to him. The suddenly intimate gesture was both startling and comforting.

"Let me think," he said. "It's a lot to take in. Certainly I have met plausible rogues, as your Mr. Lewis seems to be. But I have little acquaintance with attempts to communicate with the dead." She sat very still, surprised at the reassuring embrace and hoping he wouldn't let go.

"I feel I have escaped something dangerous," she murmured, settling against him, "but now Lydia is further and further from me, and I am very concerned about her. Perhaps I should have stayed so that I could persuade her away."

"Did you try?"

"Oh yes, I did. Of course I did, more than once. But she dismissed my concerns. She feels a calling, you see, and Aunt Madeleine was so very angry when she heard of my doubts that she commanded me to leave. In fact, she might be as responsible as Mr. Lewis for the fact that I was left in the hands of that Mrs. Wentworth."

Jed gave a rueful smile. "It's hard to convince a person to change their mind about something that is so meaningful to them. I doubt that Lydia or your aunt was easy to persuade, since they believed that they had summoned spirits, and that you simply couldn't see them. Mr. Lewis must be a very strong personality."

"Well, his tea is certainly strong. I wish I knew what was in it."

They sat quietly for a time. The wind dropped, the hot sun shone

on the dirt road, and despite his slow pace, Horace's hooves raised little
puffs of dust. Their road had shifted northward and at this point ran
parallel to the Erie Canal towpath. The stretches between towns were
pocked with makeshift structures designed for rest for the canal workers and with taverns and lodgings of decidedly lesser elegance than the
hotels that Mr. Lewis and Madeleine had reserved. Stables and the occasional blacksmith forge had been erected for the horses and mules that
plodded along pulling their floating burdens. Through sparse stands of
newly grown trees they could see the canal full of long, flat boats, some
of them packed with people.

"When we first left Troy, I thought we might travel across the state
on a canal boat," said Jane. "I thought it would be so direct, but Aunt
Madeleine refused. And she didn't want to take the new rail journey
either."

"From what I've seen, much of the boat traffic is commercial. Goods
going west, grain shipped east, and so forth. The people traveling don't
look very comfortable, though I guess it depends on the boat. Now
and then I've seen what look like excursions full of well-off folk, and
I'm sure the boats they take are nicely outfitted. But mostly, I've seen
immigrants moving west and laborers looking for work along the canal.
I doubt your aunt would have liked that kind of company very much."

"No, probably not. But if we had taken a boat, we might already be
in Rochester with her cousin and none of this would have happened."

Both of them had the same thought at that moment: And we two
never would have met. But neither said it.

"You're absolutely right that she would never approve of that mode
of travel for either herself or for Lydia and me," Jane continued. "It
wouldn't be at all proper for respectable women or young ladies. Far
more acceptable to be crammed into a jolting coach all by our proper
selves. However, the last weeks have made me wonder if I really count
as a respectable young lady anymore. After all, Lydia and I are both or-
phans with almost no money. We would have been described as impoverished if it weren't for Aunt Madeleine and Uncle George. We might
still consider ourselves proper young ladies, but I think that somewhere
along the way, we might have lost our claim to be too respectable for a
canal boat."

Jed laughed and gave her shoulder a squeeze before taking the reins
in both hands again to guide Horace onto slightly higher ground. "The
canal workers can be pretty rough, although most of the people trav-

eling are just heading for what they hope will be a better life. You'll probably see a lot of them when we get to Buffalo. There is a lot of opportunity for work along the canal and its various ports of call. When you're poor and on the road, it's hard to look respectable."

Buffalo. Jane wondered if Lydia and their aunt might be waiting for her when they finally reached Rochester and if they would persuade her to stay with them. The thought that she would have to make yet another decision about her journey was too daunting to consider after the events of the last few days. Once again, she put the thought from her mind and concentrated on the moment at hand. She surveyed her soiled dress. "Well, I have to admit that I would like to have a bath one of these days and to change my clothes. I think I've been in this dress for... Well, I'm not sure how long. Mr. Lewis's tea has rather scrambled my sense of time."

"Also," said Jed, "we're heading west. I've come all the way from Connecticut, and I've formed the impression that the farther one goes, the more the need for respectability fades away. Or maybe it just doesn't look the same." He gave Jane a smile.

"That's encouraging," she said. "Maybe if your mural project is successful, we can buy our way back to respectability. Or its outward appearance."

"Well, if appearance is all that's missing, it is easily retrieved," said Jed. "I have every hope that my rich client will like the design I have planned. We shall paint together and delight him with the result."

Jane savored the word *together*. Jed hadn't said much about her story yet, but he didn't seem appalled, nor did he indicate that he was sorry she had joined him on his way westward. She wondered how much money would be needed to retrieve respectability after days on the open road, especially after nights when she might find herself sleeping in the back of a wagon.

And if anyone should come to know of that arrangement, how many would believe that the young man by her side had really slept outside on the ground, bedded down on a cushion of pine needles beside his horse?

33

Portrait of an Unknown Man

An echoing thud. And then— *"Dan!"* His mother's voice calling from three floors below.

Dan dropped his tools and flew down the stairs with visions of her lying on the floor beside a collapsed ladder, bleeding from the fall, gasping in pain. So alarmed was he that when he saw her standing upright and whole by a display case, his relief turned to anger.

"What?"

"Just look what I've found!" She was gazing at a picture in her hands.

Dan bent over to catch his breath, hands on his knees, pulse hammering in his ears. "What?" he said again. Priscilla looked up.

"You didn't have to run."

"I heard a crash. Thought you'd had an accident."

"Oh no, sorry I scared you. That packing crate tipped over rather noisily. I knocked it over in my excitement. Fortunately, there was nothing left inside. But look at what I found at the bottom."

Priscilla held out an oil painting, a portrait of a man. A wide gilt frame surrounded the image of a gentleman of early middle age, steady gaze, full lips, dark hair springing back from a high forehead. His shoulders were broad and square, he was clad in a high-collared shirt and a dark jacket, and one arm was crossed over the other in a stiff gesture that a better artist might have rendered as informal and lifelike. Dan looked at it, unimpressed.

"What am I looking at? Who is this?"

"Study it more carefully." Priscilla held the picture closer, an eager smile on her face. Her son still looked perplexed and a bit annoyed after his needless dash to the rescue. "Oh, come now, Dan, see what he is wearing!"

Dan peered. And then he saw. He took the picture from her and brought it over to a window where the light was better.

"The buttons. That button. Can it be the same one?"

"I'm almost positive," said Priscilla. "Craig forwarded me a photo he took after it was cleaned." She scrolled through the images on her phone. "But I hardly need a picture to remember, such a shock it was to see a button jammed in that poor girl's teeth. Yes, here it is. The very same style, don't you agree?"

Despite its long years underground, the button's decoration had emerged clearly after cleaning and was distinct in the photograph. As was its painted image in the portrait before them: a waistcoat with large round brass buttons adorned with a pattern of three oak leaves.

"Holy shit!" said Dan.

"Language, dear."

"You're right! It looks exactly the same. A perfect match. How common do you think these buttons were back then?"

"I'm not sure. I haven't seen one like it before, so I imagine it's a bespoke design. It's rather decorative for a man's garment, in my view. Most men favored a plainer style. This one might have been a bit of a peacock."

"Who was he?"

Priscilla consulted the manifest from the shipment. "There is no name given for the sitter. The title is merely *A Gentleman of Utica*. Well, I suppose that makes sense, since it comes from the Munson Williams Proctor there. My friend Antonia arranged for a loan of three works that they've had in storage. I don't think it's been on display for years."

"Any way to find out his identity?"

"Possibly. I certainly intend to investigate. In fact, I'll call her right away. Your friends will be interested too, don't you think? As will Craig. I intend to ask him to loan the button itself for the exhibit; I'm sure he won't object. We can put it on display in one of the vitrines, maybe on a raised cushion to draw attention to it. And we'll hang the portrait just above. Won't that be dramatic? This discovery ought to increase our visibility, given the public interest in poor Lucille. Perhaps we ought to extend the hours of the opening to accommodate more visitors. I'll have to order more hors d'oeuvres."

❧

"I knew it!" said Karen. "I just knew that Lucille had something to do with Bigwell House. That's what I said the other day, remember?"

"Well," said Dan, "so far the connection is coincidental. She was found near here, and this portrait shows a matching button. But there is no evidence that she had anything to do with the house. And even more, there is no evidence that the man in this picture was ever here either. Remember, the painting is on loan from another city."

Jasmine, usually the skeptic, was inclined to agree with Karen. "How could there not be some connection? Too many things line up for it to be merely a coincidence. We know that she died here. Okay, it was down the street and on the next block, but still, so very close by. And the timing is right for a real connection too, because Bigwell House was being finished then and those trees were being planted, so Lucille had to have arrived at the scene around then. And I don't know how the man in the picture got here, but his button certainly did!"

"A button like it got here, certainly, but maybe lots of men wore them," said Dan. "We can't be sure that this painted button is the one that ended up in the ground." He spoke with disinterested caution, but privately he felt a growing delight at this new thread that kept the search for Lucille moving forward. It was both creepy and thrilling to think that he held in his hands the portrait of a murderer.

"Sherlock Holmes says there is no such thing as coincidence," said Jacob. "And I tend to agree. We just aren't sure what the connections are yet, but they are sure to be there."

"Oh, well, if Sherlock Holmes doesn't believe in coincidence, then there can't be any for sure," said Dan with an ironic smile. But his skepticism was sliding away, and he was happy to let it go.

His mother entered the room. "Antonia's going to do some digging and call me back. She thinks there is a record of the family that donated the painting. And I was also just on the phone to Craig. He is as excited about this picture as we are, and in fact he's on his way this very moment with the button. We can place it in the case right away and lock it up. What a good thing that you all are here. Let's choose the best place for this portrait, and then we can adjust the position of the display cases so that it hangs right over Lucille's button. Over there between the windows, don't you think? Here, Jacob, if you lift this side of the cabinet, Dan can manage the other. Move it carefully, please, it's rather heavy."

As he picked up his end of the glass-topped case, Dan caught Karen's eye and shook his head good-humoredly. He never failed to admire his mother's ability to commandeer people to her own ends. But she did it so well that her purposes always became theirs as well. Perhaps her technique wasn't really manipulation at all, just excellent timing.

34

RUMINATIONS ON THE ROAD

CANANDAIGUA, NEW YORK. AUGUST 4, 1851

"You've been gone a long time."

"Yes, I'm sorry. That took much longer than I thought it would." Jane wearily set her easel on the ground and leaned against the wagon, her face lifted to the sky. "But the woman really wanted the picture finished right away, and she gave me two dollars for it. Two dollars for one of my daubs! That's the first payment I've gotten since the other day when I exchanged a theorem for a basket of eggs. There isn't much market for theorems. Every schoolgirl does them. So I jumped at the opportunity to paint for this woman, and she offered me such a good price. Besides, it's a beautiful afternoon. I hope you weren't bored."

"Not at all. I repaired the traces and rearranged the wagon. It should be more comfortable tonight."

Jane looked down and smiled shyly at the thought of a newly comfortable wagon. Their attempt to share the narrow sleeping mat during a sudden storm two nights previously had ended in companionable hilarity and not much sleep. The oiled canopy over the wagon imperfectly kept out the wet, and the heavy tree cover had provided only a little protection from the downpour for poor, patient Horace. But the two of them lying uncomfortably in the cramped space had suggested stirring possibilities.

"Where did you go?" Jed asked. He was occupied removing a stone from Horace's right front hoof, so she could not see whether his face betrayed that a similar thought had crossed his mind.

"I thought I would be taken to her house, but it turned out that she wanted a mourning picture. She led me to a small cemetery behind the church up there on the rise. It really wasn't necessary for me to be there, as one tombstone looks much like another and can be drawn from description. It's not like a portrait. But for some reason, she was intent on having me in the very place where her husband was buried so I could render his headstone exactly. I think it meant something that I was drawing at his grave so I could copy the stone itself and not paint one that simply resembled it. How could I say no?"

"A mourning picture. You mean the kind with willows and tombs and urns?"

"Yes. And I added two figures standing beside the stone that are supposed to be her and her daughter, although since their faces are veiled they could be any women at all. She cared less about rendering her own figure than about the grave marker, oddly enough. I had to copy the inscription exactly too. The design is a common formula, but I am pleased with the result, as was she. I expect that my picture might also become the model for an embroidery."

"Why?" Jed put down the horse's foot and looked at her quizzically. "If she has the painting, why bother also with an embroidery?"

Jane laughed. "Spoken like a man. Or at least one who is also a painter. I'm sure you've seen pictures hanging on walls that are actually stitched rather than painted. They require a great deal of skill, and you sometimes have to step very close to see the fine threads. There are certain kinds of stitches that render things like leaves very well, especially the narrow, pointy ones of weeping willows."

Horace's foot restored to his satisfaction, Jed hitched the horse to the wagon and they climbed aboard. The weather had turned hot, and they kept the canopy in place overhead to protect them from the torrid sun. Both were becoming tanned, an appearance that would have prompted disapproval from Aunt Madeleine, who might comment that she was beginning to resemble a farm hand. Jane wondered again if the others had resumed their journey westward and might be in Rochester by the time that she arrived herself. Perhaps they were still meandering a more circuitous route to call upon spiritualist communities and summon the dead. She missed Lydia. Every thought of her brought a pang across her heart, a little knife cut of memory and regret.

Jane glanced back into the storage area behind the seats and saw that Jed had removed his equipment to a far corner and covered it with a blanket. The sleeping mat was neatly rolled, and her bags had been arranged to serve as pillows. Suddenly, she remembered that they were not yet fully packed.

"Oh, wait! Stop a minute. I forgot something!"

"What? What could you have left behind?"

"Not left behind, but…" Jane stood on the seat and reached over the top of the canopy. She removed her newly washed chemise, stiff from drying flat but smelling fresh from a vigorous application of soap, a rushing bath in a stream, and a cleansing breeze. It was an intimate garment to hold in her hands so close to her companion, but it would be far worse to have it blown off and lost.

"I forgot that I had washed out some more clothing this morning. I spread it up here to dry when you were out finding breakfast."

Jed barely glanced at it. "Oh, I'm sorry. I didn't realize it was still up top. I hope we can find another convenient spring tonight. I should do some washing-up of my own."

What a pleasure it had been yesterday to find that narrow, cool stream pouring over smooth rocks. They had stopped for Horace to have a drink and then had entered the water themselves to cool off. Washing yourself while fully clothed wasn't the most efficient way to get clean, but the stream had served efficiently as both bath and laundry. Fortunately, that stretch of countryside was sparsely populated, and Jed had moved discreetly back to the wagon, his own clothes still dripping, while she wrung out her skirt and changed into dry clothing.

Just to the north of them, the busy canal waterway plied its business, but they had chosen a quieter route to Canandaigua. On their way out of town, they passed by the foot of the low hill where Jane had drawn her mourning picture. The edge of the cemetery was visible through a crown of trees.

"The woman who desired a mourning picture lost her husband less than a year ago, and she is still grieving," she said. "I believe that the picture will give her some solace. But if Lydia were here, she would urge her to join a séance and communicate with her husband's spirit, continuing the bond that was broken by death. Is that desire so wrong?"

Jed did not answer immediately. This was his habit. At first, his silence had made her uneasy, but now she recognized it as a pause for thought.

"My father wanted me to go into the ministry," was his unexpected comment. "My schooling was aimed at that. But I prefer working with my hands with a practical end in mind. Studying is good in its way, but thinking by itself, and reading about what others think, and then preaching about what they think and what others thought long ago, that didn't appeal to me. Nor did the obligation to convince others of the rightness of my teachings and the wrongness of their beliefs. The truths of religion seem to me to escape certainty."

"Was your father disappointed?"

"At first, yes. But my brother took up the study, so all was not lost. I take after my uncle as far as what I like to do. And they—Uncle Rufus and my father—are fond of each other, so my choice to pursue my uncle's interests fit the family model."

"And what, exactly, are his interests?"

Jed laughed. "Well, just about everything as a matter of fact. He is a man of wide imagination and boundless energy. He is an inventor, an experimenter, a scientist. And an artist. He excels at murals for houses, and his work is in much demand. Lots of people prefer it to wallpaper. In fact, as I told you before, it is a commission of his that he delegated to me to execute in Buffalo. He has moved on to other projects and hadn't the time to do it himself. I hope the man who is paying the bills won't mind the substitution."

"And your uncle trained you?"

"Yes. Actually, he trains anyone who wants to read his manual. I'll show it to you soon. It's at the bottom of my bag. His directions are pretty easy to follow, as you'll see."

Jane waited to see how this information would address her question about the spirit world, at the same time taking in the idea that she actually might go with Jed all the way to the end of the canal and help him paint someone's wall. Would she go or would she tarry in Rochester? The question that she had postponed thinking about would shortly be unavoidable.

After another long pause Jed resumed. "But anyhow, the reason I mention the ministry, is that during my studies I had occasion to read a lot about the soul and death and the afterlife. I was less interested in how you avoid hell—some preachers these days make it seem inevitable, so why bother even trying—than I was about the nature of the soul. If it is entirely separate from the body, then when the body dies, how could we who are still stuck on earth ever reach it again? On the other hand, if there is a trace of material left, as your Swedenborg seems to think, then perhaps there is a way to bring it back into our physical world."

"I wish I had brought that book with me. Mrs. Sibley gave it to me to read, but I don't think she meant for me to keep it."

"I haven't read any of his writings," said Jed. "I'm just thinking out loud about what might be possible."

"So you think that the spiritualist quest, calling for the dead to appear, is a reasonable one?" Jane persisted.

"No, I didn't say that. Only that it might not be as lacking in science as it sounds at first."

A small concession.

"But, Jane, if the souls of the dead are eager for communication with the living, why would it take a medium like your cousin or Mr. Lewis to bring them out of hiding? Why do they just not appear to those who desire them?"

"I don't know. I wish I understood it better."

"What did Lydia say about it? What does she make of this ability to communicate?"

Jane sighed. "She is ecstatic, a real enthusiast. And if you could see her at a séance, you would not doubt that she believes that spirits visit her. It's hard to describe, but she falls into a trance and grows pale, then her cheeks flush and she gasps. It's almost as though she is on the brink of floating. And when she speaks, it is in a voice quite unlike her own. It is no wonder that she feels taken over by another. She is no fraud, I am sure. She may be mistaken, or misled. But she truly believes."

"And she would never send you away, no matter how much you doubted."

"No. Never. She loved me. She loves me."

Despite the closeness of her companion, Jane suddenly felt very alone. She was driving in the middle of a place she had never been, the road stretching indefinitely beyond, the horizon limitless, the population sparse, and her only friend this one young man. She thought of the bustling household in Troy with its social gatherings and the daily calls from friends, of an aunt who once was almost like a mother, and an uncle who, to all outward appearances, had been fond of them all. Only a few months had passed, but that part of her life now seemed to have happened long ago. Did her memories record things as they had truly been, or had there also been deception there that had gone unnoticed?

After another long pause Jed spoke again. "And you know, even if there is truth to spirits, that doesn't mean that frauds might not decide to take advantage of people's beliefs, manipulating their griefs and desires for their own ends."

"That's true enough. Lydia was saddened by my doubts, but she hoped I would someday come around. But Mr. Lewis, he was angered by them. And then after the last séance, Lydia simply dismissed the proof I found of his deception. But he wasn't so casual. Even though he denied my evidence, he seemed to fear it. And, frankly, I am afraid of him."

"With good reason. No wonder he separated you from the others. You might have scuttled his plans."

"And perhaps some of his income. My aunt was selling her jewelry. I don't know how much of what she got went into his pockets."

"Do you think his schemes are his alone? What about his sister?"

That remained a vexed question and a sore point for Jane.

"I don't know. I simply don't know. But I hope that she is a true believer. It would be better to believe in something false than to pretend so that others would be taken in. I never liked Mr. Lewis very much, but Mrs. Sibley was kind to me. And she also liked my paintings. At least, she said she did. She encouraged me to paint, to draw, to be independent. In fact, she's the one who instructed me to consider myself an independent woman of the future. Whatever that might mean. I heard her words in my head the moment I refused to go with Mrs. Wentworth. But at the same time, Mrs. Sibley did not like the fact that I harbored doubts about the spirits. Not in the least. And I have to say, doubting constantly when everyone else was convinced left me quite uncomfortable. I tried very hard to believe."

There was another silence before Jed snapped the reins and Horace picked up his pace. "Well, I tried to believe in my vocation in the ministry for a time too, if only to please my father. But I came to think that sometimes doubt is better than conviction."

35

DECISION

Jane awoke gasping. Shreds of nightmare lingered: Lydia walking down an ever-lengthening path, her slight form growing smaller and smaller as the light grew dim, Jane's legs so heavy and slow that she could not run after her. Her breathing labored, her heart pounding, her steps stumbling. And Uncle George, his face translucent white, grinning horribly as she staggered and fell.

She sat up and untangled herself from the light blanket that served as her bedding. The stars were out, but in the heavy, moist air they glimmered faintly as if behind gauze. In the dark of a pine grove nearby, Jed had lain down on an oilcloth tarp, his bedroll flung back in the hot, still night. She took her blanket and clambered out of the wagon and lay down beside him on the cushioning pine needles. He stirred briefly at her presence but did not wake. She matched her breathing to the rhythm of his until her heart calmed and she could sleep again.

As the sun rose they both awakened. Jane sat up and brushed needles from her hair. She saw Jed looking at her quizzically.

"You are a man of few words, Mr. Porter," she remarked, "even at a moment like this." He smiled and raised his eyebrows. "I had a bad dream," she explained. He nodded, understanding.

They turned north on a road that would lead to Rochester, and the closer they came to the canal the busier the area became. Woodlands and old farms lay over the hills, giving way to newer settlements with their shops and taverns and stables. Increasing numbers of men tending mules and horses, repair stops for boats and gear. Loading docks. Long warehouses. And travelers, some looking well-heeled and confident, others with the wary look of strangers in a strange land. From time to time their wagon was passed by a faster carriage, larger and better equipped to convey vacationing families. Jed speculated that they were likely heading to Niagara Falls, the wonder of the world that attracted so many visitors. A few were accompanied by their Black maids and manservants, probably some of them free and some enslaved.

There was a cloudburst along the way that turned the road to muck, and Horace lost a shoe outside Clyde that required locating a smith to forge another. Even after the sky cleared, the air was so humid it was like breathing under water. With unhurried patience, Jed studied the canal lock, then removed his camera obscura from the wagon and sought to find a good vantage for sketching. Dissatisfied with what the mirrors could capture, he put away the equipment and took paper and pencil and drew freehand, rendering the lock's gates, noting the time it took to fill with water, the height the boats were raised, the time afloat before the water reached its height and the next floodgates opened.

Jane didn't bother taking out her paints. It wasn't territory that offered much in the way of paying customers desiring their portraits. But she took pencil and paper and sought a vantage for sketching. Mrs. Sibley's instruction cards were humidly stuck among her papers, and she took out a few and used them as models to render the scene of dockworkers, loaders, passersby. She was hopeful that she might soon learn to capture what she saw without the restrictions of standard poses or stencils to organize what met her vision. But her renditions were clumsy, and anxiety about what lay ahead in their journey hampered her concentration.

"My pictures won't sell well here, and probably trying to paint at this point in our trip would be fruitless," she said when Jed returned to the wagon. "But I have little money left."

"You shouldn't worry," he replied. "I have enough, and there will be plenty more when we reach our destination."

"Thank you," said Jane, uneasy to be his dependent but not knowing what alternative there was. Am I truly going all the way to Buffalo? she wondered.

Horace newly shod, they continued on a narrow road that paralleled the towpath where mules and horses plodded pulling their floating cargo. The sun pounded, heavy clouds brooded before them on the western horizon, and the still air gave no relief from the damp heat.

Their slow progress gave Jane time to reflect about the past many weeks and to ponder how things had come to pass with Lydia. She was now utterly apart from the one person whom she had considered the center of her world. It was painful to think that Lydia might not be suffering as she was, a likelihood that revealed an imbalance in their friendship that Jane had never even suspected might be there. She did not wish her cousin distress, but its probable absence made her feel bereft.

Unanswerable questions piled up: Would the others have reached Aunt Madeleine's cousin before she did, and would they be glad to see her after all she had done? Even if they were happy to resume her company, would she really want to stay there? The decision to join Jed had been made in a moment of panic to get away from Mrs. Wentworth and to put some distance between herself and the dangerous Mr. Lewis. Despite the tempting prospect of Jed's mural project in Buffalo, Jane had vaguely assumed that she might depart the wagon at Rochester and rejoin her cousin and aunt. The more she got to know Jed, however, the more she desired to stay with him, curious about what would happen should she follow him onward. His steady patience, his wide interests, the way he looked at the world both with and without his camera obscura—she would miss all of that should she leave his company.

The nearer they drew to Rochester, the more anxious Jane became about what she might find there, and where Lydia might be, and if Aunt Madeleine had sold all her jewelry, and what had happened when they discovered she had left with Jed. Had they tried to pursue? Had they been upset? Had they breathed a sigh of relief? More questions roiled in her mind, mostly centering on Lydia: was she happy and, above all, was she safe?

She voiced her concerns from time to time, worrying that she would become tedious. But Jed only said, "I'm sure you did all you could. People can be hard to persuade." His placidity in the face of her mounting worries began to exasperate. After snapping at one of his calming statements, which she followed with a groveling apology, she bit her tongue and forced herself into a silence that rivaled Jed's own.

He was the one who broke it. "Why don't you take the reins for a while. It'll be something to take your mind away from your cousin. I feel like walking for a bit, and Horace should get used to other hands guiding him. He's an easy horse, but you need to pay attention or he'll start to amble off to find something to eat, and before you know it we'll be in the weeds. Here, hold them in both hands, not too tightly."

He hopped off the slowly moving wagon and continued on foot. Horace looked back with curiosity and slowed as though hoping for another rest, but a comradely smack on his haunches made him resume his steady pace. Jane concentrated on the horse's clopping rhythm and tried to calm her agitated thoughts.

One question would not let go: Would Lydia already be in Rochester, and would she want Jane to stay? The hope that she would vied with Jane's own desire to stay with Jed. Deciding to leave Seneca Falls and avoid the fearsome Mrs. Wentworth had been easy. Deciding to part company finally with her cousin and best friend would be much harder. Yet another thing to worry about, she thought with irritation. Could Lydia possibly be as concerned about me as I am with her? Probably not. Mr. Lewis has consumed her attention; she sees him in her future, not me. She worked on resentment for a while as a palliative to anxiety, but she realized that with every mile they came closer to Aunt Madeleine's cousin in Rochester, the nearer she herself was to yet another momentous decision.

It was late afternoon by the time they reached that city and early evening before they located the address Jane had for the cousin. The maid who answered the bell was disinclined to permit entry to a disheveled girl disembarking from a dusty wagon, but the housekeeper recognized her name and invited her into the hall.

The family was not home. Neither Madeleine Talmadge nor Lydia Strong had arrived, nor had there been any recent communication as to when they might. However, a letter had arrived for Miss Jane Woodfield just the day before. And the trunks that had been shipped from Troy had arrived safely and were waiting for them in the backroom.

Jane hadn't expected a welcoming party, but the absence of the family that supposedly would afford her a new home, as well as the fact that Lydia had not yet arrived, left her bewildered and unsure of what she ought to do.

The housekeeper seemed slightly unsure as well. With her dusty skirts, Jane was not entirely suited for the pristine parlor, but she was a weary traveler and deserved refreshment. The woman invited Jane into the airy kitchen and gave her something to drink while she read the letter.

Dearest Janie,

What a surprise to find you gone from Seneca Falls! You must have been more dazzled by Jed Porter than I realized to have gone off with him like that. Auntie is most disapproving, and Mrs. Sibley raised her eyebrows, but when she read your note to her, she only said "a woman must make her own decisions." She is enigmatic, is she not? (And how does it feel to be considered a woman instead of a girl? I have wondered that myself. But on that topic, more anon.)

We have had some most exciting sessions here that I would detail for you in person, but they are too momentous to try to write about, so I shall have to wait until we are together again to tell you all that I have seen. But how I wish you could have been with us the night before last! Uncle G. appeared most definitively, even you would have had no doubt, and with his latest communication, Auntie feels in a position to return to Troy to press her case with the lawyers again.

I might go with her, or I might not, as Mr. Lewis has invitations upstate that look most promising. (I am inspired by your boldness, dear cousin! Going off with the dashing Jed Porter like that.) I might decide to go with Alexander rather than Auntie. Certainly, he desires that I do so.

In any event, we shall be delayed in our travels and will not take up residence in Rochester till some weeks hence. I believe Aunt Madeleine has written her cousin about that. Or if not yet, she surely will soon.

So stay put when you read this letter, dear Janie, and I shall see you whenever our paths take us that far west. How I miss your company!

I do hope that you are well and happy, and painting up a storm. With very much love,

Lydia

Jane pored over the letter, seeking to decipher its implications. Lydia's tone was oddly light. Jed? Dashing? Well, why not. He was handsome enough and had a compellingly confident demeanor. But putting it that way inserted Jane's desperate disappearance into the plot of a romantic novel and failed to recognize the risk she had taken, which should have aroused at least a little concern. The message was fond, even loving, but nothing suggested that Lydia was at all worried about her cousin. Jane was somewhat hurt that her departure did not occasion more consternation than apparently it had. And Aunt Madeleine—only disapproving? Not desiring to see her younger niece again? How could her former affection have dried up so quickly?

The housekeeper approached her and inquired as to whether the letter indicated when Mrs. Talmadge and Miss Strong might arrive, and Jane shook her head tiredly.

"I'm afraid it tells me little," she confessed. "I had hoped to find them here already so that I could tell them of my change of plans. I intend to continue farther to Buffalo rather than stay here."

And with those words, Jane felt her ties with her cousin and aunt finally loosen and release. A decision once made brings relief from the anxiety of making it. Lydia has chosen her path, she thought, and so have I.

The woman was kind. If she was also curious about why the travelers from Troy had gone their separate ways, she suppressed her prying questions. Confident from years of running the large house when the family was away, she offered Jane a bed for the night and Jed a pallet in the stable where Horace was accorded a stall. Jane was grateful and glad for a bath and a real mattress. But as sometimes happens when one has become used to sleeping on boards, the bed was too soft. As she drifted into a slightly smothering sleep, Jane thought she might prefer to share the stall.

36

MR. BIGWELL

"These four walls will be the canvas for your artistic endeavors, Mr. Porter. They will, in the fullness of time, enclose the dining room. As you can see, there is already a chandelier installed overhead in the place that, also in the fullness of time—slightly fuller in this case, as the furniture has yet to be shipped—will indicate the center of the area where the table will be placed. I'm sure that you will appreciate the fact that this space will be empty while you work, for I gather from your uncle that the paints used to cover these bare walls come in large buckets, and you will need all the room you can get."

Jane turned slowly and took in the large expanse to be covered in murals. Jed stood calmly still as his employer described in detail what he wished to have painted, but his eyes darted here and there with a look that hovered between eagerness and alarm. The room was huge.

"As I described in the letter to your uncle, which serves as a contract between us, at least one wall should feature the marvelous canal that has made this city prosper. Only appropriate, don't you think, since it has done the same for me! The grain from the west all passes through our port, and it has brought about such a sudden growth of the city you could never have imagined. Perhaps this long wall is suitable for the main subject, since it is the only one not interrupted by windows. You can choose scenes as you see fit for the other three. And of course, those large French doors will need to be accommodated. Shades of blue and green, perhaps? Maybe even a winter scene, but not on the long wall. The winter months are fierce here, and the canal closes for the season. Can't pull a boat through ice. Far too much white to feature snow anyway. It is bright color we want! Only appropriate for the expanding future! I'm sure my wife will agree when she arrives."

Jane thought she had never met a man who fit his name so well as

Mr. Samuel Bigwell. For big he was, from his large head to his enormous feet with a substantial midsection in between. His hair was curly and unruly, his smile frequent and inclusive, his voice commanding and on the loud side, especially reverberant in the cavernous, empty room. His size and voice might have been domineering, but somehow his enthusiasm was so infectious that it invited one to share his gusto rather than to cower before the onslaught of its expression. She liked him immediately.

"And although it isn't in the contract," he continued, "I hope that when you are finished with this room, you will move upstairs to the top floor and paint another scene for me. Up there, I envision the mighty Niagara, even the Falls, and perhaps a small scene at the base where the river continues to Lake Ontario. I'll describe it to you later. Of course, you could travel just a few miles downriver and see it for yourself. Magnificent sight! I have designed this house rather like those one sees on your New England coast, Mr. Porter, with a sort of cupola on top. One can't call it a widow's walk here, of course, there being no vista to gaze out in search of sailors returning from years at sea. But still one can see over the trees almost to the river, affording the imagination a view of the real thing that you will render in paint."

Jed nodded agreement, murmured something approving of these design plans, and the two shook hands. Mr. Bigwell extended his hand to Jane as well, though now a quizzical look crossed his face. Apparently, he had forgotten her name and was belatedly unsure why she was there and what her relation to the painting project might be.

"Excuse me, sir." Mr. Bigwell's manservant entered at that point and the two withdrew to a corner and engaged in a low-pitched exchange for several minutes. So Mr. Bigwell doesn't always boom, thought Jane. She caught Jed's eye and shrugged with a smile.

"I'm surely glad you are with me, Jane," he said, moving closer and sharing his own quiet word. "This job is even bigger than I anticipated."

"It will be a challenge, certainly," she said. "But so much fun, don't you think?"

Jed smiled. "I'm relieved to hear you think so."

The manservant turned to leave, but Mr. Bigwell interrupted his progress. "Oh, Clancy, I should introduce you to our painters. Mr. Porter and Miss, er, this young lady. They will be here for some days, maybe even weeks, decorating these blank walls with their art."

Clancy turned and gave a slight bow. Jed stepped forward and extended his hand, and after a brief hesitation that might have indicated surprise, the handshake was returned. Mr. Bigwell looked at Jane, his eyebrows raised.

"Jane Woodfield," she said to Mr. Clancy, filling in the blank. "Very pleased to meet you. I hope we won't be very much in your way."

"I'm sure you will not," said the man with the faintest of smiles. "Please let me know if I might be of service during your stay." He executed another slight bow before nodding to Mr. Bigwell and exiting the room.

"A good man," said Mr. Bigwell in a slightly lower tone of voice than the one with which he had so enthusiastically described the walls he wished painted. "A free man, you know. Born free of free parents."

"As only it should be," said Jed.

Mr. Bigwell gave him a long look and a sharp, approving nod. He opened his mouth to say something else, but evidently thought better of it and returned to his exposition of the walls.

"Floor to ceiling, mind. And I would be delighted if you wish to continue onto the ceiling itself, perhaps with clouds, sky, and so forth, feel free. I've seen pictures of churches that do that sort of thing to good effect, but please, no cherubs flying around for me. No chubby little infants with wings. Nature is what I want. Clouds, birds, a sunset or two. The sky's the limit." And then recognizing an almost-pun, he added, "Hah!"

"The ceiling is very high," said Jane. "Perhaps we shall require a taller ladder, don't you think?"

"Actually," said Jed, "I believe we'll need to erect a scaffolding to reach the higher portions of the walls, and certainly for the ceiling. One needs a steady hand to paint, and for that a secure platform is required."

"Whatever you need!" said Mr. Bigwell. "Can't be falling off ladders in the middle of painting a picture. The builders have left ladders and boards and a few tools in the carriage house. They won't be returning until the bricklayers have finished mortaring a troublesome chimney, so feel free to use whatever you find."

"Thank you," said Jed. "We shall begin right away by assembling materials and planning the design, and in a few days we should be ready to paint."

A shadow passed over Mr. Bigwell's face as he realized that his paint-

ed room would take a good deal of time to accomplish. He was a man
who desired that tasks be accomplished immediately. But he was also a
practical person, and his ready smile quickly returned. He shook Jed's
hand again and then Jane's too, and although the afternoon was waning,
he strode off to his office to put in an evening's work.

The carriage house was set behind and offset to the side of the residence. The stables below and the living quarters above were finished
but as yet unoccupied. Horace was to share the lower quarters with only
one other horse, a sleek roan with an elegant arch to his neck. Horace
looked rather run-down and commonplace in comparison. The two animals lifted their heads and gave each other long, searching looks before
each turned to his stall and tucked into the evening's dinner of oats.

"I hope they'll get along," said Jane. "It's hard to read a horse's
expression." She was thinking how admirably straightforward animals
could be. And how complicated and indirect were the ways of humans.

"They'll be fine," said Jed, who was wondering about the sleeping
arrangements afforded by the carriage house. Upstairs there was one
bed and a room outfitted with a heavy pottery ewer, a washbasin, and a
few hooks for hanging clothes. Mr. Bigwell had not expected two artists
to arrive, just one young man. And certainly not a man accompanied by
a woman.

They ate supper in the kitchen of the residence, sharing a table with
a young maid and the cook, neither of whom were quite sure about the
newcomers who were seated at their table. Both were courteously un-
inquisitive but obviously bristling with curiosity about the relationship
of these two itinerant artists. Being unsure of the matter themselves,
Jane and Jed ate hungrily and directed the conversation to the excellent
cooking.

"Such a fine ham, Mrs. Copley," said Jed. "I haven't eaten so well
since I left Connecticut."

"Nor I," said Jane. "And such lovely, fresh greens."

"And are you, Miss Woodfield, also from Connecticut?" asked Mrs.
Copley.

"No," said Jane. "I joined Mr. Porter later to assist him on this mural
project. The house is very large, is it not? I'm sure it will be grand when
all is finished. And when will Mrs. Bigwell take up residence? Have you
cooked for the family a long time?"

All and all, Jane and Jed got more information than they needed but were satisfied that they succeeded in giving little.

They took two lanterns back to the carriage house. The shaded light shed narrow pools around them, making their shadows dance against the gathering darkness.

"You can take the upstairs, Jane, if you like," said Jed, adopting a casual tone. "After we unload the wagon completely, I'll arrange my bedroll in it and sleep here downstairs."

The quiet behind him made him turn and look at Jane. He raised his lantern and saw that she stood glaring with her hands on her hips.

"Are you accommodating Mr. Bigwell's delicate sensibilities, Jed? I wasn't aware myself that he harbored any misgivings about my presence here."

"That wasn't my primary concern, no," he replied, taken aback at her assertive tone. "I was only imagining that you would prefer to sleep up in the loft bed."

"Alone."

"Well, doesn't it seem more comfortable as well as more…more…" (fishing for the right word), "more seemly? Now that we have reached our destination?"

"Seemly? A fine term," said Jane. "Sleeping in a stable yet worried about appearances, I see. But are we not, to use a phrase appropriate to the place, shutting the barn door after the horse has left?"

Jed was silent, thinking of the warm space they had shared in the wagon for several rainy nights on the road.

"I'm not sure what to say," he replied.

"Say what you mean, Jed Porter," commanded Jane. "Don't presume that your standard silence will be understood. But bear in mind that if you are concerned about my reputation, it is far too late. There is little to be done about that any longer. That point has long passed." She drew a shaky breath. "You are a man of few words, but you are observant. Very observant. You see things that others overlook. You observe, you draw, you paint. So how, *how* could it have escaped your notice that I have already thrown in my lot with you?"

Her stern voice began to waver, so she grabbed her bags and headed for the upper rooms. She had intended a sweeping ascent up the stairs, but the bags were heavy and her exit was slowed to a less dramatic trudge.

She had left the lantern downstairs, and although the window on the gable let in a sliver of moonlight, the room she now entered was almost fully dark. She dropped her bags at the door of the sleeping quarters and stumbled to the bed, suddenly exhausted. It was little more than a mattress on a low platform, but it was thick and covered with a fresh-scented quilt. I should not be lying on the clean counterpane with my shoes on, she thought, passingly irritated that the painful episode below was so quickly diluted by this mundane concern.

After only a short while, there were quiet footsteps on the stairs and a glow appeared. The mattress shifted as Jed lay down beside her in the soft lamplight.

"I'm glad to hear you say that you have thrown your lot in with mine, Jane," he whispered. "I hardly dared hope that your decision would last this long. Beyond your escape, that is. I feared you would stay in Rochester. Or that prudence would advise you to distance yourself from the time we have spent together on the road. Or even that you might change your mind and go back east looking for your cousin. But since you declare your lot is thrown with mine, I tell you here and now, that mine is also thrown with yours."

37

SMALL THINGS FORGOTTEN

"Are you absolutely sure your mother won't be coming back here to-night?"

Karen was nervous. Not only because she was still at Bigwell House long after closing hours, but also—and chiefly—because she had just that moment slid naked under the covers of the thick, humped mattress of the large reproduction bed designed to match the one in which Mr. and Mrs. Bigwell might have slept. Four mahogany posts flanked each corner, and the ivory satin sheets were so slippery that the comforter in its embroidered duvet refused to stay in place.

"Positive," said Dan, tossing his jeans on a chair and joining her. "I've told you twice now that she hurried off to a fundraiser for local preservation groups and left me to finish making up this room. Knowing her, she'll be the last to leave too, so don't worry."

Karen thought of the first moment she'd set eyes on Priscilla Cavendish early one Sunday morning, an elegant woman still wearing the evening clothes of the night before and prepared to get them dirty in order to examine a jawbone. "So she's such a party animal that you can trust she won't return early?"

"She is. She won't be back till morning, I'm certain. She knows how to enjoy herself, I'll give her that. Plus tonight she has another item on her agenda. She wants to convince the African American Historical Society that Bigwell House was a stop on the Underground Railway, so she's also probably exerting her famous powers of persuasion and hoping that they will join forces with her about the importance of this place."

"Was it?"

"I've no idea. I guess it's possible, given what's known about Bigwell and his household." Dan wrapped his arms around Karen and nuzzled her neck. "I like your perfume."

"I'm not wearing perfume. What do you mean, what's known about his household?" Despite the assurance, Karen was still listening for the sound of a key turning in a lock or a door opening downstairs.

Dan sighed and tried to recall what his mother had been chattering about when she left. "Well, he employed a Black servant, which wasn't common at the time. Most servants of the wealthy around here were Irish and white. So her idea is that members of the household harbored escaping slaves, with or without Bigwell's knowledge, but probably with, given hints in his diaries. Maybe not in this house itself, but there used to be a carriage house behind, and Mom thinks there might have been a hidden room under the stables. But since it's paved over now, we'll never know for sure. But do we really want to be talking about this now?"

"I guess not."

Bare skin against cool satin sheets, like diving naked into water, plus the guilty thrill of making love in a place they should not be. Only one lamp burned, its glass shade in wavering colors of deep amber and green. From a small table across the room it cast its ocean light onto peacock blue wall paper patterned with vines and birds. In the dimness the ceiling seemed to hover at an indefinite height, a soothing twilit canopy for the bed below. Karen wondered fleetingly if Dan's choice of beds might be a small act of mutiny aimed at his mother, a gesture regarding his renovative labors that she had so thoroughly commandeered. The thought produced a nervous giggle, quickly overcome by the warm, urgent grasp of her companion.

Some indeterminate time later, after she had caught her breath, Karen voiced another worry. "What will she do when she finds out we've been here?"

"Why should she find out? Do you intend to make an announcement?"

"Well, no, but I presume we've left some evidence on these fancy sheets."

Dan laughed. "If we make the bed again, I doubt anyone will ever unmake it for a long time. And suppose they do years from now, there'll just be another little mystery to solve for some future student of history, like you. Besides, you're talking about a woman who once jumped drunk into the Trevi Fountain and climbed onto one of the seahorses. By her own braggy admission. I don't think she has many grounds to object to our putting this bed to use."

"Okay, maybe not," said Karen, adding after a pause, "and besides, it's a reproduction. It's not like we're defiling an antique."

That required some explanation.

"Look around this room," said Karen. "It's been decorated in the style of the mid-nineteenth century, and the furniture looks like what the Bigwells might have used. We know that because of the photos that were taken just after the family moved away in, what was it? About 1890? But none of it is old, it just looks old. The wallpaper looks like it would have a hundred and sixty years ago, but now in 2015 it still looks new, and because it shouldn't, it has a different quality. It's not like the historical items on display downstairs or like the Porter murals—those are authentic, real. It feels different to be around them. So we're not really lying in the bed that Mr. and Mrs. Bigwell slept in. Just one that looks like it."

Dan still was puzzled. "I don't get the point. So you mean that the Bigwells wouldn't mind, if they knew?"

"No, not that. But when things have lasted a long time, survived the accidents of history, they demand attention. They invite us back into their own time in a way that reproductions don't. So we have to be careful how we treat them."

Dan pondered. "I guess I see what you mean. But if the original bed were still sturdy and not too musty, I don't see why it couldn't still be put to use. And maybe the Bigwells were generous folk and would have shared their actual bed with us. Not at the same time, of course. There wouldn't have been room."

"Don't be silly, I'm serious. Okay, forget the bed, you're missing the point. Don't you sense how different this room is from the ones below us? It looks authentic, but it isn't. The rooms downstairs are different. They have an older feel. A kind of aura about them, a spirit. Real old things do that, at least sometimes. Didn't you feel something strange when you first touched Lucille's bones? And when we dug up her locket and her clothes, wasn't it thrilling to hold them in your hands?"

Vividly, Dan recalled the shock that had met his fingers when he picked up the bone and the almost electric fascination it had aroused. "Yes," he said, "with the bones anyhow. It was kind of a thrill, but darker. It felt wrong to be touching them, like I had violated something. Transgressed."

"Really? You never said. I didn't know that." They lay side by side now, touching along the length of their bodies, feeling the living warmth they shared and thinking of the desolation of bones.

"Did you feel the same way about the artifacts? The button? And also the locket and the chain?"

"Not quite. They weren't part of her, not in the same way."

"Maybe not. But it's still awesome to handle something that once touched her when she was alive, don't you think? It's one thing to hold it in your hands and examine it like a scientist. Touching her things, even wearing them, furnish another way of knowing her. For a moment I had the urge to put on her necklace. Of course, it was impossible because the chain is broken. It would need to be mended. And then it wouldn't quite be the same thing; it would be a hybrid."

"Hybrid?"

"Sure. Antiques often are. Repairs and replacement parts mean that historical objects are often partly old, partly new. For instance, if you have your great-grandfather's watch, the workings inside might be replaced, but the gold case on the outside, which is the only thing you usually see, makes it seem as if the entire object is old. You might not realize it, but it's a hybrid. Delicate things like jewelry often come apart, and new chains are put on so that they can still be worn. Like Lucille's locket. We found bits of the chain and the pendant, but the bale connecting the two is gone so it would need to be replaced."

"What's a bale?" Dan was charmed by Karen's enthusiasm.

"This thing." Karen squirmed to extract her own necklace, which had twisted to the back of her shoulders. "See this loop that connects the drop to the chain? It's called a bale. They are replaced all the time, and chains also."

Dan fingered the smooth agate lavalier that Karen frequently wore and placed it gently between her breasts. It rested on a shallow cleft of her sternum, the bone palpable beneath the smooth skin. "You've thought a lot about these things."

"Of course. It's why I'm studying archaeology," said Karen, warming again at his touch and hoping it would continue. "But sorry, I didn't mean to launch into a lecture. Sometimes I get carried away."

Dan kissed the hollow of her neck. He could feel her pulse beneath his lips. "Not at all. I like your enthusiasm. I imagine you in a year or two excavating a tomb in the desert or hacking through jungles in South America in search of lost ruins." As he spoke, he felt a pang at the distance there would be between the two of them when she set off on her own. She adventuring in Peru or Mexico or some Greek island, he remaining here and missing her and feeling static, maybe even succumbing to his mother's suggestion to work at Bigwell House.

"No, I won't be any of those places," said Karen. "I don't intend to dig for ruins, not me. I would have thought you could tell that already, given my incompetence in Lucille's trench. Come on now, I know you thought I didn't know what I was doing. I could tell by the way you stared at my feet that first day. But anyhow, I'm interested in the little things that get left behind as time goes by: jewelry, cups and plates, tools, bits of clothing. The small things forgotten. You find those everywhere, not just exotic places but where we already live. Anywhere. Here."

"Small things forgotten. Pretty phrase."

"Yes, but not mine. It's the title of a famous book. But that's my interest. Little domestic things people leave behind that get found later by people like me—like us, in fact, since you found Lucille—and make us wonder what they are, where they came from, who used them and why."

The pang began to dissipate. Dan smiled and pulled her closer. "Domestic things. Like satin bed sheets with puzzling stains."

"Oh," said Karen, then again on a breath, "*Oh!*"

Another stain later, she asked, "Do you believe in ghosts?"

"No."

"I don't mean wailing things in white that hang around attics and haunt houses. But a kind of spirit that old places take on over time, that make the past linger around us."

"Like the downstairs of Bigwell House, with the old fixtures and floors, and the murals on the walls?"

"Yes, like those. Or the cupola even, where there are only faded traces of what was once there. Places and things that are thrilling to be near because you feel you are coming closer to times long ago. Don't they seem to have a spirit of their own, kind of a life?"

"No."

But then Dan thought about how the conservators had brought the downstairs walls back to life, the images of the past growing more and more vivid under their care. And about the button and how he felt when he recognized that it matched the portrait, the realization that he held a fragment from the clothing of a murderer, that he could look into his painted eye and desire retribution. And when they found the locket that had torn loose from Lucille's throat, and the thrill of turning it over in his hands, his fingernails prying open the hinge to see the ruined slip of ivory beneath. But it wasn't like encountering a spirit, he thought, just a small thrill of discovery.

"No," he said again. And then, "Well, kind of."

38

MURALS

"'Dissolve half a pound of glue in a gallon of water,'" read Jane, "'and with this sizing, mix whatever colors may be required for the work.' My word, Jed, how many gallons will be needed for these rooms?"

"I figure at least twenty," said Jed. He stood with a lightly loaded brush, making tentative gestures at the wall before him. "Maybe more, because we'll have to have separate jugs for different colors, and then a series of jugs to add white or slip to a base color in order to lend gradients to sky and land and to make the water look transparent and flowing. There's going to be a lot of water in this picture. And sky."

"I had no idea that your mural project would be so large. What a good thing that there is nothing else in the room to get in the way of our work. Mr. Bigwell was right about that."

"His letter to Uncle Rufus only specified a mural, and I figured it would be only one wall. But I suppose you could consider a picture that crosses several planes one mural rather than three or four. I hope this won't be more than I can manage." Jed put down the brush and stepped back. "I can't figure out how to start. Or where. If we make a mistake, there will be a lot of work to cover it up and repair the damage."

Jane came up beside him, Rufus Porter's book in her hands.

"Of course it won't be more than you can manage. There are explicit instructions in your uncle's manual, and all we have to do is follow them. Remember what the title says: *A Select Collection of Valuable and Curious Arts and Interesting Experiments, which are well explained, and warranted genuine, and may be performed easily, safely, and at little expense.* See? Well-explained, performed easily and safely, although I don't know why we need be assured about safety if we are only painting. Besides, you have an assistant, remember?"

Jed smiled and gave her a quick hug. "More than an assistant. A partner. And thank goodness for that."

She continued to read. "'Strike a line round the room, nearly breast high; this is called the horizon line.' So that's where we start. Strike a line. The ceilings are so tall, we probably should use your height as our guide rather than mine."

"Actually, if Mr. Bigwell really wants us to continue the scene onto the ceiling, perhaps we should make it even higher, maybe at my eye level."

"Yes, that would give us more room on the lower section for the scene on land. Is this the wall where he wants the canal to be painted, or is it the opposite one?"

"This one. And since it will depict the most important scene, we should plan it first."

After being temporarily overwhelmed at the enormity of the task, Jed began to field ideas for the design. Discussion of details freed his stymied imagination, and they began to make some experimental daubs on the plaster, transferring ideas from paper to the wall and beginning to sketch the desired scenes on the giant canvas of the room. The picture needed to feature the terminus of the canal, the commercial slip where boats unloaded their cargo, as well as where their passengers staggered, cramped and bewildered, onto the busy shoreline. And also—this point had been emphasized—the places where the Bigwell warehouse received cargo and the distribution points where long boats loaded with grain embarked on their way east.

"That will be the biggest object in the foreground, and then…um." Jed stalled again.

Mr. Bigwell desired that the room depict both the length of the canal from east to west and the five high locks that lifted the water to the level it required to complete the transit to Buffalo, but designing both relative height and much longer length, not to mention the sharp southwest curve that the canal took toward the end, was a challenge on a surface that was also supposed to be decorative.

And in addition, Jane observed, they ought to figure in the probable disposition of furniture. Mrs. Bigwell, when she arrived, would be displeased if the monumental picture prohibited the placement of what they suspected would be proportionately large china cabinets and sideboards. Everything of this family seemed larger than normal.

"So definitely, a much higher horizon line," Jed confirmed with a confident swish of the brush. "The bottom half can be docks and streets surrounding the warehouse."

"Can we wrap the design around that window and let the change of levels at Lockport march over the frame?"

"Maybe. We could also curve the length of the canal into the distance until it disappears around some hill or other. Then it could come out later in a much narrower band of blue."

"But do we have to keep the same vantage point on all the walls? What about doing a city scene on one. That wouldn't have to recede so far toward the horizon. And what about the ceiling? Is it to be daylight? Evening? Which direction does this window face anyway? If it's east, we can depict the rising sun on the upper parts."

Jed grinned at Jane's rapid-fire questions. Rather than producing anxiety, they now fostered excitement. They spent the morning engaged in their design speculations, becoming alternately daunted and enthusiastic about the scenes that were beginning to emerge. They laid out ideas on the floor in front of each wall, using long sheets of newsprint thoughtfully provided by Mr. Clancy, who occasionally observed their work, his neutral expression gradually becoming engaged as he listened to their conversation.

"Don't forget that some of those ideas can be saved for use upstairs," he interjected at one point, surprising both Jed and Jane, who had not heard him enter.

"Oh yes, of course. I think that is where Mr. Bigwell suggested the Falls, is it not?"

"Indeed." He was carrying a small table and set it now near the doorway. "I expect you would like some refreshment. My daughter has brought you some."

In came the maid with a tray.

"Oh, thank you! Sally, is it not? I didn't know you were Mr. Clancy's daughter. I'm starving, now that you mention it, so this food is most welcome."

Jed was inclined to eat while sketching, but Sally brought in two upright wooden chairs. It was a relief to sit down after their hours of work.

"I didn't realize how tired I was getting," said Jane. The walls still looked immense, but their task no longer seemed impossible.

"Yes, mural work is strenuous. On one's feet all day and reaching high and low," said Jed, tucking into his food. "You know, in spite of all of the time we have spent discussing painting, I never asked you how you began to draw. Did you have instruction?"

"The usual sort of thing in school. Sketching and the use of theorems. Young ladies are supposed to learn how to draw in order to decorate a home. Also, there was a library at Uncle George and Aunt Madeleine's house in Troy, and it had a small shelf of drawing books that I consulted from time to time. Chapman, you know, and Peale. And a few others. Some were pretty old. I tried to teach myself a few methods from them. And then I practiced drawing likenesses of everyone around me, including Uncle George. He had a very distinctive face, so it was fun to see that I could capture a recognizable image. He seemed to appreciate my efforts, but Auntie preferred the portraits done by the other artists whom she hired."

"I'm hoping that you can be the one to add figures to the scenes," said Jed. "We don't want to have only hills and water and buildings. A few people walking here and there will add interest. Didn't you take any of the drawing books with you when you left? I know you took your paints and pencils, why not a manual or two as well?"

"No, I left them all there. They had belonged to Uncle George's first wife, you see. Her sketch books were there as well. She was quite talented. He said he didn't mind my looking at them, but somehow after he was gone, it didn't seem right to take anything that wasn't really mine. Especially—" She paused. Suddenly, something fell into place that she hadn't noticed before. A lull fell over the conversation.

"Especially?" Jed prompted.

"Especially after the reading of the will," Jane continued slowly. "I told you some of this before, but now I'm wondering whether I really understood completely what was happening at the time. As I told you, after he died, we learned that Uncle George hadn't changed his will after he married Aunt Madeleine. With his first wife gone, everything went to his sons. It seemed strange, but now—I should have thought of this before—now I put this together with the fact that shortly after their wedding, Lydia and I lost our mothers, who were Auntie's older sisters, and she invited us to live with her."

"That was only right, I suppose," said Jed. "But it was also very generous of her. And of him."

"It was. I didn't understand that at the time. Lydia and I were in a daze of grief. We didn't know what to do. Living with them seemed not only the best, but maybe the only option for us."

She paused again. Jed didn't interrupt but let her gather her thoughts.

His eyes traced their sketches on the walls, the notes they had jotted on the plaster, indications of size, quick sketches of buildings, curves where hills might block sight of the canal.

"Anyhow," Jane resumed, "when it turned out that Uncle George hadn't included Auntie in his will, the assumption was that he had been careless. Delinquent in his duties, you know, and that eventually he would have rewritten it to include her. Perhaps not Lydia and me, but her, his wife. But he did not. Auntie was shocked. Terribly shocked. She spent many days searching for another document that would prove his intent to include her, and she argued endlessly with the lawyers. But nothing was found, and the lawyers were adamant. I wonder..."

Another ruminative pause.

"Now I wonder if Mr. Bailey—that's the name of the lawyer—didn't know more than he said, and if Uncle actually might have told him that the omission was on purpose."

"But why? Wasn't he fond of your aunt?"

"I have no reason to think he was not, except for the inescapable fact that he left her nothing. That's why she seized the opportunity that Mr. Lewis presented. That is, to communicate with his spirit in hope of getting some evidence that he had wanted to leave her a legacy. That he loved her in spite of it all."

"You told me something of this on the road. But it sounds so absurd. What lawyer or court of law would accept testimony gathered from a séance?"

"I agree. And I tried to persuade Lydia of the foolish fruitlessness of this quest. But she was too wrapped up in spiritualism to listen. She also hinted once that she hoped to hear from her own mother eventually. That, indeed, might have been her ultimate goal, the real reason that she fell into the idea so readily. Besides, she wasn't particularly interested in the legacy. Mainly, she hoped that Auntie would be comforted if she could hear words from her husband. I realize now that Liddy was really concerned with Auntie, and I was too absorbed in my own sense of being an outsider to pay as much attention as I should have. And Aunt Madeleine was indeed comforted when Uncle George began to appear at the gatherings. When he seemed to appear, that is. But now I wonder if Auntie wasn't going slightly, slightly...well, slightly mad. Crazed by the injury and hurt."

It was a terrible thought.

"That would be very disturbing," said Jed, regretting the inadequacy of the statement.

"I wish I had thought of everything this way earlier," said Jane sadly. "I have been so concerned about Lydia and also worried that I was losing her. But maybe I should have been more concerned about Auntie. Certainly, Mr. Lewis has been exploiting her grief and bewilderment."

Jed had no words for that. He only placed his hand on hers and sat quietly until the young maid came to collect the dishes. She cast a curious eye over the walls, now covered in experimental swipes of pale paint and some charcoal smudges.

"What do you think, Sally? Are we making progress?" said Jane.

The girl smiled. "I'm sure you are, miss," she said neutrally, and left the room.

The morning's exertions had been more tiring than either realized, and they resumed their work in silence. Jane spent some time turning in circles and staring at the ceiling, trying to imagine how the sky could be painted. Slightly dizzy, she sketched possible designs on a corner of paper and notated color gradations and the shifting light from the windows that were set on two sides. Jed took the bull by the horns and drew a horizon line on the longest wall, correcting it twice until he was sure it was level. Although Porter's manual largely bypassed vanishing points, he marked one on each wall anyway. The room was very quiet and warm as the afternoon drew on.

"Are you thinking of Lydia?" asked Jed.

"Yes. I can't help but wonder where she is now and whether she is still as happy with the company of Mr. Lewis as she was earlier. He seemed fond of her, but he has the look of a seducer, and I don't trust him at all. Even though now his reputation is kind of dependent on her talents as a medium, I am not assured that he wishes her well. How I wish I knew how she is faring! I left her a note in Rochester telling her where we were going. And I posted letters both to Utica, in case they return to Mrs. Sibley's house, and to Troy, should she return there with our aunt. But I have heard nothing."

"It's still too early to expect a response," Jed said reassuringly. "You don't know when she will receive any of your letters, and then it will take a while for one from her to get to you here. Don't worry."

"I'll try not to," said Jane. But they both knew she would.

39

PIGEON

BUFFALO, NEW YORK. OCTOBER 5, 2015

There were less than three weeks to go until the opening, and even the imperious optimism of Priscilla Cavendish was faltering. As yet she had found no indisputable proof that the striking murals of Bigwell House were by the hand of Rufus Porter himself, nor had additional evidence turned up linking the unfortunate Lucille to the museum. Small bits of information were dribbling in, but they failed to fall into a clear pattern. Priscilla was poring over the correspondence of Samuel Bigwell hoping to discover additional communications with Porter, but so far she had only the draft letter of invitation.

The tentative convergence of Lucille's story with Bigwell House was still without foundation. The museum in Utica had informed them that the portrait on loan, tentatively dated about 1849, had been donated in 1984 by one Winnifred Owen, a collector of American paintings, who unfortunately had not indicated the identity of the sitter in her bequest. They promised to inquire more explicitly about the provenance of the painting, but their search was likely to take more time than was needed for a dramatic announcement at the opening.

At the moment the buttons, both painted and excavated, were displayed suggestively together between the central windows of the living room. But they did not constitute real evidence for a long-ago murder, and Priscilla Cavendish was too scrupulous to make a claim without further proof. How fortunate—indeed, how spectacular!—it would be if the renovated museum combined its opening with the solution of an old, cold murder case. Lucille had captured the imagination of the public, but her identity remained a mystery. Priscilla still hoped for a last-minute discovery, but time was running short.

However, on this particular morning the urgent, immediate problem confronting her was far more mundane and had been caused, not by the occlusions of history, but by a pigeon. The bird had flown unnoticed through an open, screenless window the previous Saturday afternoon and been unable to find its way out over the remains of the weekend. It had flapped hysterically around every corner of the house, leaving poop-white splotches along the polished floors and freshly cleaned oriental rugs, until it found the upper stairway and reached the cupola, where it proceeded to bash against the windows until falling, exhausted, on its back, lizard feet reaching futilely up to heaven.

First thing Monday morning, after a period of cursing dismay, Priscilla sent her son to assess the damage in the cupola and took a mop to the lower floors herself.

Remarkably, the bird was not quite dead. Dan opened a window, picked up the groggy pigeon with its disheveled feathers poking in all directions, and placed it gently on the sill, where it wobbled and blinked for a minute before staggering out onto the newly shingled eave. After several rubber-necking minutes, perhaps reflecting on resurrection and assessing its options, the pigeon flapped raggedly away, leaving Dan with clumps of gray feathers and sticky bird droppings to clean from floor and walls.

Its desperate attempts to escape had left yet more chips and scratches on the faded murals around the windows, and he fervently hoped that the newly restored paintings downstairs had not suffered similar damage. His mother might be irritating sometimes, but she had poured heart, soul, and sweat into the museum, and he wanted her efforts to succeed. He scraped drying pigeon poop into a dusty heap and swept it into a garbage bag, trying not to inhale. Who knew what bird shit could do to your lungs and sinuses. Stuck to the walls there were patches of feathers frilled with pink where the poor thing had bled.

The bird seemed to have managed to get everywhere in the small room. Each window, all four walls, the wainscotting, even the ceiling sported evidence of its panic. A splotch overhead was just beyond his reach. The step ladder was three floors below, so Dan decided to move the large chest to the center of the room in order to climb up and clean off the dangling feathers. The chest was heavy and hadn't been moved for a century, having become virtually a built-in piece of furniture. Its feet were stuck to the floor from its inert weight over the years. Dan heaved, but something more impeded its movement. He pulled harder, and harder again. His impatient tug was followed by an ominous, splintering crack before the chest jerked away from the wall in a spew of paint chips.

He stared in dismay at this new damage. The chest was an old-fashioned design, heavy and ugly, and had been outfitted with numerous knobs and latches, hinges, decorative gewgaws of no apparent purpose, and worst of all, protective brass corners. One of the latter, already bent and protruding, had caught on the top molding of the wainscotting, which had disastrously pulled away from the wall with Dan's muscular exertions.

The destruction extended only a about a foot laterally, but the vertical tongue-and-groove boards below the molding were irreparably split and would require replacement. Damn it, another job, thought Dan, tamping down useless fury. But not right now. A quick tap of the hammer would hold the fragments in place, and the chest could be pushed back against the wall to hide the mess. It would have to do for the time being. It was not something to call to his mother's attention at the moment.

More carefully now, Dan slid the heavy object to the center of the room and stepped up to clean the ceiling. With a sweep of his hand, the stuck feathers fluttered down docilely, their removal hardly worth the injury to the wall that he had caused. Dan hopped down. Evidence of frantic pigeon was nearly cleared from sight, and it would take only a little more effort now to hide the new damage. He looked again at the split wainscotting, its horizontal top molding peeled back and bent like a broken rib. And then he looked more closely, peering at the wall behind that was newly revealed.

Deep blues and greens, lush lawns and the colors of sky and water.

Heedless of splintering wood, Dan pulled more of the wainscotting away from the wall. The more he tore at it, the more he saw that the cupola mural did not end midway down the wall as they had thought. As the molding peeled off, below a dancing line of nail holes there emerged a grove of trees waving in the vivid sunlight, just as they might have looked to someone gazing out from these very windows one summer day long ago. Miraculously, the wainscotting, installed for whatever reason years before, had protected a set of images that looked to be in almost perfect condition.

His mother was grimly scrubbing a banister when he bounced downstairs. He could hear her muttering under her breath: "This place is cursed. A pigeon, a damn bird. If I find out who left that window open—" Then she saw that her son was standing at the top of the staircase and grinning widely. "What is it? Why do you look so happy?"

"Come upstairs and see what I've found," said Dan. "That bird has done us a favor."

❧

It was only right that they all be present at the unveiling. Dan called Karen and told her to spread the word. But neither he nor his mother could wait for the others, and they began removing the wainscotting as gently as they could. It was hard to resist the impulse to tear at it willy-nilly, regardless of collateral damage. "Careful! Be careful! Not so fast!" commanded Priscilla, ripping away with enthusiasm, enjoining caution but herself unable to stop.

Karen arrived almost immediately, Jacob soon thereafter, and Jasmine texted with a wail that she had back-to-back classes and they simply must take pictures and send them right away as they worked. Priscilla called in another assistant to take over the pigeon clean up downstairs and brought up an empty packing case to fill with the debris that was quickly covering the floor.

Once they had taken down the wainscotting on the first wall, it was clear why it had been erected in the first place. Cracked plaster and bulging lath indicated an ancient leak discovered long ago and simply patched and covered. The faded traces that remained on the upper part of the walls were filled with clouds and birds, presumably representing the sky above the cupola. But the pictures now being revealed, long hidden under the wainscotting, appeared to be of land and a flowing river beyond.

"Doubtless the Niagara," said Priscilla. "You could almost see it in the distance from these windows, if it weren't for all the houses and trees in between. What a pity that part of the scene is missing."

Miraculously, there was only one damaged section. As splintered wood fell away from the wall and blisters and scrapes formed on hands eager to uncover what lay beneath, views of a shore beyond the river were revealed. It was as though Canada were within reach and the streets separating Bigwell House from the river had disappeared. Shimmering water, near hillsides laden with fruit trees, and in the foreground a garden—all as fresh and bright as the day they were painted.

"Where do you suppose this is?" asked Jacob. "The scenes downstairs seemed to be near the canal, but this looks different."

"Do you think it was supposed to be the view out this very window?" mused Dan.

"Doubtful. There are no houses."

"I think it's a picture of some special event," said Karen. "Look down here on this side. There are people gathered together, and something is happening."

She was kneeling amid a pile of rubble, perilously near to nails pointed menacingly upward now that they now longer fastened anything to the wall. The others cleared a path and carefully crouched beside her—and then they, too, saw what she had found.

Three figures stood in a garden by a lake. A man and a woman were holding hands and standing side by side. Their faces were tilted toward each other, and although the image was small, they appeared to be smiling. Before them was a tall man with a book in one hand and the other raised in a gesture that might have been a blessing.

There was a moment of quiet.

"It looks like a wedding, doesn't it," said Karen. "Who could they be?"

Priscilla leaned forward suddenly, her shirt catching on a nail. She ignored the tearing sound as she pointed and said, "There's a *signature*! It is signed right there! And it says *Porter*, I'm sure it does. We've found it! Rufus Porter did sign his work after all, at least this one. This is it! Finally! We've found proof!"

She was right. Sketched in a gentle arch over the standing figures there was a leafy arbor. Long violet blossoms trailed from a heavy, twisting vine. And nestled among the wisteria was a name twined among the leaves. It was a clear and unambiguous declaration—*Porter*.

"Oh, but, Mom," began Dan. He couldn't bear to finish as he saw her face change from triumph to perplexity. She brushed her fingers against the painted arbor as if she might clear away the leaves and see more distinctly the names inscribed there.

"Definitely, it does say Porter!" said Jacob. "And there are initials here too. You're right! It's your proof!"

As the dust settled, they gazed at the mural, variously smiling, excited, and then quiet. Jacob broke the silence. "But I don't think that's an R for Rufus, do you? And there are two of them—two letters, that is. Don't they look like *J*s?"

40

LYDIA'S LETTER

"A triumph!" said Mr. Bigwell. He beamed and gazed, turned and surveyed, stepped back to see vistas and strode forward to peer at details.
His round eyes glowed with pleasure. "A triumph!"

It was all he said for a moment, and for this loquacious man to be at
a loss for more words was praise in itself.

The walls and ceiling of the dining room had been transformed
into another world, a world where hills humped toward the horizon,
buildings stood solid and tall, boats traversed the waterway. Specks in
the distance gradually became long boats towed by mules and horses
as they neared the canal terminus. As they drew close, decks crowded
with passengers came into view. In the foreground, people swarmed on
a dock, mostly men loading and unloading cargo, a few women disembarking with children in tow. Some of them appeared ready to step over
the low molding and into the room. What a pity that when the furniture
arrived, the lower portions of the mural would be covered with cabinets
and sideboards. Jane's hand had populated the mural with travelers, immigrants, laborers, businessmen. Men ready for work; women fatigued
from travel and ready to find a home; children held by the hand or
cradled in arms.

One of the figures—although not yet noticed—was Mr. Bigwell
himself standing outside his company's warehouse. A robust gentleman of amiable demeanor pleased with the prospect of the future of
the city. She had drawn him freehand, a three-quarters view, one foot
forward, arms crossed, eyes focused on cargo being unloaded from a
docking boat.

Jed and Jane had managed to surround the floor level with city streets,
the mid-sections with countryside, and the upper portions with sky. The
sky itself continued onto the ceiling in patterns of day and night, pale at

the edges, rosy at one side with the dawn and glowing at another as the day ended, and gradually darkening until stars swirled around the chandelier in the middle. With the deft shading, the ceiling itself appeared concave, as though the room rested under a gently swelling dome.

Jane stood alongside Jed and the admiring Mr. Bigwell, but her attention was fastened on the packet she clutched in her hands. A letter thick and wrinkled, poorly sealed and with the print of a wheel running down a torn edge.

Lydia.

Upon entering the room, Mr. Bigwell had handed it to her. "This post came several days ago, and the deliverer knows to hand me my papers immediately the mail bag arrives," he said. "But this one is for you, Miss Woodfield. It became mixed with my own business mail, I'm afraid. Only noticed it this morning, my apologies. It appears to have been damaged and was probably a little delayed in reaching you. Just a day or so, I'm sure. Hope you get good news."

And then he forgot the post and reveled in the glory of the painted room.

The letter trembled in Jane's hands. She itched to tear it open, but she made herself stand still while the murals were appreciated in all their detail. Mr. Bigwell paced around the perimeter, exclaiming at colors, at particular features, at the vivacity of the world that was spread on his walls. His discourse uncorked and he continued to praise their work with all the abundance of vocabulary at his disposal. When he noticed his own portrait amid the bustle of the dock he laughed with delight and shook Jed's hand like a pump engine.

"Not my work," said Jed. "That one is Jane's."

So she was the recipient of his enthusiastic encomia and his thanks. "Marvelous, my dear Jane, marvelous. What a portraitist you are! We must find you more commissions, your talents must be recognized and rewarded! You have captured the very image of myself! The spit and image, as it were." And on and on. Despite her desire to be out of the room and alone with Lydia, his pleasure was contagious and she could not but share in his delight. He spun and looked up and admired the ceiling, made several more circuits of the room.

"And now, you will be ready to tackle the cupola, no?" said Mr. Bigwell with an abrupt shift of attention as his enthusiasm moved to the projects still to be done. He swept from the room and headed for the stairs. "Let us discuss the design again so that you can get right to work.

My wife should be arriving in two weeks, and I would be glad if you were to finish by then."

Jed caught Jane's eye and intervened. "I'll accompany you and take more notes, Mr. Bigwell. We two have already settled on a design that awaits your approval before we begin to paint. But if you permit, Jane would like to read her letter. She has been anxious to hear from her cousin."

"Of course, of course!" He waved. "Take your time. Join us later when you have finished, if you please!" The voice was already receding upward. For a large man, Mr. Bigwell could move very quickly.

Jane slipped into the back garden and sat on a bench beneath the shade of a copper beech, glad that its dark spreading branches had been spared the ax when the house was built. It was quiet there, no booming voice echoing in still, empty rooms. Street traffic passed on the other side of the house. She could hear clopping hooves and snatches of conversation, but in the yard only a leisurely bumblebee murmured its way among the clover. Her heart was pounding. She took a deep breath and waited for her fingers to still.

Lydia's distinctive writing had addressed the latter, but it had clearly suffered an accident, one involving mud and water. Something like a cartwheel had ripped the edge, and a partial hoofprint in a corner indicated the plodding gait of a mule. The ink had run, and much of the address was obscured. No wonder Mr. Bigwell had not noticed right away that it was directed to her. It was a good thing that his name was well-known at the post office and that the wheel and hoof had left his street legible.

She opened the thick envelope. There were several pages, but they were folded separately into two clumps, two letters in fact. She began with the neater one, torn only slightly at the edge and legible. It was dated only *Tuesday*, but which Tuesday was unclear. A week ago? Two weeks? More? In her agitation, she couldn't recall just how long she and Jed had been in Buffalo, and the wagon trip across the state stretched to an age.

My dearest Janie,

Well, we made it to Rochester and stayed with Auntie's cousins for a week. Or I should say, we stayed at their house, for they are at their cottage in the Adirondacks for the time being, seeking fresh mountain air away from the summer heat. Mrs. Davenport most kindly prepared rooms for us, and she told us that you and Jed had spent only one night here before continuing your journey to Buffalo. How I wish you had stayed so that I could tell you all that has happened! But although writing is a poor substitute, I shall attempt to tell you all.

We have conducted a number of sessions since you and I parted in Seneca Falls. I feel more and more transported with each gathering. Try as I might, I cannot express to you the rapture that I always feel when in touch with the spirits! My abilities as a medium have increased tremendously with practice, if I do say so myself. There are times when I feel as though I still inhabit another world for hours after the séance has ended. It is as though I continue in a dream what I experienced when in communication—a state for me that is neither wake nor sleep but a kind of floating awareness. When this occurs, the spirits come, and although my sweet mother has yet to make an appearance, I trust that soon she will. And yours as well, and when that happens, all your doubts will vanish! I am convinced of it. Once one hears a voice from beyond, there can be no disbelief.

Oh, Lydia, thought Jane. How I wish I could be there and hear what you hear, see what you see. If in fact you truly see. Can you really be so caught up in the spirit world that you fail to come back to the real one after the séance concludes?

It was an alarming thought, especially as Jane recollected the increasing strength of the tea she herself had once drunk so trustingly.

That feeling was never stronger than three nights ago when Uncle George came to us once more. So vivid and clear he was. He spoke, and although it was my throat that uttered his words, it was his voice we heard. Auntie insists it was his voice. She would have known it anywhere. She was so gratified when he expressed his regret at her distress and that his love for her continued beyond the grave. She wept to hear it. As well as his assurance that, should she return to Troy, his legacy for her awaits. I cannot say that I recall his words exactly myself. Indeed, the session remains a blur to me, as I was deeply tranced. But both Auntie and the others who were present testify to his words, and they have embarked on a plan of action that, I confess, presents me with a dilemma. But more on that anon. Alexander is calling me, and I shall set this aside for a time and continue before long to finish my tale.

Yrs in haste and with much love,

Lydia

That a summons from Mr. Alexander Dodge Lewis had interrupted finishing the letter filled Jane with resentment. He managed to intrude between her and her cousin even from a distance. How readily had Lydia put down her pen at his bidding!

The second section of the letter was folded separately, and part of it was almost glued together from the water damage it had sustained. Something about its tight folds filled Jane with foreboding. With trembling fingers she picked at the edge of the paper, careful not to tear it.

She heard a window open high above where she sat, and the voices of Jed and Mr. Bigwell discussing the cupola murals floated out. For a moment, they seemed to be speaking from a different world, one that hardly matched the narrative she held in her hand. She had been with Lydia until just a few weeks before, and now with Jed's voice three stories above her, for a moment she occupied a kind of limbo in between them.

This section of Lydia's letter continued with different ink and a scratchier nib that skipped over the page now and then, and her handwriting jumped and blotted.

Thursday
Resumed several days later, dear Janie, because there has been much to do and I haven't had sufficient quiet to write. Now is my first chance. So what I had thought would be merely a final page is now a separate letter altogether.

Aunt Madeleine, as you know, has always resisted the new rail travel, but she is eager to return to Troy and lay her case before Mr. Bailey once more. So she and I are now racing east again, much faster than we traveled before. The train is most exciting, although the rails sometimes cause us to sway when we reach the higher speeds. I have to take care lest the ink bottle overturn.

So it was a train that now jostled Lydia's hand. Jane recalled the times when Jed and she had taken a road that paralleled the rails, and how swiftly the linked cars moved in comparison to the slow wagon that Horace pulled.

I am sorry to say that Alexander is not at ease with our return for this purpose, although he consented to join us on this first leg of our travels east from Rochester. (He sits aloof and grumpy at the end of the car.) This change is unsettling, as from everything he said earlier, it appeared that he endorsed Auntie's plan to plead her case to the lawyers with evidence from Uncle George himself. Last night, however, he was unexpectedly severe and pessimistic that anything we have learned from spirit testimony could be presented as a legal brief. Auntie was most upset, and I myself became rather angry with his change of attitude, and also that he had not warned her that the outcome of her transactions—he actually used that financial term—with her husband were not likely to serve as means to gain anything from the estate.

Even more disturbing than his scoffing discouragement was his tone. For his retort to her queries was almost insulting, as he declared that he had assumed mere material gain was not her purpose, but rather she sought continued communication with a loved one. I cannot tell you how shocked I was by his harsh words.

But my dilemma at least has been solved, for under these circumstances I must accompany our aunt back to Troy rather than stay with Alexander as I had thought I might.

Poor Auntie! She needs my company, for I do not believe she has the heart to go back by herself. She wept with frustration and hurt and could not be persuaded to attend the séance that followed. I myself attended with a heavy heart and an aching head, and although a spirit came, it was only the annoying Eustace, and his presence left me feeling quite sick.

In fact, a strange, sick feeling now visits me more and more. Alexander assures me that it is the unsettling effect of having a physical body so frequently in commerce with the spirit world. But I am beginning to wonder if there might be another cause.

We are arriving at a station and must descend from this car to change trains and procure some refreshment. We have rather little luggage with us, fortunately. I shall resume the letter as soon as we are on our way again.

But apparently Lydia had not been able to continue to write immediately. It was impossible to tell when she took up the pen again, but the next page of the letter was such a scrawl that Jane could hardly read it. It was not a resumption of the previous thoughts but an urgent outpouring of dismay.

Friday night

I hope that what I am writing now will be legible enough to put quickly into the packet with the earlier pages. Something rather frightening has happened, and I fear to light the candle and must write by the window in the fading light of evening. Mrs. Wentworth, whom you will remember, is standing guard outside the door, and a glow around the door jamb might bring her in to inspect us.

Auntie is asleep beside me, having taken so much sleeping powder that I fear she will not awaken in time for the train tomorrow. If indeed we will be able to take it at all.

I no longer know whom to trust, and, my dear cousin, if only I had listened to you! Here, quickly, is what has happened.

As I mentioned before, I have been feeling ill of late, and last night I could not stomach the evening tea that previously was so calming and pleasant. There was a large gathering and I felt as if I needed to perform particularly well, but I was faint and queasy, and I spilled the tea out at a moment when I thought I was not noticed. But it appears I was seen, and I had to pretend my trance. Perhaps I should merely have declared the spirits unwilling to appear, but that did not occur to me in time. When we are together again, I will tell you in more detail what I saw, or what I think I saw. Suffice it now just to admit that you might have been right. All along, you might have been right, and I was so taken with my new powers and my new desires that I could not hear your words.

In brief, here is what happened last n—

The cartwheel that had run over the letter had damaged its contents at the edge and part of the ill-folded page was torn. Jane never would know exactly what had happened that had altered her cousin's views so abruptly, but she could guess. With shaking hands, she turned over the final page, torn and smudged but readable.

Oh, my dearest Janie. Alexander is furious with me—and for so many reasons. I cannot write them all, for I would never want another's eyes to see. Only you, and I hope that you will understand, and that you will pity me rather than condemn.

Auntie is now in the hands of Mrs. Sibley, who I trust will care for her kindly. But I cannot stay here any longer. I shall leave this bulky missive here for her to post, for sensing my distress, she has volunteered to do so, and I must trust someone.

I have the Buffalo address which you left with me, and I pray you will still be there when I arrive. I fear pursuit. I have bought a train ticket, but it is a pretense. One I can ill-afford, but misdirection is necessary. There is a canal boat that should be taking on passengers soon, and I will be among them.

Pray God I shall see you soon,

L.

41

Discoveries

Sometimes one small discovery opens paths to many others, like a key for a door that suddenly unlocks a room full of answers.

Dan and Karen were experimenting with the camera obscura, she drawing him this time and having trouble with his mouth, which kept talking and smiling and moving the lines reflected on the paper. To make matters worse, her laughter from beneath the darkening hood kept fogging the lens.

From the office they heard the hurry-up conversational prompts that conclude a phone call that extends too long, and then Priscilla Cavendish uttered a jubilant yelp and dashed into the room.

"We've found him! The man in the portrait! We know who it is! The donor to the Munson Williams Proctor left a record of the sitter, and she provided information about his identity. She's sending it right over. Finally!"

She snatched the portrait off the wall, sending the hook and its nail skittering into a corner, and held it at arm's length. "All is revealed," she proclaimed to the portrait. "The secret it out! We know who you are, Mr. Alexander Dodge Lewis!" She performed a small, triumphant whirl as she delivered these words.

"You found him! The man who murdered Lucille!" exclaimed Karen, fighting clear of the hood and dashing to her side. They both gazed avidly, angrily at the portrait, accusing the image in the absence of the man.

"Or he could be just a man with the same jacket button as a murderer," said Dan, ever cautious. "Let's not get carried away."

"Oh, Dan, don't be such a skeptic! Who else could it be? Too many things converge for this to be a coincidence. I'm sure it is him. It just has to be!"

Priscilla handed over the portrait and pulled some scribbled notes from her pocket. Her hands were shaking with excitement. "We'll know more when the full acquisition record arrives, which should be very soon. But here are a few facts that I took down from the phone call: Born July 27, 1811, in Utica, New York. Property owner there, but I didn't write down the address. Son of— Oh, wait a sec, here comes the fax." Summoned by buzzing sound from the small administrative office, she disappeared to the back of the house.

"Fax?" said Karen. "Who uses a fax anymore?"

Dan shrugged. He too was studying the face in the painting. Despite his cautionary remark, he couldn't restrain his own excitement at the thought that a button and a portrait might solve a murder from long ago. He scrutinized the conventional pose, seeking to detect the character of the living man. The stiff posture flattened individuality; shoulders straight, expression slightly aloof, arms positioned awkwardly across his chest. He could have been a banker, a landowner, a doctor. If he had also been a murderer, it didn't show.

Priscilla returned with a sheet of paper in her hands. "Here we have it! Portrait of a man, painted circa 1849, artist John Singleton. Hm. Never heard of him. Wonder if that's his real name. Sounds too much like Copley." She paused, musing.

"Mom!"

"Okay: Name of sitter: Alexander Dodge Lewis. Born: Utica 1811. Died: date and place of death unknown. That's odd; I wonder why that information is missing. Commissioned by self. Previous owners: Lewis household, Winifred Owen—she's the donor to the Munson Williams. Actually, there's quite a short provenance history. This piece has been in storage a long time. And this is interesting. More about the man himself. It seems he was best known for... Oh my, how unexpected. Very strange." Priscilla trailed off again, frowning at the paper.

"What? Read on. Don't leave us hanging."

"There is a brief description here," his mother continued. "Apparently Lewis was a pioneer in the early years of the spiritualist movement in the state. That was his main occupation in fact. There's a quote here from a contemporary. He is called 'a well-known medium, respected and sought after by groups that congregate in hopes of communicating with the dead.' What do you make of that?"

The information took them all aback.

Karen shivered. "Communicating with the dead? Weird. Although in this house, maybe not."

Dan read her mind. They glanced at each other, each recalling their conversation in the room just above their heads, that vaguely illicit, exhilarating night when history had come alive. When the things around them seemed almost to speak and shadows from the past crowded near.

Karen felt her cheeks flush at the memory. "But what is the connection between him and Lucille? Do you think he was the father of her baby? Could that have been his motive for killing her?" Her words were more an expression of bewilderment than an actual question.

"I don't know," said Priscilla. "But if he was that well known, the spiritualist community around here might have more information. We're on his trail at last, I'm sure of it. Just in time for the opening too. And I know just whom to call." She disappeared into the office, leaving her son to note that even when excited, his mother said *whom*.

Karen was unsettled by a renewed and disconcerting worry about ghosts. Of course, they did not exist. She did not believe in ghosts. Of course not. At the same time, the sense of the past that had swirled around them as they lay in Bigwell's bed—the reproduction bed, she reminded herself—had been palpable. To quash the idea that the spirit world might be drawing ominously near, she knelt to the floor searching for the picture hanger. "Let's put the painting back up, shall we? I couldn't believe it when your mother snatched it off the wall. I thought she was going to do a dance with him."

"Actually, she did," said Dan, hammer in hand. He replaced the hook with a decisive smack, causing a tumble of loose plaster behind the lathing. "There, it's back up and more secure. But we'll have to change the caption."

"More than a caption. There's room on this wall to frame the whole story. Once we find out what it is. Besides, your mother has added to the things in this vitrine, so those captions need to be done again too. For example, what's this picture?"

Dan looked over her shoulder at a creased photograph, a silver print of a small, dark woman standing before a structure with an open door. The blurry side of a horse could be seen within.

"It's what Mom came back with from that fundraiser. The African-American Historical Society gave her this photo on loan. It's someone named Sarah Clancy. The picture was taken when she was an old woman, but she worked here at Bigwell House when she was young. So did her father."

"Were they part of the Underground Railroad?"

"Possibly. They don't know for sure but think it likely."

Priscilla reentered the room. "I just got off the phone from the archivist at Lily Dale. It turns out that Lewis is quite well known to them. In fact, she sounded surprised that I'd never heard of him. It took some convincing, but they're going to loan us a few documents for the gala." Dan noted again his mother's admirable persuasive powers. He gave Karen a look that said, *See what I mean?* But she was gazing at the portrait. "We can make copies as well," continued Priscilla. "However, for the opening it will be good to have the originals on display. I told them you would pick everything up tomorrow."

"Me? You've given me a long list of other things to do for tomorrow," said Dan. "I can't do them all."

"This takes precedence. I don't want to give them a chance to change their minds. Besides, it's nice down there, very pretty. You'll like it. You both can go."

"I can skip class!" said Karen. "Except, oh dear, I promised to proctor an exam. Does it have to be tomorrow?"

It did. Obtaining the materials from Lily Dale was urgent and could not be postponed. Priscilla was adamant that suddenly the solution to their various mysteries was at hand, and no time should be wasted.

So Dan went on his own, driving south first on the crowded interstate, then on a smaller highway, and finally on a long, near-empty country road. After the heavy traffic dispersed and the noise of the road abated, he cranked down a window and slowed to a leisurely speed. The warm wind buffeted the half-opened windows of his truck as if it were still summer, though the leaves were turning red and gold and some were already stripped bare. Purple asters and goldenrod stirred in the breeze as he passed. Alone with his own thoughts for almost two hours, he let his mind slowly wander through the last several years, recalling the accumulation of worries over debt, the cringing appeal to his uncle for help, the sense—which now seemed exaggerated—that his difficulties needed to be kept from his mother. And now, the greater understanding of his mother's passions that had come with being pulled into her orbit, at first grudgingly, then reluctantly, then, he had to admit, enthusiastically. It dawned on him that this gradual progression had effectively burned out the resentment he had harbored for so long. For reasons he could not completely tally, by the time he reached his destination, he was feeling abnormally content.

He was expected at the gate and didn't have to pay the usual fee for visitors to enter the small spiritualist community. The brochure he was handed contained a map, and the museum and adjacent archives had been thoughtfully circled with a ballpoint pen. He drove narrow streets with cracked and gravely pavement, admired the late blooms of the elaborately tended gardens in almost every yard, the houses themselves garnished with gingerbread decorations and steep, gabled roofs. It was as if the miles he had driven had also carried him back in time to a place still infused with an aura of the nineteenth century. Shingles hanging outside doors and on mailboxes advertised the many mediums on hand and their particular skills. The numbers of those who also provided websites blunted his sense of time travel. Spiritualism had clearly embraced the twenty-first century. He did not even consider knocking on a door to see if he could schedule a reading and obtain a message from beyond. Part of him scoffed at the very idea; a smaller but undeniable part was afraid of what he might be told.

Dan parked on a strip of gravel and climbed the steps to the museum, once a large house or possibly an inn. After the bright sun outside, he blinked in the dim interior to clear his vision and saw that the entry contained a wall crowded with photographs and sketches. He recognized a number of historical figures who, apparently, had dabbled in spiritualism, Abraham Lincoln among them. Or at least his wife. Most of the pictures were of women, including names both famous and unfamiliar: Suffragists such as Susan B. Anthony. Victoria Woodhull rang a bell. Others he didn't recognize: Cora Hatch, Grace Lewis Sibley, Achsa White Sprague.

Dan sneezed. The space was full of dust with a hint of mildew, which intensified as he entered the museum proper. He passed a man enthusiastically demonstrating the use of a spirit trumpet to three women wearing comfortable shoes in anticipation of a long day's visit. They nodded and looked at their watches. "I think the assembly starts soon," one murmured. The cramped room was divided into aisles by long glass cases full of pamphlets and more photographs; postcards of the Fox cottage; copies of spirit drawings; open, unreadable diaries scratched with faded ink; mementoes and talismans he could not identify. There were more pictures on the walls and a large stuffed bird in a corner. He sneezed again.

"Are you the man from Bigwell House?" asked a woman seated in the back room. She rose and gestured for him to enter. "We have put together several papers for you and also made some photo copies. Actually, I was hoping that you might be content to take only the copies, as the originals are rare."

Dan put on his most reassuring smile. "That's very nice of you. But please don't worry. The originals will be safe with us. Besides," he added with another smile, this one slightly self-deprecating, "if I don't return with the originals for the opening exhibits at Bigwell House, my mother will have my head. Of course, we shall note with gratitude that these materials are on loan from Lily Dale, you can be sure of that." His mother had dictated that appreciative assertion.

The woman nodded, partially reassured that a loan would not turn into a snatch.

Dan continued. "We hope that you and your colleagues might come to the evening event where these materials will be displayed." He handed over a large envelope with the engraved announcement of the reopening of Bigwell House. Priscilla had liberally distributed them already, but this one carried her handwritten invitation above the printed text.

"Thank you," said the woman, less impressed than might have been hoped. "Would you like to take a look at what we have found for you? Mrs. Cavendish requested materials about Alexander Dodge Lewis, and I'm intrigued that you have discovered his image in an oil painting. I expect that the printed copies of his picture that we have are based on that one. That was commonly done in his time, you know, to have prints made as copies of portraits. So I consulted our files and located some other materials that might also be of interest."

Dan sat at a wide library table and opened the folder. The first pages were smudgy woodcuts that did look as though they might have been modeled after the portrait at Bigwell House. There were two typed pages about Lewis, apparently photocopied many times, judging from the quality of the print. He scanned them quickly, turned them over, and then he gasped at what he found beneath.

"Mr. Lewis was among the founders of our movement," said the archivist placidly, gratified at his reaction. "And he introduced a beautiful young medium into the world. You can read about her too in those papers. The paper is very old and fragile. I've put it in a protective cover, but please treat it carefully. We have only a few copies."

Curious at Dan's stunned silence, perhaps wondering if something had upset him, she continued. "Unfortunately, they left the area soon after she came to be aware of her powers, and history does not record where they went."

Almost reverently, hardly able to believe what lay before his eyes, Dan picked up a fragile newsletter titled *The Sign*. On the page was a banner headline:

Miss Lydia Strong: A New Medium among Us

Dan tried to summon his cautious skepticism, to tell himself not to jump to conclusions, that there were many other explanations for what he was reading, many other mediums that the article referred to. But his head gave way to his heart, which was beating very hard. Suddenly he knew. Knew for sure.

"It's her! It must be her!" he exclaimed. "Her name was *Lydia*. Not Lucille but Lydia."

"I beg your pardon?"

The archivist was not used to strange young men leaping to their feet, grasping her shoulders and giving them a delighted squeeze just short of a hug. But she smiled and said, "I'm glad to have been of service." At his insistence, she promised to come to the gala opening at Bigwell House.

Only on his way home did it occur to Dan that the revelation of the button and the identity of its murderous owner might not be welcome news at Lily Dale.

42

SEARCHING

Jane waited and waited. Jed accompanied her to the docks and they watched the boats unload at the central wharf, scanning the faces of every disembarking passenger. It was a fruitless venture, for both knew that Lydia should have arrived already, with or even before the mail bag that had brought her delayed letters. But still they waited, looking carefully at the passengers with the vain hope that one of them would be the woman they sought. Sick at heart, Jed saw Jane become more drawn and despairing with every passing day. Reassuring words began to falter, and he could think of nothing to do but hold her hand as unfamiliar faces passed by.

Once alerted to the problem, Mr. Bigwell summoned his network of employees and sent out inquiries to discover if anyone had seen a slender, fair-haired young woman traveling west from some point mid-state in recent weeks. Jane found her best portrait of Lydia, still a good likeness despite the torn edge it had suffered, and transferred it onto a broadsheet to aid the quest.

The responses were prompt enough to be hopeful but too vague for certainty. Some said they recalled a young woman of that description, but not on the last leg of the journey to Buffalo. Jane couldn't imagine why Lydia would have disembarked at some earlier point in the trip, but if she had, it might explain why she had not yet arrived. Hope rekindled.

But other reports recalled that a woman matching the description might have disembarked days ago in Buffalo in the company of a tall, older man, who perhaps had joined her in transit. With that thought Jane's heart sank. She wrote desperate letters to her aunt and to Mrs. Sibley, but Lydia should have arrived far sooner than any reply would come.

Eventually, both out of kindness and from desire to have her attention directed back to the mural project, Mr. Bigwell positioned one of his clerks at the central wharf to keep a steady vigil. He dispatched two others eastward to inquire at Lockport and Albion, sending queries all the way back to Syracuse. When it was clear that Jane still could not concentrate on her painting with her mind so distraught, he sent her and Jed in a private cabin on one of his canal boats. They descended the five high locks and traveled along the waterway back to Rochester but found the house they had stayed in locked and dark. Not even the housekeeper was in residence to confirm what they knew already: Lydia was not there. When Jed asked if she wanted to continue east, Jane just shook her head.

All the searchers came back empty-handed. Even if Lydia had been seen—and the reports were by no means clear—no one could say what had become of her.

High in the cupola Jane painted in silence beside Jed, her eyes turning frequently toward the windows in the desolate hope that she might yet spy her cousin making her way toward the house.

One of the younger Mrs. Talmadges penned a brief reply to Jane's letter to her aunt. It was courteous but little else.

> I am afraid that Mrs. Madeleine Talmadge is too indisposed to attend personally to the question that you posed in your letter. But I can tell you that she was deeply disappointed that Lydia did not accompany her back to Troy. She tells me that your cousin elected to stay in the company of Mr. Lewis and believes them both to have been deceitful. She accuses them of encouraging false hopes of a sort that remain vague to me, but which she declines to explain. But it was all for their own ends, for she believes they may have eloped. Or worse, gone off together without benefit of marriage. But I assure you that she knows nothing else and desires only to keep to herself. I am sorry to report her very words: "Lydia is dead to me." Repeatedly uttered. I shall not query her further, for the health of her mind is precarious, and I advise you as well to let the matter lie.

Jane wrote twice to Mrs. Sibley, inquiring now also of her brother's whereabouts, but to those letters she received no reply. Grace Sibley seemed to have vanished along with her brother.

"Lydia is gone, Jed," said Jane one night when the wind blew hard against the carriage house. "I will not see her ever again." She could not say the word *dead*. In the faint glow of a lantern nearing the end of its wick he could see a tear make its way down her face to dampen the pillow they shared. But now there was only the one and she seemed calm.

"You can't know that," he began, trying to think of some new way to encourage hope. In truth, he believed that hope was no longer what was needed to restore her peace of mind, but he didn't have the heart to utter the thought.

"Actually, I can," said Jane. "I do know. I'm not sure how I know, but I do. Lydia has bid me goodbye."

There was a soft tapping at the windows. A light rain had come to refresh the September drought that was hastening the harvest.

"I'm sorry to say it, but I believe that's true," said Jed reluctantly. "You're probably right. And painful though it is, knowing is better than uncertainty, don't you think?"

The candle flickered and died. The night fell soft around them.

"Yes. I can stop looking now," Jane said. "I am reconciled. I won't see her again, I know that now."

Jed held his young wife close. It was a brave sentiment, and he hoped it would endure. The rain was steadier now. Its soft drumbeat enclosed them on the warm bed under the eaves. Horace dozed in his stall below. The sweet scent of hay drifted upward. Tonight there was no one seeking escape who was sheltering in the deep room beneath the stables, and all was quiet.

Jane smiled against the dark, feeling peaceful at last. Her voice was little more than a whisper in his ear. "Truly, she is gone, but I feel her close."

The wind rattled the shutter and she snuggled closer to Jed. Already autumn hinted its turn in the coolness of night, and the spiders were spinning webs around the thorns of the roses in the garden.

"Dear Liddy," she said, murmuring into his shoulder. "She is gone, and I am filled with strange thoughts. At this very moment, I feel again that she is bidding me farewell. And now I can sleep."

43

GALA

The scent of mushroom crepes drifted from the caterer's covered dishes. Cold platters of interleaved cheeses and charcuterie joined assorted crackers spread like fans across long trays. There were plates of fruit and crudités as well as dips in small silver dishes that Dan recognized had come from his mother's own dining room. A steaming terrine of tiny meatballs in sweet-and-sour sauce invited spearing with toothpicks, which were decorative and slippery and just slightly too short for convenience. Fortunately, the tablecloth was dark.

One of the vitrines had been removed to the foyer to make way for a longer drinks table in the main exhibit area—the Bigwell's former large parlor—where now a bartender smartly dressed in a white jacket was setting out glasses. The drone of a vacuum cleaner could be heard in the hall for a last pass on the carpet on its way back to the cleaning cupboard, and a tinkling crash in the kitchen signaled just why plastic glasses were preferable on crowded occasions. But plastic did not strike the right tone for Priscilla Cavendish, who had rented several trays of long-stemmed wine glasses. In the midst of it all, an inconvenient ladder stood in the center of the dining room where at the last minute, a precariously balanced docent replaced the chandelier lights with slender candle bulbs, bright enough to illuminate, dim enough to simulate small flames.

Dan and Karen stood before the long display case beneath the portrait of the jacketed man with the decorative button, its real mate positioned just below. Accusing, conclusive, definitive. A new label for the picture had been prepared declaring the artist's name as well as the name of the sitter and his dates. What he had done—what he probably did, what he doubtless did given the accumulating evidence—was proclaimed in a framed narrative newly hung next to the portrait.

They raised the heavy glass lid and propped it against the wall, its edge resting just under the picture frame. The sticky putty that was supposed to hold one of the small spot lights over the exhibits, beaming on the button and inviting comparison with its painted twin, was proving stubborn and had fallen down twice. Patiently, Dan held it in place while Karen applied another discreet glob of glue.

This display was to be the centerpiece of the evening, for its contents had suddenly amplified beyond all expectation. Dan had returned with the bounty from Lily Dale, expecting his materials to be greeted with delighted accolades. Which they were, but the delight was magnified further when he found that in his brief absence, Jasmine had unearthed a dramatic document at the Historical Society. And his mother had deciphered a particularly faded entry from Mr. Bigwell's diary, overlooked heretofore because it had been interleaved into his business correspondence, an odd organizational slip for the usually careful businessman. In just one day a flood of evidence had fallen into their hands, the fruits of their labors delivered in a bountiful surge.

Arriving with the evidence of *The Sign* in his hands, Dan had found Jasmine carefully, almost reverently, smoothing a thin, fragile page between layers of Mylar film. And the page from Bigwell's diary, which was barely readable in its original, was being copied by Jacob with a darkly inked, fine nib onto new paper.

"Great job, Jacob!" said Karen over his shoulder. "You missed your calling. You'd be an excellent forger."

"Yes, I would. Maybe there's still time," said Jacob. "But stand back and don't crowd me. I don't want to do this twice."

The elegant outcome of his pen now rested next to the faded original in the display case. The journal entry not only added names to the former occupants of Bigwell House, it presented its owner with all the warmth and sympathy of his expansive character.

Poor little Miss Woodfield (or now I should call her Mrs. Porter) is so worried about her cousin, who should have arrived here some days ago. She and Jed have haunted the docks in hopes that she was delayed in her travels, but to no avail. My heart goes out to Jane, she is so concerned. Sally says she hardly eats these days.

"Jed. One of the *J*s," said Karen. They had been over this before with Priscilla. Karen herself had inked the cards that were posted in the mural-filled dining room: *Artist: Jedediah Porter, nephew of Rufus Porter.*

"I'm sure the other *J* is Jane. Jane Woodfield. Or Porter." She had wanted to add Jane's name to the card, but Priscilla had resisted without first obtaining further evidence of another hand at work on the walls. Karen intended to persuade her and had convinced two of the conservators to help in that task. They both had arrived early and were now in the dining room gazing with justified pride at their adept conservation of the murals.

The little light fixture seemed to be holding firm this time. Karen fiddled with the items in the case, moving them from side to side, up and down, just fractions of an inch, experimenting less with rearrangement than touching them with wonder. Her fingers hovered over the damaged locket, moving it closer to its broken chain, then back so that it caught the light more vividly. Touching the past, as she had marveled that night upstairs in Bigwell's bed. Her fingers danced in and out of the spotlight. With a fresh manicure and liberal slathers of cream, her hands had shed their summer roughness. Dan admired them and imagined their smooth touch against his skin, then put away the thought to attend to the business at hand.

"Only half an hour before the opening," said Karen. "I can't believe that everything has come together just in the last few days. We really needed more time to get everything ready. Your mother must be beside herself with nerves."

"You think so?" Dan smiled knowingly. "In my experience, fever pitch is the way she prefers to operate."

As if on cue, Priscilla entered the room, her high heels tapping across the bare boards, softer on the carpets, then tapping again as she diverted toward them.

"Did you get the interior light fastened securely? Oh yes, that looks splendid. Just the dramatic focus we need. Karen, will you arrange those papers together with just a few objects in between to separate them? Oh, and maybe a photograph. Is there room? Yes, just there. But leave enough space between things so that people can stand and read together. Be sure to keep the button in the center. Next to the broadside and the locket. Oh, good, Pam. That looks much nicer. Sufficiently light but more decorative." This last comment was directed to the woman descending from the ladder, one shoe dropping from a toe as her feet felt for the treads. "Thanks so much. And, Dan, would you please put the ladder back in the basement? Better do it right away before anyone trips." Like a talking dervish, Priscilla whirled back to the kitchen to check on the drinks to be transported into the living room.

"See what I mean?"

Karen laughed and shook her head. "Gotta love her energy."

When Dan returned from the basement, Karen was still standing before the open exhibit case, gazing in wonder at what they had assembled. "So much is coming to light all at once. I can hardly take it in."

They read again the headline from the small newsletter that Dan had brought back from Lily Dale.

Miss Lydia Strong: A New Presence among Us

"A medium. They call her a 'trance medium,' so do you think she was kind of a mystic? I wonder if she foresaw her own death in one of her trances. How ironic that would be," said Karen, then added, "Poor girl."

And next to the newspaper, the definitive proof.

On his ride home, Dan had realized that by itself, the headline from *The Sign* might have referred to another new medium in Lewis's company. He had spent much of the trip trying to assemble arguments for and against the confirmation of Lucille's identity. But he need not have worried, because any doubts were put to rest by the broadside handbill that Jasmine had discovered, its date recorded, its tone of alarm still vivid in spite of the passage of time.

URGENTLY SEEKING THE WHEREABOUTS OF MISS LYDIA STRONG, TWENTY YEARS OF AGE, BLOND HAIR, SLIGHT BUILD, PERHAPS WEARING A SMALL GOLD LOCKET. POSSIBLY TRAVELING ALONE OR IN THE COMPANY OF AN OLDER MAN. ANYONE WITH INFORMATION OF HER POSSIBLE LOCATION SHOULD KINDLY CONTACT THE REPRESENTATIVES OF BIGWELL AND COMPANY.

Most conclusive of all was the picture that appeared below the pleading text, which proved beyond doubt that they had truly identified the bones. It was a portrait of a pretty girl drawn in profile, her shoulders turned slightly and her hand extended in a gesture toward a wing that might have belonged to a duck, judging from the water in the background.

It was the necklace that sealed the identification of Lucille. Crisp and detailed, it lay against the neck of the girl in the drawing, whose twisting posture seemed almost to have been chosen to highlight the locket. Even though the necklace retrieved from the earth was bent and the portrait it probably had held was damaged beyond recognition, the shape and decorative engraving were a clear match. Here before them was the very image of Lydia Strong, who had disappeared on her way to meet her cousin Jane, waylaid almost on the very doorstep of Bigwell House. Just as the button was positioned beneath the portrait of Alexander Dodge Lewis, so the drawing lay next to the locket unearthed from Lydia's furtive and unmarked grave.

Dan, Karen, Jasmine, and Jacob had debated about asking Craig Killian to loan the jaw bone that had trapped the button and proved beyond question the identity of her killer. It was Dan's voice that prevailed, and they finally agreed that exposing that pathetic bit of her body to public scrutiny was unseemly, even after all these years an affront to the girl herself. Lydia's lovely face in the picture was what the world would see, not an awful fragment of the bones she had left behind. But the proof of her murder was an indispensable part of her story. They settled on a description in the printed and framed narrative above the vitrine, alongside the grisly photograph Karen had taken when the button was still lodged between two teeth.

"Lewis must have been the father of her baby, don't you think?" said Karen. "Those little bones. She must have told him she was pregnant, and he was displeased."

"Perhaps there was more to it," said Dan. "We'll never know."

"We might. So much has been discovered in the last two weeks, who knows what else we might find. I feel that we're on the edge of learning so much more," Karen said. "This museum gala seems like a dramatic finish to all of our investigation, but don't you think there is more to be discovered? About Lucille? Lydia, that is, now that we know her name."

"I expect there is," said Dan. "In fact, I'm sure of it. There's no need to stop looking. Now that we know her name, it will be easier to locate more evidence of who she was. This opening is only one night, after all. And these things will be here a long time." He closed the lid and gestured to the objects on exhibit: a button, a necklace with a broken chain, three documents, their declarative ink visible beneath their protective casings.

"Yes. If they've lasted all these years, there is no reason to worry that they won't stay around to tell us more."

Karen leaned into Dan, the two of them uplit by the reflection from the small light glowing over the display, illuminating the evidence of that long ago death. He kissed the top of her head, breathing in the light scent of her shampoo. Later she would think of the feel of his arms as he reached out to her in the night, and she would wonder about Jed and Jane, those mural painters, and how they had met and worked and married and what happened to them afterward. And especially, she would marvel at the fact that they all, the living and the dead, had landed here at this very spot, separated by more than a century.

Heels clicked across the floor. "Oh, that looks wonderful! Just enough room to show everything to advantage. People are arriving already. Look."

From the front window they could see a steady stream of visitors, some elegantly dressed, some in jeans and sneakers; some with hair gleaming white, many much younger. Dan was pleased to see three familiar men walking toward the house.

"Oh, great, they came! There are Carl and two of my buddies from the trenches," he said. "I sent them all invitations. I hoped some of them would come."

He went to greet his digger friends and took them first to see the photographs of the gas line trench, its work halted after the skeleton was found. Their pictures were positioned in a corner, and Dan moved a nearby lamp closer to illuminate them.

"This isn't part of the central display," he said, "because the main exhibits concern Bigwell House and the murals. But as you can see, the connection with the skeleton we found has filled in a lot of the story of this place."

"There's me," said Carl, pointing to the edge of the photograph at half a man with large boots. The others smiled at the memory of Carl's burly dominance.

"My mother is over there," said Dan. "Sometime this evening, she'll be coming over to thank you for your help. No need to remind her that we found the skeleton completely by accident. At the moment, she considers our efforts to have been on behalf of the museum, never mind the gas mains. Just say, 'You're welcome.' And be sure to have something to eat. The catering is really good."

The crowd arriving at Bigwell House was larger than expected. Public curiosity about Lucille had sparked interest in this historic mansion and the family that had once lived here. The rooms filled quickly. Most went directly to the dining room to admire the extensive murals. Dan could hear his mother directing the overflow to the cupola to examine the smaller paintings there. He was fairly certain she had commanded Jacob to stand guard upstairs as soon as he came in, and Jasmine had been pressed into service passing a tray of hors d'oeuvres. Ben Cavendish entered and gave his wife a kiss. Dan couldn't see what job he was handed, but the man quickly disappeared in the direction of the kitchen.

He beckoned his mother over to a window. She appeared with Karen at her side. "I had to pry Karen away from the exhibit so that more people could see the display," Priscilla said. Karen laughed. It was an expression of shared delight, for she had been nowhere near the vitrine when Priscilla grabbed her elbow and towed her over to Dan.

"Look out the window," he said. Among the visitors arriving were a man and a woman toting professional-looking cameras and hand-held microphones.

"Looks like we'll be on the news," said Dan. "Congratulations, Mom." He gave her shoulder a hug and was surprised to see a slight tear form in her eyes above the wide smile.

"I could never have done it alone," she said. "Thank you both so very much. And your friends too. I am so grateful." Priscilla bestowed two quick kisses before striding through the gathering to greet the media at the front door. Over her shoulder she added, "I should have hired two bartenders. Dan, perhaps you could help serving the drinks for a little while?"

Dan laughed, moved to the bar table, and started pouring.

LAID TO REST

FOREST LAWN CEMETERY, BUFFALO. NOVEMBER 1, 2015

The coffin was a narrow wooden box of the sort that would have borne her had she been buried in her time. Surrounding the newly dug grave were wreaths and urns overflowing with flowers that abide through the fall, late dahlias, chrysanthemums, goldenrod, sprigs of bittersweet with their bright berries.

The first speakers were representatives from the Historical Society and from the Bigwell House Museum. Since their findings had been dispensed over two months of reportage, they opted for brief summaries of what was now known about the fragile skeleton unearthed so unexpectedly. Priscilla Cavendish spoke of the button and what it meant and gave a brief account of how the young woman's skeleton had been identified and how she had died, crediting Professor Killian and his graduate students for their discoveries. A hastily summoned representative from Lily Dale, apparently undaunted by the disclosure of murder by one of their own, added a hazy statement about passing to a higher realm. If those assembled felt unease about the spiritualism that surrounded the story, it was not in evidence. A minister from one of the blander Protestant denominations then intoned the familiar words of Christian burial, using language as neutral as possible in deference to the fact that the decedent's full religious beliefs were unknown.

The small team of archaeologists had pooled their resources and chosen a grave marker. The young woman's death had been unnoted when it occurred, her first burial was furtive, and her tombstone should reflect that sad history. Therefore, they agreed, it should not be a conventional monument but a stone that would represent the place where she died. There was a brass plaque already incised to be fastened to a large piece of fieldstone that had been taken from the ground where her bones were discovered. The bedrock that had been her hidden crypt now held notice of her brief life.

Lydia Strong
1831 – 1851
Laid to rest November 1, 2015

The gathering was larger than expected and included members of the news media hauling cameras as well as curious citizens who had followed the story as it unfolded. Dan, Karen, Jasmine, Jacob, and Craig Killian clustered together garbed in sober suits and black dresses. They had decided the occasion demanded formality. When the time came, they stepped forward and scooped handfuls of earth from the mound ready to fill the grave. Dan was the first to scatter the earth over the coffin, followed by Karen, Jacob, Jasmine, and Craig. None of them spoke, all silenced by the sudden need to suppress tears. After all, they were the ones who had come to know her.

The afternoon was waning and the air was chill. Long shadows of monuments and gravestones stretched across the cemetery. The wind stirred the high branches of trees, casting flickering shadows on the ground, and a final scatter of falling leaves danced in the breeze. As the mourners—if mourners there remain after so many years—dispersed, the first colors of the setting sun lit a trail of fragile clouds drifting low in the cold November sky.

"What a long time to have to wait for a funeral," said Karen shakily. "I'm glad we finally discovered who she was. It would have been too bad if she were buried as Lucille."

She and Dan still lingered by the new grave. Dan nodded and squeezed her hand. He was thinking: What if the gas mains had never been replaced? What if he had never found her? And who else might be down there, forgotten and alone?

"Laid to rest," he said, repeating the words on the grave marker. "It suggests she'd been restless until now."

Karen was silent. It was sad to think of Lydia's troubled spirit awaiting discovery of her bones.

The wind rattled the brown leaves still clinging to the oaks, and shadows flickered across the grass. Dan glanced over his shoulder, his expression puzzled.

"What is it?" asked Karen.

"Nothing, I guess. I thought I saw something in the trees." He stood listening, scanning the branches overhead.

Karen smiled and said teasingly, "Maybe Lydia is watching. I'd like to think that she could know what we've done."

The sky slowly darkened to violet as the sun slipped beneath the horizon. Dan and Karen stood quietly for a little while longer before making their way to the parking lot and their waiting friends.

Author's Note

I have lived in Buffalo for many years and have traveled back and forth across the state on the highways that parallel and intersect the old Erie Canal, but no matter how familiar a place, no one can return to the past. In order to evoke this area in 1851, I have dug around written histories and photographic sources. I am most grateful to my historian husband, David Gerber, who was generous and helpful with my many questions, and to whom this novel is dedicated.

While this is a work of fiction, there is one background character who really lived: Rufus Porter, the author of the drawing and painting manual that Jed and Jane use when they paint the murals of Bigwell House. His *Valuable and Curious Arts* is quoted in the text. Like Dan, I myself once built a camera obscura based on his instruction. I have also experimented with the drawing techniques that Jane employs in her portraiture and can confirm both the uses and the limits of such aids that she and Jed observe.

Here are some sources that offer insights about this fascinating period of history.

Braude, Ann. *Radical Spirits: Spiritualism and Women's Rights in Nineteenth-Century America*, 2nd edition. Bloomington: Indiana University Press, 2001.

Cross, Whitney R. *The Burned-Over District: The Social and Intellectual History of Enthusiastic Religions in Western New York, 1800-1850*. Ithaca and London: Cornell University Press, 1950.

Deetz, James. *In Small Things Forgotten: An Archaeology of Early American Life*. New York: Anchor Books, 1996.

Dunn, Edward T. *Buffalo's Delaware Avenue: Mansions and Families*, 2nd edition. Buffalo, NY: Buffalo Heritage Press, 2017.

Gerber, David A. *The Making of an American Pluralism: Buffalo, New York 1825-60*. Urbana: University of Illinois Press, 1989.

Morganstein, Martin and Joan H. Cregg. *Erie Canal: Images of America*. Charleston SC: Arcadia Publishing, 2001.

Porter, Rufus. *A Select Collection of Valuable and Curious Arts, and Interesting Experiments, which are well explained, and warranted genuine, and may be performed easily, safely, and at little expense*. Concord MA: J.B. Moore, Printer, 1825.